C R Y S T A L I R I S

& The Solenscint in the Mirror

book two

BLAIR M. SHADOWS

*For the ones who get it—loneliness
isn't the absence of people,
it's the absence of the only hands you crave.*

Crystal Iris and The Solenscint in the Mirror

Crystal Iris

Book Two

Blair Shadows

LEBLON PUBLISHING

ONE

I watch the smoke drift out the window, vanishing right after wrecking my lungs. I'm not proud of this new habit, but at least I can call it French.

I don't know what possessed me to buy a pack from the bodega under the hotel months ago. I'd never smoked a cigarette before—not once. And I've had more than enough reasons to.

But things have changed. I've changed.

And—it was my birthday.

And this. Is. Paris.

Oh yeah—also, I'm stuck in a nightmare.

It's not just my mood—or my birthdays—that have gone darker. The thoughts have, too. The ones I thought I could bury. They're tipping the scale now. I'm drained from fighting them. Tired of resisting the cravings—the dangerous ones.

Ever since I checked out of that hotel, everything's gotten worse. The changes are subtle, but they're there. A bit grayer each day. A little less of me in control.

I'm exhausted. Burned out from trying. And dangerously close to giving up—to letting the prism take over completely. My mind. My body. My decisions.

After all, according to my mother, there's no point in fighting it. Control was never an option.

It's been exactly six months since I boarded that plane. Since I said goodbye to everyone—and everything—I ever knew and loved.

Six months since the prism's presence grew stronger. Since I became terrified of what that meant.

I arrived in France with few belongings and even fewer plans.

The excuse I gave immigration for needing a long-term visa was far from the truth—though it could've been, once. A year of research. That's what I told the tall, pale man who barely looked up during my extension interview. A sabbatical. A harmless art historian in need of time.

Why hadn't I done this years ago?

Because back then, I wasn't running.

But now... I'm not traveling. I'm hiding.

Any hope I had of figuring things out—gone.

Simply put: I'm fucked.

Alone. Hopeless. And very much fucked.

The burn of this poisonous stick blurs reality enough to keep me hooked. Just enough to dull the edge. To make me forget—if only for a split second.

At least the girl next door is happy. I can hear her getting railed through the thin walls of this shitty building. Her moans echo, the thrusts easy to count. At least someone's enjoying the night.

Outside, it's too dark to see anything clearly but people moving through the streetlights. But the sound carries. Laughter. Glasses clinking. Music from the bar downstairs—loud, like no one has anything to regret.

The city is always showing off. Couples touching like nothing could break them. Kids up past bedtime. Conversations spilling from open windows.

A motorcycle tears past, engine revving as it disappears down the street.

Out there, life continues.

In here, I'm just trying to make it to morning.

This isn't how I imagined seeing Paris for the first time. I was supposed to come with someone. The one. Being alone here feels wrong—yet here I am, a ghost in the most romantic city in the world.

I wait for the tears, like every other night. But nothing comes. Perhaps I'm finally empty.

I left the hotel weeks after arriving, once I realized I wouldn't be able to afford it for long.

Without a job, I've been draining my savings little by little—but only what was mine to begin with.

A few days after I disappeared, a large deposit appeared in my account. Aaron. I know it was him. It had to be. Maybe he sent a message to explain, but I never saw it.

I got rid of my phone before I even left the airport. I didn't know if phones could be tracked, but I wasn't going to risk it. Same with my laptop. I drowned it in the airport sink until I was sure it fried.

I wasn't simply cutting ties—I was erasing them. I needed everyone back home to forget me. For their own good.

And as for the money Aaron sent, I made myself a promise: I wouldn't touch a cent.

I hate that I left without an explanation. But maybe that's for the best. Maybe this way, he'll finally let go.

How am I supposed to do that?

A painful knot tightens in my chest as I let myself wonder—was Hoyt moving on? A part of me—a selfish part—hoped he wasn't. That part wished he was still stuck. Just like me. And like this damn window.

"Fuck," I mutter, wincing as I yank it down with one hand, my other hand still putting out the cigarette.

I wonder what my mom would say if she saw me now—her

little ballerina, high on nicotine, cursing, and very much wearing her precious necklace.

Forever connected.

Her words echo—etched in my mind since I read them on the plane.

I sit on the creaky old bed and read her letter for the millionth time.

Words I no longer need to read. Words I'll never forget.

The prism and I are one.

And just like clockwork, the crystal starts to hum. Low, steady, pulsing—like it's expecting me to do something. As if I need a reminder.

I've started to accept that perhaps I really am losing my mind —exactly like the healer in Salem warned me.

Maybe I'm running out of time. Out of sanity.

I force myself into my night routine.

Next step: James's words. I was surprised to find his pages in my suitcase when I opened it months ago.

Aaron must've scooped everything off my nightstand and thrown it in. I smiled at the strange collection he left me.

My lip balm—the rosemary scent like déjà vu, dragging me straight back home. I haven't dared apply it. I've been saving it, only opening the cap when I desperately need a reminder that my life there was real. That the people were, too.

A stretched-out hair tie, now perfectly molded to my wrist. A worn bookmark from Harvard's library. A crumpled receipt from brunch with Akira—she'd drawn a little heart next to her tip. And James's pages. They're wrinkled now, warped from nights I passed out on top of them.

It's become a ritual: T-shirt. Cigarette. James's words. Sleep, if it comes.

I glance at myself in the old vanity mirror. I barely recognize the woman staring back. Dark circles hollow out my eyes, my cheekbones too sharp, my skin so pale I look almost blue.

I run my hands down my shirt—Hoyt's shirt. I've had it since my time in Montana, when his home was mine too. I'm sure Aaron wouldn't have thrown it in... if he knew whom it belonged to.

Every part of me aches for human touch—for Hoyt's hands. Would I ever feel them again? After what I said to him, I don't deserve to.

I hate knowing I hurt him. If he only knew... I'd do anything to keep him safe. Happy. Whole. Because this... this life, if I can even call it that—I wouldn't wish it on anyone.

This is what I chose: solitude. And it's worse than I thought.

I keep thinking of that Gabriel García Márquez line: *"He really had been through death, but he had returned because he could not bear the solitude."* A passage I now understand with my soul.

Of course I didn't expect to make friends here. I don't even speak French.

But this is the first time in my life I've gone days—weeks— without speaking to another person.

I always thought I liked being on my own. Turns out it was just a hurt heart pretending not to need anyone.

I came here with one plan: to make a plan. But I quickly realized—I have no idea what I'm doing.

I don't want to stay in Paris. But I can't go home either. I could travel again, try a different country—one where I actually understand the language. But that would require effort.

And I'm too tired. Tired in my bones. Maybe it's my new diet: croissants, wine, espresso, and nicotine. Or maybe it's the fact I haven't slept through the night since Boston. Either way, traveling is out of the question.

As depressing as it is, I've worked hard to get used to it. The walls are thin, the carpet's musty, the windows don't seal, the heat groans, and the neighbors are unbearable— But it's home.

At least for now.

I'm only allowed to stay in France for a total of eight months.

Two left until I have to start over somewhere else. Unless... I come up with a miracle. Or a job. I'm counting on the miracle. Because a job would make this real.

I lie down, hoping for another dream. Sometimes they're just that—dreams. Fantasies. Scenes I let myself play out: soft, wild, even sexual.

But then there are the other ones. The magical ones. Those feel different. Darker. Twisted in ways I can't explain. But in those... he feels real. Like he's actually there. I'd endure whatever fucked-up thing the magic throws at me, as long as I'm not alone. As long as Hoyt's there.

And so, I close my eyes and wonder, *will he find me tonight?*

Two

Hoyt

I don't know who or what I'm looking for. Just that I'm moving with purpose. The crowd parts—then swallows me again. A kaleidoscope of velvet, shadow, and motion.

A bird. A feathered mask with beaded plumage so tall it nearly scrapes the chandeliers.

A long nose, gold-tipped, Venetian.

Laughter like wind chimes. Eyes—too many eyes—framed in crystal, smeared eyeliner, blood-colored glitter. Faces glide past like ghosts, half-sane. I'm not sure they see me. Or that they're even real. This place doesn't feel like mine. Feels like I've been dropped inside someone else's dream. *The fuck is this?*

Above, the ceiling disappears into smoke and candlelight. Below, the floor glows—crushed glass? Diamonds?

No footsteps echo—only the low thrum of music and magic, and the hum of something ancient, coiled beneath my skin.

In the crush of sequins, perfume and endless towers of champagne flutes, I ache. Not for drink. Not for a woman's touch. For something I can't put words to, but my body sure as hell knows. I feel my prism pulsing—not with pain. Not this time. With the hard edge of anticipation for something that feels mine, even before I've taken it.

"Well, hello, sir," purrs someone behind a feathery mask.

A woman tilts her head. Her lips are black. Smiling. The tone is thick with sweetness—almost cloying. It begs for attention. But my body's already turning away.

Something's calling me.

The music swells—Beethoven, then jazz, then techno—each beat crashing into the next like they're fighting for control. The tempo isn't just erratic. It's alive. It thrashes. Pulses. Seduces. Matching the rhythm of my prism, like the song is being chosen by something lodged inside my chest.

The strings tighten as my breath catches. The bass drops when the ache flares low in my spine. I don't hear it anymore—I feel it. Like I'm a drum someone else is playing.

I reach for a glass from the champagne tower—a pyramid of crystal so tall it seems to defy gravity. The stem is ice-cold in my hand, already damp. The liquid inside glows faintly and tastes like citrus and gold. Sweet. Biting. It fizzes across my tongue and slides down my throat like fangs. Not quite alcohol. *Not quite real.*

I glance down.

I'm in a tux again. Tailored. Heavy. Familiar. Black silk lapels. Cufflinks shaped like coins. Shoes so polished I can almost see the mask on my face reflected back.

This isn't a gala I remember.

The guests move like dancers. Or dolls.

And no one touches me.

A velvet curtain parts in front of me—thick and red, like the inside of a mouth. It moves as if it sensed I was coming.

I step through.

The air shifts. Heavier. Scented with perfume and something muskier underneath—wet silk, blood-orange, candle wax melting too close to skin.

I move past a mirrored pillar and find them.

Two figures pressed together, halfway undressed. Her skirt's shoved up, legs spread. His hand is all over her, slow like he's got nothing but time. Their masks are fancy—horns, jewels, faceless. She moans like she hasn't been touched in years. And he grins like a bastard who knows he's in control.

I turn away, throat tight. This isn't about shame. It's recognition—of a hunger I know too well. This entire place feels and looks like a play, a woman's fantasy. Nothing like any dream I ever had.

I don't belong here.

Am I hiding? Or am I hunting?

The question barely forms before breath brushes the shell of my ear—close. Too close.

"I like them." The voice knows me.

I start to turn, but I don't even get a chance to see—

"You look good in antlers."

Then it's gone. No footsteps.

I catch my reflection in the glass.

My hands lift to the mask—antlers, long and sharp, like bone grown wrong. I feel them. Regal. Savage.

I used to collect antlers like these—back in Montana, when the woods still felt like mine. When Luke was alive. We hunted deer at dawn. Two brothers, one bow. One shot, if we were lucky.

That was before the prisms. Before his started whispering to him. Before the voices took him someplace I couldn't follow.

I haven't picked up a bow since. But something in me remembers.

I keep moving. I don't know why.

But when the music halts, the crowd moves as one—toward something.

Outside.

I follow.

We're not in the ballroom anymore.

The walls dissolve behind me and suddenly I'm in the woods.

A forest stretches in every direction—vast and breathless. The air is colder here.

Tall pines, black and towering, spiral toward a sky that looks painted in oil.

The moon hangs silver—bright enough to buzz, but cold. No heat. Just watching.

The clearing is ringed in torches, flickering low in iron holders shaped like claws. I see masks with horns. Masks with beaks. A man in a wolf pelt drags his fingers through the dirt like it's ash. A woman with a serpent mask pours something red onto her gloves. Every branch overhead bends slightly inward, as if to listen.

No music now. Only breath.

"Let the hunting begin," someone declares.

Their voice echoes like a command.

And the crowd breaks. Masks scatter. Feet run. Some slither, some crawl, some howl. It's not panic. It's instinct.

The forest accepts us. And it closes.

I go with them.

I hear men laughing—inhaling against bark like animals.

Then I do it too.

And then...

I smell her.

Not perfume—no. It's the rosemary lip balm she wore. Faintly sweet. A little medicinal. It mixes with whiskey and the petals of the iris bouquet I gave her in Boston.

It's her.

It's her.

And like a drug, it takes me.

I lose myself in it.

I need more.

Every tree pulls me forward. Each wrong turn makes me hungrier.

All around me, others do the same — crawling, panting, masked in jewels and fur.

This is a ritual.

My shirt clings to my skin. I'm sweating.

The indigo glow of my prism pulses through me—and even here, even in the woods—

it looks expensive. Dangerous. All screams, fucked up old money magic.

And then a real scream cuts through the dark. High. Human. Raw. A woman.

I freeze. My instincts fire—go to her, help her, run toward the sound.

But I don't.

My feet move the opposite way. I try to turn. I swear I do.

My shoulders twitch like they're fighting a harness—but I've already lost.

I'm not running anymore. I'm being pulled.

My hands find the trees. Palms scraping bark like I'm trying to hold onto something—anything. Splinters bite under my nails. Blood smears on wood. But I can't stop. I don't want to stop. Because the air has changed. It's thicker now. Stickier. Saturated with her.

It's not memory. It's her. The scent is viscous. Real. Warm skin.

It coats my throat and it floods my lungs.

And my body answers like it's starving. My spine arches. My mouth parts.

She's close.

Too close.

I want to scream.

Bite.

Rip something open.

But I stay silent. All the noise stays inside me, cracking bone.

So I run—frantic—because this wait can't wait any longer.

This curse... it will take me if I don't take her first.

Right before my body tears itself apart, I see it—her violet light, suspended in air.

"No, no, no…" I whisper.

Not the light. Not the prism.

I want her.

I need her—

Her hands. Her skin. Her mouth, saying my name like it used to mean something.

But I move closer anyway.

The violet light pulses mid-air—like a spell in progress.

I step closer.

One step. Then another.

"There you are," says a voice behind me.

I turn.

And she's there.

Her voice is calm.

Too calm.

Torn silk clinging to her hips. Fingernails, bloodied. Red hair tangled like vines after a storm. A lace mask veils her eyes, but not the expression beneath. Not the knowing. And all I can think about is ripping the rest off and pinning her down, holding her in place and sinking my teeth into her, tasting what's mine, giving in like an animal.

She's standing perfectly still, like she's been waiting for hours.

Like she's not surprised to see me at all.

"Iris?"

Her name slips out—like a confession. Not a question. A hope.

But something in my bones begins to shake. Because she's close now. Too close.

And if this is a dream, then it's the kind that knows how to lie.

"What took you so long?" she asks.

Her fingers lift to my mask, tracing the bone ridge.

It can't be her. She wouldn't touch me like this.

But just before that realization can break me—I inhale again.

God. That scent.

My body reacts before I can think, cock straining like it's been waiting for her my whole damn life.

Her lips graze mine.

And I feel our prisms touch.

Violet and indigo collide—gold-white sparks flaring between them.

Something magnetic pulls at the center of my chest.

I forget how to breathe.

She says something I can't hear.

Or maybe I do—and I'm just not ready.

And right before I take her—make her mine—

I wake up.

THREE

"WE DO NOT REMEMBER DAYS, WE REMEMBER MOMENTS." – CESARE PAVESE

The knock jolts me awake—obnoxious and way too loud for whatever ungodly hour this is.

I push off the blanket and shiver. The room's cold, and the draft cuts through my bare legs.

I instinctively wrap my arms around myself, though it does little good.

Still half-asleep, I stumble toward the door, mind racing with irritation.

My fingers fumble with the rusted lock—always stubborn, always jamming when I need it to work quickly.

Who the hell knocks like that this early?

I crack open the creaky door.

The woman from downstairs stands there in a frayed night-gown and slippers that look older than the stairs.

"Le loyer," she says flatly.

She barely speaks English, but when I showed up with a wad of cash and pointed at the faded ad on the door, she just nodded and led me upstairs.

I'm staring blankly at the peeling floral pattern on her robe when she thrusts her hand out, palm open. "Money."

"Oh. Right." I blink.

I motion awkwardly for her to wait and retreat into the room, stepping over dirty clothes, my mind foggy and slow.

I dig through the mess—sweater, pillow, yesterday's jeans—until I find my bag under my jacket.

The cash is folded and slightly damp from whatever else was in there.

I hand it to her without ceremony.

She takes it without a word of thanks, mumbles something in French I can't make out, tucks the bills into her robe pocket, and turns away. The stairs groan under her weight as she disappears back down.

Another rent paid. Another month gone.

What day is it, even?

I drag myself back to bed, sink into the mattress, and pull the covers over my head—knowing full well I won't be able to fall back asleep.

I beg my brain to shut off, to dive into oblivion.

But it's no use.

And that dream I just woke from—it's still with me. Not like a memory. Like a wound.

The forest. His mask. The heat between us.

I remember every breath.

Within each dream, I feel them getting heavier, harder to shake off.

And that scares the hell out of me.

Then reality sets in.

Paris.

Alone.

And no one's coming.

* * *

There's only one thing strong enough to pull me out of this confinement.

Coffee.

And the thought of going without it is worse than the paranoia I've developed lately.

I blame that—my fear of noise, of people—on the incident with Darion.

My hatred for him grows by the minute.

I throw on my sweatshirt and scan the floor for my sneakers. The only comfortable shoes I have.

Somehow, a stupid pair of high heels made it into my suitcase.

I'll never forgive myself for buying them, let alone for the precious inches of space they stole.

I wanted to blame Aaron for the dumb choice, but I knew I'd given him an impossible task. Everything I have right now is because of him.

I've been meaning to check out the thrift store near the market, but it's never open when I'm nearby.

I could've gone shopping in one of the nice boutiques across the center square—

But I refuse to waste money. I need to make it last.

I tiptoe down the stairs, careful not to hit the squeaky ones.

If I'm not quiet, the little poodle on the second floor starts barking—and that means his grouchy owner will come out yelling. Mostly French, but the meaning's universal: Go away.

The streets are calmer now. Early risers sip their coffee and read their papers.

I'm surprised by how many still opt for the physical news here —something I only notice because of the rustling pages. Headlines I can't seem to care about anymore.

The city feels paused, waiting for the day to begin. Or maybe... that's how I feel before coffee.

I have to walk six blocks to Café au Lait, the only bakery near me willing to make an American latte. It's a small, unassuming place tucked between a florist and an old building.

The sweet, yeasty scent of fresh pastries greets me the moment I push open the door. It's comforting. Familiar, even if the faces inside change every day.

The barista knows my order by heart now.

He never asks for more than a nod, and I'm grateful for that. No small talk. Just the warm, sweet relief of a latte that tastes like home. Without appliances in the apartment, I'm at his mercy. There's only so much instant coffee a person can take.

"Good morning!" says the friendly Julien.

"Bonjour," I reply with a small wave.

"The store next to the market—do you know when they open?" I ask.

"Who knows. Whenever Odette feels like it. She's... a little strange," he says, already turning to take another customer's order.

"Thank you," I say, and head out with my coffee in hand.

Along with my strength, I seem to have lost my care for appearances. I catch a glimpse of myself in a car window as I pass and barely recognize the face staring back. I look miserable.

The thought lingers, but I shove it aside. As though it's irrelevant.

I nearly trip, catching myself just in time when my foot hits an uneven patch of pavement.

The jolt reminds me how little attention I've been paying to my surroundings.

The streets here—weathered and cracked—hold a history of their own.

They seem to whisper the stories of everyone who's walked this path before me. People who've lived, loved, and left their marks on this city.

I lift my gaze, distracted by the irregular shapes of the buildings. Each one feels like a piece of art—distinct, with its own character. The way the façades lean into each other—some grand and ornate, others plain and modern—without competition.

Even in this tiny, tucked-away side street, Paris remains undeniably beautiful.

It's in the details. A place that holds so much, even in its quietest corners.

I haven't left my apartment much for this exact reason.

I refuse to walk around like a tourist in search of happiness.

Refuse to pretend everything is fine.

I need a plan.

And until I come up with one, I'm not allowing myself to get distracted.

Even if it's painful not to make it to the Louvre. To be so close to the Mona Lisa and not take one peek.

But that's the reward, I tell myself daily.

"Hello, do you speak English?" I ask the woman sweeping the floor.

Her long skirt does a better job than the broom in her hands.

"No," she replies without glancing up.

"Shoes?" I ask, pointing to my own.

She gestures to a wall in the back.

The place is packed—antique furniture crammed together, objects stacked haphazardly, with no sense of categorization. Wherever something fit, it stayed. No regard for order.

Chairs are piled on top of one another. Tarnished mirrors lean against crooked tables.

Dusty vases rest on faded rugs.

No system. Simply the feeling that everything here is waiting to be uncovered.

I make my way to the bins of shoes, dragging my fingers across cracked leather and chipped porcelain as I pass.

I pull out one pair, then another—scuffed toes and mismatched heels.

After trying on a few, I come to a simple conclusion: the shoes on my feet are perfectly fine.

I kick the bins closed, the scent of old fabric lingering in the air as I stand up.

I continue my rounds through the store, weaving between fur coats—once glorious, now dulled by age—and racks of old hats, some too extravagant, others too worn to be useful.

I can't help myself.

I'm completely mesmerized by the things around me.

It's more than the refreshment of seeing something new after being trapped in the same apartment for so long.

It's that I would've loved to spend the whole day here, browsing.

This was the kind of thing I used to love back home.

And now, I can't help but notice how pointless it all feels.

Still, the historian in me can't help herself.

I pick up a bronze brooch nestled among the other pieces on the counter.

It's Art Nouveau—its intricate, flowing lines a delicate testament to a time when beauty and nature seemed to fuse into one.

The brooch is shaped like a fairy, her wings unfurling in graceful, sweeping curves.

I've always admired the mystical, romantic style that flourished during the Belle Époque. Orchids, lilies, snakes, and dragonflies are etched in delicate relief on the silver tray beside me—each piece capturing the essence of nature's wonders, twisted into something otherworldly and elegant.

I hold the brooch up to the light, marveling at the way the bronze glints—its vibrant sheen now softened by the passage of time. The curves of the design speak to something fantastical.

I trace the details of the fairy's face.

Then an unexpected voice snaps me out of it.

"No touching," says the older woman, tapping my hand.

I quickly put the brooch back and apologize.

I must look like someone who can't afford anything here.

If only she knew—I would've been a frequent customer in another life. My past life.

I step back out into the street, scanning for another store—hoping to find one with a friendlier owner.

After passing a couple of churches, I realize I've reached the farthest I've been from the apartment.

I take a turn into an alley and spot a mime performing on the street.

His white face paint is already fading, the lines around his mouth cracking.

I must've been staring, because he winks.

I glance around, unsure it was meant for me.

It was.

I'm about to keep walking when he steps in front of me, and I almost jump back.

He quickly mutters an apology in French.

Maybe a normal person wouldn't have reacted so abruptly.

But I haven't felt normal in a long time.

My body's shaking, and I'm struggling to catch my breath.

The striped man looks embarrassed, but still hands me a flyer.

I take it, and he steps aside.

I'm still trying to steady myself when I look down.

It's a flyer for a live music night.

I toss it into my purse, not knowing what else to do with it.

I turn around, deciding I've done enough venturing for one day.

My breath slows, catching up with my steps as I make my way back home.

I stop at the market to pick up a few things—some fresh fruit, a carton of eggs, and a few other odds and ends.

I take out extra cash from the ATM, just in case. I've debated whether that's smart—even an ATM swipe is traceable, but one withdrawal beats ten swipes. Cash feels safer.

I'm munching on a piece of baguette when I notice movement out of the corner of my eye.

A dog.

It's following me, its tail wagging weakly but still full of hope.

I slow my pace, and for a moment, I wonder if I'm imagining it.

But no. It's real.

Sometimes I feel like I'm being watched. Hunted. Haunted.

I have to double-check constantly that the things around me are actually real—like the red pulse I often catch in the reflection of windows.

Real. Not just panic. Not just fear that Darion has found me again.

The dog keeps his distance, watching me intently.

Feeling a mix of sympathy and curiosity, I pull a piece of salami from my bag and toss it toward him.

He sniffs it for a moment, then devours it in seconds. His ribs show through his coat. His fur is scruffy and matted. He looks like he hasn't had a proper meal in days—maybe longer.

A pang tightens in my chest as I watch him, his eyes still fixed on me.

Pleading. As if to say, *Is that all?*

I glance around quickly, noticing that no one else seems to be around.

The loneliness of it hits me—this dog is only trying to survive in a world that doesn't seem to care.

Just like me.

And yet, I know someone else would be a better fit to help him right now.

"Sorry," I mutter under my breath. "I can't even take care of myself."

My heart twinges again, but I can't change the reality of the situation.

I give him the rest of my salami and pick up my pace, hoping he'll move on.

Hoping someone else will find him—someone who actually has their shit together.

The dog hesitates, his gaze still locked on me.

Then, slowly, he turns and walks away, his head hanging low.

I keep moving, guilt and helplessness—the image of that lonely creature stuck in my mind as I make my way home.

By the time I reach my building, I'm completely exhausted.

The couple of miles I walked felt more like ten.

I almost slip going up the steep stairs.

A door creaks open somewhere nearby, and I use what little strength I have left to rush the rest of the way.

I can't handle another interaction right now.

I'm fussing with the lock when the door next to mine opens.

Marie—at least, I think that's her name, from the breathy sounds through the wall—steps out with that easy Parisian confidence: messy knot of dark hair, slip dress hanging on like it belongs to the street as much as to her.

I've just finished unlocking my door when she turns to me.

"Bonjour," she says.

I look at her. "Bonjour," I reply, still out of breath.

Then she says something else—still in French.

"Sorry," I say, already pulling open my door. "English only."

"Oh, you are an American," she says, like she's finally figured me out.

"Yes," I reply, almost apologizing for my own nationality.

"Are you living here? Alone?" she asks, continuing the conversation like we're friends.

"Yes," I say quickly.

"Here for work?"

At this point, I'm just waiting for her to leave so I can shut the door.

"No. I'm just living here. Not working."

"Huh." She keeps eyeing me.

I have no idea what her attitude means, but I don't care.

I close the door without even saying "good day."

Let the world judge me.

I have bigger problems.

Like *what the fuck I'm supposed to do with my life.*

Four

"We are all in the gutter, but some of us are looking at the stars." – Oscar Wilde

It's one of those days when I can't hold a single thought in place. They ricochet between catastrophes—*what if they find me, what if I never go home, what if this is who I am now.* I try to calm down, but nothing works.

I'm pacing around, impatiently searching for my lighter in the mess I call an apartment. It's really just a studio: one wide, open room with an old bed and a bathroom the size of a coffin. The sink is always clogged. The shower spits as if it's as angry as I am.

The kitchen matches the place perfectly—like someone designed it to look as rusted, cracked, and miserable as possible. But at least everything works. Mostly. And the rent is cheap. That's what matters.

I finally spot my bag slumped against the wall, like it's been hiding from me. I lunge for it, muttering half-formed curses as I tear through the contents. Lip balm, old receipts, a crushed protein bar, loose change—none of it what I need.

Maybe I really did lose the damn lighter this time.

A crumpled piece of paper flutters out and lands at my feet like it's been waiting for this exact moment.

The flyer.

I smooth it out between my fingers.

Chandelier: Live French Jazz.

I check the date twice. Tonight.

I glance at the clock ticking lazily on the side table.

If I leave now, I could still make it.

I don't let myself overthink it. I shove on my shoes and head out—then find the stupid lighter in my jacket pocket.

Figures.

I puff on the cigarette like it might bring clarity, but I know better. Perhaps a bit of fresh air will knock something loose in my brain.

I've spent the entire day in bed. Crying. Thinking. Crying again. Trying to come up with one positive thought and failing. Looks like my body's replenished its reservoir of tears.

I'm walking aimlessly when I look around and realize I've managed to get myself lost.

"Excuse me?" I ask a woman sitting on a bench, but she ignores me.

"Pardon?" I try again, this time in French. She turns.

I hold out the flyer. "This place—do I turn here?" I ask, pointing toward the narrow street ahead.

She shakes her head and points the opposite direction.

"Merci," I say, heading where she directed.

I'm halfway down the block when something shifts in the air. A tightness, a prickle on the back of my neck.

I glance behind me. Nothing.

I take another drag and keep walking.

But the feeling doesn't fade—it sharpens. Like I'm being watched.

Paranoia, I tell myself. Since the fire... since Darion... that hunted feeling never really left me. Sometimes I even dream I'm being followed. Sometimes, I wake up convinced it wasn't just a dream.

I quicken my pace. Turn a corner. And that's when I know for sure—someone's behind me. Closer now.

My legs move faster.

Another turn. Dead end.

"Shit," I breathe.

I spin around—too late. A figure stands there. Large, unmoving. A man, probably, by his size. I can't see his face, only a sliver of dim lamplight glinting off something metallic at his side.

A cane?

But it's the shadow beside him that turns my blood cold.

Because it isn't his.

It moves independently. Wavering and bodiless, like smoke pressed into the shape of something human.

I blink—and for the briefest second, something flares in the dark. A thin red light, sharp and unnatural. Could that be...

My prism stirs. Not in warning—but recognition. A subtle pull in my chest, magnetic and familiar. The same way it reached for Hoyt's.

But this isn't Hoyt.

Before I can understand—the shadow lunges.

I stumble backward. I try to scream—but something covers my mouth.

I don't know if it's the figure, the shadow, or some force in my own brain shutting me down.

And then—

Nothing.

When I open my eyes, the world is blinding.

I'm on the ground. The street's cold beneath me, wet with something I don't want to know. My palms are scraped. My lip tastes like blood. The world still feels slightly tilted—like it's not fully real.

A ring of strangers looms above me. Shadows shift. Voices blur.

"Are you okay?"

I flinch, scrambling backward.

"We're not going to hurt you," a man says quickly, hands raised, stepping back. "You speak English?"

I nod, dazed. "What... what happened?"

"We heard you scream."

He kneels, offering a hand. A woman beside him crouches too.

"You were calling for help," she says, gently.

I blink at them. My head pounds. I don't remember making a sound.

"You sure you're alright?" the woman asks. She looks young. They all do—early twenties.

"Yeah," I lie, pushing myself up. The world tilts.

"We can walk you home if you want," the guy offers.

"No," I say too fast. Too harsh.

I don't want to go home. I don't want to be alone. But I can't admit that out loud.

I reach into my pocket and pull out the flyer. "I'm on my way to—" I say, holding it up.

"Oh—the Chandelier?" the girl says, recognition lighting her face. "We're headed there too. Come with us. It's safer than wandering around alone."

I hesitate. But the group behind them is mixed—friends, laughter, the smell of cigarettes and something fried. Harmless. Warm.

I nod once. But my body doesn't relax.

The back of my neck still tingles, like something's watching me. Like the presence is still there, just one breath behind.

Was it real? Or is my traumatic past finally getting the best of me?

I have a feeling I got lucky tonight, even though I'm not sure what happened.

Chills come and go in waves. I let out a shaky sigh and force my feet to follow theirs.

"Good," the girl says, "I'm Bella—Isabela, by the way."

"I'm Iris."

"Nice to meet you." She gestures to the others. "That's Tommaso—he goes by Tom. And Rocco. And Anna."

"Are you all Italian?" I ask, though I'd already guessed from the way they slip into Italian between sentences.

She grins. "Sì. But Tom lives here."

Tom nods at me, then mutters something in Italian to the others as we start walking. There's something familiar in the way he carries himself—like I've seen him in passing before.

"Where are you from?" Bella asks, falling into step beside me.

"America, Boston."

"I told you," Tom calls from ahead. "I can always tell."

"Are you visiting?" Bella asks.

"No. Kind of. I'm here temporarily."

I hate that answer. I hate that I don't have a better one.

"And you?" I ask her.

"I'm here for the weekend," she says. "From Milano."

We turn onto a livelier street, neon flickering above cobblestones. My shoulders slowly unknot.

"Here we are," Tom says, pointing up.

A glowing sign reads CHANDELIER. Music hums through the door. The building reflects warm amber from the inside.

I glance behind me one more time before we step inside. Nothing. Still—I don't let myself exhale fully.

At least I'm not alone.

FIVE

"THE BEST WAY OF KEEPING A SECRET IS TO PRETEND THERE ISN'T ONE." – MARGARET ATWOOD

The heavy wooden doors swing open, and the music spills out like a flood. It hits me harder than caffeine, sharper than adrenaline. Like a switch flipping inside me. Every dormant part of me stirs. Cells fire awake.

I stop in the doorway, stunned—letting it wash over me.

It's not just the music.

It's the familiarity.

The comfort of chaos.

I haven't been to a bar since I landed in Paris. No clubs. No dinners. Not even late nights out. I've been hiding, keeping my head down as much as possible.

Bella's call snaps me back. "Come on, you'll love Celine."

The bar is packed. Round wooden tables crowded with people, each group louder, rowdier than the next. I clock the empty stage.

We weave through the crowd. The group gestures for me to join them.

The moment I sit, the noise shifts—my body's here, my mind is somewhere else.

"Are you meeting anyone here?" Tom asks, pulling out the chair beside me.

"No," I say. "Tommaso, right?" I try to recall the names.

"You can call me Tom."

"Thanks, Tom." I offer a small nod as I settle in.

He says something in Italian to the others and disappears into the crowd.

Minutes later, a waitress appears to take our order—apparently, Tom already told her he was covering the round.

"Salute!" Bella grins beside me, lifting her wine glass.

For a moment, I let myself think of Akira—her bright smile, the way she always toasted too early and too loudly.

I shut it down fast.

My past needs to stay behind, sealed behind ironclad doors. I can't afford the melancholy.

I'm getting good at this. Shutting it out. Numbing it down.

I take one sip of my wine and excuse myself to the bathroom.

The cold water I splash on my face brings a flush to my skin. I grip the sink, stare at my reflection.

"What the hell happened?" I whisper.

No answer.

Only a headache blooming behind my eyes.

I lean on the porcelain edge, weighing my options: I could leave. Go home. Curl up in that miserable apartment and spiral. Try to figure out if tonight meant something—or if I'm finally slipping. Or I could stay. Let the music dull the panic. Let the wine smooth the edges.

Pretend—for one night—that I'm not unraveling.

Option two seems... easier.

Even if it's a lie.

By the time I return to the table, the music stops and the lights shift.

Like everyone else, I turn toward the stage.

A woman in a silver dress stands in the spotlight.

She turns and acknowledges the crowd.

Then she sings.

I've heard it before—muffled through the thin apartment walls. My neighbors played it often.

"Look at him—Tom is so talented!" Bella beams, pointing toward the stage.

I follow her gaze, confused—until I spot the pianist. Tom.

His fingers barely graze the keys, but the sound is anything but gentle. It's rich. Intense. Effortless and aching. Like emotion made audible. It nearly brings tears to my eyes.

When was the last time I felt like this? Truly *felt* anything?

Tom plays. Celine sings. And for the length of the song, I forget everything.

The people around me.

Where I am.

Who I am.

Each note reaches somewhere deep—like it was written for moments I lost, for places I've never been, but somehow remember.

The room fades.

It's just me and the music.

The sudden cheer of the group around me shatters the silence.

I blink, jolted, and clap along.

The warmth of the bar rushes back in.

Another round of drinks and appetizers appears at our table. The chatter swells again but I'm still somewhere in the echoes of that song. The notes linger.

We raise our glasses—*à la nuit*—and I actually smile. The taste of French jazz still sweet on my tongue.

I'm halfway through my wine when Hoyt slips into my thoughts.

The antlers. The way I touched him in the dream.

I blink it away.

By the end of the night, Celine makes her way to our table.

"You sang beautifully," I tell her.

"*Merci,*" she replies, smiling as she thanks the others around us.

Tom joins a moment later, and it hits me: I'm the only outsider at this table.

I suddenly feel out of place. It's time I get back to my headquarters.

"Thank you for saving me tonight," I say, standing.

"Leaving already?" Celine asks across the table.

"Yes. I think I'm tired. But again, thank you—for everything."

I turn to leave when Tom stands too.

"I'll walk you home. I'm tired anyway."

I want to tell him it's unnecessary.

But maybe a part of me is still a little disturbed.

"You played beautifully tonight," I say as we step outside.

"Thank you," he replies, calm and quiet.

"You really don't have to do this. You should stay with your friends," I add, glancing at him from the corner of my eye as we walk down the dim, cobbled street.

"No worries," he says, hands tucked into his coat pockets, voice easy. "I'm seeing them again tomorrow. And if you were my sister, I'd hope someone would walk her home after a night like that."

He gives me a faint smile.

"You have a sister?" I ask.

"Three, actually."

"Do they live here? In France?"

He shakes his head. "I'm the only one out here. Came for work. Well—came because of Celine, really. I think she can make it big. She's insanely talented."

"She really is something," I agree.

"She doesn't simply sing. She feels every note. You can tell it's personal. That kind of honesty on stage? It's rare. I think it's going to take her far."

I picture the way Celine's voice filled the bar—how it made everything else disappear.

"So... are you two... together?" The words slip out before I can stop them. I immediately regret asking.

He glances at me, a flicker of surprise in his eyes—but it fades quickly. His lips curve into a small, sincere smile.

"No, nothing like that," he says, shaking his head. "We're friends. I've got a girlfriend—Marie. She couldn't make it tonight. Work."

I nod, relieved and embarrassed all at once.

"What part of Italy are you from?" I ask, needing to keep talking.

"Milan," he replies. "And you? Where in the States?"

"Boston."

We fall into a comfortable silence with the soft pulse of the Seine in the distance.

"Thank you, by the way," I say as we reach my building. "For the drinks. And the food. They said you paid."

"Oh sure," he says with a shrug. "They came all the way here to see me—seemed like the least I could do."

"This is me," I say, a little embarrassed as we approach my building. It's seen better days, and I suddenly feel self-conscious about the cracked stucco and broken entry light.

"You live here?" he asks, eyeing the door.

"Yes. Temporarily," I add quickly, already spinning an excuse. "The building... has some character."

"Interesting," he says.

"Why?"

Instead of answering, he reaches into his pocket and pulls out a key. Then—without ceremony—he slides it into the lock and pushes the door open.

"You're kidding," I say, staring at him. "We're neighbors?"

"Looks like it," he says, holding the door for me.

"I live in 6B," I tell him, still trying to wrap my head around it.

"6A," he replies, heading for the stairs.

I blink. Of course. The guy whose music keeps me up at night. The girl I saw in the hallway—Marie—that was his girlfriend.

"How haven't we met yet?" he asks, unlocking his own door.

"I don't get out much," I say with a shrug.

"Oh no," he says, wincing. "Now I feel terrible for being so loud. Playing music at all hours..."

"Don't worry about it," I reply. "I don't sleep well anyway."

He doesn't quite believe me. The apologetic look he gives me says as much.

"Well... good night. And thank you again," I add.

"No problem," he says, and I slip into my apartment.

I want to believe the worst is behind me tonight.

But the second the door shuts, the truth settles in my chest like a stone.

The air is thick with that smell again—rotting, sour, stagnant. My mood tanks on impact. I glance toward the overflowing trash can, my stomach twisting.

How had I gone this long without noticing?

I tie the strings in a shaky knot, the plastic stretching ominously. It's overstuffed—contents bulging, the bag nearly splitting in my hands.

I haul the bag and try to tiptoe downstairs to the trash chute, praying it holds.

It doesn't.

Halfway down the hall, the bottom splits open. Glass crashes to the floor, echoing down the stairwell like a grenade. A bottle of something sticky and alcoholic bursts—right on my neighbor's welcome mat.

Fantastic.

I scramble to gather the mess, muttering curses under my breath.

Too late.

His door creaks open, and the yelling begins—rapid-fire

French and furious gestures. There's some relief in not understanding what he's saying.

I stammer out an apology right as his tiny dog bursts through the doorway, yapping and sniffing frantically at the trash-strewn hallway.

It's chaos: barking, glass rolling, food everywhere, angry French raining down and then, as if summoned by the disaster, Tom steps out of his apartment.

He doesn't even ask—he just kneels and starts helping.

Fifteen mortifying minutes later, the hallway is clean and the trash is finally dumped. I'm fairly certain Tom now knows more about my diet and lifestyle than anyone should. Unfortunately, you really can judge a person by their trash.

"Thank you for saving my life again—twice in one day. I guess I owe you now."

He laughs, brushing his hands off. "Don't worry. Gérard's mean to everyone," he says, jerking his chin toward the neighbor's now-silent door.

"Iris?" Tom calls as I'm about to close my door.

"Yeah?" I pause, turning back.

He hesitates, then asks, "Have you ever been to the Catacombs?"

The question catches me off guard. "What?"

"The Catacombs," he repeats, leaning casually against the doorframe. "Probably not your thing. Not exactly for the faint of heart."

I blink at him. "No. Haven't been."

He nods like he figured. "We're all going tomorrow night. Marie, Bella, Rocco. Celine and I were invited to play at a private event. It's... sort of a secret show. Very selective. Fancy crowd, candlelit everything. One of those things people only hear about if they're supposed to be there."

He pauses, then adds carefully, "They didn't say anything about how many guests. So if you want to come..."

He trails off like he's not sure how much to say, then finishes with, "If you feel like getting out."

There's a softness in the way he says it, measured and cautious. Like he doesn't want to push. Like he's worried I'll take it the wrong way.

Do I look that isolated?

That... breakable?

"Thank you, but... I'm not very fun to be around right now," I admit honestly.

Tom nods. "I get it. If you change your mind, I'm heading out around seven."

"Thanks, Tom. But I think I'm going to have to pass."

"Alright. Good night," he says, slipping into his apartment.

"Good night." I close my door for the last time tonight.

I go straight to bed, worn out from the unexpected outing. I have to admit—it was nice. Having someone to talk to. More than a few words. A small break from my breakdown.

But it doesn't last.

I toss and turn, the sheets twisted beneath me, my body soaked with sweat. My head is pounding.

How am I supposed to sleep with this damn light around my neck?

The prism glows brighter than ever—like the freaking sun at this time of night.

I've lost what little control I thought I had over it. Not that I ever really had any. With this much sweat dripping down, there is nothing I can do to turn it off.

I press a hand to my chest, trying to calm my breathing. But the light doesn't dim.

I don't even have a reason this time.

I can't blame a nightmare—at least, not one I remember. I try to sit up. Why am I so dizzy?

My legs slide off the bed like they weigh more than they should. I push myself upright.

I need water. My mouth is bone dry.

I didn't even finish a full glass of wine at the bar. I can't possibly be hungover. I try to reason with myself, but the logic doesn't land. My body feels strange—off.

I shuffle toward the kitchen, passing the old mirror above the dresser—and freeze.

I scream.

My own reflection stares back at me, but for one split second I could've sworn there was something else: a shape, a shadow, a figure standing right behind me.

I stare harder. Nothing now but me, wide-eyed and shaking.

"What the fuck..." I whisper.

My chest is tight. My pulse won't slow. I press a hand to my sternum and force myself to breathe.

I move to the sink, fill a glass with water, and down it in a single gulp.

Another.

I close my eyes.

In and out.

It's barely a habit anymore, but I whisper the words anyway. "In and out."

Of course there wasn't anything in the mirror.

I tell myself that again as I step closer to it. Just my own reflection. Nothing more.

Is being alone making me lose it? Or has the prism's energy finally started to take over?

The thought lands like a weight on my chest.

If I'm losing it, *who would even notice?*

No one's watching. No one's coming.

My hands tremble, reaching for the only thing I have left that might calm me down. I have no alcohol left. Just this.

I head toward the window, reaching for my cigarettes when I pass the mirror again, and the sight of it sends my nerves into a tailspin.

That oval thing has always creeped me out, but tonight it looks like it's watching.

I can't relax with it exposed.

I glance around, spot a dirty sheet crumpled on the floor, and toss the cigarette between my lips so my hands are free. I grab the fabric and climb onto my toes to cover the glass—stretching toward the top of the frame.

And that's when I see it again.

A shadow. Behind me.

Clear this time.

I whip around, heart hammering. The sheet slips from my hands.

I slam into the lamp, knocking it over.

The prism flares to life against my chest, its light pulsing wildly as sweat pours down my back.

My breath is jagged. My hands frozen.

I force myself to move, to look again. Back to the mirror. Slowly, cautiously.

There's nothing there.

Only me. Shaking. Eyes wide. Alone.

It's gone. The shadow's gone.

The prism dims.

If not for the full moon flooding through the window, I wouldn't see the broken shards of the lamp beneath my feet. I step over them, barefoot, trembling, and sink onto the edge of my bed.

What the hell is happening to me?

I crawl under the covers and bury myself in silence.

I stare at the ceiling, refusing to blink.

Eventually, the darkness wins.

My eyes close.

And sleep takes me.

SIX

HOYT

For a moment, everything is still.

Glass everywhere—not a room, not a cell. A prism.

I don't know how I know this. I just do.

I lift my hand to touch the wall and freeze.

My hand isn't a hand.

It's softer. Hairless. Angled wrong. My skin is ash-pale, multi-colored. My fingers end in feelers, like some sickening insect. My chest flickers in the reflection like it's made of wings.

I lean closer to the glass and stare into eyes that aren't mine—bulbous, endless, not human. *Moth eyes.* Glowing. Watching everything and nothing all at once.

And then instinct hits.

I fling myself forward—into the glass.

It doesn't budge.

Again.

And again.

Each strike harder. Desperate. Wild.

Something inside me wants out. Something knows she's close.

The third strike leaves a crack.

Before I can hit again, a hand slices through the crack.

Not to stop me.
To reach for me.
Feminine.
Her hand.
I land in her palm like I was made for it. Her fingers curl slowly —possessive, unhurried—and I'm caught in the warm cage of her skin.

She lifts me toward her mouth.

"What took you so long?" she asks, eyes gleaming.

"What?" My voice is nothing but air.

"I was waiting to see if you had what it takes... to get out and find me."

My wings twitch, angry with urgency. I want to get closer. I want to flee.

"Shhh..." Her breath fans over me. "So desperate."

I try to fly.

She cups her hand tighter, locking me in.

"Where do you think you're going, moth man?"

"This some kind of dream?"

"I don't care if it is."

"Let me go now." I rasp, unsure of what I even mean.

"Why would I?" she says, voice low. "We're only getting started."

She pins me gently against the glass wall with two fingers— careful, but not kind.

It burns.

My wings twitch.

Suddenly we're the same size again.

I'm human again.

She steps in and presses her mouth to the center of my chest.

It burns like a brand.

Leaves a mark straight over my heart.

I grit my teeth on the hiss.

And still—

"Don't stop," I growl.

So she doesn't.

She kisses lower. Slower. One after the other—branding me with every pass of her mouth.

I reach for her.

This time, I grab her wrist and hold her there. Her lips are pressed to my ribs. I can feel her smile against my skin.

"Still desperate?" she murmurs, not looking up.

"You're the one on your knees."

Her laugh is vicious.

She drags her teeth across my abs. Once. Just enough to make me flinch.

"So. Pretty," she says.

"Fucking suck it already," I order.

She undoes my jeans. Doesn't touch. But stares. Like she's considering every way she can torture me.

My cock's already hard.

But I keep my eyes on her. Let her see I'm not breaking.

Not yet.

"Are you sure?" she asks, voice wicked-soft.

"You want me to make you?"

She doesn't answer—but raises one brow, teasing.

I run my thumb along her jaw. Slow.

"Suck it like you did in the shower," I say, rough and low. "And don't stop until there's nothing left of me."

Her lips part.

"What if it burns?"

"Then set me on fire."

She doesn't move fast.

She moves like she has all the time in the world to destroy me.

Her mouth clamps down on my cock—hot, wet, sucking me deeper.

I catch my reflection in the mirror behind her: my grip in her hair, her lips stretched around me, spit shining on my length. The sight almost knocks me out harder than the feel of it.

I fist the glass with one hand, teeth bared, hips jerking against her throat. Every drag of her tongue is visible—slick, obscene—her cheeks hollowing as she takes more of me.

I feel the heat all the way in my spine, but I can't tear my eyes off the mirror. Off her. Off what she's doing to me.

My hips jerk forward. She presses me back.

"Not yet," she warns.

Her nails dig into my thighs—enough to keep me still.

And still I need.

"Fuck…" my voice breaks.

She groans against me and my grip on the mirrored wall falters.

"You're mine," she whispers, short and flat. "All mine."

Her mouth seals around me again.

My hips jerk. I cum loud and raw, nothing human about it.

She doesn't flinch.

She swallows and keeps looking at me.

A single glowing drop of indigo slips from the corner of her mouth, trailing down her chin like blood.

"Like a moth…" she murmurs, licking it off her skin.

My knees give.

And she watches me fall.

Seven

"The world is full of obvious things
which nobody by any chance ever
observes." – Arthur Conan Doyle

By the time I get up and glance at the clock, it's already past noon. I stare at the floor, half-hoping it was all another dream—but the broken lamp is still there. Proof that it happened. Proof that I'm actually insane.

And it's not just the shadow in the alley, or in the mirror. It's the dreams. I can still feel the glass cage. His wings. My mouth on him. *How can dreams feel this real?*

The water in the shower is only mildly warm, but it helps. A little. Enough to clear the grogginess clinging to me like a second skin. With the way I've been sleeping, I'm not even sure I remember what rested feels like.

I almost convince myself to go out for coffee—maybe the walk will help, maybe I'll feel human again. But even that feels like too much effort today.

I sit on the bed, trying to decide, but exhaustion wins. I lie back down and stare at the ceiling, hoping the low hum of the old refrigerator will lull me into real sleep.

I probably would've stayed there all day if it weren't for the knocks. Sharp. Insistent.

Again. And again.

My rent isn't due for weeks. Whoever it is clearly doesn't take a hint: I'm not in the mood for company.

"What?" I snap, yanking the door open.

It's Tom. And Marie. Standing in the hallway like I should've been expecting them.

From the look on their faces, I must look worse than I thought.

"Oh," I say, blinking. "Hi."

Right—I know people in Paris now: neighbors. Are they going to be the kind that don't leave you alone? Because honestly, that'll make me move faster than a haunted mirror.

Tom offers a polite smile. "Just wanted to check—see if you've changed your mind... about coming along?"

"We heard a scream last night. Everything okay?" Marie asks gently.

I want to tell her I've heard her screaming too—though I'm pretty sure mine sounded like something out of a horror film, and hers... well, hers is usually followed by moans. Loud, unashamed moans.

Part of me wants to ask what kind of kinks they're into, because these two? They don't sound nearly as vanilla as they look.

"Yes," I say instead, forcing a shrug. "I knocked over the lamp."

I gesture vaguely behind me, and both their eyes drift past me into the apartment. I know exactly what they're seeing—and it's not good. I've never lived in a messier place, and I once shared a dorm with a girl who didn't believe in doing laundry.

"So..." Tom says, changing the subject. "Are you coming?"

For fuck's sake, Tom. I'm not fucking coming.

But instead of saying that, I press my lips into a tight smile. "No, thank you."

"Why not?" Marie presses. "It's going to be fun! You don't want to miss it."

"I'm not into parties," I mutter. Not into people, either. Or loud noises. Or being perceived. But I manage to silence the running commentary in my head.

"You can borrow one of my dresses," she offers brightly.

For the love of... I don't even know this woman!

"Look," Tom says, more serious now. "We thought it might do you some good—to get out a little."

He glances at Marie, then back at me. "Grief can take you down if you're not careful."

"Grief?" I echo, startled.

That's what they think this is?

"I know the signs," Tom says quietly. "I... lost someone too."

He's not just talking to me. He's talking to Marie, too. She reaches over and takes his hand, squeezing it tight.

I let the words sink in.

I guess I am grieving. Not a person exactly—more like... myself.

The old me. The sane, put-together historian with a job, friends, an apartment, a life. *She's the one who died.*

"I'm..." I start, but I don't know how to finish.

"Come on!" Marie says brightly, breaking the moment. She grabs my hand before I can stop her and tugs me down the hall toward their apartment.

I'm too stunned to protest.

Before I can say anything, I'm inside their place. The door clicks shut behind me.

Marie's already rummaging through her closet, pulling out a dress with practiced ease. My eyes wander for a moment, taking in the space. It's a tad bigger than mine but includes a separate bedroom. There's a lived-in comfort to it.

Marie's taste is simple. Clean lines, soft fabrics. Nothing like the extravagant designer pieces I used to wear to Aaron's galas.

The thought brings a rush of memories—and with it, the weight of those years. Back when luxury felt less like a choice and more like a chain.

"I think this one will look beautiful on you," she says, holding up a long-sleeved dress in a soft floral print.

It's delicate. Pretty. Too spring-like for my cold bones. And at least two sizes too small.

"I don't think it's going to fit," I say, still fumbling for an excuse to get out of this.

"Of course it will," she replies breezily—like physics will bend to her will.

"I'll give you some privacy," Marie says, slipping out and leaving me alone in her bedroom.

I stand in front of the full-length mirror. Even though I've told myself a hundred times that what I saw in mine was simply a trick of the mind—just sleep deprivation, stress. Either way, mirrors and I are no longer on good terms. I glance away and turn around.

"Need help zipping up?" Marie calls from the other room.

"Just a second!" I shout back, stalling.

Maybe going to the catacombs is exactly what my foul mood needs. At least I won't be sulking alone. And honestly, I've run out of excuses to give my two annoyingly kind neighbors.

I force myself to change.

"Okay," I call finally.

To my surprise, the dress fits. Actually fits. And I'm not even filling it out. I blink at my reflection, a quiet realization settling in: I must've lost weight.

"I told you it would fit," Marie says, stepping in and zipping me up. She turns me toward the mirror like I'm a client on a makeover show. I immediately look away. She notices—probably assumes I hate how I look. *She's not wrong.*

"Take a seat," she says gently. "Let me fix your hair."

I'm too tired to fight back.

She starts working through the knots, slowly and carefully. I wince a couple of times, and each time she murmurs an apology, like she's brushing a child's hair.

"Why are you guys helping me, really?" I ask, my voice slightly above a whisper. "You barely know me."

Marie doesn't pause. "Tom said you weren't doing well. It's nothing, really—but we're neighbors. We can't just sit by while you cry all day and night. You're alone and..."

I blink. "You heard me crying?"

She hesitates. Then nods. "Yes. But you don't have to be embarrassed. Like I said, we understand."

I want to disappear into the floor.

They've been hearing me cry? Every night? It never even occurred to me. I've been drowning in it, and they've been right there, listening.

Marie clears her throat gently. "Okay. I think we're ready. Just need..."

She glances down at my bare feet.

"I've got shoes," I mutter, already stepping toward the door.

One last favor from the man who dressed me for display—then hated the attention.

EIGHT

I can't believe this is happening. A party. Of all things.

My heels click too loudly against the ground. With every step, I curse under my breath. My legs wobble like they've forgotten heels. A mistake. I knew it the second I put them on.

"I know, heels, right?" Marie loops her arm through mine to steady me.

"It's been a while," I mutter, clutching her tighter than I mean to.

Paris feels calm tonight. The air carries that faint mineral chill of early spring. I let my gaze drift over streets I haven't dared to explore—not really. Not since that night. My birthday.

I was so angry to be spending it alone. Even worse than the year before, when my father showed up with this cursed necklace and set my world on fire. Because this time, I had plans. Hoyt was supposed to take me out to dinner. We were going to stay at the hotel with the pool again. I wanted nothing more than to spend every minute of it with him, underwater—bodies weightless, curse weightless.

But instead, I did the only thing I could do here, alone. I drank. Until I couldn't stand. Until I couldn't remember. And then I smoked my first cigarette, working through the pack like it might eventually taste right.

And then came the dream. The one that told me he was still out there. Waiting.

I woke barefoot in the street. Cold. Shaking. Still searching for him. Out of my mind.

I haven't been out at night much since.

I hesitate now, a breath catching in my throat. I could turn back. Slip into my apartment. Lock the door. Tell Marie and Tom I can't do this.

But my feet keep moving.

Down the metro stairs.

In the train car, I clutch the railing as the floor jolts beneath us. My heels are a liability. My dress feels too long, too fragile.

"Only two more stops," Tom says lightly, as if we're heading to a rooftop bar and not the city's graveyard.

I nod, forcing a polite smile.

"So... you're playing tonight?" I ask, if only to fill the silence.

"Yes. I'm nervous, actually. The hosts didn't say much—besides that it's... exclusive."

"Exclusive," I echo flatly.

I glance at Marie. She's far too happy for someone heading into a city of bones.

The train lurches, and my hand shoots out to steady myself. For a heartbeat, the tunnel lights stutter and die.

In the glass across from me, I see him.

A man. Perfectly still on the empty platform. A cane in his hand. His face lost in shadow. Watching as the train barrels past.

I blink.

Gone.

Not real, I tell myself. Just nerves.

"Have you guys ever been to the... Catacombs?" I ask, my voice lower than I mean it to be.

They both shake their heads.

"It's honestly so creepy," Marie says from my right, tucking her hair behind her ear like we're chatting about movie times. "I don't even know how they're allowed to throw a party down there. I didn't think it would even fit that many people."

"Rich people," Tom says with a dry laugh. "They get bored. They need... weird."

"Right."

My lips twitch into something that isn't quite a smile.

"This is it," Tom announces as the train hisses to a stop at Denfert-Rochereau.

I glance at the rush of Parisians pouring past us on the platform—scarves, tote bags, boots clicking against tile. Moving like they know exactly where they're going. Unlike me.

I step off quickly, afraid of the doors snapping shut behind me.

Tom's friends wait near the exit, fidgeting like they're about to step into some pop-up club—not a tomb. Their energy makes my skin crawl.

"Iris?" Bella's voice cuts through the noise.

She's staring at me—like she's trying to reconcile the girl from yesterday with the one standing in front of her now.

"Hi, Bella," I manage as she leans in to kiss both cheeks. The European thing. I'm still not used to it.

"Wow, you clean up nice," she says. Her eyes flick over my borrowed dress with open surprise.

"Ha. Yeah." My smile feels tight. Plastic.

Relief washes over me when Tom waves for everyone to follow him.

We walk a block and a half until we reach a nondescript doorway—steps vanishing into darkness.

"It's said more than six million people were buried down there," Rocco says quietly from my left.

His English is careful, each word slightly clipped like he's testing it on his tongue before letting it go. I glance at him fully. He's younger than I thought—dark curls tumbling into his eyes, shoulders slightly hunched as if trying to take up less space. There's a nervous energy about him, the kind that makes you instinctively step back to give someone room.

He's trying, though. To speak my language. To keep pace. And when his words falter, one of his friends leans in—offering a quick translation from Italian with a small, encouraging smile. Rocco nods and picks up again.

"Six million?" I echo, startled.

"Macabre, huh?" Marie says, a little too brightly. I can't tell if she's nervous or amused.

"Very," I murmur.

At the entrance, Tom exchanges a few quick words with the guards—explaining why he's brought extra guests to a supposedly exclusive event. In the end, they wave us through with nothing more than a cursory glance and a tight nod.

At the threshold, a tall man in a black coat hands each of us a white taper candle. The flames tremble against the draft curling up from below.

"Is there no electricity down there?" I ask, adjusting my grip so the hot wax doesn't drip on my skin.

My prism is cold against my collarbone. Too visible. I should've hidden it. Another bad decision for the growing list.

"Yes," the guard replies in a clipped French accent. "But not tonight. The tourist lights are only for the public. Your hosts insisted on keeping this event candlelit. More traditional. More... respectful." The way he says *respectful* carries a faint bite. Like he doesn't believe it. Or maybe he's seen too many groups like ours—laughing, posing with skulls for pictures.

"I love it," Marie says brightly, too brightly for the air down here. She cradles her candle like a glass of champagne.

The descent begins.

The catacombs breathe around us—an endless network of galleries and ossuaries, stretching beneath Paris like the roots of a tree. The temperature drops with every step, a damp chill coiling around my ankles.

Each step sends a hollow echo bouncing off the stone. Bones jut from the walls in disturbingly precise arrangements—femurs stacked like firewood, skulls balanced one atop the other like bricks. The patterns are disturbingly artistic. I catch sight of a heart shape made entirely from jawbones. A cross of skulls stares back at me. Some grinning wide, others fractured at the temple.

It's impossible to believe this was ever open to tourists.

Tom leans close, lowering his voice. "This isn't the usual path. The hosts have access to the restricted galleries—tunnels even most Parisians have never seen."

The candlelight throws long, wavering shadows across the uneven walls and low ceilings. I watch each one, second-guessing my sanity. Guests ahead of us vanish and reappear as the tunnels twist. I can barely make out the couple who entered before us.

A carved sign looms above the next archway, the letters softened by centuries of damp.

Arrête! C'est ici l'Empire de la Mort.

Marie leans over and whispers, "It says, *Stop—this is the Empire of Death.*"

My fingers graze the prism at my collarbone. It's warm now—faintly pulsing.

The feeling is familiar, it reminds me of my time in Montana. Back then, I'd felt it too—the way the prism seemed to breathe when it touched bare soil, as if the earth's energy was feeding it. But here, the sensation is denser. Not life-filled like the fields around Hoyt's ranch. "There are too many tunnels," Rocco mutters, his voice tight. "How do we know which way to go?"

His candle flickers violently as if agreeing with him. I glance at him—he's pale, sweat pooling along his hairline despite the cold. For once, I don't feel like the only one losing it.

"We follow the black line," Tom says evenly. "It's painted on the ceiling. They told me to keep my eyes on it."

We all tilt our heads back at once, raising our candles to catch the faint streak of paint. It's barely there—a guide winding along the ceiling.

As my gaze lifts, vertigo sweeps through me. My balance falters.

And out of nowhere—fingers catch my elbow. Gentle. Steadying.

I whip my head to the right, already forming the words *thank you*.

But no one's there.

Chills race across my skin. I scan the shadows. No one could've moved away that fast. Not in these tunnels.

"Are you okay?" Marie asks from my left. She's watching me, brow furrowed. "You look like you've seen a ghost."

"Well..." I gesture vaguely to the walls.

"Right," she says, but there's a flicker of doubt in her eyes.

"I'm a little lightheaded," I lie, gripping the candle tighter and shifting it subtly away from the prism. One wrong move, and I know how easily it could pull me under.

"Here." She rummages in her purse and produces a granola bar, the crinkle of the wrapper loud in the hush. "Eat something."

I nod, taking it. My hands tremble as I peel it open with my teeth. Perhaps it really is low blood sugar.

I bite down. Sweet. Dry. Utterly out of place. The simple act of chewing feels bizarre in this underworld.

A hysterical laugh flares in my head. I choke it back. Blood sugar. Right. Like a granola bar's going to fix this.

We keep moving. Side chambers branch off the main path, their ceilings so low the others have to duck. I'm relieved we don't linger. Even glimpsing them feels like trespassing.

"What exactly is this place?" Bella asks suddenly. Her voice ricochets off stone walls, too bright, too alive.

Tom doesn't answer. He just shrugs.

In the silence, the words slip out of me before I can stop them.

"These tunnels were originally dug by miners," I hear myself say, my voice cutting through the hush. "When Le Cimetière des Innocents overflowed, the city needed a place to relocate the remains. The stench was so bad people said it hung in the streets like sour milk. Cart after cart brought the dead down here. Later, other cemeteries followed."

It isn't until the group falls quiet that I realize how loudly I've been speaking. All eyes flick toward me.

"I... like history," I mumble, heat rushing to my cheeks.

Maybe it's the snack. Maybe not. But for the first time in months, I feel her. The old me. The professor. The one who could stand in front of a lecture hall and own it. The one with answers. It's almost comforting. Almost proof she's not entirely gone.

We turn again, lowering our heads beneath a low archway. Ahead, a cavernous space opens up. Large enough to hold fifty people or more.

Though transformed for tonight's concert, it's still undeniably a cave. The walls are rough stone, damp to the touch. The ground dips and rises unpredictably beneath our feet.

Hundreds of flickering candles light the room. Some sit haphazardly on the rocky floor; others perch precariously atop a tall table in the center, their wax spilling in thick, molten drips.

There are no chairs. We all stand. Waiting.

I don't need to step fully inside to know I've made a mistake. Too many candles. The prism at my collarbone has gone from warm to thrumming.

Even on my best days, I would've struggled to hold steady in a place like this.

But now? With my pulse already erratic and the prism tightening its hold like a noose...

I should turn back.

I don't.

Celine tests the microphone in the center of the room. Her black leather dress gleams with every movement. She's all sharp lines and cool precision—untouchable.

This space—the vaulted ceiling, the walls lined with bones—feels utterly wrong for music. And yet... it's mesmerizing. Almost beautiful in its morbidity.

It doesn't feel like a concert venue. It feels like a set piece. The kind of scene in a film where you already know—everything is about to go horribly wrong.

"Hi." Celine's heels click softly as she approaches, surprisingly steady on the uneven stone. "I didn't realize you were bringing so many guests, Tom."

It's impossible to tell if she's irritated or merely surprised.

"They've been waiting for us to start," she adds with a faint smile, nudging him toward the piano waiting in the corner.

The hosts—whoever they are—clearly have money to burn. Waiters drift between the standing guests, trays balanced perfectly, offering champagne flutes and whiskey glasses. The rich amber of the whiskey catches the candlelight. The sight of it sends a hard twist through my stomach.

I haven't touched whiskey since Hoyt. Since that night. Since...

His mouth on my skin.

His tongue tracing the line of spilled liquor like it was his to claim.

The memory hits hard.

I glance around for an escape. A corner. A door. Anything.

There's nothing.

Champagne feels safer. Softer. I almost wave it off, but my nerves are shredded, and the bubbles will help me fake calm.

This isn't a party. Not really. It's a performance—an hour-long spectacle with no food, no bathrooms, no way out. Only us. And the dead.

I overhear someone whisper behind me —something about the acoustics. About how the walls themselves amplify sound.

And then Celine sings.

And I understand.

Her voice pours into the cavern—rich, sad, and lingering a

fraction too long in the air. Every note ripples out, catches on the stones, and folds back in on itself. It's not just haunting. It's possessed. Like the voices of the dead are weaving under hers, amplifying every sound.

Around me, the guests fall silent. Spellbound.

And the dead? They're listening. They are singing.

Tom's fingers glide over the piano keys slowly. The sound slithers through the narrow corridors, then returns back into the room like a whisper that doesn't quite belong. Eerie. Beautiful.

For a moment, it feels almost like an out-of-body experience. But no—I know what that really feels like. This is different. Not detachment, but immersion. A sinking.

The press of bodies around me sets my nerves alight. After months alone, even this small gathering is too much. The hum of breathing, the faint rustle of clothes, the stifled coughs—it's all amplified in the tight space.

And then there's the room itself. No windows. No air circulation I can feel. Just rock, and bones, and us. Buried alive together.

A wave of nausea rises hard and fast. I press a hand to my stomach, and inhale slowly. But even the air tastes wrong—thick, metallic, laced with candle smoke. How are we even breathing down here?

My eyes flick to the rows of candles. They're everywhere. But when I focus, I notice it: a faint plastic sheen on most of them. Battery-powered.

I let out a shaky breath. At least that explains why we haven't suffocated yet.

It's fine. It'll be over soon. Only a few more songs, I tell myself. Then I can get out of this tomb and breathe real air again.

I turn my attention back to the room—and that's when I see them.

The couple.

They're dressed like they've mistaken this candlelit crypt for the Palais Garnier and tonight's concert for the opera of the year.

The woman's fur coat drapes perfectly over her narrow shoulders. Her blond curls are coiffed so precisely they look sculpted—locked in place with enough hairspray to outlast an apocalypse. Large jeweled earrings swing as she claps, her lips pressed into a perfect red—no, crimson—line.

Beside her, the man mirrors her opulence. His tuxedo is razor-sharp, fresh from a tailor's hands. Even his mustache is a masterpiece—waxed and curled at the ends like an aristocrat from another century. Perhaps they shared the hairspray.

The other guests are elegant too, but this pair... they radiate ownership. They're standing slightly apart, their vantage point perfect, like the room was arranged for them alone.

I tip up my glass as I watch them—too distracted to notice it's already empty.

And then—movement. A shadow flickers across the smooth curve of the glass. For a split second, it feels like an eye staring back at me.

My fingers tighten on the glass. I nearly drop it, the sound of shattering crystal and horrified glances flashing in my mind.

I set it down too hard and push away, slipping into the darkened hallway.

My stomach lurches violently.

Please—not here. I beg my body.

Not in this place. Not with these walls. The sound would echo and bounce back to a room full of strangers.

I press a hand to my abdomen, willing the nausea to pass. But the smell—the damp, moldy air thick with the faint tang of decay—only makes it worse. My breath comes too fast. Too shallow.

Oh God. I'm not going to make it.

And then—impossibly—a breeze. Cool. Gentle. It crosses my cheek like a hand.

I freeze.

There are no windows down here. No vents. No reason for air to move.

The second I try to focus on it—on where it's coming from—it's gone.

I swallow hard, forcing the rising bile back down. My hand braces against my knees as I drag in a desperate breath.

"Are you okay?"

I jolt.

Rocco stands a few feet away, his candlelight carving nervous shadows across his face.

"I think I'm going to be sick," I whisper.

"I don't blame you." Rocco's voice is soft, almost embarrassed.

"I'm not feeling great either. It's this place..." He gestures vaguely. "It's wrong—enjoying ourselves down here. Among them. They deserve respect."

I study him for a beat.

"Why come at all?" I ask.

He shrugs—small, sheepish. "I don't know. Everyone else was going. I didn't want to be the weird one. They'd have called me scared. Never let me live it down."

I glance at him fully now. He looks younger than he did yesterday—soft edges, nervous hands. He can't be more than twenty.

"Honestly? I think *not* being scared of wandering an underground cemetery is the actual weird reaction," I say dryly.

That earns me a faint, grateful smile.

"I'm heading out," I tell him. "Will you let them know that I wasn't feeling well?"

He nods quickly. "Sure. Wish I could leave with you."

"Why don't you?"

"I... can't. I'll wait. It'll be over soon."

"Sure. It was nice meeting you, Rocco."

"You too."

I turn, candle in hand, and step back into the darkness.

My heels click softly on stone, each sound swallowed whole by the tunnels. I move as fast as I can—though in reality, it's little more than a cautious shuffle. *Stupid shoes. Stupid sense of direction.*

The black line on the ceiling is my lifeline now. I tilt my candle upward to keep it in sight, heart pounding with every twist and turn.

The tunnels feel longer than they did coming in.

On my left, a wide chamber opens up. Relief surges—

—and dies just as quickly.

It's a dead end.

My chest tightens.

Don't panic.

Worst case, I retrace my steps. Back to the music, the candles, the people who don't even know I've gone.

I spin too quickly and my skirt tangles around my legs. A draft flares past—

—and snuffs out my candle.

Darkness crashes in. Total. Absolute.

"Shit." The word ricochets off the stone.

Okay. Think, Iris.

I strain my eyes against the black, but there's nothing. Not even the faintest outline of my hand when I wave it in front of my face.

And then—

Something brushes my shoulder.

I jump.

It felt… solid.

"Hello?" The whisper tears from my throat before I can stop it. Too soft. Too afraid. Part of me prays no one answers. The other part is terrified they will.

The hairs on the back of my neck stand straight. Goosebumps ripple across my skin like a warning.

I sidestep blindly, desperate to get away from… whatever it was. My heel catches my dress. The fabric yanks tight—

—and suddenly I'm on my knees.

My palms slap the ground as I catch myself. They skid across grit and something softer.

My stomach lurches. Bones. I've touched a fucking—

The candle rolls away with a hollow clink, lost to the darkness.

I scramble after it, hands groping blindly, but it's pointless.

I couldn't have grabbed one of the battery-powered ones, could I?

I can't stay here. I have to keep moving.

There's no one here. Just me. Just my mind cracking under pressure. That's all this is. I repeat it like a mantra, though it does nothing to help.

I push to my feet, forcing my hands to trace the wall. Lightly. Barely grazing the surface. The rock is wet beneath my fingers— slippery with what, I don't let myself wonder.

Find the main tunnel. Find the light. Keep moving.

Eventually, my eyes catch it—a faint glow far ahead. The party room. It's still there.

I can make it back.

And just as I force another shaky breath, a thought cuts through the panic.

The prism.

It can light up.

My fingers fumble at my collar, pulling the chain. I hesitate— for a second—then lean down and spit on the crystal.

The droplet hits. Crude. Desperate. But it works.

Light bursts forth—brighter than any candle, sharper than any torch. Violet and alive, it spills over the walls, crawling across the bones like veins beneath translucent skin.

It's more than enough to find my way out.

The glow seeps into empty eye sockets, pools in hollow rib cages, snakes through neat stacks of femurs until the whole chamber breathes faint violet. As if the prism isn't simply lighting the space but pulling something from it.

I realize, it's feeding.

No—it's connecting.

A sound.

Distant. The creak of wooden wheels. The scrape of shovels against stone. A grunt of effort as a burlap sack is heaved from a shoulder. It hits the ground with a muffled clatter.

Bones.

I blink, heart hammering.

Figures stir faintly in the glow—men in rough coats, faces streaked with soot and sweat. Shadows of the past. They move with weary precision, dragging carts, unloading human remains into these endless halls.

I know this history. Of course I do. *Les Innocents.* The overcrowded cemetery, emptied under cover of night. Cart after cart of the dead, carried here to rot in secret.

But this... this isn't memory.

The prism thrums warm against my chest, its light steady now.

"Is this... you?" I whisper to it. My voice sounds foreign in the suffocating dark.

The workers fade like smoke. The sound of wheels dissolves into silence.

I'm alone again.

The glow dims.

Had I imagined it? Some hallucination spun from my professor brain—history bleeding into panic?

Or had the prism—somehow—shown me?

Fucking hell, I need to get out of here.

Nine

"Mystery creates wonder and wonder is the basis of man's desire to understand." – Neil Armstrong

I fumble with the locks, hands shaking so hard I can barely get the key to catch. Adrenaline still screaming through me. I'm not even sure how I made it back here.

The door finally clicks shut. My fingers fumble over the bolts, sliding them home with a tremor. Only then do I sag against the wood, a sigh tearing out—too sharp, almost a sob.

My heels hit the floor with a dull thud. I stumble to the bed and collapse onto the mattress. My eyes go to the door—at all the locks I've fastened like they're some pathetic barrier against what I really fear. But the truth is, what I fear isn't out there. It's in here. Inside this apartment. Inside me.

Perhaps I should've left the door wide open.

My gaze snags on the mirror across the room. One glance and a fresh wave of tremors rips through me. I don't trust what might look back. I lunge for the nearest blanket and drape it over the glass, smothering it like a wound that won't stop bleeding.

I peel off Marie's dress and drop it to the floor. It's ruined—stained and torn, a casualty of whatever nightmare I stumbled through tonight. I'll pay her for it later.

My fingers find the soft cotton of Hoyt's t-shirt crumpled by the pillows. I pull it over my head, not caring that it hasn't been washed.

Wrapping my arms around myself, I press the fabric to my face. But it's not just touch I'm craving—it's him. All of him. And in the silence, his absence presses down like a weight I can't shake.

Flat on my back, I've memorized every spiderweb stretched across the ceiling. Still, I stare at it like it owes me answers.

My body feels wired, restless. My thighs press together tight, but it's no use. It's the hormones—fucking ovulation turning me feral—or maybe it's the damn dreams still haunting me like a cursed fairytale.

But it's more than that. It was the whiskey earlier. One glimpse and my brain betrayed me, dragging me back to him—his mouth hot on my skin, licking every drop I poured down my breasts like it belonged to him. His hands gripping my hips hard enough to leave bruises, dragging me closer like he could tear the curse off me with sheer force. The way he fucked me with his fingers. The way he kissed like he was starving, like the world didn't exist beyond us. And his tongue—God, his tongue—

I bite my lip as my hand slides lower. My fingers find my pussy, and I whimper before I can stop myself.

This isn't enough. It'll never be enough.

My eyes flick to the wine bottle on the counter. God. The thought alone makes my thighs clench. Too much. Too desperate. I hate myself for even considering it.

I swallow a curse and grab the nearest thing instead—the smooth handle of my hairbrush. It's ridiculous. But the second I insert it between my thighs, I'm already too far gone.

I'm so tired of missing him. Of craving him until my bones ache with it.

I circle my clit lazily, imagining his voice low in my ear—rough with need. *"Fucking suck it already."*

The stretch makes my hips jerk, breath coming in shallow gasps. I fuck myself harder, chasing the memory of him—his weight pinning me down, his mouth swallowing every sound I made.

It doesn't take long. My body knows these memories too well. The orgasm hits fast, white-hot and mean. I bite back a sob as it tears through me, pleasure and grief crashing together. It leaves me trembling. Empty.

So unsatisfying.

I was furious at Darion—for stealing my life, for ripping Hoyt out of it. Even if I'd been the one to end things, it never felt like a choice. It was a sacrifice, a quiet kind of violence I'd committed to keep Hoyt safe. So I blamed Darion. I blamed his fucking family— my fucking family—for forcing my hand.

And still, I would give anything—anything—to see Hoyt again. To hear his voice. To feel, even for one second, what it was like to be his.

I don't even remember deciding. One moment I'm flicking the lighter, lighting up a cigarette—the next, I'm moving like I've already surrendered. *I need to see him.*

Without a candle in this apartment, I grab the metal lighter. Its tiny flame flickers as if it knows what I'm about to ask of it. Will it hold long enough?

I have to try.

In the bathroom, I crank the faucet until cold water gushes into the sink. My hands shake as I dunk the prism, watching the droplets bead and roll off its surface.

A weak little voice whispers, *don't do this.* It doesn't stand a chance. Not against the cigarette dulling my fear. Not against how fucking horny I am.

I sink down onto the bathroom tiles, legs crossed on the cold floor. It's the only place I trust not to burn if the lighter tips.

I take another drag, watching smoke curl and writhe in the air like it's alive. The nicotine hits hard, smoothing my doubts, loosening my grip on reason.

Just one look, I promise myself. *One quick look.*

I stub out the cigarette on the tile and flick the lighter to life, setting it on the tub's edge. Flame and water. Together. The prism hums faintly at my chest, recognizing the elements.

I close my eyes. My pulse trips over itself as I wait for the inevitable pull.

Every other time I'd done this, it had felt effortless—like slipping between the cracks of the world.

Not tonight.

Tonight, it's like moving through tar. Thick. Suffocating. The prism doesn't only hum—it pulses, syncing to my heartbeat, like it's trying to warn me off. Or claim me.

Maybe something changed after Darion. That was the last time I traveled this way—the night I burned everything to get free. Maybe I carried more scars with me than meets the eye.

The thought splinters as water and flame finally pull me under.

There is no floor beneath me. No breath in my lungs.

I'm light. Violet and trembling.

I hover high in the pines. The forest stretches in all directions, muted by snow.

And then I see him.

He's turned away—thank God—too focused to notice the soft flicker trembling high in the trees.

His back rises and falls with each breath, broad and heaving. The axe arcs overhead, catching a shard of pale moonlight, before slamming down with a violent crack. Wood splinters. My awareness shudders. Every grunt he lets out rumbles through the clearing—low, raw, primal. The sound vibrates through the air and through me.

I flinch with each blow.

Hoyt works as a man possessed. The pile beside him has grown into a mountain—enough to heat a mansion for years. It's overkill. Spring is almost here. But this isn't about the cold. This isn't survival.

His jaw clenches. Muscles strain beneath the flannel stretched tight across his shoulders. His sleeves are shoved up to his forearms, fabric bunched as veins rise with each swing. Steam curls where his body heat meets the cold air. The moonlight catches in the damp sheen of his hair, darker at the edges from sweat.

I drift closer, unthinking. It's gravity. I don't even realize I'm doing it until I find myself hovering behind a thick pine trunk. But then I hide, sliding quietly to the side, careful not to snap a twig or disturb a leaf.

He can't see me. He can't know I'm here.

He doesn't pause. He just keeps swinging—harder, faster, like the world will fall apart if he stops.

I want nothing more than to see his eyes—once, even if it's the last time. But the second he sees me, everything I've done—every lie, every cold word—will come rushing back. He will suspect I'm up to something, and he'll come looking.

Otherwise, why break his heart if I was only going to haunt his woods like a coward? I can't risk it.

I stay still like the branches hanging above.

I lose myself in him—his grunts, his strained breaths. My awareness responds instinctively. The sweat trailing down his neck, the sharp tang of split wood—it's all so him. So devastatingly him. And yet... unreachable.

Then—

In a single, devastating motion, he turns.

His eyes lock on me—and it's like being struck. Everything I've fought to bury detonates at once.

Shock flashes across his face, raw and unguarded. Then... recognition.

The axe slips from his grip, thudding into the snow.

It doesn't matter how fast I pull myself back. It's too late. I'm too late.

His voice follows me, echoing in my ears, laced with disbelief and hurt.

"Iris?"

A beat.

"Iris!"

I stumble backward in my apartment, breath hitching. "No. No, no, no." My hands clutch at my hair. "Shit!" I start pacing—frantically—like I can outrun the reality.

And then, I hear them—Tom and Marie—back home. Their voices drift through the paper-thin walls, every laugh and clink of glass hitting like a hammer in my skull. I shut the bathroom door, praying it would mute them, but it barely dulls the noise.

I had managed to stay away for this long—months of control, of quiet withdrawal—until those two dragged me out. To a fucking party. Where the dead were waiting for me.

If it weren't for that place—its darkness, its suffocating air—I would have held the line. I would have stopped myself tonight.

My stomach twists, violent. The thought of what I've done—of Hoyt's face when he saw me—turns the nausea sharp. I barely make it to the toilet before it all comes up. Again and again, until there's nothing left but acid and regret burning my throat.

And then they start. I should be used to it by now. Their cat and mouse game. Tom's voice is always low, coaxing. Marie doesn't seem bothered that I'm right next door. She's way louder. I hear the slap of skin on skin. A thud. Then laughter again.

The bile rises again, sour and burning.

I double over the sink, gripping the edges hard enough to make my knuckles ache. My reflection stares back at me—pale, sweat-slick, hollow-eyed.

And then—

Movement.

My pulse spikes

A shadow unfurls across the mirror like spilled ink creeping outward. It has shape—human—but wrong somehow. Stretched. Warped. The head tips as if it's watching me.

I blink hard.

Gone.

Of course. Of course it's gone.

Just my nerves. Just my brain fracturing.

I stumble out of the bathroom, needing space, air—anything to drown out the sounds next door. I cross to the window and shove it open. The cold night air hits me, clearing the fog for half a second.

And that's when I see him.

A man. Below. Walking slowly down the narrow street.

A cane in his hand. His hat pulled low. His face hidden in shadow. But there's no mistaking it—he's looking up.

Right. At. Me.

The world narrows to that small slice of street, to the sound of his cane tapping against the cobblestones.

Tap. Tap. Tap.

And then he passes beneath a streetlight. He doesn't pause. Doesn't break his stride. He keeps walking, fading into the dark.

I slam the window shut and stagger back, my hands shaking.

God. What is happening to me?

I collapse onto the bed without even pulling the covers back.

* * *

It's the knock that wakes me. Again.

"Iris? It's me—Marie," she calls from the hallway.

By the time she says hello, I've already unlocked the door, still half-asleep.

"Oh. Hi." My voice is hoarse, and I rub my forehead, trying to blink the fog away.

"I brought coffee," she says, holding it up like a peace offering.

"Coffee?" The smell hits me in the best way. My hands move on their own, pulling the door wider.

"You didn't have to…" I murmur, unsure why she's even here.

"I feel awful. I heard you getting sick—yeah, these walls are basically paper. And Rocco said you weren't well. We never should've dragged you out like that. God, that place… among the dead? So insensitive." She's rambling now, her voice a tangled mix of guilt and nerves.

"It's fine, Marie." My words come out flat. Too tired for niceties.

"Oh no, you are not fine. Look at you." She presses the cup into my hands like it's medicine. "Here. Drink."

I take a cautious sip—and nearly choke. It's strong. Way stronger than I'm used to. Pure espresso. Nothing like the sugary lattes I drowned in back home. But it helps.

I open the fridge, find some milk that's still drinkable, and pour it in. The coffee turns a muddy beige.

Marie watches with faint amusement. "Ah. Americans. You don't drink it black?"

"More like… beige," I mutter, taking another sip.

She sets a paper bag on the counter like it's fragile cargo. "Chocolate croissants. Best in this *quartier.*"

I wasn't planning to eat. I wasn't planning to do anything. But the smell unfurls in the air—buttery, rich, decadent—and before I know it, I'm tearing off a piece. One bite and my mouth waters for more.

"Thank you," I mumble, wiping crumbs from my lips with the back of my hand. No napkins here. No pretense of manners anymore.

Marie glances around and wrinkles her nose—not unkindly, but enough for my stomach to knot. Is it the laundry pile? The cigarettes? Or the faint trace of vomit I thought I'd flushed away?

"What you really need is fresh air," she says brightly, like it's a cure-all.

"I'm fine." I step toward the door, already retreating.

But she cuts me off gently, her voice softening. "Iris, please. Let me make it up to you. Just one little stroll? A garden?"

"A garden?" I echo. There's no park nearby—I checked before.

"Well, we've got options." Her hands flutter nervously. "Jardin des Tuileries?"

"Oh no." My head shakes hard, almost violent. "Not the Louvre's garden. Anywhere but there."

She blinks. "Oh. You said you liked history last night, so I thought..."

Why is she trying so hard? Why does she care? I'm not a project. I'm not a charity case.

"I can't go there," I say, my voice sharper than I mean.

"Okay," she says, holding up her hands. "Another garden? Or... maybe a museum? It's a little chilly—"

"No museums!" It comes out louder than I mean. Too loud. "Sorry. No museums. I... I can't." My throat tightens. I can't explain it, even if I tried.

She hesitates. "You're new to Paris, right? What haven't you seen yet? The Tower? Notre Dame?"

"I haven't been anywhere."

Her brows knit in disbelief. "You haven't even seen the tower?"

"No." Flat. Unapologetic.

"Why not?" she asks softly.

I pause, fighting to keep my expression neutral. But the words press heavily against my ribs.

"Because I refuse to pretend I'm okay. I refuse to accept that this is my life now. That I'm... alone."

Marie's eyes glisten, but she masks it quickly. Before I can step back, she's too close, pulling me into a hug. My body stiffens at the contact. I almost spill the coffee.

"I'm so sorry, Iris," she whispers.

I can't remember the last time someone hugged me.

She pulls back, trying a small smile. "Let's get you out. The Tower has healing properties, you know."

I want to fight her. To push her away. To tell her she doesn't understand—no one does. But some small, desperate part of me wonders if this might be my last chance to claw back a piece of myself. Anything would be better than staring at mirrors or lighting another cigarette. But I know the truth. I can't outrun last night.

TEN

"The past beats inside me like a second heart." – John Banville

Tom joins us for what Marie dramatically calls "the grand tour of Paris."

I hadn't even wanted to leave my apartment today. Yet somehow, here I am—standing on the sidewalk, staring at two motorcycles like they might bite.

What Marie fails to mention—until we're already outside—is that her "tour" involves riding through the city on two wheels.

"Come on! It'll be fun!" she says, grinning as she fastens a helmet under my chin before I can protest. She's younger, probably by a few years, but acts like I'm the one who needs babysitting. Fighting her is exhausting.

"I... I've never—" I start, meaning to admit I've never been on a motorcycle and never planned to.

"Well, perfect day for firsts," she chirps, practically bouncing with excitement.

"*Mon amour*, go slow with her, okay?" she calls over her shoulder to Tom, who's perched calmly on his bike like this is nothing.

"I thought I was going with you," I say, confused.

"My bike's too small. Only fits one," she shrugs. "Don't worry —Tom's careful. He'll take good care of you. Right, Tom?"

He gives a small nod, silent but steady. Oddly, his lack of enthusiasm reassures me.

"Nothing to worry about," he says finally, his voice low and even.

"You guys really don't have to do this." I try one last time.

"It's going to be fun!" Marie calls back, already pulling away, her hair catching the wind like she's in a movie.

I hesitate, stiff and awkward. Where do I sit? Where do I look? More importantly, where the hell do I put my hands?

"Where do I... hold on?" I ask as I clumsily climb onto the back of Tom's bike.

"Here." He gently takes my hands and places them around his waist. "Hold tight. Don't worry—you won't hurt me."

I rest my hands lightly on his jacket, every muscle tense. There's no choice now—either grip him or fall off. Before I can rethink, the bike roars to life and lurches forward. Instinct kicks in, and I clutch him like my life depends on it.

A few blocks later, I dare to open my eyes. I hadn't even realized I'd been shutting them so hard until a dull ache pulses behind them.

Paris blurs—colors, lights, and people flashing by too fast. I try to take it all in. After all, this is the city I once dreamed of, read about, longed for so long.

But none of it feels real.

Tom slows as we glide onto a wide boulevard.

And then I spot it.

The Eiffel Tower.

It rises impossibly high, its iron lattice cutting into the pale sky —imposing and beautiful all at once. Bigger than I imagined. Graceful in its defiance.

Built at the end of the 1800s... My mind drifts, piecing

together fragments I once taught. A temporary showpiece for the 1889 World's Fair. Hated at first. Dismissed as an eyesore. But it endured. More than endured. It became Paris itself.

I let its quiet majesty settle into me. This isn't just steel and rivets—it's defiance turned legacy. Proof that brilliance can stand tall, even when the world doubts it.

And perhaps... I need to do that too.

Hiding had its purpose. It dulled the noise, softened the fear, made the chaos feel manageable enough. But nothing's changed—not really. I'm still running. Still looking over my shoulder.

But I can't run forever.

Possibly the only way forward isn't retreat—it's confrontation.

Standing here, in the shadow of something once dismissed as impossible, I feel it—a quiet call to bravery. Maybe I don't need a perfect plan. Maybe I just need one reckless, unflinching moment of courage.

"La dame de fer... she's beautiful, isn't she?" Marie asks softly.

I slip off the bike and plant my feet on solid ground. For the first time in months, the earth holds me steady instead of tilting beneath me.

Then the crowd hits—waves of bodies pressing in on every side. Since when did I have a problem with groups of people? I try to shake it off, but the truth is, I've had a problem with everything since I set foot in this country.

"The Eiffel Tower is the most visited monument with an entrance fee in the world," Tom says calmly, like he's reading from a guidebook. Easy to believe, judging by the sea of tourists swarming around us.

At least we're outdoors.

"There are restaurants on the first and second levels if you want to grab a bite," Marie adds, gesturing to the iron giant as if it's nothing. Her enthusiasm hasn't dimmed an inch.

"When the lights come on, they say you can hear angels," she adds with a little grin.

We slip into Madame Brasserie, settling at a window table with appetizers and drinks. It's too early for dinner, but the place is quiet enough to feel like a pocket of calm.

The view is staggering—Paris sprawled out beneath us in muted grays and soft golds. I can't stop staring.

"Thank you," I say finally, glancing between them. "You didn't have to do this. But... I'm grateful. It's beautiful."

I sip the diabolo menthe Marie ordered for me. It's sharp and sweet, the kind of drink that burns just enough to sting. My stomach still twists uneasily, but I tell myself the sugar might help. Help me relax. Help me forget last night—even if only for a few hours.

"Of course, I know we just met," Marie says, her voice softening as she glances between Tom and me, her smile warm, almost protective. "But you can count on us."

"I know how hard it is," Tom adds. His tone is steady, but there's a weight behind it—a weariness I recognize all too well. "Being in a new country. Alone. It gets heavy fast."

"When did you move here?" I ask.

"Italia's close, but Paris felt like another planet at first." His fingers trace the rim of his glass absently. "I met Celine five years ago. I was nineteen. She was playing at a café—just her and an old guitar. I wasn't planning to stay, but..." He exhales, a faint smile tugging at his lips. "I couldn't leave. Something in her voice—it hooked me."

I nod. After last night, after hearing her—really hearing her—I understand how someone would drop their entire life to follow that sound.

"She's the brave one though," Tom continues. "Traveling alone. Singing to strangers. I wanted to be near that. So I left everything behind and followed her."

Marie watches him with open affection, her fingers brushing his arm like she can't not touch him.

"Last year we stopped moving. Celine wanted to come home.

Paris is her city. For me..." His voice softens. "I'm still figuring out how to belong here."

"You seem like you do," I say quietly.

A faint, almost reluctant smile. "That's mostly Marie. Without her, I'd still be lost."

"How did you two meet?" I ask, my gaze slipping between them. Marie's fingers rest lightly on Tom's arm—a small, intimate gesture that says more than words ever could. But it's the way he looks at her—like she's the gravity holding his whole world together—that leaves no doubt he's already found his home.

Marie shrugs, her smile softening. "He was playing at a benefit I was helping with. I'm an assistant, I was running around like a headless chicken." She laughs at the memory. "But the second I heard him—I knew I had to say hello."

She glances at Tom. "Everyone comes for Celine, but it was his music that pulled me. It felt... different. Like he was playing just for me."

I lift my glass, the movement automatic. "You do play beautifully, Tom."

He gives a modest smile as they both raise their drinks. "Salute," they say in unison.

"Salute," I echo, clinking my glass gently against theirs.

"To new friendships," Marie adds, her grin wide and infectious.

We sip quietly as the sun sinks lower, amber haze spilling across the city in soft ribbons.

"Everyone needs to see this," I say softly. "At least once in their lifetime."

It's breathtaking. And for a split second, it almost seems like enough.

"Look, I know it's none of our business..." Marie says. "But we're here if you ever want to talk."

"Thank you." I swirl the last sip of my drink. "I... I wouldn't even know where to start."

Marie leans in, her elbows on the table, her expression soft but probing. "There are only two reasons people move far away from home alone, Iris. You're either running from something you did..." She tilts her head slightly, her voice dropping. "...or someone."

"I think..." I hesitate, feeling their quiet eyes on me. "I'm running from both," I admit, my voice barely above a whisper.

They don't press. The silence that follows isn't awkward—it's thick with understanding.

The lights bloom across the Tower and spill through the restaurant windows, making the glass look like mirrors of fire. Perhaps Marie's right. Maybe something—small, fragile—is stitching itself back together inside me.

By the time we're slipping helmets over our heads again, I surprise even myself when I say, "Being out... it helped."

"Then let's keep going!" Marie says, her voice bubbling with so much enthusiasm it's almost contagious. She's one of those rare people who lights up every space she enters—brighter than any tower or streetlamp.

"What? And go where?" I ask, though my protest is half-hearted now.

"Let's continue our tour!" Tom chimes in, handing me my helmet with an easy grin.

"Saint-Germain-des-Prés," Marie suggests, her eyes practically sparkling. "We'll weave through the little streets—it's magic at night."

Tom nods, already straddling his bike.

And so we go.

Saint-Germain-des-Prés is alive in a way I didn't expect—like a living, breathing canvas. Artists linger in doorways, paint-smeared hands clutching brushes and cigarettes. Couples stroll arm in arm, their laughter rising like soft music into the night air.

As we glide past, my mind drifts to the history buried here. The abbey once a stronghold for Viking forces during the siege of

Paris in 845. They dismantled parts of it to repair their ships, reinforcing their siege.

This place remembers every invasion, every fire, every moment of survival. Maybe that's Paris's magic—it doesn't erase its scars. It carries them like art.

As we continue, I glance down narrow alleyways twisting between buildings. Some lead to hidden cafés, the scent of strong coffee and buttery pastries curling faintly through the chilly night air. Others open onto dimly lit bookshops that look forgotten by time—places I used to dream of wandering, back when Paris was still just a fantasy.

Marie gestures ahead, her voice as bright as ever. "Let's head toward the Luxembourg Gardens! It's not too far—we'll even catch a glimpse of the palace."

We pass through the gates of the gardens, once the playground of Parisian elites in the 17th century, built at the whim of Queen Marie de Medici. I catch sight of the Medici Fountain—its stone figures hidden. Legend says its waters hold magic, or so the stories go.

The prism warms against my skin, a reminder I can't keep pretending everything is fine. Sooner or later, I'll have to face it.

Perhaps it's time I stop surviving and start seeking answers. Even if that means finding the last person I want to see again. *Even if it means confronting my father.*

Marie and Tom weave their bikes down another narrow street and we begin our journey back.

Shockingly, I'm feeling calm. Maybe it's Marie's relentless warmth or Tom's steady smile. Whatever it is, a strange stillness settles in my chest—fragile but real.

And then I see it.

The kind of sign you can't ignore. A tattoo shop.

Before I can second-guess, my hand lifts on its own. "Stop here," I say, my voice firmer than I expect.

Tom slows, glancing at me in the rearview mirror. "You sure?" he asks as the bike eases to a halt at the curb.

"I... I can find my way back from here. Thank you," I murmur, sliding off the bike. The words sound bold, but my hands are trembling as I pull off my helmet.

Marie pulls up beside us seconds later, her eyes already alight with curiosity.

"What's going on?" she calls over the engine.

"I... want to..." The words crumble before they're fully formed.

"Get a tattoo?" Marie supplies, one brow arched high.

I let out a shaky laugh, startled by how easily she reads me. "There's someone I..."

"Say no more." She's off her bike before I can stop her, a grin tugging at her lips.

"Take mine back, Tom. We'll ride yours home," she says, tugging off her gloves with a breezy finality.

"No—you don't have to come with me," I protest weakly.

"Of course I do," Marie says, passing me toward the shop door. "We're friends now, remember? Getting a tattoo together—it's the perfect friendship milestone."

I let out a short laugh.

"Okay, so I'm thinking this little flower." Marie taps a design in the book, her tone light, almost teasing.

"You're really getting one?" I ask.

"Of course. I've already got a few—what's one more?" Marie smiles. She reminds me of Akira. Younger, softer around the edges, but still—Akira. The same effortless boldness, like the world could never bruise her. How many times had Akira begged me to get a tattoo with her? I'd always laughed her off. Always said no.

I slam the memory shut before it can drag me under.

"Does it hurt?" I ask.

Marie glances up, amused. "A little. But it's worth it."

I nod vaguely, eyes drifting—not to the books filled with flowers and butterflies, but to the thin, tender skin right above my hip bone.

The memory flashes, uninvited: Hoyt in the shower, his rough hands gripping my thighs as he pulled my underwear down with his teeth. His mouth hot against that exact spot, his low growl vibrating through me.

"There was someone," I say before I can stop myself. "Back home..."

"His name?" Marie asks casually, still flipping pages.

"Hoyt." The name burns on my tongue.

"Ex?"

"Yes. Ex."

Marie finally lifts her gaze, her eyes soft with something I can't name. "What happened?"

I force a smile. "We were from different worlds. And he's better off without me."

She doesn't hesitate. She reaches across the counter and squeezes my hand like we've known each other for years. "I doubt that."

She flips another page. A moth stares back at me, its inked wings delicate and dark, as if they might crumble under a breath.

"That one," I say. The words slip out fast, certain.

The needle burns as it carves permanence into my skin. And I let it. I let it hurt—because this is exactly what it feels like to be the flame. Destined for loneliness. Dangerous to anyone who dares come near.

When it's over, Marie leans forward eagerly. "Let me see."

I lift my shirt to show her the tiny moth inked low on my hip, tucked near my bikini line.

"Looks amazing. And much better than a name. Never a good idea, trust me."

I smile. "I thought about it, actually. But this... it means something to us. To me." Marie studies me for a long beat. "I like it. But most people don't get tattoos about their exes. What aren't you telling me?"

"Maybe another time," I say softly.

She nods. No judgment. No pressure.

And I wonder if—perhaps—the tower really does have healing powers.

Eleven

I'm halfway into Hoyt's shirt before I catch the faint sour smell of sweat and sickness clinging to it. The fabric sticks unpleasantly to my skin. With a grimace, I peel it off and toss it aside—maybe a little harder than necessary.

I reach for one of the oversized t-shirts I've been living in. The kind Aaron hated. He preferred me in matching silk pajamas—his neat, perfect little fiancée, polished and pliant. I used to work so hard to play that part. Now I can barely remember her.

The corner of the blanket draped over my mirror catches my eye. I hesitate, fingers twitching.

I tug the fabric away and the moth stares back at me. Ink-black wings curled low on my hipbone. My fingers ghost over the tender skin.

A faint smile tugs at my lips.

I drop the blanket back over the mirror and crawl into bed. The weight of the day presses me flat against the sheets.

I let myself hope—stupid, reckless—that I'll see Hoyt in my dreams again.

What's he doing right now?

Did seeing my prism light shake him—or does he hate me for it?

Does he hate me for the words I left him with? Or did he see through them? See the lie beneath? Could he tell?

Did he come looking for me anyway, even after I told him not to? Or... did he let me go too easily?

Does he ever think of me?

Does he dream of me the way I dream of him?

I reach for James' pages. The familiar creases find my thumb, the paper soft and worn from too many nights like this. I flip to the introduction and let his words flood the room like a ward.

The term supernatural didn't exist for the ancients. There was no line between seen and unseen, no word to diminish what they knew in their bones: power runs beneath the skin of the world like blood under flesh.

It wasn't until the medieval mind—afraid of its own hunger—tried to lock the unknown behind words (paranormal, supernatural) that we began pretending magic wasn't natural.

But strip away the names, the denial, and you'll see the truth. We've never been separate from it. Humanity's history is soaked in rites meant to pierce the veil—blood rites, sex rites, the kind that make your body the altar.

This isn't about ghosts alone. Or witchcraft. It's about bodies—two, sometimes more—bound in pacts of pain and ecstasy. Hands gripping so hard they leave bruises. Teeth breaking skin. Mouths pressed where the body aches most. A tongue sliding across your throat.

The ancients knew: the fastest way to touch the divine is through flesh. Pressure. Breath stolen by a hand at your neck. Nails scoring down your spine. Blood drawn—not enough to kill, just enough to remind you you're alive. Vessel. Offering. Key.

There are rituals carved into bloodlines, pacts whispered in candlelit rooms, prayers mouthed against sweat-slick skin while power flows

between bodies like current. Call it witchcraft if you must. But it's more. Astrology. Alchemy. Divination. Botany. And yes—sexual. This is natural magic. Not the safe kind. The kind where your orgasm isn't the reward—it's the lock breaking open.
If you think I'm speaking in metaphor, you're not ready.
But if something in you stirs—low in your belly, sharp as hunger and fear—then you already know.
You're already marked.
And this book didn't find you by accident.

A scream slices through the quiet.

It freezes me in place. My pulse thunders so loud I almost miss the sound of paper crumpling in my fist.

Marie.

Not the moans and laughter I've heard too many nights—her teasing Tom, their little games echoing through these thin walls.

This wasn't playful.

Too raw. A sound ripped from someone trying—and failing—to survive.

What the fuck?

For half a second, a sick thought snakes in: *Did Tom take it too far?*

Then comes the sound I can't mistake.

A heavy thud.

Glass shattering.

I don't move. My body won't let me.

My breath scrapes in and out, shallow and jagged. Maybe I imagined it, like the shadow in the mirror and the dark figures at the edge of my dreams.

I force myself upright, every muscle stiff with terror. The cold air bites my bare legs as I tiptoe to the bathroom and press my ear to the thin wall between our apartments.

Footsteps.

They move with a terrible calm. No voices. No Marie. No Tom. Just those footsteps... circling. Stalking.

Then nothing. Except—no. There: one set of footsteps, moving toward their front door.

My breath catches. I stumble back, nearly tripping over the rug. *Call someone.* The thought slams into me, useless and cruel. There's no phone.

What do I do?

Go to them? Or stay put?

My stomach churns at the thought of opening my door. My fingers hover over the lock, trembling so hard I can hear the metal rattle. Even my breathing feels too loud, like it might give me away.

Then—a soft scrape.

Paper slides under my door.

Cousin,
Thought you could hide forever? Cute.
Your neighbors? A pity. But I've got your attention now, don't I?
One hour. Notre-Dame Cathedral.
Or I'll make sure your boyfriend suffers a slow, agonizing end, too.
Don't keep me waiting. You know I hate that.
Tick-tock.

P.S. He sure does love you. Shame if he died thinking you didn't.

The paper flutters against my bare feet.

"No," I whisper. Then, louder: "No. No. No."

My shaking hands fumble with the lock. The door groans as it swings open.

Their door—right beside mine—is cracked open. Too open.

I shouldn't.

I can't.

But I do.

"Marie?" My voice comes out a cracked whisper. Too quiet. Too late.

The apartment is still.

Then I see them.

Marie is face down, her body twisted in a way no living body should ever be. One arm bent beneath her awkwardly, the other outstretched like she'd tried to crawl. Her hair fans out in a dark halo on the floor. And there—on her wrist—the delicate flower tattoo she got only hours ago. Fresh ink. Still slightly raised, like the skin hasn't yet healed. The little bloom looks absurd here—bright, innocent. Out of place against the brutality of her death.

A sound tears from my throat—half sob, half gag—as I drop to my knees beside her. My trembling fingers press against her neck, searching for a pulse I already know isn't there.

I don't need touch to tell me. The room already has.

She's gone.

Tom isn't far. He lies on his back, eyes wide and glassy, mouth slack in a silent scream.

Panic is frozen into his face—pure, undiluted terror. His hand stretches toward Marie's, like he was reaching for her in his last moments.

There's no blood. No wounds. Just stillness.

The kind of stillness that feels like it might drown me.

My throat tightens. My instincts scream—call for help, do *something*. There's no one. Even if there were—it's too late.

Too late for Marie's easy laughter.

Too late for Tom's quiet steadiness.

Too late for the only people in this city who were kind to me.

I stagger backward, my hand gripping the doorframe for support.

The clock on their wall ticks too loud.

One hour. That's all he gave me.

One hour to cross Paris.

There's no time to mourn. No time to process the horror staring back at me.

If I don't move now, Hoyt—

Don't think.

I can't let myself imagine what will happen if I don't make it to that church in time.

I can't.

Move.

Survival mode clicks on like a switch.

I leave their door open and their bodies lying there.

One second. That's all I give myself. I grab my purse. I shove on shoes.

On my way down, I slam my fist against Mr. Gérard's door so hard his dog explodes into frantic barking.

Someone will find them. My friends. My friends' bodies. My friends' dead bodies.

It's my fault.

And if anything happens to Hoyt—

No. Don't. Not now.

It doesn't matter how Darion found me. Only that he did.

And he got Hoyt—how?

None of it makes sense. Nothing does.

The thoughts tangle and blur—panic and reason bleeding into each other until I can't tell them apart.

Had any of it even been real?

The taxi reeks of old cigarettes and cheap cologne.

"Faster," I rasp. "Please, please faster."

I lose count of how many times I say it, my voice breaking each time.

My nails dig half-moons into my palms as the streets blur past.

The metro would've been quicker—if I knew the way. But there's no margin for wrong turns. No margin for getting lost.

The driver does his best, but I'm still barely on time. There are only minutes left on the clock when the cab jerks to a stop.

I shove crumpled euros at him and fling the door open.

Notre-Dame looms from the darkness, bigger than I could've imagined.

I'm a doll at the feet of a castle. A gothic castle out of some dark princess story—if those even existed.

The restoration hides most of the damage, but not all. It's hard not to think of the fire—how even this fortress of stone once burned. Proof that nothing is untouchable.

I slow for a second, my shoes skidding on the wet cobblestones slick with rain. Every inch of the cathedral speaks of centuries, of kings and conquerors, of prayers unanswered.

My eyes drag upward without permission. I'm searching.

The gargoyles.

Those grotesque stone sentinels leering down like they know. Twisted mouths stretched in eternal laughter—as if they can see straight through me.

But there's no time for awe. No time for fear.

Run.

I don't even know where I'm running. Only that I have to.

I drag my gaze down, force my legs forward. My heart pounds louder than the bells overhead. Time is slipping through my fingers like water.

I slip in behind a group of tourists, their chatter a distant hum. The massive wooden doors swallow me whole as I push past them, my shoulder grazing the carved saints and demons standing vigil.

I don't look.

I can't.

Is this even the right place? The right entrance?

Why here? Why Notre-Dame?

Why did Darion murder Marie and Tom instead of coming for me directly?

And how the hell did he get his hands on Hoyt?

The questions claw at my skull, sharp and relentless. Nothing fits.

I rush through the main hall.

People linger everywhere—some kneeling in silent prayer, others frozen mid-step, their gazes tilted skyward. Phones and cameras rise like offerings, capturing what seems to them like a once-in-a-lifetime moment.

The patterned tiles beneath my feet stretch endlessly, their intricate geometry creating a dizzying illusion of infinity. They are worn with age, evidence of centuries of footsteps.

Above me, the arches soar so high they seem to pierce the sky. I've never felt smaller.

The grandeur presses down, suffocating. I feel more insignificant than ever. I know that feeling—it's been my companion for months—but here it's crushing.

The stonework is alive with detail—every surface carved, every arch etched with ancient symbols I don't have time to decipher.

Breathe.

Move.

The unease builds with every step.

The cathedral looks like it's watching me. Waiting.

I scan the cavernous hall—right, left, center—eyes darting over marble columns and rows of pews. My mind, unhelpful, spits out facts I don't need: Napoleon was crowned here—the coronation site, a stage for kings.

My breath comes ragged, desperate.

"Darioooonnnnn!"

The scream tears out of me, echoing against the stone like shattering glass. Heads turn. People scatter, their gasps and murmurs swelling like a tide.

I don't care. I keep moving.

The stained glass windows loom above.

They watch me run like an audience, as if I'm a gladiator sprinting toward the lion.

I draw in a desperate breath, ready to scream again—when a hand clamps around my wrist.

"Come with me if you want to live."

Twelve

"Not all those who wander are lost." –
J.R.R. Tolkien

The voice is creepily low.

Fingers wrap around my arm—too tight. My skin aches where he grips me, the pressure hard enough to leave bruises.

I whirl, jerking against the hold. The stranger is wearing a coat, face concealed by the hood.

"Let go of me!" I hiss. The sound ricochets off the cathedral's stone.

"Quiet," he snaps, words rapid and clipped. "You don't want them to find you."

Them?

"What—" I choke out, confused.

"Trust me. I'm your best chance of making it out of here alive."

"No. I can't—I have to find him. He's got my boyfriend...," I say, still trying to twist free.

"You're so out of your depth." His grip tightens as he pulls me toward a side hallway, shoes silent against the ancient stones.

Panic claws at my throat. I don't know this man. I don't have time for this.

"Let me go—now!" I wrench back with all my strength.

He releases me—abrupt, like he's decided to let a wild animal lunge at the cage walls.

But he's calm. Too calm.

"You have the violet amulet. You're the seventh possessor. And if you want to see your boyfriend alive again, you'll listen to me."

I freeze.

"Who are you?" My voice wavers.

"Not here. We need to move. Now."

"I can't. I can't leave. Darion said he'd—"

The man wheels on me, his hood shifting just enough for me to peek at his face.

"And what's your plan, Iris? March straight to the Seers? You think Darion's going to hand your... boyfriend over like a good little soldier?" His tone is a low snarl now. "What makes you think he'll ever let either of you walk away?"

He knows my name.

But before I can ask how, a voice slithers in behind me—mocking, venomous.

"Well, well. Look who's still breathing after all."

I don't have to turn. I can sense his presence like a draft through a cracked window.

Darion.

"It's been a minute, Iris," he drawls, a smirk in every syllable.

I turn to face him.

Anger floods my body. My fingers curl into fists at my sides, itching to claw that smug look off his face.

But Darion's not the same man I last saw.

He's changed—more arrogant now, disgustingly disheveled like he's been drunk on his own power for months. A jagged scar cuts across his face, thick black stitches holding the ruined skin around his left eye shut. He looks monstrous. And yet, he still smirks, like he's already won.

I swallow hard, forcing down the rage boiling in my gut. I can't let it rule me.

Hoyt. Focus on Hoyt.

"Where is he, Darion?" My words come out sharp. "Tell me he's safe."

His grin widens, teeth flashing in the cathedral's dim light. "He's fine. For now."

"What did you do to Tom and Marie?" My voice cracks, but I steady it. "They—"

"Pity," he cuts me off with a shrug. "But necessary. Poison's elegant—clean, untraceable. The refined man's weapon."

Something inside me twists violently.

"Now," he says, stepping forward slightly, his shoes ringing against the tile. "Come with me, or your boyfriend will get a front-row seat to what I'm capable of next."

"You could've come for me directly, Darion. You didn't have to hurt them."

"Sure. I tried that, remember?" His tone drips with mockery. "But you're slippery, Iris. Always running. Always hiding. Not anymore."

His eyes flick to the man standing at my side, still half-shrouded in his hood. "All you have to do is walk away from... him." He tilts his chin at the stranger like flicking off an insect. "Come with me, and you'll be reunited with your pretty boy soon enough."

My jaw tightens. "Prove it. Show me he's safe. Where is he?"

Darion doesn't answer right away.

Instead, my attention snags on the three men flanking him. Their hoods hang low. Each wears the same heavy coat as the stranger beside me. And on their sleeves—

An eye.

An elongated eye stitched in silver thread. Inside, a prism shimmers, its iridescence shifting from violet to blue to green as they move. Around it, tiny specks of gold swirl in a broken circle—like a halo cracked open.

"He's back home," Darion says smoothly. "In our family

estate—Morgrave Hollow. It's time you saw the place for yourself. He's waiting there." His smile curls. "A proper little family reunion."

My stomach turns. "What? Where the hell is that? I don't believe you."

"Back in New England." His tone is infuriatingly calm, like he's explaining directions to a child. "We'll call him on the way— soothe that bleeding heart of yours. Let's go."

I take one shaky step toward him—

And the man beside me finally speaks. His voice cuts the air like a blade.

"She's not going anywhere."

I whip my head to him, startled. "I'm sorry," I snap. "But I am. I don't even fucking know you."

Darion chuckles—a low, sinister sound that echoes off the cathedral's stones.

"It was good seeing you again, Comhghall," he says, almost playfully.

I take another step. Then another.

That's when it happens.

A cold weight wraps around my wrist.

My breath shatters in my chest as I glance down—

A shadow.

It's not possible. Not real.

But it is. Dark and coiling like smoke, a hand-shaped mass of blackness grips me tight. My skin prickles where it touches.

Before I can scream, another tendril snakes around my waist, pinning me.

No. No, no, no. Not now. Not here. I can't be losing it now—this isn't real. It can't be real.

"Let her go!" Darion barks suddenly.

The shock almost knocks the breath out of me. *He... sees it too?*

"Walk away, Darion," the hooded man says, thrumming with authority. "Before things get ugly again."

Why are they acting like me being held by something invisible is... normal? Seen?

"Iris," Darion calls, his tone taunting now. "Do you want to see your boyfriend? Then use that fucking thing around your neck and let's go!"

I fight against the hold, every muscle screaming for escape—but something's changed.

The shadow not only binds me but it also moves. Tendrils coil around my wrists, my ribs, my throat. One brushes my lips, tasting my fear.

Each one acts with an intelligence I can't name. Not mindless. Not chaotic. Calculating. Like hands that know exactly how much pressure it takes to hold without breaking.

I gasp, but the sound barely escapes. My lungs heave against the constriction. Air slips away, mercilessly. The darkness isn't just around me—it's pressing inward now, into my veins until even my thoughts splinter and static hums in my skull.

The shadow is alive. Aware.

And it's not letting go.

The cathedral tilts and warps in my vision. Stained glass smears into a kaleidoscope of colors, the ripples distorting everything.

And then I feel it—my prism.

For a split second, hope flares. It's helping me.

But no.

The pulse isn't fighting the shadow. It's *feeding* it. Amplifying its power until I can feel it sinking into my skin, wrapping tighter.

A choked sound claws up my throat. My limbs go heavy. My body betrays me—too weak to fight, too weak to scream.

The shadows drag me down, into a blackness deeper than anything I've ever known.

The last thing I feel is my prism's pulse pounding like a second heartbeat—fast, eager.

Then—

Nothing

* * *

Where am I?

Panic as memory rushes back—the cathedral, Darion, the shadows wrapping tight like ropes. Did he take me? Did I black out, only for him to drag me somewhere worse?

But when I turn, it's not Darion.

The hooded man sits beside me, motionless, his head bowed. For a moment, I almost think he's asleep—until I see his jaw clench. His fingers twitch against the cane propped at his side.

The cane.

My stomach knots. I blink hard, but it's still there. The same sleek, polished cane I've been catching in flashes for weeks—reflected in shop windows, hovering in the corner of mirrors, disappearing down alleyways as I turned too late to catch the man holding it.

No. No, it can't be.

This isn't real. This is like the shadows. The whispers.

But now it's here. In the open. Solid.

"Where's Darion?" I almost crack on the question.

No answer.

I glance around, desperate for clarity—for Darion, for the other hooded figures, for any explanation of what the hell just happened—or is still happening.

Is any of this real?

I drag my gaze upward to the stained glass.

Focus.

There—Christ crowned in thorns. Apostles and saints rendered in jewel-toned glass, their faces almost otherworldly. Angels rising, their wings unfurled. In the borders, delicate flowers bloom—typical medieval ornamentation meant to echo the Garden of Eden.

I search for anything darker, and there it is: small figures near the edge of one panel, twisted in agony, tumbling into flames—a glimpse of the Last Judgment. Not demons, not really, but sinners falling headlong into damnation.

Classic Notre-Dame. Sacred narrative layered with the quiet hand of its craftsmen, who hid nature and humanity in every corner.

History. Facts. Proof I'm not losing my mind.

It's real. Tangible. My breath shudders out. Okay. Maybe this is actually happening.

"Where's Darion?" I repeat.

"Shhh," the man murmurs. "Quiet."

"Who are you?" The words tumble out before I can stop them.

"I said quiet." His voice lashes, sharp as a blade. Not shouting. Controlled.

He doesn't look at me—his body wound tight as if holding something back.

I inch backward, scanning for an exit. The nave stretches too far, too open. I can't see a door, but I don't care. I need to move.

"You're not safe," he says suddenly. "They're still here."

"Safe?" My tone pitches higher. "I didn't want to be safe. I wanted to go with him!"

"You wanted to die?" His words cut like ice. "I thought you wanted to save your boyfriend."

"I do want to save him!" My hands curl into fists. "What happened? What did you do?"

"Long story. We don't have time for it."

I shove myself to my feet.

His head tilts slightly, the hood shadowing his face.

"I don't need your permission," he says. His tone drops, low and final. "But this will go a lot easier if you come willingly."

And right as I start to back away—ready to bolt—a faint glow flickers at the edge of my vision.

Red light.

It spills from his right hand, faint but alive. Familiar. Too familiar.

My breath snags. *I know that glow.*

A prism.

A ring prism, wrapped around his finger like a special piece of jewelry.

"You have a—" I choke on the words.

"We need to go."

I tear my eyes from the glow and spit out, "I told you—even if I knew you, even if I trusted you, which I don't—I'm not leaving."

He exhales sharply, a flash of frustration tightening his jaw. "We both know you have no idea what to do."

I glare at him, my body tense to run. "I don't need you."

"You do," he says flatly. "If you walk out there alone, the Seers will have you bleeding on a marble floor before you even know you've been caught."

"The Seers?" I snap. "What the hell are you talking about?"

"The society."

"What society?"

"It doesn't matter." His head jerks toward the darkened nave. "We need to move. Now. The police are circling. And if the Seers aren't already watching us, they will be any second."

"I'm sorry, but there is no way in hell I'm going anywhere with you."

His head tilts, almost disappointed. But he doesn't argue.

Instead—something shifts.

From beneath his coat, darkness leaks. Slow at first. Then faster, pooling and stretching across the floor. A long shadow, detached from his body, creeping toward me like it has a mind of its own.

I stumble back, but the thing is faster. It snakes around my ankle, then my wrist—cold and impossibly solid.

"Stop—" I say as I shake against it. "What are you—"

The shadow tightens. A second tendril darts up, curling around my arm, dragging me forward with slow, unyielding force.

"No! Let go of me!" My feet skid against the stone floor. I yank hard, but it only makes the grip bruising.

He doesn't turn, doesn't even raise his voice.

I scream—raw and panicked. But before the sound can fully escape, a sliver of darkness splits off, rising like a hand and pressing over my mouth.

My eyes go wide. I can feel it—*solid*.

The man finally stops walking. His tone is calm, almost bored:

"I'll let it go. But only if you stop screaming. Will you?"

I force myself to nod, my body trembling so hard my teeth nearly chatter.

The shadow peels away from my lips, retracting in a slow ripple. The tendril on my wrist loosens just enough to keep me upright.

"What part of me helping you are you not understanding?"

"I can't. OK?" I tremble. I'm close to breaking now—grief and fury boiling together. "I don't know who—or *what*—you are, but I came here to find someone. I'm not leaving without him."

The man exhales through his nose.

He drops his hood.

He's older than I thought—mid-sixties, maybe. His face is lined, angular, with shadows carved deep into the hollows of his cheeks. Streaks of silver thread through close-cropped black hair. His skin—deep brown, smooth despite the years—seems to drink in the glow from the stained glass overhead. And his eyes—black, sharp, unflinching—fix on me with the weight of someone who's seen the worst of the world and survived it.

"Your boyfriend isn't here." His answer is tired. Weighted.

I look at his cane again.

I've seen that cane.

The one I've glimpsed in mirrors. In alleys. I thought I was losing my mind.

But it was him.

"You "

"Yes," he says simply. No explanation. No apology.

"How do you know about Hoyt?" I demand. "Even if he's not here, Darion has him."

"I will answer all your questions. But not here. We don't have time. I know Darion. I know what he's capable of. And I know he's not alone. If we stay, they'll send more. I can only shield you for so long. If you go to Darion now, you'll be handing him your life. He won't even keep his end of the deal. That's not how this works."

I'm shaking my head before he's finished. "You don't know that."

"I do," he snaps. The calm cracks for a moment, and something cold and lethal flashes in his eyes. "You think I got this far without learning how to survive them?"

My voice sounds thin even to me. "Why should I trust you?"

"Because if you don't..." His tone drops low. "They'll find you. And they won't bother making it quick."

I take a deep breath.

"You want answers?" he asks, softer now. "About the amulets? About what's happening to you?"

I don't answer. I can't. My mind is screaming and the prism—God, the prism won't stop pulling. Pulling like it did the night it drew me to Hoyt in Alaska.

"You want to save him?" the man presses. "Then stop fighting me and move."

I'm shaking when I whisper, "Yes."

"Good." His expression doesn't soften. It doesn't need to. "Then don't look back. It's time we both get the help we need."

My feet move. I don't remember deciding. One step. Two. My rational brain still screams, but the prism's pull is stronger. It's already made the choice for us.

I don't bother pretending I can't feel it anymore. It pulled me to Hoyt once. Now it's pulling me again.

Perhaps I'm meant to follow this man.

Or maybe I'm about to make the biggest mistake of my life.

Thirteen

"THE SCARIEST MONSTERS ARE THE ONES THAT
LURK WITHIN OUR SOULS." – EDGAR ALLAN POE

I hover at the edge of the car door, my fingers brushing the cold metal handle. The night air bites at my skin, thick with exhaust and faint rain. My body screams to move—to run—but where would I even go?

Comhghall waits inside as still as a statue. His hands rest lightly on the steering wheel, but there's a strange readiness in his posture. The faint red glow of his prism has faded now, but I still sense it—like an echo pulsing in my own chest.

"Get in," he says. Not unkindly but not pleading either.

I hesitate. *This is insane.* I don't know him. I don't know where we're going. He could be leading me straight into another trap.

But I slide in anyway.

The door shuts with a solid thunk that feels disturbingly final. My pulse thuds in my ears as he pulls us away from the curb.

I swallow hard, the silence stretching as the cathedral fades in the rearview mirror.

"Where are we going?" I ask, my voice sharp from the effort of holding it steady. "Who are you? How do you know me?" The questions tumble out too fast.

His eyes stay on the road.

"To my place. You're not safe in the city."

"That's not an answer."

"I'm Leon Comhghall. And I know you because of the prismatic amulets. They... connect us. Unless you know how to block the signal. Which—you don't."

I turn to the window, watching Paris dissolve as we speed down slick cobblestones. The city's golden glow recedes, swallowed by the wet black of night.

I press my palm hard to my thigh, willing my hands to stop trembling. "You're saying they're like... trackers?"

"Not quite." His sigh fogs faintly in the cold air. "It's more complicated."

"Try me."

He doesn't answer. Just keeps driving. The wipers click in a slow rhythm.

I fold my arms, trying to sound steadier than I feel. "Magnets, then? Pulling each other?"

"Not magnets." Leon's tone is maddeningly calm, like a teacher correcting a child. "They're conduits. And unless you learn to shield yourself, they're always broadcasting a signal."

"Yeah, sure."

His eyes flick to me in the rearview mirror—sharp, assessing, and somehow patient. "Think about it. Do you really think I found you by accident?"

"How do you know Darion?" I snap.

Leon's hands tighten fractionally on the wheel. "I know more than you think. And I know Darion doesn't stop at one victim. If he has your boyfriend, then we don't have time for your ego, Iris. He will spare no one."

I tear my gaze from him, turning to the window. But my reflection stares back—pale, hollow-eyed. "You sound like you know him well."

Silence.

My throat tightens. "You do, don't you? How?"

Still nothing.

"Answer me!"

His jaw flexes once. Then, finally:

"Because I used to work with him."

I turn toward him, my seatbelt digging into my shoulder. "You're one of them?"

"No," he says precisely. "I was never one of them. But I know their playbook. I know how far they'll go. And I know how to keep you alive."

A bitter laugh catches in my throat. It comes out too sharp, too fragile. "So what—you're my bodyguard now?"

"Think of me however you like." He doesn't even glance at me. "But don't be reckless enough to think you can do this alone."

The car hums in silence except for the faint rumble of tires on wet asphalt. Paris is gone now. Outside, the countryside stretches black and unknowable, broken only by passing street lamps.

My thoughts slip sideways, useless and random. Work mode. Vermeer. That soft chiaroscuro light I loved—illumination falling across a peasant's cheek, a servant's hand paused mid-task.

I'm staring at the blur of hedgerows when he cuts through.

"I'm sorry about your neighbors."

It's so quiet I almost miss it.

My head snaps toward him, heat flaring under my skin. "You're sorry?" The words tear out, sharp and cracked. "You—" My voice falters.

"I tried to get there sooner," he says finally, his tone low, tight with something—guilt, maybe. "I didn't realize Darion would escalate that fast."

My breath catches. "You were watching us?"

He doesn't flinch. Doesn't look at me. His knuckles are pale on the steering wheel. "I had to be sure," he says. "You weren't the only possibility. There are others with prisms."

"You were... what? Spying on me?" The words taste like acid. "Why didn't you—"

"You think it's that simple?" his tone sharpens—controlled, not quite angry. "I couldn't risk approaching too soon. I needed to know if you were... ready."

"Ready for what?"

"Ready to listen. Ready to learn."

For a long moment, I stare at him, but his gaze stays locked on the road, unyielding.

"So what now?" I whisper.

"Now?" He exhales through his nose, his expression shifting—softening almost imperceptibly. "Now we turn the table." His eyes flick to me briefly before returning to the dark ribbon of asphalt. "You're not the only one carrying a prism, Iris. And you're definitely not the only one Darion's hunting."

I drop my gaze to my lap. My fingers toy absently with the chain at my neck, the prism cold and heavy against my skin.

Without warning, Leon veers off the road. The tires crunch over gravel, and the sudden shift jerks me against the seatbelt. I brace a hand on the dash; heart leaping.

Ahead, a lonely gas station glows under sickly fluorescent lights, buzzing like trapped insects. Leon kills the engine and sits still for a moment.

"Stay here," he says, finally.

"Why?" My fingers tighten around the door handle, ready to bolt.

"Trust me on this." His voice is almost gentle—but there's no room for argument in it.

Before I can reply, he's out of the car.

The door shuts, sealing me inside.

I should run.

My eyes dart to the ignition, but the keys are gone.

Even if they weren't, what then? No phone. No map. No plan.

I don't even know which way is back to Paris—let alone how to get Hoyt back.

Movement catches my eye.

A flicker—no, a shadow.

It stretches across the glass of the store window, impossibly long. It moves like Leon's had in Notre-Dame.

Then he's back. The driver's door opens and he drops a bottle of water and a chocolate bar into my lap.

"Eat," he says. Quiet. Firm.

I twist the cap and take a sip, the water cool against my raw throat. The chocolate stays untouched in my lap.

Leon pulls the car back onto the road, his eyes flicking to the mirrors. "I think we're clear."

A wave of emotions crashes through me—dread, exhaustion, and something else I refuse to name. *Hope.*

"Your... shadow?" The words claw their way out, disbelief thick in my throat.

He glances at me, his eyes briefly softening with something like understanding. "You can do things, can't you? With your prism. Unnatural things."

I hesitate. "Yes." The word slips out small, shaky—less an admission than a question.

"Same." He shifts, hands loose on the wheel. "I can... extend a part of me. That's all. Like that story—the boy who didn't want to grow up. Remember? His shadow?" He makes a vague gesture. "Turns out not all fairy tales are fiction."

"So, the shadows... in the mirror. In the alley. That was all you?" I need him to say I'm not crazy.

"Yes." He doesn't hesitate. "I never meant to scare you. I was trying to figure out the best way to approach you." His voice dips lower, rough around the edges with something I can't quite name. Regret? "I didn't realize how much danger you were already in. I didn't know Morgrave was after you. Or that the Seers were." He exhales sharply. "I should have."

"Morgrave?" I cut in, my pulse spiking.

"Darion. It's his last name."

Not Morris. Morgrave. Of course he lied. And so did my mother. Morgrave, that was her maiden name.

My thoughts fracture. "Continue."

"Darion and the Seers have been after me too. For a long time. At first, I thought the filum might make things easier. But you—" his gaze sharpens slightly—"you're never calm enough to bridge. You were scared of the mirror, and then you barely left your apartment."

"Bridge?"

"The prisms. Connect them," he says, like it should be obvious.

I stare blankly. "What are you talking about?"

Leon exhales through his nose. "Okay. Let's back up. What do you actually know about the prisms?"

I take a deep breath, forcing the words out. "They shine when wet. With fire I can... travel. They mess with your head. And I can't take it off. Ever."

"Right," he nods slowly, his expression unreadable. "So basically nothing."

My head jerks toward him. "Excuse me?"

"It's not an insult," Leon says. "You know the ABCs. It's time you learned the rest of the alphabet."

"You're sticking with this child analogy?"

A faint breath of a laugh escapes him—barely there. "Sorry. I... I'm a father." His jaw tightens. "Was."

The silence that follows is heavier than the car itself.

"I'm sorry," I manage finally.

He nods once, curt.

"Tell me the rest. The other letters."

His mouth twitches—not quite a smile, but close. There's a flicker of energy now, like a teacher who's been waiting years for someone willing to listen. I'm familiar with the feeling.

"I don't even know where to start."

"How about this filum thing?"

"Okay... you know when you mix water and fire, and it lets you travel to find another prism? You said you've done that?"

"Yes." My voice tightens.

"Well. Hanging from the light, there's a thread. A filum. Only another possessor can see it. If you pull it toward you, you can... connect. Prism to prism."

I blink at him, baffled. "That makes zero sense."

Leon exhales slowly, like he's reminding himself to stay patient. "Didn't expect it to. Perhaps we start with something else."

"Please do."

"Do you at least know how to turn your prism's light on and off?"

"No. I have no... control. Not that I think control's even possible. It comes on whenever I'm—" I hesitate, shame rising like bile. "—vulnerable. And wet."

His mouth tugs. "Then that's lesson one. Control."

"Lesson?"

"Of course. You'll need many."

I bite back a bitter laugh. "I don't need lessons. How are we going to get Hoyt back?"

Leon's hands tighten on the wheel.

"Your plan is to rush in blind and hope Darion hands him over? You'll get him killed. And yourself."

I flinch but don't look away.

His eyes flick to mine. "Learn first. Then you get him back."

My gaze drifts to the window. As crazy as the last few hours have been, what was the alternative? This man might have answers —about the prisms, about Darion. Maybe even a way to get Hoyt back.

Best case? I get answers and Hoyt back.

Worst case? I die.

No—worse than that: Hoyt dies. Because of me.

Exactly like Marie. Exactly like Tom.

Tears sting my eyes. I blink them away.

And I have to admit—the idea that Darion would just let Hoyt go because I showed up? Hard to believe. This is the best plan I've got. But something in my gut keeps whispering: there's no time for lessons.

"How do you know Darion? How long have you been running from him? I need to understand what we're dealing with." He cuts through my spiral of thoughts.

"He's my cousin," I say finally. "My mother stole this prism from his father a long time ago, and they've been hunting it ever since. I ran away months ago. I..."

"What?"

"I didn't think they could find me. Didn't think—"

"Didn't think what?"

"Didn't think he'd find Hoyt. I broke up with him—to protect him. I thought if we weren't together, they wouldn't find him."

"And you think Darion took your boyfriend to use as leverage?"

"Yeah... I guess. He'd do anything to get the prism. But—"

"But what? Can't you finish a sentence for once?"

I flinch. Then exhale. "It that it doesn't make any sense. Hoyt has his own prism. If Darion got a hold of him, perhaps he got greedy. Wanted both."

"Your boyfriend has a prism?" The car jerks slightly.

I think for a second if I should. "Yeah. The indigo one."

Leon says nothing.

"You seem surprised," I say, my voice sharper than I intend. "I thought you knew all about me. That you'd been spying on me."

"I first found you last year, after I caught a rumor about the violet prism being awoken," Leon says after a long beat. His voice is reluctant, but there's a faint warmth there too—like he's speaking a memory aloud for the first time. "I didn't know who it belonged to, not then. Only that it was strong—different. I followed the signal wherever it flickered, hoping it would lead me closer. I'd been searching for you ever since. So imagine my surprise when, months later, I saw you in Paris. Stepping out of a cab, your sadness written all over you, prism shining plain as day. You weren't even hiding. I remember standing there on the corner, coffee in hand, amused that I'd chosen that day to wander into the antique store."

"Once I was sure," he finishes quietly, "I stayed close. I was waiting for the right moment to reach out."

He stares at the road for a beat too long.

"So you and Locklear?" he asks finally.

My heart skips like a stone across water.

"Yeah," I whisper. "You know about him too?"

Leon lets out a low whistle, his shoulders sinking slightly back into the seat.

"Well," he says, almost to himself, "this just got a hell of a lot more complicated."

"What did?"

"The plan to get him back." Leon shoots me a glance, his expression unreadable. "Let's hope Locklear knows how to use his prism better than you."

"What?" My voice spikes, sharp with anger.

"You couldn't even defend yourself. You—"

"I don't even know what this thing can do!" I snap, louder than I mean to.

He doesn't respond immediately. The silence stretches between us.

"Then you'd better learn. Fast."

I don't reply.

"You're like a newborn who doesn't realize it has legs," he continues. "It doesn't know it can walk."

The words sting because they're true. I press my nails into my palms, staring hard at the dashboard. A newborn. That's exactly what I am in this world of magic and shadows and secrets. And all I want is to cry to mommy. But mommy's long fucking gone.

"How are you going to help me get him back?" I ask, forcing my voice steady.

"One step at a time."

"I don't have time for steps. Tell me everything you know."

Leon remains calm. "I'll tell you... but not tonight. You've been burning on adrenaline since... If you don't rest, you'll break before we even begin."

I open my mouth to argue but stop. He's right—not that I'll admit it. My brain is foggy, every thought spiraling back to the same image: Tom and Marie on the floor, lifeless. Would the police even find their bodies? Or had Darion already erased all trace of what happened?

The car slows. My head lifts and I spot a cottage tucked deep in the hills. It sits low against the landscape, its crooked windows framed with ivy climbing like grasping fingers. Faded blue paint softens the stone exterior, giving it a quiet, almost deceptive charm.

As the car stops, the door to the cottage swings open. A woman stands in the threshold, a shawl draped over her shoulders. Her voice cuts across the night:

"Where the hell did you go?"

Her gaze sharpens as it lands on me stepping out of the car.

"And who the hell is that?"

Fourteen

"Those who do not believe in magic will never find it." – Roald Dahl

"Will you just take a seat?" Mel says for the third time, her accent clipped and her tone sharp. She stands with her arms folded, the soft firelight flickering off the edges of her shawl. "You're pacing holes into my rug."

I ignore her. The little cottage looks too small, feels too warm. I can't stop moving. My sneakers thud softly against the wooden floorboards as I circle the room like a trapped animal. "I'm sorry," I snap. "But do you have any idea what I'm going through? No—you don't. So excuse me if I can't sit down and sip your coffee like we're having a cozy little chat. The person I care about most in the world is probably—" My throat tightens. I can't say it. "I can't sit still while he's out there."

"Now, let's all calm down, shall we?" Leon's voice cuts in. Calm. Measured. The kind of voice that might've soothed me if my veins weren't crawling with panic. "Mel, give the girl a minute."

"I need to check on him," I blurt, spinning to face them.

"What?" Leon's brows knit together. "What do you mean?"

"I need to make sure he's okay. Maybe Darion was lying—

maybe Hoyt isn't even—" The words tumble out too fast as I fumble through my bag.

"You haven't checked?" Leon's tone sharpens slightly, the first crack in his careful calm. "I agreed to help you under the assumption that you had confirmed Darion had him."

"I don't have a phone. I don't even know his number off the top of my head."

"Look him up." He tosses me his phone with a flick of his wrist.

"I have a faster way," I say, gripping the lighter in my pocket like it's a weapon.

"If you mean what I think you mean…" Leon warns.

"Do you have a candle? It's easier with one," I ask.

"No." Mel's tone is a knife. "Absolutely not. You're not doing that in my house."

I meet her glare with one of my own. "I have to."

"You will not," she snaps. "Leon! Shut it down. Now."

"You can't stop me." I glance around for anything that might help.

"What if you're trapped?" Leon's voice rises—not with anger, but with a sudden, urgent weight. "You don't understand the risks. If something happens,… like it or not, I'm involved."

"We're involved," Mel corrects sharply, her eyes still locked on me.

"What are you talking about?" My fingers tighten around the lighter.

Leon exhales slowly, like a man explaining fire to someone who's never seen it. "Traveling the aether path is dangerous—even for those with a lifetime of experience. Something tells me you don't have that."

"I've done it before. Many times." I argue. "I'll be quick. Just a glimpse to make sure he's—" My throat threatens to close. "—not…"

I grab the cup of water from the table and dunk my prism in it.

From the looks on Leon and Mel's faces, I know they're not going to cooperate. But I don't have a choice. I have to do this.

Before I can flick the lighter, Leon's shadow lashes out—fast as a whip—and the lighter vanishes from my grip.

"Give it back!" I shout, spinning toward him. But Leon's eyes open calmly. The lighter is gone.

"Will you just listen to me?" he says, not angry—just tired.

I press my lips into a thin line, fury simmering under my skin. "I told you—I've done this before. There's no harm in it."

"I wish you were right," Leon says softly. There's no mockery in his voice, only a weary truth. "But we've already established you don't know nearly enough about the prisms to make that call. And... there's another way."

"Another way to travel?" I demand.

"Yes."

"How?"

"Mel?" His gaze flicks to his wife. She exhales like a woman who's lost this argument before and vanishes down the hall.

"Take a seat." He pats the worn cushion beside him.

I hesitate, my legs still thrumming with the need to pace. But finally, I drop onto the couch, my knees bouncing like they're still trying to run.

The room smells faintly of woodsmoke and something sweet —chocolate probably. A brass clock ticks steadily on the mantel, each click measuring out my rising impatience. Trinkets and old photographs clutter the shelves, one of a laughing child caught in a shadow's looming shape.

"Remember when you saw me in your mirror?" Leon asks, breaking my spiral.

"You mean the shadow reflection?"

"Yes." His gaze sharpens, studying me like he's weighing every word. "Ideally, we'd test your temperament first—choleric, sanguine, phlegmatic—but I can tell you won't wait for that."

I scowl. "Wait—you mean like the four temperaments? Blood, phlegm, black bile, and yellow bile?"

He nods once, as if this isn't the most absurd thing I've ever said out loud.

"That's ancient medicine, Comhghall. Galen. Hippocrates. The idea that mood and personality have anything to do with body fluids is—" I let out a short, humorless laugh. "—ridiculous."

I shake my head, gripping the edge of the seat harder than I mean to. "Jesus. I got in the car with a lunatic."

Unbothered, Leon reaches for the bowl on the coffee table and peels a chocolate bar free from its wrapper. He snaps off a piece and pops it into his mouth like this is the most casual thing in the world.

"Eat," he says, handing me another piece.

"I'm good."

"It wasn't a request. Specific nutrients." He breaks off another square. "Trust me. Your body will thank you. Maybe you should also have some—"

I take it reluctantly and chew, the chocolate thick and sweet on my tongue. "So what, chocolate unlocks magic now?"

He smiles, amused. "In a way. It helps steady your nervous system. Think of it as preparing your body for what comes next."

Mel returns, hefting a large wooden-framed mirror from the entryway. She sets it against the couch across from us with a sharp clunk.

"You can't be serious," I mutter. But my reflection stares back —me and Leon side by side. A chill prickles over my skin. This can't be happening.

"This is safer than fire and water," he explains. "Darion knows how to trap in the aether path. So does the Society. But with mirrors, we don't enter fully. We watch. We gather information. And we stay tethered."

"You're saying I can... spy through the mirror?"

"Exactly. You won't be able to interact. But if you need eyes on your boyfriend—this is how."

I swallow hard. Spy on Hoyt. Relief and dread knot in my stomach.

"Deep breaths, Iris," Leon says gently. "Panic will only cloud your prism."

Mel places two metal bowls filled with ice water on the table. "Be fast," she warns. "I hate this part."

"Here's how it works." Leon dips his ring prism into one bowl until its edges glow faintly red. The light deepens into a dark, blood-red pulse. "When your prism touches the ice, watch for a golden speck—*the Solenscint.* Tiny. Almost invisible. Focus on it. Let it pull you."

"Golden speck?" I echo, my voice thin as I clutch the bowl tighter to my collarbone. My fingers tremble as I lower my prism into the icy water.

The reaction is immediate. A jagged violet glow erupts, spreading in fractal patterns like stained glass catching fire.

Leon says, "When the speck appears, think of him. Hold him in your mind until the connection forms. Then open your eyes into the mirror. But listen carefully—this isn't like water-fire travel. It's heavier. Denser. The prism energy will press against you, like it's testing if you belong. You'll feel it in your lungs, in your veins. Don't fight it—or it'll crush you."

A chill races down my spine. "That's... comforting."

"Stay calm," Leon warns, his tone razor-sharp. "Breathe slowly. If you panic, it'll consume you."

Before I can ask how long it'll take, I catch a glimpse of Leon in the mirror. His eyes are closed, but his shadow waits inside the glass—longer, darker, stretched into impossible shapes.

The violet light from my prism flickers violently, dimming until it's nearly extinguished. I stare down, heart hammering, as a single golden speck appears at its center—tiny as dust, glowing like molten sunlight.

It's mesmerizing.

"Iris! Now!" Mel snaps me back.

I slam my eyes shut.

Hoyt's image crashes into me like a wave. Him in the bathtub. My thighs straining as I ride him, his hands steady on my hips, his voice low and wrecked: *You feel so good.*

Our prisms sparking golden light as they linked, showering us in specks like falling stars. His face—perfect in that moment, lips parted, eyes half-lidded, like he couldn't believe the curse could feel like this. *Like magic.*

I feel him everywhere now—in my fingertips, in my throat tight with longing. My body remembers him. The way we fit. The way I could never get enough. What I wouldn't give to ride his cock until I was raw. My brain doesn't even hesitate—it flashes to his thumb on my clit, pressing down so hard I wasn't sure if those golden specks were even real.

God, I need him alive.

I force my eyes open, pinning them on the speck in the mirror. My chest tenses. I whisper in my head like a prayer: *Please, please... be alive. Whole. Please.*

The second my gaze locks on the golden speck, agony ignites.

It's like a lightning strike tearing through my skull, down my neck, straight into my core. The air is gone. My lungs seize as my body convulses, the weight pressing down so heavily I swear my ribs will snap.

"Calm down. It's not real. You can breathe." Leon's voice doesn't touch my ears—it thrums in my head, deafening and distant all at once.

I'm suffocating.

"I'm here," the voice says again.

"Leon?"

"Yes. Now listen—we can't stay long. Look around. Do you see him?"

This isn't like the prism travels I've done before. Not even close. Gone is the lightness, the float. Here, everything is dense. My eyes shift side to side in this frozen limbo.

"Quickly, Iris," Leon urges. "You'll burn out if you stay too long."

I force my gaze to sweep the space. A bar—or something like it. Flashes of movement, noise on noise—laughter, music, glass clinking. But it's fractured, like I'm peering through warped glass. Faces blur and smear, their features refusing to hold still.

Where the hell are we?

And then—

"...one... two... more... please."

Relief slams into me so hard I nearly forget how to breathe.

Hoyt.

He's there—hunched against the bar like it's the only thing holding him upright. His dark shirt clings to broad shoulders, damp with sweat or spilled whiskey, the collar loose enough to show a flash of skin that makes my stomach hurt. His hair's a mess, strands falling into his eyes as he tips back another shot in one smooth, practiced motion.

There's a looseness to him I've never seen before. The sharp edges are dulled—drunken laughter rumbling out of him as Broc claps him hard on the shoulder.

That laugh—low, wrecked, unrestrained—hits me like a goddamn freight train.

He's alive.

He's drunk.

He's fine.

"Is that him?" Leon's question slices in, faint and tinny.

"Yes." My voice is barely there. "That's him. Black hat."

"Fantastic," Leon says. "Let's go, then—"

But then I see her.

She's laughing too—long blonde curls spilling over a sparkly bra that looks like a second skin. She's all petite confidence as she slides closer to Hoyt, her arm brushing his as she reaches for the second shot in his hand.

And he doesn't pull away.

He watches her toss it back, his gaze steady as she slams the glass down.

Then—he smiles.

Not big. But enough. Just enough to hollow out my chest like he reached in and ripped my heart clean through my ribs.

His fingers flex against the bar. His shoulders shift—not toward her, not fully. His gaze drifts lazily across the room.

And then—his eyes lock on mine.

No.

No no no—he can't see me. I'm not here. I'm not there.

But it feels like he does.

Those green eyes freeze in my direction, narrowing ever so slightly, a flicker of something passing through them—confusion? Recognition?

My lungs seize.

The air tears out of me in a violent rush.

I can't move. Can't think.

And then I'm yanked back—hard.

"Easy!" Leon booms through my skull, snapping me loose. "Iris—breathe. You're out. It's over."

The world lurches violently as my vision shatters into black static. My body hits the couch like dead weight, cold searing through my veins as if I've been plunged into ice water. I gasp, sucking air like I've been underwater for hours. My throat burns raw.

Mel's worried face looms above me—only to harden back into that familiar mask of irritation. The mirror now sits propped against the wall, its surface dull and lifeless. The bowls of ice are nothing but puddles.

"What happened?" I rasp, my lungs clawing for air.

"You're okay," Leon says, infuriatingly calm. "I should've

tested your temperament first, but... you made it through." His mouth twitches in what might be a smile. "And great news, huh?"

Mel crosses her arms so tightly it looks painful. "Did you find him?"

"Yeah." My voice comes out weak, hollow. I want to smile, to be relieved that he's alive—laughing, drinking, *fine*. But the relief curdles too fast.

Anger surges up, hot and bitter. I'm here, tearing myself apart over his safety, and he's about to get a fucking lap dance? I want to scream, to burn the whole cottage down, to shatter every damn glass in this room.

"And? Is he okay?" Mel presses.

"Yeah," I manage on a shaky exhale. "He's fine. Darion doesn't have him."

Leon lets out a low laugh, tipping back in his seat. "He was at a bachelor party! A lively one, too." He chuckles again, almost delighted, and sips from the glass of water Mel shoved into his hand.

I collapse deeper into the couch cushions. I don't know if it's relief or pure rage making my head spin. A bachelor party. Of course. The girl's outfit makes sense now—she's a dancer. Maybe even a stripper.

"Did he see us?" I ask suddenly.

Leon shakes his head. "We reflect our prism's light through mirrors and glass. To the people around, it's nothing but a rainbow—a harmless glint of color."

"But I saw your shadow in my mirror," I snap.

"That's because you have a prism," he says. "Otherwise, you'd have seen nothing but scattered light. Again, we'll cover it all later."

"But Hoyt has a prism too," I bite out.

Leon pauses. "Ah. Right. He might've seen... my shadow." He shrugs. "But if he did... Oh well."

"Oh well?" The words tear out of me, sharp enough to cut.

"We can focus on your training now," Leon says smoothly, as if my world isn't falling apart in front of him.

"My what?"

"Her what?" Mel asks, irritated.

"Your training, of course." Leon is smiling now—like this is a game and I'm the newest piece on his board. "Tomorrow. We start tomorrow."

"I'm not going to sit here eating and sleeping like everything's fine," I bite out. "You're going to tell me everything you know—now."

Leon doesn't flinch. Doesn't even blink. "Mel will prepare the guest room. You'll do as I say. Eat. Rest. And tomorrow, you can ask me anything you want."

I open my mouth to argue, but he cuts me off.

"You've been surviving so long you've forgotten what it means to fight for yourself. You deserve better than scraps, Iris. You deserve a real chance—and I can give you that."

"We don't have a guest room," Mel says flatly. "The study's full."

Leon's gaze slides to her, calm as still water. "We'll fix up this room, then. It's got a door and a pull-out couch. Perfect."

"And if I refuse?" My fists clench in my lap.

"Feel free to leave," Mel snaps.

Leon's dark eyes find mine. "That is... if you can really deny yourself the answers you came here for."

I hate this—hate how right he is. There's no winning this. I'm starving, shaking, and my rage is dangerously close to consuming me.

But Hoyt is alive. More than alive—he's enjoying himself. The thought of his green eyes following that girl's movements makes something sour and ugly bloom in my stomach.

I sink deeper into the seat. "Fine."

FIFTEEN
HOYT

I don't know where I am. The sound of my boots on wet ground echoes sharp—lonely.

The corridor stretches out in both directions, endless and dim.

At first, I think I'm surrounded by solid walls. Claustrophobic. No way out.

Then I see them.

Doors.

Lined one after another, barely distinguishable from the dark wood around them.

Camouflaged.

I run my fingers across one.

It speaks.

Open me. She's here. Wet. Waiting.

Another one pulses under my touch.

You haven't seen her like this.

I almost turn it. But I fight it. Harder than I want to admit.

The next whispers—coaxing, smooth.

You won't be sorry to enter me.

They beg to be chosen. Promise things I ache to believe. I want them all. I trust none of them.

Some have no handles at all. Sealed shut like a warning—or a dare.

I consider forcing one open. Taking it down.

But the gold knobs call to me.

And what they offer... is impossible to resist.

My hand trembles as I touch the next one. Because what it offers proves this has to be a dream:

You can touch her here.

I open it.

The light hits me first—warm like summer in Montana. We're parked in the field behind the barn. The windows fogged. The engine off. Her bare legs drape across my lap—one hand curled into my shirt, the other toying with the chain around my neck. She's flushed from the heat. Hair wild.

Her sundress is hiked up high, riding her thighs. I look down and see the pale edge of her panties is damp—clinging.

"Come on," she whispers, tilting her hips up. "You gonna just sit there or—"

I kiss her. Hard. Desperate. The kind of kiss that says *I missed you*, and *I need to forget everything else.*

Her hand drops to my belt, fumbling with the buckle, her laugh breathy and eager. My cock's already straining against my jeans, the friction maddening.

She shifts, thighs spreading wider, and I slide my hand up her leg, pushing the fabric aside—her pussy hot and dripping, melting into my hand.

"Fuuuuck," I groan against her mouth. "You're soaked."

"Harder," she whispers.

I hook a finger around the edge of her underwear. Slide it aside to—

Crack. The windshield splinters like ice under a tire.

A bird—bloody, broken—slams against the glass and slides down, slowly.

Iris screams. A scream so sharp it shatters the other windows.

The air thins. Pressure slams into my chest.

And then—something worse.

A shadow. Fast. Too fast.

It spears through my ribs, and I don't even feel pain, only the cold certainty that my heart's been pierced.

The door behind me slams shut.

I spin, gasping—but I'm alone. Just her voice. Everywhere. Nowhere.

"You'll be stuck here forever... dreaming of me."

Like a promise.

"No happy endings. Not for you."

I find the handle again—shaking—and wrench it open.

Back in the corridor. Sweating. Breathing hard. I press my forehead to the wall.

There's no way I'm opening another one.

But then—

I scrape my hand along the knobs.

She's soaked here.

She wants you to fuck her here.

She'll beg to taste you here.

She loves you here.

My knees buckle. And I turn it.

The blast of sunlight almost knocks me back. Montana. High noon. The air smells like warm grass and river rock. She's out front, barefoot in the grass, garden hose in hand. Tank top soaked. Shorts slung low on her hips.

She doesn't see me at first. She's laughing—spraying a horse. *Her* horse.

Mona tosses her head beneath the stream, hooves shifting in the grass, the white of her coat catching rainbows in the sun. Iris runs her hand down the mare's flank like she's done it a thousand times.

Then she turns. Sees me. And smiles like the sun itself might get jealous.

"What took you so long?" she asks, voice breathless with joy—like I've come home. Like I was always supposed to.

Before I can answer, the water hits my chest, and I flinch—cold. Shocking.

She giggles—runs.

I chase.

She shrieks, twisting the nozzle, but I catch her waist mid-laugh—lift her clean off the ground. Water sprays wild across both of us as she squirms in my arms, drenched, kicking.

"Put me down!" she screams, laughing too hard to mean it.

I don't.

I slam her against the porch post, kiss her like it's the only way I'll survive.

She moans into my mouth, arching. Her legs wrap around me, slick thighs squeezing my hips.

The hose hits the porch and keeps spraying, forgotten.

"You're soaked," I mutter, dragging my mouth down her neck.

"So are you," she pants, grinding into me. "Wanna do something about it?"

I do.

I tear her tank top clean in half. The cotton rips like wet paper.

She gasps. Not scared—turned on.

I drop to my knees. Drag her shorts down.

She's already dripping, and the taste of her—sweet and salt and something I'll never recover from—makes my vision blur.

I tongue her deep, and she cries out. Her hands fist in my hair, pulling, shaking.

"Hoyt—"

And then... the hose jerks. Like it's alive. Slithers.

It wraps around her ankle and yanks her backward—hard.

I fall, try to grab her, but she's gone—dragged into the grass by something I can't see.

I run, shouting her name, but the yard is gone. It's all doors again. All knobs.

And her voice, whispering through the cracks—

"I'm not yours to keep."

My throat burns. My hands shake.

But I keep on going.

Addicted to her—but not her body.

No.

It's the idea of *us* that hooks its claws in me. The dream of a future where we make it. Where *us* is possible.

And so I reach for another door.

I try many knobs until one hums—low and certain:

In here... she never left you. And you never let her go.

It's just a dream, of course—I know that now. But I hope I never have to wake up from what waits behind this door.

I turn the knob.

We're in the kitchen. Rain taps softly against the windows.

She's perched on the countertop, legs swinging—one of my old t-shirts barely covering her thighs.

I'm flipping pancakes at the stove, shirtless and still a little sweaty from sleep.

Her coffee mug sits beside her, forgotten—because she's watching me like I'm the only thing she's ever wanted.

"Smells good," she says, licking her lips.

I glance over my shoulder. "You mean me or the pancakes?"

She grins, tugging the shirt off one shoulder. "Yes."

I walk over, place the plate beside her, but she tugs me between her knees instead. My hands find her hips like I never stopped touching her.

And when she kisses me... it's slow. Sweet.

Her hands slide down my chest. She leans in—lips grazing my ear.

"I want you right here. On the counter. With syrup. You still hungry?"

I groan into her mouth, fingers already slipping beneath the hem of her shirt. "Starving."

But then the smell shifts.

Smoke. Burning.

She gasps.

I whip my head toward the stove—but it's not the pancakes.

The smoke is coming from *me*.

My fingers—blackening, cracking, turning to ash as they brush her skin.

I can't even look at her. I stare as they disintegrate piece by piece—until there's nothing left of me to hold her with.

And then I wake up.

Still starving for her.

"Fucking nightmare."

SIXTEEN

"THE PHOENIX MUST BURN TO EMERGE." –
JANET FITCH

I wake up with the smell of burning still curled in my nose. But it's just the dream. Again.

They're getting worse. Or deeper. Or realer. Perhaps Leon knows if it's prism-related. Or just Iris-related.

The ceiling above me is unfamiliar—wooden beams. I blink into it. I lift the collar of my shirt and inhale. I need a shower. Desperately.

I barely slept. Mostly I only lay here, craving a cigarette. But without my lighter, I only stirred with the need. No toothbrush. No clothes. No clean underwear. And somehow, I've never felt freer. At least I had the sense to grab my purse. Passport and wallet —check. I'll miss my mom's letter. James's pages. Hoyt's T-shirt. But I can't go back to my apartment. I'm sure it's being watched— by the Seers and, hopefully not by the police too.

I may have lost everything I own. Everyone I love. But under the ache, there's a flicker of hope.

On that note, I follow the trail of coffee in the air.

"Good morning," Leon says, handing me a glass of orange juice when I find him in the kitchen. He already seems too alert for this hour.

"Please tell me you have coffee," I mutter.

"Not even a thank-you, girl?" Mel asks, appearing behind him with a raised brow.

"I'm sorry. Thank you," I say, shifting my weight. "You... saved me from walking right into Darion's arms."

"You're welcome," Leon replies, lifting his mug—which I realize contains coffee. "And no coffee for you."

"What?" My voice pitches higher than I mean.

"First lesson," he says, setting the mug down with finality. "No substances that can affect your concentration. Not until you've mastered it."

"I can't do that. I need coffee." I turn to Mel, begging with my eyes. "Please tell me he's messing with me."

"No coffee, no alcohol, and definitely no cigarettes," she says, wrinkling her nose. "You stink of them, by the way. A shower might be in order." She looks at Leon, who nods.

They have to be kidding me.

"Look, I'm really grateful. But I don't need training. I need answers. As soon as you tell me what you know, I'll be out of your hair. You don't have to worry about me."

"Nonsense," he says, entirely unbothered. "You're staying here. You're learning to control the crystal. And then you're going to help us."

"Help you?"

"Yes. Help us end this. Once and for all."

"End what?"

"The witch-hunt," Mel says, passing me a piece of toast. "Now eat, girl. I'll get you fresh towels."

I don't know what's more infuriating—being treated like a disobedient child or being drafted into a training program I never signed up for.

"I can't help you. I can't stay. I..." I begin, but the truth clogs my throat. I don't know what to say. I have nowhere to go. No life.

No plans. No friends. No idea what comes next. But I can't possibly stay. *Can I?*

"My visa's about to expire," I mumble. "I don't have clothes. I have nothing..."

"If you want answers, this is how it's going to be," Leon says, already heading for the door. "Shower. Then meet me at the shed. We'll fix the visa and the clothes."

Of course I want answers. The questions have only multiplied since yesterday. I almost let myself forget about the curse last summer, when I moved in with Hoyt—almost believed I could live a normal life with him, even with the constant reminder that we couldn't touch. From the moment we met, the need for answers took a back seat. I shoved it aside. My feelings for him were all that mattered. I dreamed about our future.

I kept telling myself we'd cross that bridge when the time came. Well, the bridge is gone. Burned to ash behind me. I didn't just cross it—I dove off it. Headfirst into disaster. And now, the only proof it ever existed is the smoke curling in the air behind me. A life I once had, smoldering somewhere in the distance.

The shower is hot. Gloriously, perfectly hot. I scrub my skin like I'm shedding the past six months down the drain. Real towels. Actual shampoo. Moisturizer that smells faintly of almond and bergamot. I brush my teeth, then my hair and almost feel human again.

Someone is offering to help me.

I'd be an idiot not to take it. I know that.

But I can't shake the grumpiness crawling under my skin.

I look at myself in the mirror. Mel's clothes hang loose on me —soft and oversized.

Who the hell needs underwear anyway? Commando it is.

I find Leon by the shed. He's sitting on a log, motioning for me to join him.

"Why are we outside?" I ask, shivering as I cross the yard. The air is colder than it should be. I wrap my arms around myself and blow into my hands.

"Because the cold is a great teacher," he says.

"Oookay." I shake my head and sit down, teeth on edge.

"Good," he says. "If you don't fight me on everything, we'll make progress much faster."

"How... what is this witch-hunt you were talking about?"

"You're not the only one on the run. I've been running my whole life."

"From what?"

"From whom," he corrects. "You know anything about secret societies?"

I want to say no.

But the truth is—I know plenty.

"I was an art history professor," I say. "You'd be surprised how much I actually know about them."

"Fantastic!" He grins, far too energized. "Tell me everything."

"No. I'm the one who needs answers, remember?"

"Right." He stands and starts pacing like he's about to deliver a lecture. "I might be telling you things you already know, but here we go. Since... well, since forever, people have gathered in secrecy to protect something. Or someone. You've heard of the famous ones?"

"Like the Ku Klux Klan? Freemasonry? Molly Maguires?"

"Right. And beyond the student, political, and religious ones, there are those my father called family tree societies."

"Like the precursors in Egypt?" I ask.

He tilts his head. "You'll have to tell me what that is."

"Ancient religious orders—Egypt, Rome, even indigenous tribes. Their mysteries were guarded through bloodlines. Sometimes you had to be related to even participate."

"Exactly. What else do you know?"

I don't even realize I've slipped into teaching mode until I hear my own cadence change.

"There's a lot. I know that in 19th-century Europe, there was this explosion of interest in Egyptian, Greek, and pagan mysteries. Anthropology, religious history, all of it. Some secret organizations formed directly out of those obsessions—some even tied to major historical events. The fall of Robespierre, for example. Membership was usually exclusive—based on status, belief, and lineage. Honestly, they're not even that secret anymore. Books—even movies—ruined that. There were even rumors about one at Harvard."

"Right. I knew you taught there."

My stomach twists. "How do you know that?"

"I've been looking for you. For someone to help me. It's good to see you're smart—it'll make things easier. And yes, there are secrets buried on every major campus. Have you heard of the Arcana of Light?"

"No."

"Darion's father is part of it. So was mine. The members call themselves the Seers."

"The witch-hunt?" I remind him.

"Right." His tone darkens. "It's said that many secret societies were founded to either protect—or hunt—the seven amulets throughout history. Formed by knights, kings, presidents..."

"You're saying more people know about the prisms?"

He blinks at me, stunned. "What do you mean?"

"Up until yesterday, I thought it was just... my parents. My boyfriend—ex-boyfriend," I correct, forcing Hoyt's name back down my throat. "And a handful of others."

"You really believed the most powerful objects on Earth were known to a handful of people? Your inner circle, more precisely?"

When he puts it like that...

"To be fair," I say, "I thought they just glowed. And caused a few... creepy side effects."

He raises an eyebrow. "Iris, for a history professor at one of the world's top universities, that's a shocking underestimation. The seven amulets aren't only sacred—they're weapons. And there are many, many people hunting them. Darion and the Seers are only one faction."

I let that settle. My mother's letter had been clear: there's no going back once blood seals the prism.

If people are hunting the amulets—and mine is bonded to me—then they're hunting me. Forever.

"Iris. Iris." Leon cuts through the spiral.

I blink up at him.

"I know what you're thinking. But panic won't solve anything, will it?"

"How..." My voice cracks. "How am I supposed to live like this? Constantly on the run?"

"It's not easy. The path isn't easy. But I've chosen to see it differently." He lowers himself back onto the log beside me. "My father taught me that when a prism finds you, it's a responsibility. A gift. You're chosen to protect it."

"A gift?" I stand suddenly, hands clenched. "This is anything but a gift. It's a fucking curse. Hoyt was right."

"Who's Hoyt?"

"He's—" I kick a branch at my feet. "My ex. Locklear. The one you found yesterday."

"Ah. I'm not good with names. Especially first names."

He shrugs like he didn't just dismiss my entire emotional life in one breath.

"There's so much to explain. So much we don't understand yet. But if you're going to survive this, you need to learn to control your emotions."

"My feelings have nothing to do with this," I snap.

"Don't they?" His tone stays maddeningly calm. "How are

you supposed to control the prism's power if you can't even control your feelings for your ex-boyfriend?"

"There is no controlling it!" I shout. "There's no off switch!"

"Of course there is." His tone doesn't rise to meet mine. "What do you think I'm doing right now?"

"What?"

"If I wasn't controlling it," he says, "how do you think I'd be able to go about my day without the shadow running the show?"

I stare at him, thrown.

"There's skill, and there's mania. I can show you the path to both. It's up to you."

"Come in now!" Mel calls from the house. "Lunch break!"

I want to say I'm not hungry. But my stomach growls in betrayal.

* * *

When was the last time I had a real meal? I bite into the croque monsieur with a moan—crisp toast, melted cheese, salty ham, and a golden crust of béchamel.

"Slow down, girl. You're going to choke," Mel says from across the table.

"Sorry." I wipe my mouth with a napkin. "It's been a while since—"

"You ate?" she offers.

"Since I've been around people," I say.

Her expression softens. "What happened to you? Leon said you've been hiding. That they're looking for your prism, too."

I nod. "I left home in a hurry. I've been alone ever since."

"I'm sorry," she says. "We know the feeling."

I glance between them. "I still don't understand what you want from me."

I've decided to play nice. At least until I get answers. After that, I'm gone.

"As I said," Leon says, chewing slowly, "people know about the prisms. Dangerous people. They won't stop until they have them. It's always been this way."

"Unless..." Mel adds.

"Unless?" I echo.

"Unless... we destroy the prisms." Leon's voice is steady.

I freeze. "Destroy them?" I cough, choking on a bite of bread.

"Yes," Mel confirms. "Once and for all."

"And... that's possible?" I ask. "You can destroy them?"

"According to the prophecy," Leon says.

My pulse quickens. "What prophecy?"

"You never heard of it?" he asks, eyes wide. "I thought..."

"I heard it existed. Darion mentioned something. But that's all."

"Finish your food," Leon says, already pushing his chair back. "I'll show you."

I stuff the last bite into my mouth, wash it down with the rest of my water, and stand.

"Done."

He chuckles. "We should probably throw in a lesson on patience while we're at it."

Mel waves him off when he tries to clear the table. "Go. I've got this."

"Thank you," I tell her, already following him out.

SEVENTEEN

"Time, the devourer of all things." – Ovid

The study is tucked away in a quiet corner of the cottage. A large desk sits under the window, its surface cluttered with notebooks, old coffee cups, and pages stained with ink and age. One narrow window overlooks the garden. Books fill every shelf and even spill beyond them. Piles stack against the walls and along the floor, precarious and overgrown.

And on the far wall—like a detective solving a murder—are photographs, newspaper clippings, maps, scribbled notes, red thread. It's a conspiracy of history and obsession. I step closer.

Some of the photographs are of me in Paris.

Leon has been tracking the other prisms—hunting them, exactly like Darion.

I have too many questions to begin.

He pulls a yellowed page from the middle of a stack.

"There are many versions of this text," he says. "But this one's the oldest I've found. Originally written in Latin. I had it translated years ago. It's called *The Reflective Prophecy*—or *Prophetia Reflexiva*."

He hands me the page. I read.

On the day of the fuse, the crystals will shine and dull by the hand of the rainbow. The fate will be his who dares to act, and the price she will pay will be death, which will spare none.

I read it again. Then a third time.

"I have entire volumes of commentary written by philosophers trying to explain that passage," Leon says. "Most agree it means the crystals can be destroyed—but only once fused again."

"Where was this found?"

"In the collection of Geoffrey of Monmouth."

"King Arthur's Geoffrey?" I ask.

"The one and only."

"You do know Geoffrey of Monmouth wrote fiction, right? Like a king pulling a sword from stone... dragons... Merlin?... Why would we believe this prophecy isn't just more of that?"

Leon smiles faintly. "Again, this is one of many. I could show you similar messages written across centuries—some hidden in Egyptian tombs, some carved into sixteenth-century woodcuts. I'm no historian, but my father was. He dedicated his life to gathering all this. I'm simply continuing the work."

"How did you come across your prism?" I ask him.

"It was passed down. My father possessed it before me."

"You mean... he wore it?"

He nods. "He told me that once he died, it would be mine—that I'd become the next protector. He trained me for it my whole life—how to carry it, guard it, use and live with it. There was never really another way for me."

"My mother asked me never to put mine on," I whisper.

"But you did anyway?"

"I didn't know until it was too late." I glance around the room at the books, threads, and evidence-strewn walls. "It seems like I've missed an entire history course."

Leon shrugs. "Most people wouldn't believe magic exists even if it bit them in the ass. Almost everyone encounters it at some point. Some call it religion, some call it miracles, others call it madness. But magic? It's everywhere."

He glances at the window, eyes distant.

"That's the tragedy, isn't it? People overlooking the magic and letting the mundane win. Dangerous, really."

His words remind me of James's pages—how he wrote that the supernatural is always around us, waiting. If only we bothered to look.

"So..." I motion to the chaos on the walls. "You're hunting all the prisms. And then what?"

He exhales. "I don't know yet. There's talk of a ritual that must be performed, but I haven't found the details. First, I have to find the prisms."

"And you think you can? Sounds like plenty of people have tried before you. For... centuries?"

"I don't think I'm better than them. Perhaps luckier." He gives me a look. "After all, I found you. Perhaps the prisms... like my plan."

"How many others have you found?"

"I have theories about most of them."

His answers are vague, and every one leads to ten more questions. Still, I keep asking. And he keeps answering—in riddles. Or maybe they only sound like riddles because I'm still on the outside looking in.

I pick up a nearby page. A sentence catches my eye.

Violet is the most bent color in a prism; it has the shortest wavelength of visible light.

I drift around the room, absorbing the fragments. People. Places. Possessors. Possessions.

"Is there really no way to take it off?" I ask, clinging to my last sliver of hope. "To control it enough to remove it?"

Leon looks at me, then slowly sinks into the chair. "No.

There's no such thing as taking it off. It's bonded to you. Forever. The only thing that separates a possessor from their prism is death. Unless you're ready to die for it, I suggest you start listening."

"I am... it's just—"

"What?"

"Well... Hoyt and I. We couldn't touch. Because of the prisms."

"What do you mean?"

"He would burn. Every time I touched him. Unless we were underwater."

I sink into the velvet chair across from him.

Leon doesn't respond. He starts pacing, thoughtful, until Mel walks in with a tray of herbal tea and warm scones.

"Any progress?" she asks, setting it between us. Her food always makes me feel... cared for. I hadn't realized how much I needed that.

"Not much," I admit, taking a bite.

"Iris?" Leon says.

"Yes?"

"Put out your hand."

I hesitate, then extend it. He places his palm gently on mine.

"What happens when I touch you?"

"Nothing," we say at the same time.

"So the burning..." I begin.

"Must be something with his prism, not yours."

"It actually used to hurt me too. The first time."

"And then it stopped?"

I nod.

"Interesting." That's all he says. He joins me again and lifts his cup.

A dull ache throbs in my forehead. I want to blame the flood of information, but let's be honest—it's withdrawal.

From the substances I'd grown used to leaning on: nicotine, alcohol, caffeine.

Little poisons that dulled the buzz in my brain just enough to function. Or forget.

I glance at Leon.

All of a sudden he looks too pale, as if the color has drained from his face without warning.

"Are you okay?" I ask him.

"Age is catching up with me," he mutters.

He rises slowly, leaning harder on his cane than before.

"Feel free to keep reading," he says. "But when you're done— when you're convinced—will you let me train you?"

"Train me to do what?"

"To use and control the amulet. I can't do this alone, Iris."

I want to press him. But he looks worn down. Almost sick.

"Sure," I say to end the conversation.

"Okay. See you tomorrow."

Mel follows him out. I catch the worry in her eyes before she disappears.

A part of me is grateful to both of them—for finding me, for feeding me, for giving me somewhere to land.

But another part of me wants to scream. To rebel. To kick my feet like a toddler.

I'm irritable, and I know it's the withdrawal. "No coffee. No alcohol. No drugs," Leon reminded me again tonight when I asked.

Leave now and stay lost... or stay and finally understand this cursed magic. It's not much of a choice.

Hoyt doesn't seem to care that I'm gone. Everyone is fine. How arrogant of me to think I mattered that much.

I didn't. I don't.

I need to do this for me.

The training Leon's offering might be the only real hope I have.

I linger in the study, sifting through the chaos. Most of it is incomprehensible—half—translations, obscure references, unindexed texts. But a few things catch my eye: a series of sketches that match the shape of Hoyt's prism. A torn letter from someone named G. Armitage referencing "the fifth host." A list of names I don't recognize. One of them is crossed out in red: Iris.

I keep going.

Eventually I drift to the bookshelf and run my fingers along the spines. I haven't picked up a book in months. When I first got to Paris, I tried. I searched for answers in pages, hoping words would rescue me. But the silence only enraged me.

I threw the books at the walls.

I didn't realize how angry I'd become. The kind of anger I didn't know I was capable of until Darion. He didn't just take the people I loved—he took the things I loved.

Reading had always been mine. My refuge. My world.

But now?

Now everything feels pointless.

One book stands out. A children's book, worn and soft: *Two Ducklings Lost Their Mama*. I brush my fingers over the faded velvet cover. The corners are peeling. It was loved once. Cherished.

I picture a mother reading it again and again at bedtime, the way mine used to.

And then I remember what Leon said—he was a father.

God, I really hope that he meant they had a falling out. Something repairable. Not... final.

A pang of guilt hits me hard. I've been living under their roof. Eating their food. And I haven't asked them a single thing about themselves.

I open the book. The illustrations are faded now, their colors washed out by time.

I read a page that stops me.

"Look down deep, inside your heart,"
said Ducky, "that's where we'll never be apart.
Mama's love is always near,

even when she might not appear."

"Her love's like sunshine, warm and bright,
guiding us through day and night.
Mama's never really far away,
she's always with us, every day."

Tears slip down my cheeks before I can stop them. I close my eyes and let myself remember—my mother's voice. Her warmth. The way she used to tell me I had nothing to fear. That we were in each other. That we were always connected. That a mother and child are never truly apart. I used to think she only said that to comfort me. To make me stop crying. But... it worked.

Since reading her letter on the plane, I've been angry at her, too. Angry that she put me in this position, even if she tried to warn me. If she hadn't given me the necklace, none of this would've happened.

Then again... I never would've met Hoyt.

Still, I wonder—

What would my life look like if my father hadn't reappeared a year ago?

Would I still be with Aaron? Married by now? Thinking about children of my own?

Would I be happy?

Or would I be crying myself to sleep?

The door creaks open quietly. Mel steps inside with a bowl of soup and a blanket. Her eyes go straight to the book in my lap— and in that second, something flashes through her. Pain.

But when she sees the tears on my face, her expression softens.

"Are you all right?" she asks gently.

"I'm fine," I say, wiping my face with my sleeve. "Cute book."

"Lily loved it," she says.

"Your daughter?"

She nods.

"How old is she?"

"She would be thirty-six."

"Oh... I'm so sorry."

"She loved stories. Always asked for one more. I remember being so tired some nights, just wishing she'd fall asleep already." Her voice cracks. "But now? I'd give anything to read one more book with her."

Tears rise again. This time, I don't try to stop them.

"I'd give anything to have my mom read to me again, too," I whisper.

Mel slowly sits beside me.

"You lost your mom?" she asks.

I nod. "When I was little. She got sick."

"I'm sorry."

I hesitate. "What happened to Lily?"

Mel inhales. The breath shakes on the way out.

Mel folds her hands, staring at the blanket in her lap.

"We had to move for the fourth time that year. Lily was six. We were used to the constant uprooting by then. We told ourselves it was an adventure—that we were giving her the gift of the world, even if we were just trying to outrun the worst parts of it."

She swallows.

"Leon had only had the prism a year when I got pregnant. He was still learning how to manage the shadow. We were young, broke, terrified... but Leon was a dedicated father. We tried so hard to make it work."

I nod, gently. I can tell she hasn't told this story in a long time.

"We had systems," she continues. "Checklists. Protocols. Lily's insulin kit was always first. But that night... Leon came home pale. Said someone had spotted him. We had to go. No time to think, just grab what we could. Catch the train. Cross the border."

Her voice drops.

"We didn't realize it was missing until hours later. Somewhere between Belgium and the ferry to Ireland. We called every hospital we could once we got off the train, but it was rural, off-season, and too late."

I can barely breathe.

"She died in my arms," Mel says, eyes glassy. "Because of the prism—because of what it demands. Maybe now you can understand why all of this is so important to Leon. And why it terrifies me."

Tears stream down her cheeks.

I reach for her hand. "I'm so sorry, Mel."

She shakes her head. "Leon blames the hunt."

"But he talks about the prisms with such reverence. Like he loves them."

"He's torn. His father trained him his whole life to be a possessor—it's all he ever knew. He used to tell Lily how wonderful and magical it was. That the world held secrets most people never even dreamed of. But after we lost her... he changed. Said this kind of power doesn't belong in a world like ours. That we don't deserve it. That it should be destroyed."

"And what do you think?"

She looks up, surprised. "Me?"

"Yes. What do you think about the prisms?"

"I don't think Mother Nature makes mistakes," she says softly. "Who are we to decide what should exist and what shouldn't?"

"So why go along with Leon's plan?"

She exhales, long and slow. "Because it kept him alive. After Lily, he stopped eating. Stopped speaking. It was like he'd vanished too. But then he found this prophecy... and he came back to life. I let him believe I believed. Because it gave him something to live for. Even if there was no hope for me anymore."

"You didn't kill her, Mel. And neither did he."

"Maybe. But we're both broken. Don't let it happen to you too."

She squeezes my hand.

"You're a possessor, Iris. Whether you like it or not. All you can do now is learn to live with it."

"It's hard to believe there's no way out."

"Oh, I hoped there was. Prayed, begged, searched." She looks away. "But you'll have to come to that truth on your own. We all do."

She stands and gently brushes her hands against her skirt.

"Get some sleep. You don't have to figure everything out tonight," she says, and walks away.

Eighteen

Hoyt

Blackwater stops. Just—stops.

One second we're riding through morning fog. The next, he's frozen — ears twitching like he hears something I can't. Then he rears with a sound I've never heard from him before—half fury, half fear—and bolts backward, tearing through damp earth.

"Blackwater!" I shout, already off the saddle. "What is it?"

But he's gone. Vanished. Swallowed by the mist like he was never real. No trail. Just gone.

I stand there, fists clenched.

This isn't Montana. The trees aren't right. The slope of the hills bends too sharp. This isn't my land.

I take a step forward. My boots don't hit pine needles. They hit stone.

The forest is gone—replaced.

Massive doors rise in front of me. Arched. Half-eaten by vines.

These doors don't belong in my world.

(They're from mine.)

The thought stings like smoke in my eyes. I didn't think that.

"Hello?" I say as I look around.

(Shhh. We're not meant to be here.)

I whip around, looking for someone. There's no one.

"This isn't happening," I mutter. "Not these fucking dreams again."

I clench my jaw.

Ball my fists.

And slam them into the doors.

They don't budge. I shove harder.

They swing wide. Slow. Mocking.

(You should've kicked the damn thing in.)

Her voice.

Soft. Slippery. Inside me.

"Get out of my fucking head."

(You can actually hear me?)

"Loud and clear. Fucking nightmare."

Inside, my boots echo on the smooth marble.

A museum. That's what it looks like.

I've never set foot here. And still—

(Neither have I, but I know: it's the Louvre.)

I shut my eyes and beg my body to wake up.

I don't.

I keep walking. Faster now.

No guards. No tourists. No lights. Only a thousand silent eyes staring down from the walls.

I pass painting after painting, but one makes me stop.

A woman. Lifeless. Her limbs too human to be divine. Red drapery behind her like a shroud of velvet blood. Her feet are bare. Her hair clings to her neck like she was dragged from a river.

I know this painting.

(You don't. It's me who does.)

The words bloom in my mind like memory—*The Death of the Virgin.*

(She doesn't look like a saint here.)

I grit my teeth.

(Go closer. I want to see it.)

Of course she does.

I don't move.

But my feet do.

Because when it comes to her, I never fucking listen to myself.

I step closer, squinting at the shadows. The longer I stare, the more the colors begin to shift. The red begins to move, slowly bleeding toward the woman's skin. Her face blurs slightly—like something underneath is trying to come through.

"This place isn't right," I mutter. "None of this is right."

(*What's happening?*)

Her voice again—whispering like she's worried, like she's innocent.

It makes me want to hit something.

I keep moving, looking for a way out. Out of this place. Out of this dream. Away from her.

The room opens up into a space filled with white marble sculptures. They tower around me like judges, frozen mid-sentence. Silent. Pale. Watching.

Even their stillness feels... wrong.

I move between them, breathing hard through my nose.

I hate the quiet.

In the center of the room, raised on a pedestal like it matters more than anything else—*Psyche Revived by Cupid's Kiss.*

I stop.

Of course it's this one.

(*I love this one.*)

I scoff, loud enough to echo.

"Fucking hilarious."

(*Why?*)

"Because you said it was about love and trust. I remember your little story well, the one you told me when I picked up the statue from your shelves."

(*And?*)

"And you don't know the first thing about either."

The statue's wrong now.

Cupid's wings—cracked and blackened.

Psyche's mouth—open, but not soft.

There's something dark across her ribs. A bruise? A stain?

They don't look in love.

They look like they were caught in the act.

And punished for it.

The air stills.

I'm running out of patience.

Then the other statues move.

Eyes shift. Heads tilt. A stone hand reaches toward me and freezes. Then another. And another. A man in robes lifts a broken arm. A woman leans forward, fingers extended, lips parted like she might scream if she could.

And for a second, I wish she would. Just to break the silence.

Suddenly, an ivory girl near the far wall raises a trembling hand and points.

The girl's finger shakes toward a corridor.

It's black. Endless.

And I walk into it like I don't have a goddamn choice.

The moment I step inside, the temperature changes.

The air shifts. No—it suffocates.

A single light flickers on.

The walls are lined with paintings.

Their frames sag. The canvases drip. I pass a landscape that collapses into itself, trees slumping like they've given up. The brushstrokes twitch if I stare too long.

And then—

(I didn't mean to hurt you.)

The thought isn't mine, but it hits like a knife between my ribs. It slides in, uninvited.

"I told you, get the fuck out of my head."

Silence.

The corridor ends with a single frame. Hung low. Alone.

The Mona Lisa.

Smaller than I imagined. But somehow, she owns the space. That face—watchful, smug.

Until her smile stretches — slowly, too slowly — and she blinks. I jolt back.

Her face shimmers—no, shifts. The lines blur. One eye turns green. The other, hazel. Her skin starts to melt. Color bleeds from the canvas like fever-sweat. Crimson to gold. Brown to violet. It runs in thick, slow tears.

"What took you so long?"

The voice comes from the dark behind me.

Real. Close.

Not in my head.

I whip around. Hard. Boot skidding across the slick floor.

Nothing but flickering shadows. Walls closing in with heat.

"Iris?"

"You told me to get out of your head," she says. "So I did."

The air thins. My ears start to ring.

Above me, the lights die—one by one.

Not fast. Mocking. Like someone dimming the world just to watch me crawl.

Shapes twitch at the edge of my vision — to the left, behind me.

I turn around—teeth bared—but I'm always too fucking slow.

I reach out. "Where are you?"

"I'm here."

"I can't see you."

"You don't have to see me to feel me."

I do feel her. That's the goddamn problem. She's everywhere. In my lungs, in my skin, in the spaces between my thoughts.

My chest tightens like it already knows the damage coming.

"I can't see anything."

"But when you close your eyes," she says, "do you see me?"

I stop.

Clench my jaw.

"Because when I close mine," she whispers, "you're always there."

A breath grazes the back of my neck.

Real. Her.

I turn, ready to tear this dream apart with my bare hands.

But there's nothing—only heat, thick and oppressive.

"Tell me where you went."

It's not a plea now; it's a command, but she doesn't answer.

I close my eyes. My voice shakes with restraint. "Iris."

"I can't."

Distant. Receding.

"Why not?"

"Because I'm protecting you."

"Bullshit."

"It's not."

"I never fucking asked for your protection."

My breath comes hard. My fists curl tighter.

"I don't care if you tear me apart."

The words rip out of me. "Just tell me where you are!"

Still nothing.

No echo.

Only heat.

Relentless. Consuming.

Nothing.

My skin sizzles. My clothes cling like they've melted to me.

"Iris," I snarl. "Say something."

Still.

My hands tremble. I drop to my knees; they hit the floor with a crack.

"FUCK!"

I slam my fist down. Once. Twice.

The floor splits beneath me.

I want to wake up.

But I can't.
I can't breathe.
I'm burning. Dying. Drowning in her silence.
"TELL ME!"
I scream it. Voice gone ragged.
"TELL ME WHERE YOU ARE!"
The dark eats it.
Devours the sound whole.
And right when I think the dream will bury me alive—
Just when my body starts to fold and there's nothing left to burn—
Her voice comes.
Close.
Clear.
"Come find me."

Nineteen

I toss and turn, the dream flickering in and out of focus. Another one.

My pulse won't calm. Neither will the cravings.

I'm too rattled to fall back asleep. I sit up, breathing through it, trying to ride it out.

It doesn't pass.

By one a.m., I'm sweating. Shaking.

I need something.

Just one last drink. One more cigarette.

Then I'll let Leon train me. Then I'll get clean. Then I'll be the put-together version of myself again.

Tomorrow.

I pad down the hallway barefoot, careful not to wake anyone. My fingers tremble. The kitchen is cold and unfamiliar, but I know exactly what I'm looking for.

I find it tucked in the back of a cabinet—dusty, unopened, definitely not meant for me.

"Don't be saving this for anything," I whisper.

I dig out a corkscrew and light my last cigarette off the stovetop burner.

The flame flares—sharp, judgmental.

Outside, the air bites colder than I expected. I sit on the steps anyway, hunched over, shielding the wine bottle with one hand.

I sip. I smoke.

The tension in my spine finally begins to loosen.

My thoughts don't. They just get louder.

Marie's laugh.

Tom's sweet, perfect smile.

Hoyt's voice in the dream—cruel and pleading.

I look up, hoping for stars. But the clouds have taken everything. Even the moon.

I let the smoke burn my lungs on purpose.

What would Akira say now?

She begged me to look into the prisms. I brushed it off. Thought I could keep my normal life and hide this thing under my shirt.

Then I met Hoyt. Thought I could love him.

Thought I could handle this.

I smoke the cigarette down to the filter. Then, I drain the bottle.

By the end of it, I feel worse than when I started.

Not clean. Not clear.

But ready.

If Leon wants to show me how the amulets work—fine.

I'm out of distractions.

Out of illusions.

And maybe Leon's right.

Destroying them wouldn't be such a bad idea.

* * *

A scream wakes me. *Was it my own?*

For a second, I forget where I am.

I sit up too fast. The room lurches sideways. My head pulses like something's trying to claw out of my skull.

Shit. I drank too much.

Did I have another dream? But no... it wasn't Hoyt.

I lean back, palms braced, begging the room to stop spinning when I remember what I was dreaming about.

With whom.

Aaron.

Being hunted too. With me. Here in France.

And Darion's voice—calling out for us. Motorcycles.

Chaos.

I press a hand to my forehead.

And then—

The realization hits.

I lurch to my feet. Everything spins. I grab the side table and hold on.

My pulse is spiking again—too fast, too loud.

How did I not think of this?

Darion doesn't know about Hoyt.

He thinks I'm still with Aaron.

Aaron, who everyone thought was my future.

Of course Darion knew about us.

If they've been watching me for years—

That's who he meant.

My boyfriend.

Not Hoyt.

I stumble through the house like a woman possessed, yanking open drawers, cabinets—searching for anything. A lighter. A candle. A goddamn match. Nothing.

"*Shit.*" Aaron doesn't have a prism. This won't work for him.

Fine. The mirror it is.

I grab a cup of ice from the freezer, plunging my prism into it. My hands are shaking so badly that I almost spill it.

"Come on," I whisper. "Come on, give me something."

I stare at my reflection in the hallway mirror.

The gold speck finally blooms—slow and reluctant.

I press my palm to it and push.

I don't think.

I don't breathe.

I just go.

The shift hits hard.

Rougher this time. Slower.

Shapes blur. Stretch.

I can't orient myself.

My vision dips in and out—

I'm too drunk.

Too weak.

My body doesn't have what it needs to do this.

I choke on my own breath as the world slams into place.

I'm in a room.

Dark.

Sparse.

There's a figure in the corner—crumpled, broken.

His head is bowed, arms wrapped tight around his knees like he's trying to disappear.

He's bruised. Bleeding. His shirt is torn. One shoe missing.

I can't see his face fully, but I know that posture. I know that body.

Aaron.

My chest aches.

I'm not in the room with him.

I am the glass. The window.

No matter how hard I try to move, I can't. I'm only here to watch.

To listen.

Then—footsteps.

Voices echo from the hallway outside his cell.

I can't see them.

But I hear everything.

"She'll come."

"You're sure?"

"She won't be able to help herself."

"He doesn't look so good."

"Then give him less."

A pause.

"My father will finally give me the credit I deserve."

I recognize it's Darion's voice.

I recoil inside the glass.

He didn't lie. He never meant Hoyt. He meant Aaron.

The boyfriend he thought I never left.

I want to scream. To shatter the glass from the inside.

But I can't even blink.

"We're almost out of the antidote," one of them mutters.

"Then don't fucking waste it. Skip today's dose."

My vision wavers. The reflection buckles. The mirror magic is unraveling—too fast, too rough.

My pulse spikes. My body seizes.

And it all tears apart.

Darkness floods in.

My chest convulses. My brain screams. My whole body is on fire.

A flash of silver. A thread.

It yanks me back like a whip.

"Stupid girl," Leon's voice is harsh.

I blink up at him from the floor.

"My... head..." I croak, weak.

Mel is beside me.

"Don't move," she says gently. "Just breathe."

"What the hell were you doing?" Leon snaps, his face pale and his hands shaking.

"I—" I try to sit up. The ceiling spins.

Mel presses me back down. "Lie still."

Leon holds up the empty wine bottle like it's Exhibit A. "Really?"

"I needed to check on him."

"You could've died, Iris."

"I just..."

"What?"

"I had to. Darion..." I blink hard. "He wasn't lying—he does have Aaron. I didn't know until the dream. I thought he'd taken Hoyt, but he didn't. He has Aaron."

"Who the hell is Aaron?" Leon asks, squinting like I'm speaking underwater.

"My fiancé. Ex-fiancé," I slur.

Mel gently presses a cold towel to my forehead. "Lie back," she says. "You're overheated."

"I thought we had done that already," Leon mutters, rubbing his temples.

"It was the wrong guy," I mumble, gesturing vaguely. "Like—wrong ex."

Leon scoffs. "Wrong guy?"

"Yes. Darion wasn't lying, Leon. I saw him. He had him. And he's all—" I mime a crumpled figure. "Like that. On the ground."

"She's drunk," Leon says flatly, turning to Mel. "Not making any sense."

"I think she means Darion took someone," Mel replies. "And it sounds like he's in bad shape."

"You didn't eat," Leon cuts in. "Didn't sleep. Drank a bottle of wine. Then tried to mirror-travel. What part of this plan sounded good in your head?"

"We checked on Hoyt yesterday," I say slowly, like it's a major revelation. "But Darion took Aaron. And... I think... he's been... poisoning him."

"Okay," Leon says, exhaling. "So Darion does have one of your exes."

"Aaron and I were together for years," I say, eyes closing. "Engaged. Darion didn't know we broke up. I guess."

"And Locklear?" Leon presses.

"After Aaron," I say, head wobbling. "Actually, they overlapped a bit... Things were... messy. Well... I broke up with Hoyt before moving to Paris..."

Leon stares at me like he's aged a decade. "Perfect. A love triangle. That's exactly what we needed right now."

"I have to go," I say, trying to stand again.

Mel plants a hand on my chest. "The only place you're going is back down. You're as drunk as a pirate at a rum party."

Leon slides a glass of water toward me. "We'll talk tomorrow. When your brain works again."

I want to argue. Want to fight. Want to do something.

But I can't even make it to the bathroom.

I simply throw up into the bucket Mel sets in front of me.

Over and over again. Until all I can taste is fear.

TWENTY

"Man is not what he thinks he is, he is
what he hides." – André Malraux

"You are so stubborn. I just didn't think you were stupid,
too!"

"Mel, will you look at me? It's going to be okay, I promise."

"Don't make promises you can't keep."

"You're right. But I will be okay. Alright?"

I wake up slowly, like I'm surfacing from the bottom of a
lake.

My mouth tastes like acid. My head's a war drum. Something's
sticking to my skin—sweat, shame, maybe both. I don't know how
long I've been on the couch.

I hear them. Not far away.

Mel's voice, hushed but furious.

"You can't be serious."

Leon doesn't reply right away.

"You can't take her there. She nearly died last night—You
nearly killed yourself at Notre-Dame, remember? What the hell do
you think is going to happen this time?"

"I can't let her go alone."

"Why not?" Mel snaps. "She's strong. You said it yourself."

"She's not ready."

"For God's sake, Leon, you are going to get both of you killed."

"I can handle myself. I've done it before."

"It was different then."

"Why?"

"Why?" her voice breaks. "Because you were twenty years younger, that's why!"

"I'm not dead, Mel."

"You will be."

"You don't understand—if I don't go, she won't make it. If I go, maybe I can stop this from turning into another fucking funeral."

Something slams on the counter. "Goddammit, Leon."

Silence.

"Then I'm coming with you."

"You can't."

Mel's voice drops, low and steady.

"And why not?" I hear her ask. "All these years, you always make me stay. Why?"

"Because if you're there, I'm weak," Leon says. "And they know that. They always know. All they have to do is touch you, and I won't be able to fight back."

He exhales, long and tight.

"That's how they get to people like us—the ones with power —through the ones we love."

"Love makes you weak," Mel says bitterly.

"No," he says. "It makes you breakable."

A long silence. Then, quieter: "I can't lose you too, Leon."

"Come here."

I wait until the arguing fades before I push myself upright, fighting off nausea.

My limbs are shaky. My throat's raw. But I can stand.

Barely.

When I step into the kitchen, they both freeze.

"You don't have to come," I tell Leon. "I can do it on my own."

He arches a brow. "After last night? Forgive me if I don't trust your judgment."

"I'll be fine."

"Iris, you told me yourself—you don't have what it takes to kill someone. That the only reason you got out last time was because you set the place on fire. You could've gone through them. But you didn't. You said you were trying to find a way out without blood."

I remember what I told him in the car.

That it took everything in me not to go through Darion in that warehouse. That I'd considered it.

But the truth is—I'm not a murderer. Not even for revenge. Not even when they deserve it.

Killing my cousin, killing his father...

I've imagined it. Fantasized about it. But I know I'd never be able to follow through.

"I know what I said."

"And what changed?"

"Me," I say. "I have."

"No, you haven't. You are not a killer."

"I'll find another way," I say, trying to make myself believe it. "Again."

He narrows his eyes. "They won't hesitate, Iris. They have guns and trained men—they've done this before, many times."

"I can't leave him there," I say.

Mel steps forward, softer now. "Let's think this through."

I look straight at Leon.

"What if it was Mel in that room?" I ask.

He stiffens.

"You wouldn't hesitate," I say.

"No," he admits.

"But he's not the one, is he?" Leon asks quietly.

I understand what he's really asking.

"No. But he loved me, and I've ruined enough already. I can't let him die because of me."

Leon sets down his mug. "I'm coming with you."

"Leon—" Mel warns.

"We need her alive," he tells her.

"Need me?"

"I told you," he says, meeting my eyes. "I can't do this alone. I'll help you now. You'll help me later. Seems fair."

Mel's jaw tightens. "You're limping. You're old, and now you want to walk straight into a gunfight with your worst enemy?"

She looks at me.

"I'm sorry, Iris. But you're on your own."

I nod. I understand. I don't blame her.

Leon gently takes her hand and presses a kiss to her knuckles.

"Mel... I saved her once. I can do it again."

I think of Notre-Dame.

I still don't know how he got me out. All I know is—without Leon, without his shadow—I have no idea how I'll get Aaron out without trading my life.

"Don't worry," he tells her. "I have no plans to die before we destroy those prisms."

She doesn't answer.

She doesn't even look at him.

But she starts packing his bag anyway.

* * *

"How long have you been in France?" I ask Leon as we wait to board.

He doesn't answer right away, eyes flicking to the departure screen like he's memorizing it. "Long enough." he says.

I raise an eyebrow.

He exhales. "I was born in New Orleans. My mom was French

—Sorbonne educated. My dad was American. They moved to France when I was ten."

"Because of Darion's father?"

"In part. My father knew what was coming. He believed the real Seers—the last ones with uncorrupted ideals—were hiding in Paris. Said the U.S. had become too fractured, too exposed. But Paris... Paris still kept its standards. He believed the Arcana of Light never left Notre-Dame."

"He was really part of it?"

"Yes."

"What do they have to do with Notre-Dame?"

Leon exhales slowly. "It was a place for them to meet. To hide. To perform rituals. The Arcana of Light needed places that were old, quiet, powerful—and forgotten. Notre-Dame offered all of that."

He pauses, watching a family pass by on their way to another gate.

"The cathedral was rebuilt in the 1800s after the fire, but the foundations beneath it — beneath the Île de la Cité — go back much further: Roman ruins, early Christian vaults, medieval chambers no one talks about. They're not part of the official catacombs, but there are tunnels, crypts, even old sewer lines that connect deeper than most realize. They don't advertise it, but they're there."

He glances at me.

"A sanctuary. A prison. A vault—depends who you ask."

I frown. "So you've been here ever since?"

"Mel and I moved around a lot at first. We lived in Bruges. Vienna. Naples for a while. But then..." His voice trails. His jaw tightens. "We lost Lily."

His grief hits like a shadow crossing the sun.

"We stayed in Ireland for a bit. Quiet place. That's where we laid her to rest." He clears his throat. "But in the end, I needed to be close to the Arcana. Close enough to intervene, to observe. So we came back to France."

"I'm so sorry about Lily, Leon. Mel told me."

He nods slowly. "I never got to bring her to America. I wanted her to see it."

"I meant you know... I'll do what I can to help you."

He just nods once, eyes still on his phone—like it's easier to look at that than at me.

I should be anxious. Dread should be curling in my stomach like a snake. But there's a strange calm in my chest. Perhaps because—for once—I'm not running.

Scary, yes—but also freeing.

I even stopped at the airport shop to buy a few clothes—underwear, hand lotion—then felt almost human again, if it weren't for the hangover.

Leon checks his phone for the hundredth time.

"Your mom..." he says, distracted. "What did she tell you about the prism, anything besides the letter?"

"Nothing."

"What about your dad?"

I shake my head. "Apparently my dad knew too. But he never said anything either."

"So you really went into this blind, huh?"

"Yep." I lean back against the hard plastic seat. "Which is why I'm so desperate for answers now. What exactly does this training entail, anyway?"

He finally puts his phone down. "There's a process: exercises to regulate your emotions, separate them from the prism's pull, and learn how to guide the energy while tapping into its properties."

"And how long will it take?"

He shrugs. "Depends on you. My father started teaching me when I was five. I had nearly two decades of training before I ever put the prism on."

My jaw drops. "You're joking."

"I'm not saying it'll take twenty years. But I can't give you a timeline either."

I sigh, rubbing my temples. "And what if I fail?"

He glances at me sideways. "Didn't you say you can't touch your boyfriend? The newest one?"

My head tilts. "Yeah..."

"Well, perhaps with training..."

My heart stutters. "Wait. Are you saying—"

"I'm not saying anything for sure. I don't know enough about what happens when two possessors fall in love. But when I touch you—nothing happens. That tells me it's not just your prism. Maybe it's something you need to do. Maybe it's him. Maybe it's both of you."

"So... you think there's a chance? To..."

"I think it's worth finding out."

TWENTY-ONE

"THE MORE YOU KNOW, THE MORE YOU REALIZE
YOU DON'T KNOW." – ARISTOTLE

"Yes, I know the place," Leon says again, like he's answering a question I've already asked three times on this flight. "Frank's place."

"Who's Frank?"

"Your uncle."

I blink at him. "Oh." The word feels too small for the weight in my chest. "I guess we're not only... rescuing Aaron."

"What do you mean?"

"I'm meeting my mother's family too."

Leon looks at me.

"What's it called again?" I ask.

"Morgrave Hollow—an estate, a large property."

"How do you know it?"

He doesn't look at me when he says, "Because once, a long time ago, my father and Frank had a bad encounter over there."

"What happened?"

"It ended with people dead." His voice flattens. "My mother. Frank's mother. Neither of them deserved it."

The words drop like stones between us, and I want to ask more—

"Later," Leon says, cutting it off. "Right now we use this time for something more important."

The cabin hums around us—overhead vents pushing stale air, a flight attendant clinking glasses a few rows up. Every seat is filled, knees jammed close, strangers murmuring over the drone of the engines.

Leon leans back, folding his arms. "Now that it's you and me, we're going to practice."

"Practice what?"

"Control. Detaching emotion."

I raise an eyebrow. "From what?"

"From everything. You said Aaron's worth saving, right? Worth the risks, this trip?"

"Yes. He saved me once too."

"Then you'd better learn fast. The prism is strong, but it doesn't care about right or wrong. It answers to your rawest intentions—what you truly want, not what you think you should want. If you don't learn to control your emotions, it will act on them before you do. And that," his eyes lock on mine, "is how people die."

I sink lower into my seat. "Sounds... comforting."

"You need to take this seriously. You can level a city without meaning to if you lose control. You need to be steady. Calm. Know exactly what you're telling it to do."

The idea that I'm wearing something capable of that kind of destruction makes my stomach twist. "So... how do I stay calm while storming into a hostage situation?"

"Practice," he says simply. "Let's try this: I'll throw something at you. Try shutting it down."

I shift uncomfortably. "Okay."

He doesn't ease me in. "Your neighbors—dead on the floor."

My breath catches. "Seriously?"

"Exactly. Control it. I don't mean don't feel it—feel it, and then shut it down. Fast. Shove it behind a door, lock it in a cage—whatever works. Lock it in your mind, not your chest. If it settles in your chest, it turns into anxiety. And your prism? It'll sense it. Remember: blood woke it. It's directly connected to your heart and every beat."

I try to imagine what he's saying. I'm used to shutting things down, but not like this. Not on purpose. My body only ever did it when the memories were too much, a reflex to survive something I didn't want to remember.

Leon watches me too closely. "Your father shows up after all these years."

The door in my head rattles. "That one's harder."

I picture an iron door and shove the image inside. My palms still sweat.

"Your fiancé cheating on you."

"He never did," I snap before I can stop myself. The words land too fast, too defensive.

Leon doesn't blink. "Still made you react. That's my point."

"It's because I—" My throat locks around the words. "Because I was the one who…" I swallow it down. He doesn't need to know that part.

Leon doesn't pause. He just keeps pressing, somehow knowing exactly which wounds to prod—even if we've only known each other for days.

"Lock it down, Iris," he says quietly, like it's the simplest thing in the world.

"Easier said than done," I mutter.

"It is," he admits.

I lean back. "Can we try… good memories instead?"

"First kiss."

A smile tugs at my mouth before I slam it behind the door.

Leon nods once. "Good. But you blinked. It's harder with good ones. Makes you want to stay there."

"I don't think I can do this," I admit.

"You don't have a choice. Lose control, and we both die."

I blow out a breath. "Then maybe you should teach me how to fight instead."

Leon tilts his head. "Fight?"

"You know—punch, stab, set something on fire. Something useful for surviving."

"The most useful thing you can do is not let the prism take over. Your only job is to get in and out with Aaron. Not get revenge. Not scream at Darion."

"You think I can just stand there and do nothing?"

"I think," he says, "you want to burn that place down the second you see it. I can see it in your eyes."

He's not wrong. The thought of Darion breathing the same air as Aaron makes my hands ache to break something.

"If you don't control your temper," Leon warns, "you'll ruin any chance we have. Learn the elements later. Hide your light later. Fight later. Right now, you need to be calm enough to walk into the lion's den and back out without waking it."

"Sounds like I'm already screwed," I mutter. "Because I want him to pay."

"You're better than that." He leans his head back, ending the conversation. "Now close your eyes, and keep practicing."

Leon is asleep within minutes—arms crossed, head tilted like we're in first class. We're not.

I try to follow his instructions, but my hangover claws behind my eyes. My palms press against my forehead. All I want is to be off this plane, moving, ideally with a cup of coffee in my hand. One glance at Leon tells me coffee's not happening. He might grant me an herbal tea if I ask nicely enough.

The sight of Boston rising below looks wrong. I never thought I'd be here again so soon—not like this.

We've got a short layover before connecting to Portland,

Maine. I keep my hood up in the terminal, watching families and students pass, some in Harvard sweatshirts. They're all blind to me, blind to the shard of power looped around my neck.

When we board the connection to Portland, the cabin is half-empty. I take a whole row, stretch out, tell Leon I'm going to "practice." Really, I want to block out the engine hum, the recycled air, and the truth clawing at my ribs—Aaron might not be alive by the time we get there.

When I wake, the flight attendant is telling us to fasten seatbelts. My neck aches from the armrest. Leon's already scrolling through his phone, jaw tight, eyes shadowed like whatever's on that screen isn't meant for me.

* * *

The drive from Portland to Bristol is just over an hour, but it drags. Maine in early evening is all gray sky and dark water, cottages hunched behind bare-branched trees. Harbors sag with lobster traps. Gulls cry into the wind.

We pass weathered beach houses with FOR RENT signs swinging in the breeze. For a second, I imagine vacationers here in the summer—bare feet in the sand, beers sweating in the heat—while we casually drive straight toward a prison cell. I shove the thought down before Leon can read it on my face.

"There's so much you know that I don't," I say. "You can't expect me not to ask questions."

"All in its time, Iris. I'm not keeping secrets. I'm simply picking the right moment. You're far from ready... and I..." His tone dips, rougher now. "...maybe Mel's right. I might be too old for this."

For a moment, I swear I see worry in his face.

"You can get us out, right? Like whatever you did at Notre-Dame?"

He keeps his eyes on the road. "Do I have a choice?"

"Just answer me one question," I say.

"What?"

"You knew about the fire and water. And the travel."

"Yes. It's how I found you—and some of the other prisms. Properties of the earth."

"So this... property... it works for all prisms?"

"Yes, it's not special to mine or yours. Why?"

"Because Hoyt told me nothing happened when he tried. When he tried to find me."

Leon doesn't flinch. "He lied."

The words hit harder than the cold air pressing against the windows.

"He wouldn't." My heartbeat spikes. "You don't know him like I do—he wouldn't."

Leon's expression doesn't change.

The denial burns hot in my chest, impossible to shove behind any iron door.

"Iris." His voice hardens. "Focus. Again... Your emotions, I'm warning you."

"Right," I say, but the knot's already unraveling, thread by thread.

Could Hoyt travel, too? Could he have lied about it?

I'm still angry at him for—God, I don't even know—being happy without me.

Pathetic.

He deserves to be happy. That's why I left.

We drive another twenty minutes in silence, my thoughts chewing themselves raw, before Leon swings into a gravel driveway.

"We need to stop here," he says.

I glance around, confused. The place looks like it's been sitting at the edge of the world for decades—weathered cedar shingles, bleached-silver by the salt air, a bed-and-breakfast that seems to have been here forever.

"Why?"

"Because I'm not walking into Morgrave Hollow without an hour of rest and a warm meal." His mouth twitches. "Could be our last, you know."

"Very funny. We're this close. Aaron looked like he was hanging by a thread. I can't—"

He cuts me a look sharp enough to shut me up. "Also—we're meeting someone."

"Who?"

"Help." He's already reaching for the door handle. "Can we please go in? I need a bathroom."

A peeling sign out front reads The Driftwood Inn in faded blue paint. A buoy sways on a rusted chain beside the door. I can smell the ocean before I even step out of the car. Inside, the air is a mix of coffee, salt, and old wood. A brass bell jingles when Leon pushes open the door.

The woman at the desk—white hair in a messy bun, knit sweater with loose threads—greets us like she's known us forever.

I think about walking right back out, heading for Aaron alone. But I know better. I need the help, even if waiting feels like betrayal.

Apparently Leon planned this stop from the start. Two rooms, booked in advance. He hopes we can return here with Aaron. A hospital is out of the question, he says—too public. We'll need a doctor willing to come to us.

My room smells faintly of lemon cleaner and sea air. The walls are painted a pale, worn blue, the kind that dares you to relax. A quilt with frayed edges lies across the bed. Through the thin curtains, I can see the lot and the road beyond it. Gulls scream overhead, impatient, like they're warning me not to settle in.

Leon told me to keep practicing. I gave up hours ago.

I sit. I pace. Every time I blink, I see Aaron on the floor of that cell—arms wrapped around his knees like he's trying to disappear.

The knock on my door is so heavy it rattles the frame.

I pull it open—and the air leaves my lungs.

He fills the doorway, broader than memory, shoulders like he's been hauling the world by hand. A black shirt clings to him, stretching over muscle I don't remember, hair longer now, brushing his forehead in a way that shouldn't make my chest ache.

Twenty-Two

"True love is like ghosts, which everyone talks about and few have seen." – François de La Rochefoucauld

"What... are you doing here?" My voice comes out low, unsteady.

Hoyt doesn't move. Doesn't blink. Just stands there in the doorway, blocking out the hallway light. His gaze holds mine for a beat too long, like he's weighing the cost of his words.

Behind him, Leon says, "Inside."

It's not a suggestion.

Hoyt finally shifts, moving past me without looking down, and the heat rolling off him makes my breath stutter. He stops inside the room, standing still, like he doesn't know how to be around me.

Leon, on the other hand, claims the chair by the window, leaning back like he owns the place. "You two are... acquainted."

"How dare you," I snap at Leon, surging toward him before I even realize I'm moving.

The floor tilts in my vision as his shadow breaks away from the wall. It lunges, solid where it shouldn't be, cold fingers wrapping my arms. My muscles lock. I jerk against it, shoes scraping the floor, but the grip only tightens.

"Let me go—" My words come out in shreds as I twist, but it's

175

like trying to fight smoke that's decided to become steel. The air between us vibrates with my frustration, the strain dragging sweat to the back of my neck. "You had no right. How dare you drag him into this."

Behind me, Hoyt's voice cuts in, rough enough to scrape. "I take it she doesn't know you asked me to help?"

I whip around to him. "No. I didn't know. You'd be the last person I'd call."

Something flickers across his face—not quite pain, not quite anger—gone before I can be sure.

Only then do I see where his eyes are fixed. Not on me. On the thing pinning me.

"Can anyone fucking explain what the hell I'm looking at?" He's pointing directly at the shadow, like he's ready to put it down.

Leon doesn't answer right away, just smirks like Hoyt's reaction is exactly what he wanted. Slowly, the shadow peels itself off me, retreating until it stretches harmlessly along the wall again. My knees nearly give when my feet are fully mine again.

"The fucking shadow?" Hoyt's still staring at it, his disbelief sharp enough to cut.

"That's my prism's gift," Leon says smoothly. "Care to show me yours?"

Hoyt lets out a low laugh, nothing amused in it.

"We could use another possessor's help, Iris," Leon says, maddeningly casual. "Honestly, I didn't think you'd be this upset to see your boyfriend."

"We're not—" I start.

"We're not anything," Hoyt finishes for me, flat and final.

It's the lack of hesitation that stings.

He looks different. Harder. Hair longer, beard thicker; arms and shoulders built like he's been training with vikings, every inch of him carrying a weight I don't recognize.

"I hope you brought with you a useful gift... because—" Leon begins, but Hoyt cuts him off.

"Lucky for me, my prism didn't come with gifts," he says. "Only curses." His chest rises and falls with each breath, the solid curve of his biceps pressing against his sleeves.

"Impossible," Leon replies, studying him like a puzzle. "But fine—if you don't want to show me, don't. We don't know each other yet. What I *can* see is you won't have any problem carrying Aaron out of there. Strength counts for more than you think tonight. If you can move fast and quietly, even better. My shadow can only buy us a short window once we're inside."

Leon stands, brushing invisible dust from his hands. "Now, I'm going to give you both a minute while I check on that meal I ordered us."

"Leon! We have to go—now!" I snap. "We can't sit here eating while Aaron's in that house. Every second we wait—"

"I'll be right back," he cuts in, tone steady, already heading for the door.

"Leon—"

The door clicks shut behind him, and the room seems smaller without him in it.

We stay quiet for what feels like an eternity. The air between Hoyt and me is a taut wire I'm afraid to touch.

"Hoyt—"

His eyes lift to mine, and the word dies in my throat. There's no welcome there. No softness.

"I'm sorry," I try again.

"Don't waste your breath."

My chest tightens. "What?"

"Keep your sorry," he says, voice as flat and cold as possible. "Save it for someone who still gives a fuck."

The words hit me, knocking something loose in my ribcage. I swallow down everything I want to tell him—about why I left, why I lied, why I can't stop thinking about him.

The door opens again before I can speak, Leon stepping in with a paper bag that smells faintly of fried food.

"Here it is," he says like he's returning to a perfectly normal conversation.

"I'm not hungry," I tell him.

"Then don't eat," he replies easily, already turning toward the door. "Let's go."

I trail them out.

Hoyt's chosen the largest car he could find—something black and hulking, the kind of vehicle you drive when you expect trouble. He takes the driver's seat like it's his by right.

I slide into the back, Leon up front, unwrapping his food, acting as if we're on a casual road trip instead of heading into god-knows-what.

Hoyt starts the engine and Leon gives him the address.

"So..." Leon says between measured bites, as if the air in here isn't razor-thin. "Without much time, and not knowing your prism's gift"—he tips his head toward Hoyt—"and since Iris doesn't know a thing about hers, I'd say our best chance is to avoid being found at all."

Hoyt keeps his eyes on the road, hands steady on the wheel.

"We park a mile out," Leon continues. "Walk in under cover of the woods. I go in with the shadow and assess the situation. With any luck, Darion hasn't called in reinforcements."

"We should call the police," I mutter.

Leon glances at me briefly. "I've told you—if the police become aware of the prisms, we will be the ones taken in. I can only extend my shadow for a short time. You'll both need to be in and out quickly, or I won't be able to divert enough attention. Iris, your focus is the antidote."

Hoyt doesn't respond.

"Do you have questions?" Leon asks, calm as ever.

"None," Hoyt says flatly.

I lean forward. "None? You don't want to know why Darion has Aaron, or why I left, or how I met Leon? Nothing?"

"No," Hoyt says without looking at me. "I don't fucking care about any of it. I'm here because I don't want another death on my conscience. Even if the prick probably deserved what he's got himself into. You said you just needed someone to carry him out, right?" He glances at Leon.

"Yes," Leon says evenly.

"Then that's all I'm doing. I carry him out. Then I'm gone. You can all go about your crazy shit without me."

My hands knot in my lap. "Why?" It's all I can manage.

He doesn't answer, and I shut my mouth as well. Fine. I had bigger things to worry about at the moment.

The rest of the drive is silence, broken only by the soft crinkle of Leon's food wrappers.

The drive isn't long, but it feels like an endurance test—three people, three silences, each for a different reason.

When Leon finally tells Hoyt to stop, he eases the car onto a narrow strip of gravel that crunches under the tires.

"Here," Leon says, reaching for his cane. "We walk from here. Stay close."

We step out into air so damp it slicks my skin instantly.

Leon locks the car and starts forward, cane tapping, unhurried but steady. "And for the love of God, try to keep your lights down."

It takes me a second to realize what he means: *our prisms.*

The fog wraps around us. A glow blooms in my peripheral vision. I glance down. Sure enough, soft violet light is bleeding through my shirt.

Beside me, Hoyt's is doing the same—indigo flickering along the edge of his collarbone.

"Shit," I whisper.

"Breathe," Leon says without turning. "And stop thinking

about anything that will make it worse. Your emotions will feed it."

Easy for him to say. Every time Hoyt shifts beside me, my body remembers more than it should, and the light surges—as if it knows him too.

My boot catches on a slick root, and I stumble forward. Before I can catch myself, Hoyt's hand is on my arm, steadying me. Warm, solid, there.

For half a heartbeat, panic sparks—then I realize he's not recoiling. The damp clinging to my clothes, the mist on our skin, it's enough to keep the burn at bay.

His grip lingers a second too long before he lets go.

"Thank you."

"Thank the weather."

The moment is gone as quickly as it happened, but my pulse hasn't gotten the message. My prism glows hotter under my skin, violet spilling into the fog before I force it down again.

We push into the trees, branches dripping overhead, mist curling between the trunks. Leon moves like a man decades younger, cane finding invisible roots and stones before his feet do. He never once stumbles.

My light flickers again. Hoyt's flares brighter for half a second. Leon glances back to murmur, "You'll get us spotted—both of you."

For a stupid second, I want to trip again—just to feel his hands on me.

By the time the trees begin to thin, my nerves are raw from trying to hold the glow down.

Ahead, the mansion looms above the cliff. Four stories of weather-stained stone, its outer walls mottled with lichen and streaks of salt from years of sea air. The roofline bristles with chimneys, some leaning as if the wind has been trying to tear them down for decades. Narrow windows glow unevenly, their light warped by thick, old glass.

We stop inside the tree line. Leon drives his cane into the wet soil, closes his eyes, and goes still.

The shadow at his feet begins to move, stretching out over the ground in a thin, unnatural line. It glides away from him, hugging the earth as it heads straight for the mansion.

The woods hold their breath.

I clamp down on mine, trying to smother the violet light. Beside me, Hoyt's prism pulses once—sharp, indigo, startling—before dimming again.

I pray Darion has been patient, that Aaron is still alive, that this won't end before it begins. But the longer Leon's shadow is gone, the more my stomach turns. How are we supposed to walk in and take Aaron without being seen? All the questions I'd buried on the drive here flood back, relentless.

Hoyt watches Leon like a man expecting bad news.

I'd kill for a cigarette right now.

"Why did you come?" The words slip out before I can stop them.

"I told you why." Hoyt replies.

"I don't believe you. You came all the way here to what? Carry Aaron and then leave?"

"That's right." The flatness in his tone lands hard.

"Hoyt, I never meant to—I was just trying to—"

"I told you I don't care." His eyes stay fixed on the place Leon's shadow vanished. "We shouldn't be talking. Whatever he's doing, he needs concentration."

My prism flares again at the sound of his voice. I force it down, my teeth clenched.

He won't even let me explain?

Time drags. The mist thickens, swallowing the distant hush of the sea. I chew the inside of my cheek until I taste blood, forcing my focus anywhere but on Hoyt.

Suddenly, Leon's eyes snap open. Even in the dim light, something in his face has shifted—tighter, graver.

"What? Is Aaron okay?" I ask desperately.

"He's alive. It's…"

"What?"

"It's Darion," Leon says slowly. "He's dead."

"What?" Hoyt's head snaps toward him, his prism flaring bright in the air.

"The house is empty," Leon continues. "I searched every room. No one's there. No one alive. Only Aaron—still locked in the cell."

TWENTY-THREE

The doors are already open. Heavy wood, iron-riveted, creaking just enough to make the hairs on my arms lift. Like the house can't decide if it's welcoming us in... or warning us off.

I look up from the threshold. If a house could speak, this one would scream: *Enter at your own risk.*

The floor groans under our shoes. Even though Leon says the place is empty, I feel like I am being watched.

We step into the foyer.

A grand staircase curves along the wall, its bannister catching the faintest glint of light.

This can't be the place my mother grew up.

And yet—

The thought roots itself.

She never talked about her family. Never said where she was from or why she left. I was too young to ask before she died, and then my father did a great job avoiding the questions. But now, standing here—this creepy old house presses against something in me I didn't know was hollow.

"This way," Leon says, moving ahead.

Hoyt steps forward first; the thud of his boots makes me wince.

I hesitate a moment longer. We pass closed doors and darkened hallways, and I can't help wondering what's behind them. What rooms belonged to my mother's childhood. What kind of life she ran from. I don't know why, but part of me wants to see for myself —only to understand what this place is.

"Iris," Hoyt calls for me.

I follow them until I see Darion lying face down in the living room, his blood soaking into the thick, ornate rug beneath him.

The room itself is too clean. There's a leather armchair angled toward the cold fireplace, a half-full glass on the side table. A full decanter sits untouched on a mirrored tray. Everything is expensive. Neat.

I blink, trying to make sense of it.

"Who could've done this?" I ask, my voice barely audible.

No one answers.

"We need to get Aaron," Leon says, already turning from the body. His tone is steady—but I hear the edge in it now.

"Right," I echo, forcing my feet forward.

The house is immense.

We follow a hallway that stretches on.

We reach a narrow stairwell at the end. Leon doesn't pause before descending.

It's damp down here. The kind of cold that sinks into your sleeves and stays. I keep close to Hoyt without meaning to.

The basement opens into a corridor lined with stone. At the far end: the familiar iron door. The same one I saw in the mirror. The memory of Aaron inside, bloody and fading, hits me hard.

We stop in front of it.

I press my palms flat against it. The metal is cold, unmoving. It's still locked.

"Aaron?" I call through the door. No answer. "Aaron, can you hear me?"

Nothing.

I turn to Hoyt. "Can't you break it down?"

He gives me a look. "It's fucking metal, Iris."

I turn to Leon. "Can you—?"

"I'm not a wizard," he cuts in. "We need to look for the key."

"Great, it could be anywhere," I mutter.

"Let's split up." Leon advises.

"I'm not letting you out of my sight," Hoyt says immediately, following me before I can argue.

Leon doesn't waste time. "Fine. I'll search down here."

We head back up the main staircase. The banister is cold under my hand, polished smooth from generations of people I never knew. I try not to picture my mother's hand here.

I feel Hoyt's presence near me—so close yet so cold. I let my frustration out.

"I don't need a bodyguard," I say to him.

"I told you, I don't need any more deaths on my mind."

I want to say something mean, but I know he means Luke, and I can't make myself push him.

The first door opens into a bedroom.

A king-size bed dominates the space, its velvet coverlet perfectly smooth. The sheets are silk. Red. Too red. They scream sex or power—or maybe both. I wrinkle my nose at the strong perfume hanging in the air.

An ashtray sits on the nightstand, next to an empty gold-rimmed glass. The drawers are empty. Whoever stayed here last cleaned up after themselves. Mostly.

I rummage through the dresser anyway. Nothing.

"We're not going to find the key just lying around," I say. "We need to check Darion."

Hoyt stiffens. "You want to search the body?"

"We have to. He might've had the key on him."

He doesn't argue.

I'd never seen a dead body in my life—and now this is the third I've come across in a week.

We go back downstairs, and my body tenses again the moment we step into that room.

Hoyt crouches beside Darion. I scan the floor for something to use. "Here," I say, handing him a fireplace poker.

He hesitates, then uses it to tug at the coat and check the pockets. Nothing.

"Turn the body," I say, my voice slightly above a whisper, trembling with something between fear and disgust.

As he rolls Darion's lifeless form, a fresh gush of blood spills from the wound in his chest, the dark liquid pooling across the floor in a grotesque shape. My stomach turns. My breath catches in my throat. My hands fly to my mouth, the taste of metal lingering as I fight the urge to scream.

Breathe, I tell myself.

As Hoyt shifts Darion slightly I see it—tarnished metal, long and thin, ending in a key.

"There," I whisper. "The chain."

Hoyt slips the poker under the chain and lifts it gently. The sound it makes when it slides free will stay with me forever—soft, wet, wrong.

We run.

By the time we reach the door again, Leon's shadow is already there. Moments later, the real Leon joins us.

The sharp scrape of metal on stone echoes as I push the iron door open. The stone walls are slick with condensation. I watch as Hoyt and Leon rush to Aaron—

But I can't move.

Can't breathe.

Because my prism is doing something on its own.

Its brightness surges, spilling violet light across the walls—not just glowing, but feeding, pulling.

Like in the catacombs.

Because this isn't a regular basement. The walls are cut straight from the cliff—salt-wet, mineral-rich, ancient.

It's connecting to the mortar and the minerals, drawing from something hidden here.

Hoyt and Leon slow, glance back—but they don't seem to see what I do.

A girl running barefoot across the stone floor, dress torn, red hair streaming behind her.

A voice in the dark: "Vivienne—!"

My breath stops.

My mother's name.

But just as quickly—gone.

"Iris." Leon snaps me back. "We have to move."

I nod, dazed.

Aaron's slumped on the floor, barely conscious. Barely alive.

I crouch beside him, touch his face. He doesn't flinch.

His body's here.

But he isn't.

"We need to move faster," Leon says.

Hoyt drops to one knee and hauls Aaron's weight over his shoulder. He doesn't ask for help, but I move beside him anyway, trying to ease the weight.

"There," I say, pointing to the two glass jars in the corner.

Leon goes to grab the vials and the needle resting beside them.

As we step out, the waves crash against the rocks—and I feel it all pressing down on me.

Aaron. The past. And what's still ahead.

TWENTY-FOUR
"THE DARKER THE NIGHT, THE BRIGHTER THE STARS." – DOSTOEVSKY

"I'll go find a doctor," Leon says, already halfway out the door.

"Thank you," I murmur.

He pauses. "You got any cash? I might have to... encourage some discretion."

Hoyt nods. "In the car." He follows him out without another word.

I'm alone with Aaron.

His breathing is shallow. His face looks like it's been dragged across stone—bruises blooming along his jaw, a split down his chin that'll definitely scar. His eyes stay shut, fluttering once, maybe twice. I reach for his hand, but there's no response.

Two glass flasks sit on the nightstand—one pink, one clear. No labels. No instructions.

I crack the window and light a cigarette.

I snatched the pack from Darion's living room like a guilty thief. But right now, I don't care. I need something to hold. Something to burn.

Salt air creeps in—cool and thick with ocean mist.

Aaron breathes behind me. Slow. Fragile. But alive.

My hand shakes as I take the first drag.

I hear the door and I don't have to look to know it's him.

"Since when do you smoke?" Hoyt asks, roughly.

I take another drag. "Since I stopped caring if it kills me."

He doesn't answer.

I turn to face him.

His gaze scrapes across me like it hurts to look.

Then—he walks forward.

Holds out his hand.

I pass him the cigarette, careful not to let our fingers touch.

He doesn't say thanks; he just brings it to his lips, inhales, exhales, and mutters—

"Tastes like shit."

"Yeah," I say. "That's kind of the point."

He hands it back. For a moment, our prisms pull toward each other—a flicker of light between them. We both freeze.

Suddenly he steps back and leans against the wall. Close enough to feel. Far enough to hurt.

We don't speak for a long time.

"I thought you were leaving," I say finally. "You did what you came here to do—you got Aaron out."

"I'll wait for Leon."

"Right. Gotta keep that conscience clean."

He doesn't flinch and turn to stare out the window.

He stays against the wall. I stay by the window. The cigarette burns down between my fingers. I let it. Let it sting.

After a moment, I cross to sit beside Aaron. His face is still pale. Sweat beads along his hairline.

Hoyt watches before turning away.

I wonder what he sees when he looks at me. If it hurts. If it matters. If he's already decided I'm not worth it.

He still doesn't know I lied.

Still thinks I'm with Aaron.

"I don't think Leon should've gone alone," I say, mostly to fill the silence.

"He can handle himself."

"It's been too long."

I glance at Aaron. His breathing is getting shallower—unsteady, wrong.

"Hoyt—" My voice catches. I move to the window, scanning the lot. "Hoyt, something's wrong. He's not breathing right!"

Hoyt's already moving.

We both crowd the bed. Aaron lets out a gasp—then nothing.

Panic spikes in my throat. "He's not breathing! He's not—"

"Move," Hoyt snaps.

I stumble back as he grabs one of the glass vials, draws the liquid into the syringe, and presses it into Aaron's arm—calm, controlled.

"You don't know what's in that—"

"I know he's dying," Hoyt growls. "So it doesn't matter."

A beat.

Then Aaron jerks.

Gasps.

Coughs.

Color floods his face like a slow sunrise. His chest rises. Falls. Rises again.

I sag forward, tears blurring everything. "Thank God."

Hoyt exhales—sharp, shaky. "Lucky guess," he mutters.

I look at him. *Really* look.

His knuckles are white from how tightly he's gripping the chair. His hair's a mess. He looks like hell. And still—he saved him.

"Thank you," I say. "For everything."

He doesn't respond right away. Without even looking at me, he says, "Leon's back."

I turn—and sure enough, the door creaks open a moment later.

Leon enters with a man behind him. Mid-fifties maybe, with a graying beard and a posture that screams reluctant accomplice. A leather bag dangles from one shoulder, worn and overstuffed.

The man scans the room—bed, vials, bruised body. He sighs. "I should've asked more questions."

"You didn't," Leon says as he heads for the chair. "You took the money."

"You said he was sick, unresponsive, not..." The doctor's voice hardens.

Leon shrugs. "I said he needed help."

"That's not the same thing."

The man turns to me. "What the hell did he take?"

"We don't know," I say. "He was injected with something—we found these flasks near him. We tried one. It worked."

"Worked?" He lets out a dry, barking laugh. "Worked how? Do you even know what was in it? Could be a stimulant. A paralytic. An experimental hormone. Could be sugar water laced with something worse. It could kill him."

"I know," I say, quieter now. "I know. But he wasn't breathing. We didn't have time..."

The doctor steps closer, picks up the flask, turning it in his hand like it might whisper its secrets. "There's no way to identify this without a lab."

He looks at Leon. "He needs a hospital. Machines. A toxicologist. Not... whatever this is."

Leon folds his arms. "You take him to a hospital, he dies. The cops show up. Questions get asked. People disappear."

"He could still die here," the doctor mutters, checking Aaron's pulse.

I nod, too quickly. "He's right, Leon. We're guessing. What if it wasn't the right one? What if we only delayed it?"

Leon sighs through his nose. "Iris. We're in the middle of nowhere. You want to drag him across state lines with a needle in his arm and no story to cover it? Be my guest. *If* we make it out alive."

The words land like a stone in my stomach. I tremble.

Hoyt cuts in. "Easy, old man. No reason to cause panic."

I blink. Turn toward him. He's still by the window, arms crossed, but now his gaze is fixed on Leon.

Leon steps closer to the bed, eyeing Aaron with a strange detachment.

"Don't you find it strange," he says quietly, "that they left the door open? That Darion was just... there? No guards. No lock. No protection."

My stomach clenches.

"It was like they wanted us to find him," Leon continues. "Wanted to see who'd come for him. And they let Aaron live. Why?"

I can't answer.

"Where's Frank?" he asks, voice dropping. "Why would someone kill your cousin—the same day you were coming here—unless they already knew you were involved?"

His eyes lock on mine.

"We weren't lucky to get out of that house alive." Leon settles it.

The doctor sighs, pretending not to listen. He kneels beside the bed, peels back Aaron's eyelid, checks his pulse.

"Is he... gonna be okay?" I ask.

The doctor pauses. "He's stable, for now."

"What can—what should we do?" I ask again, desperation leaking into my voice.

"If we were certain this was the antidote," he says, "I'd tell you to keep giving it to him—small doses, no more than a syringe every four hours. But since we're not..."

"For how long?" I cut him off.

He hesitates. "Until he wakes up. Until... something changes. If it worked once, it might stabilize him again. Or it might kill him. You're gambling either way."

Hoyt finally speaks. "Can we call you if something goes wrong?"

The man hesitates. "That depends."

"On what?" I ask.

"On whether there's another payment."

Hoyt steps forward, pulls a wad of cash from his back pocket. "There will be."

The doctor takes the money and tucks it into his coat without looking. "My family needs it. Doesn't mean I like taking it."

Leon nods toward the door.

"You're not the only one trying to do what needs to be done," he says. "Door's that way."

I step forward.

"Please, stay the night—to make sure..."

The doctor looks at me for a long moment.

"If I stay, I become part of this—and can't do that."

The doctor stands, gathers his bag. "Good luck," he mutters on his way out. "You're going to need it."

The door clicks shut behind him.

Leon exhales—long and frayed. "I'm going to get some sleep before my heart actually gives out."

"You sure it's safe?" I ask. "For us to stay here?"

"It's not," he says. "But it's safer than driving through the night. You two get some rest too."

He turns to leave, then pauses at the door.

"Remember the deal," he says, looking at me. "I help you, you help me. Don't try anything stupid."

I hear Hoyt shift behind me.

"Are you leaving?" I ask.

"I'm going to sleep in the car," Hoyt mutters.

My chest tightens. "Hoyt, wait... can we talk?"

His hand is already on the doorknob. "I have nothing to say to you, Iris."

He pulls the door shut behind him.

I flinch at the sound.

I turn back to Aaron.

The rise and fall of his chest is the only proof I have that he's still with us.

I sink into the chair beside the bed. Everything aches—my body, my mind, my hope.

I reach for Aaron's hand, but I'm thinking of Hoyt's.

And all the reasons I can't reach for him.

Twenty-Five

I try to sleep, but it's impossible. Hoyt is outside. Darion is dead. Aaron is lying next to me with poison still in his veins. Not even a normal person could sleep through this.

It's nearly daylight by the time I finally drift off. When I wake, the sun is already pouring through the window like it has no idea what kind of night we had.

I turn to look at Aaron.

He doesn't look worse. His color hasn't changed, but his breathing is steady. That has to count for something.

I stumble to the shower and let the water scald the night off my skin. I want it to burn something clean—fear, guilt, confusion. All of it.

Leon's words echo in my head like a warning bell: *We're not safe anywhere.*

He's right. We still don't know who killed Darion. Still don't know who's coming after us next.

How do you make a plan when the whole world is a trap?

I scrub harder, like I can scrape the dread out of my skin.

When I'm done, I towel off and pull on the new clothes I

bought at the airport. Plain. Comfortable. They don't make me feel good, or safe, or in control—but at least they're clean.

Back in the room, I draw a dose from the clear vial to inject it into Aaron's arm. My hands shake the entire time.

I've never used a needle before. The syringe feels heavier than it should—foreign, too medical. I hold my breath as the needle breaks skin, whisper an apology I don't even fully hear, and press the plunger down slowly.

There's no sign it worked. No confirmation. Only the unconscious rise and fall of Aaron's chest.

I exhale slowly and tell myself it's enough—for now.

Still, I make a mental note to ask Leon to call the doctor again. Just to be sure. Just to feel a little less like we're gambling with Aaron's life.

I leave the room quietly, and the smell hits me before I even reach the landing. I follow it without hesitation.

I round the corner and find Hoyt already at the small table, one hand wrapped around a chipped mug. He doesn't look up— eyes narrowed like he's watching the fog itself for threats.

"Morning," I say, keeping my tone casual as I pour myself a cup from the carafe.

He lifts his mug in silent reply. Sips. Doesn't speak.

I take the chair across from him and let the silence stretch. The coffee is bitter and cheap, but it's hot—and it gives my hands something to hold. Something to do besides tremble.

Hoyt shifts slightly in his seat, and I remember what he said the night before. That he was leaving once Aaron was stable. Maybe this is the moment. Maybe he's simply waiting to say goodbye.

"I know you're leaving," I say, watching the steam rise from my cup. "I just wanted to say thank you. For the money. And everything."

He doesn't respond. Keeps sipping.

"Enjoy," Leon mutters, appearing behind me. "That'll be your last cup for a while."

Hoyt looks up. "The hell's that supposed to mean?"

Leon shrugs and gestures for us to follow him. "Come on. We've got planning to do."

We follow Leon back into the room where Aaron lies still, pale against the sheets. Leon closes the door behind us and takes a long breath before speaking.

"I think I have a plan," he says, crossing to the chair and dropping into it. "We need to go off-grid for a while. Somewhere quiet. Remote. I need time to train you both—show you how to actually use the prisms. Control them."

He glances at Aaron.

"In the meantime, we keep checking Morgrave Hollow. Watch the house through the mirror. Try to figure out who killed Darion... and why they let us walk out alive."

The words hang in the air too long.

Hoyt scoffs. "Yeah. No. I don't think so."

Leon's gaze sharpens. "What?"

Hoyt pushes off the wall. "This isn't my problem. I got Aaron out. That was the job. Whatever this is now—mirror spying? prism boot camp?—it's not mine."

Leon doesn't flinch. "You're already involved."

Hoyt laughs, bitter. "So what?"

"There were cameras in that house, Locklear," Leon says. "You think no one's seen your face? Think again. You're on the board whether you like it or not."

Hoyt curses under his breath and starts pacing.

"I'll take my chances," he mutters.

"Let him go," I say quietly. "Enough people got hurt already."

Hoyt pauses slightly, and his eyes flick to mine. But then he looks away.

Leon's voice drops. Low and deliberate. "How about your family?"

That stops him mid-step. He doesn't turn. Doesn't speak. But I see the way his fingers curl at his sides.

Leon keeps going.

"Because whatever's happening—it's not staying contained. If someone's willing to torture Aaron and leave Darion's body like that... they won't hesitate to come for the people you love."

"We'll be fine," Hoyt snaps, but it lands thin.

Leon shrugs. "Very well. I guess if you can walk away from her... again."

He turns to me.

"Then go."

That lands like a stone in the room.

Hoyt doesn't move, but something in him shifts.

He crosses his arms. Leans back against the wall.

Says nothing.

But he doesn't leave.

"And where are we even supposed to go?" I ask, trying to keep my voice steady.

Leon leans forward, resting his elbows on his knees. "Somewhere remote. Isolated. Near the ocean."

He glances between us.

"Water calms the body. Calms the mind. And that matters—because your emotions affect the prism. The more stable you are, the more control you'll have. And we're going to need control."

Silence settles between us for a beat.

"The Isles of Shoals," I say before even thinking about it.

Leon raises a brow. "What's that?"

"Cluster of islands off the coast of Maine and New Hampshire. You can only get there by boat. No cars. No cops. Only... rocks, waves, and time."

Leon nods. "Sounds perfect."

* * *

A couple of hours later, the doctor returns—summoned again by Leon.

I meet him at the door, nerves buzzing beneath my skin.

"Thank you for coming back," I say. "I... needed to be sure."

He nods and steps past me with his worn leather bag. "Of course."

We follow him into the bedroom.

Aaron stirs slightly as the doctor leans over him. It's a small movement, but it's something. I catch my breath, watching the doctor's face as he moves quickly—checking pulse, pupils, reflexes.

"He's improving," the doctor says after a few tense minutes. "Stronger heartbeat. Breathing's more even. He should wake up soon."

Relief floods through me.

"So... he's really going to be okay?"

The doctor meets my eyes. "He's not out of the woods. But he's moving in the right direction. He could use an IV."

"No hospitals," Leon cuts in, firm.

I exhale slowly, letting my body believe it for a moment. Letting myself imagine that maybe, just maybe, Aaron will be okay.

Leon stays by the door, arms folded. "We're leaving soon."

The doctor glances up. "You sure that's wise?"

"No," Leon says. "But staying here is worse."

We're heading somewhere remote—far from hospitals, far from help. Too far, if something goes wrong. But I don't say it out loud.

The doctor sighs and rubs a hand over his face. "If you need me again, you know how to reach me."

He packs up without waiting for more questions.

And I just hope we know what we're doing.

* * *

We don't waste time after that.

The rental car isn't our problem anymore—Leon paid the doctor to return it for us. Less contact. Less risk. We're taking Hoyt's car instead.

Before we can disappear to some remote island, we have to stock up. Food. Clothes. Medical supplies. Phones. Batteries. We need everything.

As we step into the store, Leon mutters under his breath, "Keep your head down. Let's split up. Don't draw attention with what we're buying."

It's one of those rare moments where, despite the chaos around us, I let myself feel a flicker of gratitude. *At least money isn't a problem.*

"Thanks again," I tell Hoyt quietly, accepting the cash he hands me. "For... everything."

He gives a small nod. Expression unreadable.

Inside the store, I push the cart slowly, letting the fluorescent lights and background music lull me into something like calm.

We have a plan. Aaron is safe. Hoyt is... here.

Even if everything couldn't be more twisted, at least I'm not doing this alone.

I grab the basics—clothes, hygiene stuff, painkillers, bandages. I force myself to walk past the wine aisle without looking. Past the cigarettes behind the glass counter.

Keep moving, I tell myself.

Leon handles the electronics—burner phones, chargers, batteries. Hoyt's cart is all food and water.

We don't talk much, but we stay close. I'm still nervous he might change his mind. Walk away on a whim.

By the time we reach checkout, it looks like we've bought half the store.

We haul everything back to the car. The sun has climbed higher now, glinting off the windshield like a spotlight. I round the passenger side, arms full of bags—

And stop.

Aaron is awake.

Wide-eyed. Trapped in the back seat. Breathing hard, like he's been yanked from a nightmare.

His eyes lock onto mine the second I open the door.

"Iris?! What's happening?"

His voice shakes. Every syllable lands like a punch.

I drop the bags and pull him into a hug before he can spiral further.

"You're... okay," I whisper into his hair.

He pulls back slightly, squinting against the light. Eyes darting. "Darion?"

I freeze.

"You got me out?" he adds, like he's not sure if it's real.

I squeeze his hand. "It's a long story. But you're safe now. I promise."

Hoyt appears behind me, tossing something into the trunk. Aaron sees him—and his confusion only deepens.

"Where are we?" he asks, voice still weak.

I hesitate for a second.

The words are heavy, like a door I can't close once I open it.

"Prepare yourself," I say softly. "What I'm about to tell you... it's going to change everything."

Aaron blinks. Confused. Scared. But trusting—because he has no other choice.

I glance at Hoyt, then back at Aaron.

"My necklace," I say. "Turns out... it does more than shine a little light."

And then—sitting in the backseat of a car in the parking lot of a too-normal store—I finally stop lying to him.

Twenty-Six

There are nine islands in the Isles of Shoals, scattered like bones off the New England coast. After an hour of research and tense debate, we land on Smuttynose Island—a rugged spit of land, barely developed and mostly abandoned; utterly perfect if your goal is to vanish.

Its rocky terrain and crumbling infrastructure make it ideal for disappearing. But it isn't isolation that makes my stomach twist.

It's the island's history.

Smuttynose isn't just remote—it's haunted. Not in the ghost-story sense (or so I hope), but in the real, blood-on-the-walls kind of way. A double murder. Two women slaughtered in the dead of night. The case made national headlines. Some say the wrong man went to prison.

Leon doesn't seem to care. Hoyt doesn't ask questions. And Aaron—still recovering—simply nods along.

But me? I'm not so sure we should be hiding on an island that's already soaked in violence.

The drive to the port is long and mostly quiet. Aaron's still pale, slumped in the back seat, chewing ibuprofen and watching the trees blur past like he's trying to convince himself this is real.

Eventually, he breaks the silence.

"Look... even if everything you're telling me is true—which, honestly, you have to forgive me for still processing—I can disappear on my own. I don't need... training."

His voice is low. Defensive. Like he's needs to reclaim something—control, perhaps. Dignity. A sense of choice.

Something in Hoyt shifts. He doesn't say anything, but I can feel his focus sharpen—as if Aaron just confirmed something he'd been wondering about for a while.

Leon, still driving, doesn't flinch. "You're not only here to disappear."

Aaron scoffs. "What does that mean?"

"It means," Leon says, calm but firm, "we need your help."

"What?" Hoyt and I say it at the same time, both of us turning toward Leon like he's lost his mind.

Aaron blinks. "Help with what?"

Leon keeps his eyes on the road. "With training them."

A beat of silence.

Me. Hoyt. Aaron. All staring at each other like we've all entered a new phase of the nightmare and no one told us the rules.

* * *

The Moonlit Trawler sits at the edge of town like it's always belonged there. A crooked sign swinging in the breeze. From the parking lot we can already smell the sea—and fried clams.

Inside, the place is warmer than I expect—cozy, coastal, familiar. Nautical maps line the walls, alongside photos of fishermen with proud, wet catches.

Only a couple of locals sit at the bar. They glance up when we walk in—four strangers with tired eyes—and fall quiet.

Leon leads us to a table by the window. I slide into the booth across from Hoyt. The gulls outside scream like warning bells. The waves crash against the dock by us.

The waitress approaches. Young. Freckled. Blinks twice at the sight of us before pasting on a smile.

"I'll have the lobster roll," I say before anyone else can speak.

She jots it down and glances at the others. Leon orders water for all of us before I can even think about beer.

We eat mostly in silence—forks scraping, paper napkins crumpling. Everyone's avoiding eye contact, but we're all thinking the same thing: once we step off land, there's no turning back.

Aaron picks at his plate like food might still betray him. Hoyt only touches his fries. Leon, as usual, devours everything like it's his last meal on Earth.

Finally, Leon speaks.

"So—ferry or private boat?"

Aaron wipes his mouth with a napkin. "I can probably manage a small boat... on a good day."

"We should buy one," Hoyt says, barely looking up. "If Aaron can handle it, it's better than being at the mercy of ferry schedules."

"I was going to say: the ferry," I admit.

Hoyt shakes his head. "We need the ability to leave on our own terms."

Leon leans back. "Agreed."

I nod slowly, trying not to think about how much this is starting to sound like the beginning of a heist movie.

The waitress returns with our check. Her eyes linger on us again. Too long.

When she leaves, I murmur, "We should get moving. People are starting to notice."

Leon finishes his water in one long pull. "Exactly why we're getting off the grid."

* * *

We find a man on the docks with a weather-beaten face and eyes that suggest he doesn't ask questions if you pay him enough.

Leon does the talking. Shows him a wad of cash. No names. No paperwork. Just a handshake, a glance at the horizon, and a muttered "follow me."

He leads us down a rickety wooden pier to a modest fishing boat—paint faded, hull scratched, but engine solid. A bit small but it'll get us there.

Aaron runs his hand along the rail, inspecting it like he's looking for something to trust. "She'll do," he mutters.

Hoyt tests the balance under his boots and nods.

We pay the man not only to sell us the boat, but also to guide us halfway and show Aaron the route—the safe passages, the rocks to avoid, the channel markers hiding in the mist. The man agrees with a grunt, tosses in a few life vests, and starts the motor.

We leave the mainland behind.

The sky is gray. Water slaps against the sides of the boat, restless. I sit near the back, my fingers curled around the rail, eyes on the shrinking shore. Only water and gulls now.

Aaron watches every move the man makes—how he angles the rudder, how he reads the currents. He's still pale, but focused. Steadier than he was this morning.

He grew up around boats—Cape vacations, yacht clubs, summers on the water with his parents pretending not to fight. I'd seen him dock a sailboat with one hand and a lemonade in the other.

It was second nature to him.

Even now, after everything, I can see the muscle memory kicking in.

Leon is quiet. For once. He's staring out at the open sea like it might tell him something.

Hoyt stands near the bow, jacket whipping in the wind, jaw tight as stone. He hasn't looked at me once since we got on board.

Smuttynose appears like something summoned from a story I

was never meant to be in. A black, jagged silhouette on the horizon. Steep cliffs, wind-twisted pines, patches of gray rock and dark brush. There's no welcome sign. No marina. Just sharp edges and crashing surf.

I feel a chill creep over me.

The boat slows as we draw close. The man points to a narrow inlet between two rock faces. "That's your entry," he says. "Stick to the left. The right side'll tear your hull out."

Aaron nods, memorizing every detail.

I glance up at the cliffs—uneasy. This is the site of real horror. Two women were bludgeoned to death. The surviving woman swore she knew the killer, but not everyone believed her. They hung a man for it anyway.

The man helps us dock and gives Aaron one final round of instructions—steady voice and quick gestures. Aaron nods along. Then the man steps into the smaller skiff that followed us out here, unties the rope, and pushes off without another word.

Within seconds we're alone—just the four of us, standing on a rocky, sea-slick shore with nowhere to go but forward.

Leon simply stands there, leaning on his cane, eyes scanning the coastline. Hoyt doesn't wait—he's already unloading supplies from the boat like it's just another Tuesday. I don't move—not yet.

"I don't like this place," I murmur.

Leon throws a pack over his shoulder. "That's exactly why it's perfect. Nobody will suspect."

"The local said there were no permanent residents," I say, scanning the shoreline. "Only a few abandoned buildings left from when people still fished out here."

Leon shoulders his pack. "We'll make do."

We start walking.

The path is barely a path—a worn strip of gravel and moss leading up a shallow rise. The island's small, half a mile across, but it looks bigger somehow.

The first building we pass is the old boarding house. It stands crooked at the island's center, half-sunken into the ground, shutters swinging loose. That's where the murders happened.

"Anywhere but there," I say, pointing toward it.

Leon glances at the house, unfazed.

We keep walking.

There's only one other standing structure. A fishing shack, half-swallowed by sea grass and set back from the path. Weather-beaten and gray, with a rusted outdoor shower slumped to the side —but it's intact. That already makes it the best option.

Leon steps ahead and pushes open the door.

Inside, the air smells like salt, smoke, and fish. The furniture is sparse: a sturdy table, a few mismatched chairs, a couch with a hole worn through the arm. One wall is lined with old fishing gear— nets, hooks, baskets. A narrow bed with a faded quilt sits in the corner.

The bathroom has a toilet and a sink. No shower.

I twist the faucet out of habit and jolt slightly when a trickle of water sputters out—rusty at first, then clear.

"I thought this place was abandoned," I mutter.

Leon shrugs. "The man on the boat said there's an old rainwater system. Cistern's probably buried out back somewhere. Said it still works when the weather's good."

I touch the stream—cold and smelling metallic, but not foul, barely a step above seawater. Still, it's something.

"So I guess we're bathing outside," I mutter, nodding toward the rusted shower pipe we passed near the deck.

"If that thing works," Leon says.

Aaron, quiet since we landed, steps into the middle of the room and slowly turns a circle, taking it all in. "You can't be serious."

"We are," Leon replies. "This is it."

"We can't stay here," Aaron scoffs. "Look at this place."

"I figured you'd prefer a five-star hotel," Hoyt says. "But I guess Prince Charming isn't keen on roughing it in a fishing shack."

Aaron glares. "You're damn right I'd prefer a hotel. Not all of us are built to live like animals. Some of us enjoy a little civilization."

Leon bites back a grin. I roll my eyes.

This is going to be a long stay if those two can't go five minutes without a fight.

Aaron moves to the other side of the room, casting a look at me—then at Hoyt. Anger, maybe. Or resignation. He thinks we're still together.

Hoyt, on the other end, stays cold. Controlled. But when he catches Aaron watching me, I see it—a flicker in his jaw, the way his hand curls too tight around the edge of the crate before letting go.

Neither of them says a word; both of them think I'm with the other.

And me? I stand in the middle.

Single. Lonely.

Hurting both of them without even trying.

Leon claps his hands once. "Then let's make it quick. The faster you both learn to use your prisms, the faster we can get off this island."

I swallow.

Leon said it took him twenty years to master his.

I doubt we'll survive twenty days here.

TWENTY-SEVEN

I finish unpacking and step outside for air. The shack is too small for all of us to be in the same room for long, especially with the tension hanging on every breath. We're all on edge. Grumpy. Tired. Trapped.

I stand at the edge of the clearing, watching the waves claw at the rocks below, when Aaron steps up beside me.

"I guess I should thank you," he says, voice flat. "For coming to get me. For saving me."

"You don't need to thank me," I say, keeping my eyes on the water. "It's my fault this happened to you."

He shifts a little closer. "I told you in the car—what Darion did. What he asked for."

I nod. He hadn't given details—just that Darion had tortured him for information he didn't have. Now Darion's dead, and no one's left to answer for it.

"I can't believe you never told me about the prism—about any of it. That's a massive secret to keep from someone you were supposed to marry."

"I didn't know how," I say quietly. "At first I thought you'd never believe me. And then…"

"Then you didn't trust me to help you."

"It wasn't like that, Aaron."

He exhales hard, staring out at the sea like it might offer clarity. "How long do you think we're stuck here?"

"I don't know. Leon's idea of training is... vague."

He lets out a bitter laugh. "You know what's not vague? Watching you and Hoyt orbit each other like magnets. Being around that is not exactly easy."

"We're not together," I say. "If that helps."

He turns, startled. "You're not?"

I shake my head. "It's complicated."

Before he can respond, Leon's voice slices through the wind:

"You two! Inside. Now! We've got things to go over."

I follow Aaron back to the shack, heart pounding for reasons I can't name.

* * *

I sit on the floor, head resting against the couch where Aaron's stretched out. Hoyt's across the room in one of the kitchen chairs. Leon leans against the table, cane beside him.

The tension between the three of us is unbearable—too much left unsaid. Too many things to explain, to confess, to apologize for. I don't even know where to start.

"Before we get into questions," Leon says, "is there anyone who could be used against you? Someone they might try to take? Iris? Hoyt?"

I blink, caught off guard. "Akira, maybe..."

"Who's Akira?" Leon asks.

"A friend from Harvard. Darion took her last year."

"She still in Boston?"

"I think so. I haven't talked to her since I left for Paris."

Hoyt gives me a look—part surprise, part... something heavier.

"You need to call her," Leon says. "Tell her to disappear for a while. We don't know who we're dealing with yet."

He turns to Hoyt. "Anyone on your end?"

"I think my family's fine where they are," Hoyt says. "But I should let them know I'm not coming back for a while."

"Use this." Leon hands him a burner phone. "No names, no locations. The fewer people who know where we are, the better."

Hoyt takes it with a nod. I hear Johanna's worried voice crackles through the speaker as he quietly explains he's with me.

When he's done, I take the phone and type in Akira's number —thankfully Hoyt had it saved in his contacts.

"Hey," I say as soon as she picks up.
"Iris? Oh my god!" Akira sounds like she might cry. "Are you okay? Where are you?"
"I'm safe. It's... complicated."
"You vanished. I've been so worried. What happened?"
"I'm sorry. Things got dangerous. The prisms—they're more powerful than we thought. And more people know about them than we ever imagined."
"What do you mean?"
"Darion took Aaron, tortured him trying to find me."
"What?" Her tone spikes. "Is he okay?"
"He's here. He's recovering. But Darion's dead. And now... we don't know who else might be involved. You need to leave Boston. Now."
"Wait—what?"
"I don't know how far this goes or how much they know. But please trust me. Get out. Just for now."
Her breathing sharpens. "Where would I even go?"
Hoyt steps closer. "Tell her to go to Montana—to Jo."
I nod. "Go to Hoyt's place in Montana. Jo's there. We don't think they know about Hoyt's prism yet. You'll be safe."
"Okay..." Her voice trembles. "But where are you?"

"I can't say. I met someone else with a prism. He's helping me."
"Helping how?"
"I can't explain it all yet. Just promise me you'll leave soon."
"I will," she whispers. "Your stuff... I packed it up. Put it in storage.
Aaron paid for it after you disappeared."
"Thank you." I pause, heart catching. "Aaron's here, actually."
"He is? Okay... I'm glad you're not alone."
"Yeah."
A beat.
"I should probably tell you... Hoyt came here. Looking for you. I told
him you and Aaron were traveling. I didn't know what else to say."
"It's okay," I whisper. "That was probably for the best."
"Broc said he wasn't doing well."
I glance at Hoyt. Still nearby. "He's here too."
"What? Are you serious?"
"It's a mess, Akira. I'll explain everything later. Please go. Today. Be
safe."
"Okay. I will. You too."

"Aaron?" Leon asks. "Anyone you need to call?"

Aaron shakes his head. "No."

"What about Mel?" I ask. "She'll be worried."

"I called her as soon as I knew we were coming here," he says.
"She's on her way."

"She's coming here?"

"Yes. I'm not sending her off alone. I don't trust anyone else
with her."

I nod. I can't argue with that.

Leon claps his hands once. "Alright. We need a schedule."

He points between us with the handle of his cane. "Mornings
are physical—training, discipline, getting your prism under
control. I don't care how tired you are. We start at first light."

He glances at me. "Afternoons, we slow down. I'll explain what
I know, answer what I can. We'll also take shifts with the mirror—

keep checking the house in case anything changes. Someone left Darion like that. Maybe we'll catch something."

His eyes sweep the room like a general assessing a half-broken squad. "And while we're at it—we need firewood. To cook, to stay warm. If the weather turns, we're going to feel it."

I raise an eyebrow, but stay quiet.

Leon keeps going. "We also need to hit the mainland again. There's a lot we forgot. Someone—two people max—will go back tomorrow. In and out."

He pauses. "Sound good?"

No one answers. But no one argues.

I swallow. This already sounds like more than we can handle.

"It's late," Leon says, rubbing the bridge of his nose. "But let's hit a few things while we're still upright. I'll answer what I can. Any pressing questions?"

I glance between Aaron and Hoyt, nerves buzzing. Where do I even start?

"You said something about the shadow," I say. "That it's your prism's gift."

Leon nods. "Yeah."

"How do I find mine?"

He leans on the table. "There's no clear way. Mine came naturally. My father had the same prism, so I knew what to expect. He trained me, but even then—it didn't take effort. Some people never awaken theirs. Others... don't survive it."

He turns to Hoyt. "What about you?"

Hoyt's voice is low, guarded. "I told you. I don't have anything. I just... feel things. When people are in pain."

"Right. Because you have indigo," Leon says. "But that's not a gift. That's your sense."

Hoyt frowns. "What does that even mean?"

Leon pauses—like he's just realized how far behind we really are.

"Okay. So," Leon begins, "each prism aligns to a sense. That's how the magic connects to the world. Think of it like... elemental translation. You don't simply *have* power. You *perceive* the world through an elemental lens—and that's how your gift emerges."

He gestures toward Hoyt. "Indigo, for example, is tied to the sixth sense—intuition, perception, emotional resonance. Red is touch. Green is hearing. Blue is vision. And so on."

I frown. "There are seven prism colors. But only five senses."

"Exactly," Leon says. "That's the issue. The last two—indigo and violet—don't fit cleanly. They're the least understood. Some believe violet doesn't align with a sense at all. That it represents something... different."

"Like what?"

He shrugs. "No one agrees. Prophecy. Chaos. Purity. Destruction. Take your pick. Whatever it is, it's rare. Dangerous. Possibly unstable."

"So... I do have one? A gift?" I ask.

Leon shakes his head. "I don't know—probably. Some gifts only emerge under stress. Some need elemental combinations—fire and blood, water and shadow. Others are tied to memory. Or trauma. I can give you the rules, Iris. But I can't force it to surface."

Silence stretches—the kind that rings in your ears.

Leon shifts. "Your turn, Hoyt. Questions?"

Hoyt runs a hand down his face, jaw tight. "That mirror thing. What was it?"

Leon's face lights up a little. "The Solenscint. It's one of the more advanced abilities—linked to the prisms. If you've got the right alignment and control, you can use mirrors or glass to observe others. I'll show you tomorrow."

"That's how you found me?" Hoyt asks.

"Partially," Leon says. "You already know the prisms are aligned with nature. Water draws light in. Fire and water together? That's how you locate other *possessors*. Not any prism—only ones that have been bonded. The moment someone connects to a prism, their light becomes traceable... unless they know how to hide it."

Their conversation fades around me. My mind spirals, looping back to what Leon said earlier.

Each prism has a gift.

What if mine hasn't emerged yet?

What if it's already inside me, waiting—tied to what I saw in the Catacombs? At the house?

"What else?" Hoyt asks, worn, but curious.

"There are endless combinations," Leon says. "Each with their own qualities. Smoke and blood. Water and stone. Fire and mist. The four core elements branch into subtypes—earth becomes dust or bone, fire becomes smoke, water becomes ice or fog, and so on."

He glances at me again. Then back to Hoyt.

"Those societies I told you about, Iris? The Seers? They spent decades studying the prisms. Pushing boundaries. Testing combinations."

Hoyt doesn't reply. He's sitting with it. Quiet. Guarded.

Leon exhales. "We don't have time for a full lesson tonight. But the basics matter. There are seven prisms, just like the rainbow: red, orange, yellow, green, blue, indigo, violet. Five align to the classic senses: touch, taste, smell, hearing, sight. Indigo is likely the sixth—intuition, empathy, emotional resonance."

He turns to me. "And violet?"

He hesitates.

"That's the one no one can explain. Some say it's sense beyond sense. Some say it's something lost. Others say... it's something we're not ready for."

The silence that follows is thick. Heavy.

"Any more questions?" Leon asks.

I shake my head.

Not because I don't have any.

But because if I hear one more answer, I think I might break.

Then Hoyt says, voice low but suddenly sharper—

"Were you... at a bar? Looking for me?"

I blink. "We both were."

"I saw you," he says, eyes locked on mine. "In the mirror. Behind the bar. Two shadows."

"You did?" I whisper.

"I thought I was imagining it. I was drunk. But they were there —two shadows. One darker than the other."

Leon straightens, suddenly alert. "Two?"

Hoyt nods. "Pretty sure."

Leon looks at me. "Interesting."

"Great," Aaron mutters, sitting up on the couch, rubbing his temples. I'd almost forgotten he was there.

"So let me get this straight. We've got magical prisms, shadow gifts, color-coded senses, mirror travel—am I supposed to just sit here and pretend you guys are not all high on some shit?"

"Aaron—" I start.

He throws up a hand. "One minute I'm getting kidnapped and poisoned, the next I'm on a haunted island with my ex-fiancée telling me magic is real. Fuck me."

Silence.

He exhales hard and collapses back onto the couch, eyes fixed on the ceiling.

"I'll explain everything," I say quietly.

Leon stretches with a grimace. "Right. You can all pick my brain again tomorrow. I'm done for the night. My bones are older than they look."

We'd already decided—Leon gets the bed. Aaron keeps the couch while he recovers. Hoyt and I get the floor.

I grab one of the thin blankets we found and toss another to Hoyt without meeting his eye.

He walks out.

Aaron lifts his head. "You sure you don't want the couch?"

"I'm fine," I say, already lowering myself to the floor.

A list starts forming in my head: pillows. Better blankets. Something to soften the floor.

But for now, the sound of waves against the rocks becomes our lullaby.

I close my eyes.

Something tells me France was just the warm-up.

TWENTY-EIGHT
HOYT

The moment I look up and see the moon—too big, too close, like it's pressing down on the world—I know this isn't real. It can't be. This is another dream. I'm starting to recognize the signs now.

The too-still air. The hum under my skin. The way my thoughts come sharper than they ever do awake. There's no weight in my chest. No ache in my shoulder. Not even the sting of her name. That's how I know it's a trap.

Because there's a kind of freedom in these dreams that's almost worse than the pain. It tells me I can move how I want. Speak what I mean. Touch what I shouldn't. And if this one's anything like the others, I already know she's here. I can't see her yet, but I can feel her. Like the tide knows who it belongs to, like a siren.

"Thinking about me?"

Her voice startles me; I spin toward the sound.

She's there. No masks, no glow, no heat shimmering off her skin—just her. Real. Normal. Almost. But the way she moves toward me isn't normal at all.

She walks slowly, like she's testing how close she can get before

I flinch. My instinct is to step back, to create space—not to protect her, but to protect myself.

She doesn't stop.

She knows I'll move first.

I keep backing up until the wood of the boat presses against the backs of my knees. One more step and I'll fall.

"Wait," I say, louder than I mean to.

She doesn't.

There's something in her eyes I don't recognize. Her usual hazel fades, overtaken by the color violet.

"Iris, don't."

But she's smiling now. Not soft, not sweet. Wicked. The kind of smile someone wears when they know exactly what they can do to you—and plan to.

She doesn't need to ask. She doesn't even need to touch me. She could bring me to my knees with a look. And if I don't fall willingly, she'll burn me down anyway.

If only she knew I'd do it gladly.

That's what terrifies me most. Not her fire, but how completely I've surrendered to it. I've tried—God, I've tried—to forget her. To shut her out. To move on.

Some dreams are just noise. Broken scenes. Kisses that turn into arguments. Touches that end in pain.

But this? This is different.

These dreams carry weight. Magic. I can taste it. Sense it pulsing in the air between us, coiled and waiting.

Right before she reaches me—before she can lay a finger on my chest, where I know the fire would start—I stop holding still.

I remember: *this is a dream.*

And in dreams, I don't have to be afraid. Not of her. Not of the pain. Not even of what I want.

So I move first. Two slow steps toward her. Not cautious— *calculated.*

I see the flicker in her expression. She wasn't expecting that. She thought I'd flinch. Fall back. Beg. But not tonight.

"What?" I say, almost a whisper, almost a threat. "Are you... scared?"

She tries to recover quickly, lifting her chin like she's still the one in charge. "What do you think you're doing?"

But I hear it. The hesitation. A crack in the mask.

"Funny," I say, circling slightly now, watching her closely. "I was about to ask you the same thing."

She doesn't answer.

So I press: "What were you doing? Walking right up like that? Thought you'd burn a hole in me and walk away again?"

Still nothing.

"Or were you going to kiss me?" I step closer. "Or touch me? See if I'd break?"

Her silence is louder than anything she could say.

And for the first time in a long time, I feel it—control. Power. The ability to *choose* what happens next.

"I wasn't going to do anything." Her answer is small, breathy.

I don't let her off that easy.

"I don't believe you."

Her head snaps back, eyes wide. "What?"

"You wanted what?" I take another step forward, closing the space between us. "Say it. Tell me the truth for once."

She falters. "I... I don't know. It wasn't like that. Your prism... I could feel it, hear it, maybe. Like it was calling me."

"Calling you?" I echo, bitter. "So you were just going to walk up and what—answer it?"

"I don't know, Hoyt."

She sounds exhausted. Desperate.

We're inches apart now. I can see every detail in her face, the way her lashes twitch, the way her throat moves when she swallows.

And beneath all of it—*pull.*

The prisms sense each other now. That invisible current sparking between us, tugging like magnets.

I clench my jaw and ask the question I shouldn't need to ask anymore.

"What do you want from me, Iris?"

"I don't want anything from you," she says quickly, too quickly. "I told you... I—"

"Don't lie again," I snap. "It looks cheap on you."

She flinches at that. Not visibly, but I feel it.

"Hoyt..."

Just my name, but it lands heavy. Her voice. Her eyes. Violet now, glowing enough to hypnotize. They're the only thing keeping me from losing control. From pulling her in and pretending for a moment, that any of this is allowed.

But it isn't real. This isn't her. And I won't let this dream become more dangerous than the world we wake up in. She already has me out there. Out in the cold, in the quiet, in the way I can't touch or breathe or sleep without her.

Here? Here I'm in control.

"Is it my prism?" I ask.

She blinks. "What?"

"I could feel your... hunger." I lean in, deadly soft. "You want this one too, don't you?"

"What are you talking about?" she says, but there's tension in her jaw now. A twitch in her fingers.

I smirk. "We can play this game if you want."

"I'm not playing games."

"You're better at them than you think," I say, circling her again.

My eyes drag across every inch of her. The slope of her shoulder. The soft rise and fall of her chest.

And then—I reach out.

Only one finger.

I hold my breath, fully expecting agony. That familiar sear.

But when I touch her... nothing.

No pain. No burn.

Just skin. Soft, impossibly soft. Warmer than I expected.

Real. Too real.

And once I start, I can't stop. My hand moves on its own, tracing the curve of her arm, the ridge of her spine, the barest touch like I'm drawing worship into her skin.

She doesn't move. She lets me. Whether it's because she likes it or because she's scared to stop me, I don't know. But here, in this strange, suspended world, she can't hurt me.

"What..." she starts.

"Shhhh."

I cut her off, pressing my finger gently to her lips.

"Quiet." My voice is calm. Steady. "Here... I'm in charge."

I circle her again, slower this time.

"I'll tell you when to speak. When to sit. When to bend over."

That gets her attention. Her head lifts, eyes snapping to mine —not in submission, but challenge.

She wasn't expecting this. She doesn't like the reversal. Her eyes glow brighter, burning with violet light, and then she laughs —not softly, but sharp, like a warning.

"Oh..." she purrs, tilting her head. "You really think you're in charge, my cursed cowboy?"

She snaps her fingers.

In an instant, the golden dress she wore vanishes—not into fabric or shadow—but into *something else entirely.*

I blink.

It isn't clothing anymore—it's skin: scales gleaming like wet obsidian, iridescent in the moonlight, snake-like.

My breath catches in my throat. I have to close my eyes for a second to stop whatever spell she's casting from pulling me under completely.

Because even here—even in a dream—she is still the one thing I can't resist. No matter how hard I try.

Her hands find my chest. The moment she touches me, I open my eyes again.

She's already gripping the chain around my neck—the prism —and with the slightest tug, she pulls me toward her.

I don't resist. I couldn't if I tried.

She guides me back until the edge of the boat catches me. The wood digs into my spine, but I barely feel it. All I see is her.

"Look," she whispers unhurried. She nods toward the sky. "She's beautiful tonight, isn't she?"

I follow her gaze. The moon is full and immense, hanging too low.

Then, slowly, she runs her hands through her hair.

She begins to sway—not in some seductive cliché, but with a strange grace that belongs only to her. Her bare feet balance perfectly on the deck, skin shimmering with that inhuman glow. She moves like she's part dream, part ritual.

And it's not the scales or the magic or the wicked smile that unravels me. It's the memory. The memory of her dancing for me that night—when everything changed. I lunge before I think, my hand closing around her neck—too tight.

I drag her face to mine, forcing her to look at me. To *see* me. To face the part of me she keeps dragging back to life. I don't flinch at her glowing eyes, or the impossible way she stares back. Because I need her to understand: I'm not afraid of what she is. Not here. Not anywhere. Not anymore.

"This ends here," I growl, tightening my grip a fraction more.

But instead of fear, she moans—low, breathy, shameless.

"Then squeeze harder," she whispers, eyes half-lidded with something between challenge and desire.

The words catch me off guard. She means it. Of course she does. And that's exactly why I release her. Slowly. My fingers slip from her neck, leaving a silence between us that feels louder than any scream.

She tilts her head, disappointed. "Pity," she murmurs, her lips curling into that maddening smirk again. "I thought we were about to start having some fun."

I turn away, jaw clenched, blood burning. She knows how to get under my skin—she *lives* there.

"What do you want from me?" I snap, barely holding it together.

She doesn't hesitate. "The same thing you want from me..." She steps closer again, voice like velvet and venom. *"Everything."*

Before I can blink, she spins and leaps.

Right off the edge.

My heart slams against my ribs as I run to the rail.

She surfaces with a splash, laughing—wild, and completely unbothered—floating like this is all a game.

No violet eyes now. No snake skin. Just her. Iris. Normal. Almost. And smiling like she knows I'll follow.

Because she's right.

I jump even though I know I shouldn't. Every part of me screams to stop, but I'm already midair, already chasing her. The water hits like glass, cold and shocking, then the waves close over me.

I grab her, pull her against me, and everything else disappears—the boat, the sky, the world. The waves rise around us, rougher now, churning with something that feels like warning. But we don't care. We want this.

"What took you so long?" She asks the familiar question.

Our lips crash together, desperate and uncoordinated, mouths open like we're both trying to breathe each other in. It's too much. It's like drowning from the inside out, like kissing someone who already owns every inch of you.

We don't stop.

We can't.

The waves keep rising, thrashing around us like they know we're breaking every rule—magical, physical, emotional. I feel her losing air, feel the fight in her lungs. I try to pull back, to break the kiss, but I can't. We're stuck. Fused. Her lips won't let go—as if the prisms have locked us together, refusing to release.

And the wildest part is—she's not afraid.

She closes her eyes.

Not in fear. In surrender.

Because maybe she knows it too: whatever this is, it was never meant to end cleanly. Not above the surface. Not in light.

The sea takes us.

Together.

TWENTY-NINE

"The most beautiful thing we can experience is the mysterious." – Albert Einstein

I bolt upright, gasping. Air. I need air. For a few seconds, I can't focus on anything but breathing. I clutch my chest, palms flat, just to feel it rise—just to make sure I'm still alive.

It's dark. The shack is silent except for the steady crush of the sea beyond. Moonlight spills through the slats in the window, too full, too bright.

Then—beside me, Hoyt jolts upright with a sharp gasp.

My body goes rigid.

He's awake.

He's gasping.

I turn toward him slowly, heart still pounding against my ribs.

"Oh my god," I whisper. The words barely escape my lips.

He doesn't speak. He simply sits there in the dark, fists clenched in the blanket, his breath ragged like he's still inside the dream.

"Fucking nightmare," he mutters.

"Hoyt?" I whisper.

His eyes find mine in the moonlight—wild, searching, uncertain.

"There was..." I swallow. "The boat. The moon. And you were—"

His eyes widen. "What?"

I blink at him.

He stares like I've spoken another language.

I lower myself slowly back down, eyes fixed on the ceiling. My voice barely carries.

"Have you had others?"

He doesn't answer right away. Then, quietly:

"Iris... are you saying we're—"

"There was one at a masquerade," I interrupt. "You had..."

He exhales through his nose. "Antlers."

Silence.

"And the museum?" he asks.

"The moving statues?"

He lies back beside me, eyes open, lost in the dark.

My face heats. I don't want to ask the next question. I do anyway.

"You remember... all of it?"

"Yeah," he says, barely above a whisper.

I press my arm over my face. The ceiling spins. My skin still burns in places where he touched me in the dream. Where I let him.

This isn't just magic.

"What does this mean?" he murmurs.

"That things just got even more complicated."

I think of every dream.

Every inch of skin. Every sound. Every breath. Every goddamn look.

They weren't private.

Hoyt saw everything. Felt everything.

A tight, aching silence stretches between us.

"Fuck," Hoyt mutters, voice low but tight, like the weight of it all just landed.

I flinch.

Then—

"What's going on?" Aaron's groggy voice cuts through the dark.

I shoot up. "Nothing."

Hoyt's already on his feet, grabbing a hoodie off the floor. Without a word, he shoves open the door and disappears into the night.

"Go back to sleep," I whisper to Aaron, my heart still hammering.

He groans and turns over.

But I stay sitting.

Because the one I can't stop dreaming about—isn't dreaming anymore.

* * *

The sun's just starting to rise when I open my eyes again. Aaron and Leon are still asleep. But Hoyt's side of the floor is empty.

I tiptoe out the door, careful not to make a sound.

I'd kill for a cup of coffee, but all we have is Leon's bag of herbal tea. He swore it would help with clarity—whatever that means.

I rub the sleep from my eyes and walk toward the beach—if you could call it that. The shore here is more jagged rock than sand, littered with old seaweed and bits of driftwood. The mist hangs low, dragging the salt with it.

Hoyt's sitting near the water, soaked. Shirt clinging to his back like he walked straight into the waves.

"Hey," I say softly.

He doesn't turn around.

"About last night..."

"Leon might know how to stop it," he says, cutting me off.

I blink. "Stop what?"

"The dreams," he mutters. "I'll ask when he wakes up."

It catches me off guard. He wants them to stop? I hadn't even thought about that. Sure, they're violent. Confusing. But they're also... ours. And the only place we can touch.

I open my mouth to say something, but before I can find the words—

"We need firewood," Leon calls from the shack.

"On it," Hoyt says. He's already getting up, walking past me without another glance.

I drift back toward the shack, digging through the box on the table until I find the tea bag labeled *Herbal Blends for Everyday*. I sigh and drop one of the bags into a metal cup.

"It could be worse," Leon says from behind me.

I look over my shoulder. "How?"

Aaron walks in from the back, towel draped around his neck. "Yeah. Worse how?"

Leon shrugs. "You could be dead."

Fair enough.

* * *

Hoyt doesn't come in for breakfast. God knows what time he woke up. Or if he even slept at all.

Aaron, Leon, and I sit around the table, eating our sad little spread of bananas and granola bars. The tea isn't awful—but it's not coffee.

"Ready for your first day?" Leon asks, handing me a water bottle.

"Ready as I'll ever be, I guess."

"What about me?" Aaron says. "What should I do?"

"I'm going to need your help," Leon replies, standing and stretching. "Come on. To the beach."

We follow him outside.

Hoyt's already there, waiting. He looks like he hasn't moved in hours.

The grass is damp beneath our feet, wet from the morning mist. My violet light flickers like a busted bulb. Across from me, Hoyt's glows steady—brighter, maybe—but just as uncontrolled.

I catch Aaron watching him.

"Now, Aaron," Leon says, tone light. "You're going to help Hoyt."

"What?" the three of us say at once.

"Hoyt, hand out," Leon instructs.

Hoyt frowns but obeys. Leon brushes his fingertip across Hoyt's palm, and Hoyt flinches violently.

"You—" Hoyt starts.

"No," Leon says calmly. "Not me. You. I can touch Iris just fine. Whatever's blocking contact—whatever burns—is coming from you."

"I'm not doing anything," Hoyt says quickly, turning to me like he needs me to believe it.

"Exactly. You're not controlling it. That's the problem. I'd bet it's tied to your sixth sense." Leon explains.

Hoyt's jaw tightens. "You think I could stop it?"

Our eyes meet. The thought blooms inside me—hopeful. Dangerous.

"We'll find out," Leon says.

Aaron shakes his head. "What the fuck is going on?"

"Hoyt can't touch another prism possessor," I say quietly.

Aaron lets out a sharp, stunned laugh. "Wait... wait. You're telling me you two haven't even been able to touch this whole time?"

I wince.

"We found a way," Hoyt snaps before I can answer. "So wipe that smirk off your face."

Leon exhales like a teacher tired of managing toddlers. "Can we maybe—just maybe—suspend the love triangle long enough to learn the thing that might actually save your lives?"

Silence.

"Let's get it over with," Hoyt mutters.

Leon nods. "Aaron, since I can't help Hoyt, it's your job now. Let's get comfortable."

"I'll stand," Hoyt says stiffly.

Aaron stands too, arms crossed.

"Suit yourselves," Leon says. Then he looks at me. "Iris?"

I nod and sit.

"Now, Iris and Hoyt, close your eyes," Leon says. "Your only job is to keep your light off."

"What?" I blink. "Leon, we're soaking wet. How are we supposed to—"

"If I can do it, so can you." He lifts his hand, flashing his prism ring. No light.

"Eyes closed," he says again, firmer this time.

"Aaron," he continues, "if Hoyt lights up, give him a nudge."

I imagine Aaron's reluctant agreement. Or maybe he's secretly enjoying this.

I close my eyes and try. Really try. I focus on the sound of the waves, the pull and retreat of the tide.

Leon squeezes my hand.

Damn. I failed again.

I try not to think about Hoyt. Or Aaron. Or what Aaron might be doing to Hoyt. Elbowing him? Taunting him? Flicking his ear?

Curiosity wins.

I crack one eye open.

Aaron's facing Hoyt now. Close. Too close. I see Aaron lean in and say something. Hoyt doesn't answer right away.

He growls something back. I catch only the last word: "Iris."

Aaron flinches.

I shut my eyes.

Nope. No thank you. Bad idea.

"Iris, Hoyt—focus," Leon says. "Don't rely on sight. The prism's energy shifts when it lights. You'll feel it, if you're paying attention. Breathe in the sea. Think of nothing else. Just the waves."

I focus harder, begging each intrusive thought to disappear.

Finally, Leon stops squeezing my hand.

A small smile tugs at my lips.

Then—squeeze.

"Shit," I mutter.

"Shhh," Leon warns.

I try again, narrowing in on the water.

Right when I think I've finally gotten the hang of it, a cold gust of wind rips across my face. I shiver and tuck my hands tighter around my knees.

Beside me, Leon shifts.

I hear Hoyt exhale—long, ragged. Aaron mutters something under his breath I don't catch.

We stay like this for hours. The magic. The silence. The not-saying-things. It's exhausting in a way that sleep can't fix.

Aaron breaks the silence. "I gotta take a piss," he mutters.

Leon stretches his back. "Okay," he says gently. "Let's... take a break."

Hoyt leaves first. No words.

Leon follows behind him, rubbing his temples like we're all giving him a migraine.

I start to rise, brushing off my hands—but before I can move, Aaron's fingers close around my wrist.

"Let them go," he says.

I glance at him, startled. His voice is soft but firm.

"I just—" I start.

"You don't have to chase him every time," Aaron says. "He's not going anywhere."

"I'm not—" I try to argue, but the words don't stick. I don't even know what I'm defending anymore.

I swallow hard. "Thank you. For helping. For being here."

He shrugs. "Yeah. Like I have a choice."

"Still," I say. "It matters."

He looks at me for a long second. Something unreadable passes over his face.

"What I don't get is..." he says slowly. "If you two couldn't even touch this whole time... then why?"

His voice drops. "Why him?"

I don't have an answer. Not one I can say out loud.

Because he saw me when I didn't even know I was lost? Because some part of me lit up the second he looked at me?

But instead, I say, "I don't know."

Aaron nods. Once. Not because he believes me but because he knows I won't say the truth.

"If you aren't together," he says, "then why is he here?"

"Leon called him. We needed someone to carry you out of there."

Aaron blinks. "So... he..."

"Carried you out."

He lets out a sharp breath. "Perfect."

THIRTY

"Water's too rough," Aaron mutters, dripping from the storm that just rolled in.

"Then we hit the mainland tomorrow," Leon says, glancing up as another leak trickles from the ceiling.

"Can we check the house?" Aaron presses. "The sooner we find out who took Darion, the sooner we can get the fuck out of here and move on with our lives."

Hoyt stands against the far wall, arms crossed. Silent. But his eyes flick to me—watching. Waiting.

Leon hesitates. "Well... Iris and I had a different arrangement."

He looks at me.

I shake my head—small, sharp. A quiet warning.

"That was between us, Leon."

Aaron narrows his eyes. "What deal?"

Leon sighs. "We should tell them. Secrets don't stay buried long."

I exhale. "Fine. But don't say I didn't warn you—they're not going to like it."

Leon nods. "Before we knew you had been taken, Iris agreed to help me..."

"With what?" Hoyt cuts in, already tense, like he knows exactly where this is going.

"Find the other prisms." Leon answers.

"What?" Aaron's voice tightens.

Hoyt scoffs—sharp and disbelieving.

"And destroy them," Leon finishes. "The prophecy says—"

Hoyt pushes off the wall. "Hold on. What did you say?"

I glance between them. "Leon thinks the prisms can be destroyed."

"Based on what?" Hoyt demands.

Leon stays calm. "Prophecies. Writings passed down through generations."

Hoyt shakes his head. "Sounds like bullshit."

"It's not," Leon says. "Every person tied to these prisms is in danger. This is the only way to keep everyone safe—for good."

Silence.

Outside, the rain pounds harder against the roof.

Leon continues, "We're barely managing basic light suppression, mirror travel, and emotional control. We don't even understand the full scope of what's going on. But yes. Eventually, they'll need to be destroyed."

"I thought you said you have to die to take these things off?" Aaron asks, frowning.

I glance at him. I think we're all wondering the same thing.

But I don't say it.

All I can do is hope Leon's plan doesn't require... that kind of sacrifice.

Leon clears his throat. "We know Darion was murdered and someone else is pulling strings. Until we figure out who, we're vulnerable. They could be anyone we know. So let's focus on that, shall we?"

I can see Hoyt's muscle twitch in his cheek.

Leon turns to him. "Locklear, you're going in with me."

Hoyt straightens. "What does that mean?"

"Before we enter the mirror, I need to assess your temperament," Leon says. "I skipped this step with Iris and... well—lesson learned."

Hoyt raises a brow. "Temperament?"

"There are four," Leon explains. "Sanguine, choleric, melancholic, and phlegmatic. Your temperament affects your control—especially under stress."

"It's an ancient theory," I say. "The Greeks believed body fluids influenced personality and behavior. Blood, yellow bile, black bile, phlegm. Absurd. Insane really."

"Perhaps," Leon replies, "but most people would say the same about everything else I've taught you."

He turns to Hoyt. "Tell me—would you say Iris is mostly happy, calm, sad, or angry?"

"What?" I blurt.

"Your loved ones know you better than you know yourself," Leon says simply.

Hoyt doesn't answer right away. He's thinking. That alone makes my pulse quicken.

Aaron cuts in. "She's happy."

I glance at him. Hoyt doesn't.

Hoyt says, quietly, "She's... angry."

Leon nods. "Good. We're narrowing it down."

"I'm all of those things," I say. "It depends on the day."

Leon shakes his head. "It's not about mood swings. We all feel joy, sadness, rage. I'm asking what drives you—what's your core emotional frequency. Now Iris, what would you say Hoyt is?"

I hesitate. "Calm."

Aaron scoffs. "He's not fucking calm. He curses every three words."

Leon, however, takes note like a therapist with a clipboard.

"Next question: Would you say Iris is steady, cautious, inspiring, or obsessive?"

"Inspiring," Aaron says.

"Obsessive," Hoyt replies without hesitation.

Leon scribbles again.

"And Hoyt—would you say he's cautious, Iris?"

"Yes," I say, and I mean it.

Leon moves on. "From the four elements—fire, water, air, earth—which one do you associate with?"

"Fire," I answer, before I can think.

"Water," Hoyt says.

Leon looks too pleased about all this.

"Alright, one more exercise," he says. "Picture the person you love most. The one you can't live without. I know, I know—touchy subject for this group. That's why it's helpful."

He looks to Aaron. "You can participate in your mind."

Aaron rolls his eyes.

"Now imagine that person you love was taken from you," Leon says. "Tragically. Violently. Imagine they were killed. What's the first thing that comes to mind? Don't give me a pretty, thought-out answer—I want your *first* response. Iris?"

I try not to overthink. "I... would look for justice. Maybe... even revenge."

"Hoyt?"

There's a long pause.

"I don't think I'd feel anything," he says.

The room goes still.

"I think it'd be... too much to process. I'd shut down. Go numb. And I don't think I'd want to live anymore, either." He lets out.

I have to look away.

Leon nods. "As I suspected. Iris, you're choleric. Angry, obsessive, energetic—but also strong, assertive, a leader. Your symbol is the lion. Hoyt is phlegmatic. Calm, supportive, cautious, intuitive. A peacemaker. Your symbol is the ox."

"What does any of this matter?" Aaron asks, already over it.

"Because depending on your temperament," Leon explains,

"there are certain things you should eat before entering the mirror with the Solenscint."

"Solen-what?" Hoyt asks.

"The *Solenscint*—the golden speck inside your prism."

I glance at Hoyt and know instantly he's remembering the water, the gold dust on our skin. I wonder if he's missing me as much as I'm missing him.

"Iris," Leon continues, "you should eat something with protein. Red meat, if possible. It'll sharpen your focus and fuel your inner strength. Hoyt, you need something grounding. A vegetable. Carrots, spinach. It'll help stabilize your energy."

"You know this is ridiculous, right?" Aaron mutters.

"No more than mirror travel," Leon replies with a shrug. Then, to Hoyt: "Go grab something to eat. And bring me one of those chocolate bars while you're at it. Lucky for me, sweets do the trick."

I head toward the cooler—a beat-up, battery-powered box Leon calls our most precious asset. The inside reeks of mildew and something worse, but the ice is still semi-frozen. I pour a few chunks of ice into two bowls, exactly like Mel did days ago.

Behind me, Leon explains the mirror process to Hoyt. He listens, but his eyes flick around—like he's trying not to look worried.

That's when it hits me. He's never done this before. Never any kind of prism travel. Unless Leon's right. And Hoyt lied to me about that.

I want to ask him about the months we spent apart—his family, the horses, whether he ever thought about me—but he won't even look at me. He's been pretending I don't exist since we got here. And I hate how much it bothers me. *If he's trying to punish me, it's working.*

Aaron mutters something under his breath about all of this being insane and slips outside. I watch him go, his shoulders hunched like he's carrying something heavier than any of us will acknowledge.

Guilt catches in my throat. He's alone in this. No prism. No magic. No shared light or visions or dream-threads tugging him under.

I hope Mel shows up soon. He could use someone outside this mess. Leon keeps insisting we need Aaron's help—and he's not wrong. None of us can handle a boat. We're relying on him more than we want to admit.

Hoyt spots the golden flicker—the cue—and I lean closer, reminding him, "Look in the mirror. Follow Leon. Picture the house."

He nods once then closes his eyes. A breath escapes his lips, and just like that, his eyes roll back—white as bone. The moment it happens, the temperature in the shack shifts. Everything goes still. Their bodies stay upright, but something essential slips out of them.

I feel it immediately—that cold emptiness. I get it now. What Akira meant when she said the worst part wasn't watching, but waiting. Watching someone you love sit there with no expression, no spark. Not really them. Even though I've done it too, it still chills me. They look like ghosts wearing their own skin.

Time slows. Every second stretches, thick and heavy, as I sit there watching them. I keep searching their faces for a twitch, a flicker, anything to prove they're still part of this world.

What are they seeing? Is someone else in the house? Has someone found Darion's body? My brain won't shut up. I need to know. And I hate that I'm the one stuck waiting. I've never been good at sitting still, especially not now, not with the withdrawal crawling back in.

I'd trade a mile-long walk for a cigarette. I'd sell my soul for something stronger than Leon's bitter herbal tea. But there's nothing. Just me. Me and the silence. Me and my thoughts. And they're both getting louder.

I start pacing. Small circles at first, then bigger, messier loops around the shack. Aaron's still outside. Probably talking to himself about how insane all of this is. *He's not wrong.*

How long are they supposed to be gone? I should've asked Leon. *What if something goes wrong—am I supposed to wake them up? Can I wake them up?*

I glance at the cracked phone screen on the table. Twenty minutes. That has to be enough. I give it five more. Then I open the door; the salty wind smacking me in the face.

"Aaron!" I shout, scanning the trees and shoreline. Nothing.

I try again. "Aaron!"

Still no answer.

I walk back into the shack, silently praying they're back.

But no. Their eyes are still rolled. Not bleeding, at least. That's something. But the longer they stay like that, the more it feels like they're not here at all.

THIRTY-ONE

"THE DARKER THE NIGHT, THE BRIGHTER THE STARS." – FYODOR DOSTOEVSKY

I'm about to spiral when, suddenly, both of them jolt. Hoyt gasps, sharp and loud. Leon's first instinct is to reach for the food and hand Hoyt a carrot, motioning for him to eat.

"What happened?" I ask, stepping closer. "You were gone forever. Did you see anything?"

"I saw your... uncle," Leon says slowly. "He didn't look well. Bedridden."

My stomach clenches. "Was anyone else there?"

Leon nods, shifting his weight. "Darion's body is gone. The room where he died—it was scrubbed clean."

My throat tightens. "So someone's been there."

Leon exhales. "It's disorienting at first, right?" he says, mostly to Hoyt, but loud enough for me too. "Like dissolving into glass. You don't walk through a house—you *become* its reflections. We had to move surface to surface. Mirror to window. Window to picture frame. Even a glass of water. Any room without a reflection? Dead end."

"It's like being trapped behind the walls," I murmur, remembering. "You see everything, but you're not... in it."

Leon nods grimly. "Exactly. We worked our way room by room. That's when we heard a child crying."

"A child?" My heart kicks.

"A boy. Seven, maybe. In one of the upstairs bedrooms. Toys everywhere."

My mind spins. "Who... who do you think he is?"

"No idea." Leon shakes his head. "Could be your cousin too. He had hair like yours—red as flame. Pale skin. Freckles. Do you know anything about your mother's family?"

I shake my head, throat dry.

Across from me, Hoyt chews the carrot too fast, chest heaving like he's trying to calm down and failing.

"The boy was clutching a stuffed bear," Leon goes on. "Rocking back and forth. Then a woman came in—nanny, probably. She rushed to him, smoothed his hair, called him honey. Asked if he'd had another bad dream."

Leon's voice drops. "But he just kept whispering into the bear."

I swallow. "What did he say?"

Leon's eyes lock on mine. "Over and over... *I saw him.*"

A chill slides down my spine.

Leon straightens, brushing dust from his sleeves like it suddenly matters. "We were about to come back when the front door opened. A man walked in." His gaze flicks to Hoyt. "You seemed to recognize him."

Hoyt's whole body goes still. His fingers dig into the table. His jaw works like he's grinding fury down to words.

"It was..." he says, swallowing hard. "It was fucking James."

He finally lifts his gaze to me.

And my stomach drops straight through the floor.

"James?" My voice comes out thin, bewildered. Like I misheard him. Like he's talking about someone else entirely.

Hoyt's eyes flash. "Your pupil, Iris." The way he says it—like poison—makes me flinch. "What the fuck are you hiding? Because I'm getting real tired of your secrets."

I slam my hand down on the table, hard enough to rattle the bowls. I'm so fucking tired of the secrets too—but even more tired of him talking to me like I'm some stranger he has to interrogate. Like I'm not—

No. I bite the thought back before it finishes.

The door opens.

The tension crackles like static.

Aaron steps inside, stopping short. His brow furrows as he takes in the scene—Leon frozen, Hoyt looming over me, my hand trembling on the table. "What's going on?"

"Hoyt!" I whip toward him, panicked. "I don't know why James was there. He was just a student. That's it."

Hoyt lets out a sharp, joyless laugh. "Just a student? And now he's lurking in the house where your cousin was murdered? I don't buy it."

My thoughts reel. Every memory of James collides in my head. I blink, stunned. "I'm telling you the truth."

"Are you?" He pauses. "Because either you're cursed with the worst luck in the goddamn world... or—" He takes a step closer. "I swear, Iris, you'd better say the truth or I will—"

"Watch it," Aaron interrupts.

His protection takes me off guard.

I snap back at Hoyt. "Funny you ask me for honesty when you've been lying to me this whole time."

Confusion flickers in his narrowed eyes.

The sting of his words crashes into me, dragging everything else down with it. All the things I want to tell him—need to tell him—press against my ribs like claws. But the anger's there too. He hasn't even given me a chance to apologize. He's been looking at me like I'm nothing. Like I'm not the girl he gave a fucking love sigil to. Like I didn't spend months aching for him.

How dare he be so quick to throw it all away.

Yes, I messed up. I know that.

But I never thought he wouldn't forgive me—not if I asked.

"I have never lied to you," Hoyt says, voice raw.

"What the fuck happened?" Aaron demands, turning to Leon.

Leon tries to explain but I don't let it go. I'm not done. Not even close.

"Leon. Tell him. Tell Hoyt what you told me."

Leon stops mid-sentence, frowning. "What are you talking about, Iris?"

"You said Hoyt must've been able to travel with his prism too. You said he lied to me."

"What?" Hoyt's voice cuts sharp, whipping toward Leon.

"Well—" Leon lifts his hands, hesitant. "Every prism should be able to travel through the aether when water and fire come together. It's one of the principle laws."

"I can't," Hoyt snaps. "I tried. I couldn't."

"And I'm supposed to believe you? Why?" I shoot back. "You don't believe me."

"I don't care if you do," he says, furious. Then he storms out of the shack.

"See?" Aaron says to Leon, gesturing at the door Hoyt just slammed. "He can't be the calm one."

Aaron's words from before echo louder than the slam itself: *"You don't have to chase him every time."*

He's right. I stay right where I am.

* * *

Time drags after the argument.

I told Leon everything I knew about James—over and over, even the parts from his book I'd practically memorized. He kept pressing, but I had nothing else to give. Eventually, he went to rest.

It was Aaron who stayed with me. He kept me talking, picking my brain about Darion, the prisms, the mirror rules, the boy. Every answer I gave led to more questions. And for each of his, I had ten of my own. The unknowns gnawed at me.

I'm chewing through another peanut butter sandwich when the door creaks open.

Hoyt.

He hasn't been back since the fight. No word. No explanation. Just gone.

The air shifts the moment he enters. Even without turning around, I hear every step he takes—heavy boots across warped floorboards. He digs through one of the bags, zippers rasping, plastic crinkling. Every sound magnified.

He doesn't say a word. Doesn't even look at me.

I keep chewing like I don't care, but every bite turns to sand. My body is so tense I start fantasizing about swimming across the ocean just to get a drink.

Mel's arriving tomorrow. Maybe she'll bring some kind of cheer. Though knowing Mel, that's not what's packed in her bags.

"I think I'm going to bed early," I say, barely above a whisper. "My head hurts."

Aaron rises from the couch and starts folding blankets. He carries them over, spreading them across the floor.

"I'll sleep on the floor tonight," he offers lightly. "I'm better now. I'm good."

The offer hangs there. For a second, I almost let him. This couch might as well be a featherbed compared to the floor.

But instead I hear myself say, "No, it's okay. My back will hurt, actually. On that springy couch."

Aaron hesitates. "Are you sure?"

"Yeah," I say, smoothing the corner of a blanket harder than necessary. "It's fine."

The truth?

I want to be closer to Hoyt.

It's stupid—we're barely speaking. But somehow, lying on the floor near him makes me feel... better. Even if I can't touch him, I can still hear his breathing. And the ache of distance is worse. So much worse.

I lie down facing the wall, heart thudding. I wonder if he's even still indoors.

And then I hear him.

His voice—low, rough, like it's been caged in his throat all day.

"Leon?" Hoyt says. "What's with the dreams? The shared ones. How the fuck do I stop them?"

I stop breathing.

Silence. Then the creak of Leon sitting up fast, his cot groaning beneath him.

"What did you say?"

"The dreams," Hoyt repeats, louder. "The ones we've been having. Iris and I. The same ones."

Leon doesn't answer.

"You're... sharing them?" His voice is tight with disbelief.

Hoyt doesn't respond.

So I do. "Yes," I whisper.

Leon exhales—fast, harsh. He stands and paces once, mind already ten steps ahead. "It shouldn't be possible..."

"It is," I murmur, lying back down, not exactly eager to hear the rest.

"What are you talking about?" Aaron remarks, slicing through the room, sharper than I expect. I'd almost forgotten he was still on the couch behind me.

Leon halts. Turns toward us like a professor about to deliver a lecture nobody asked for.

"It's called interlucence," he says. "Rare. Thought to be myth. But I've heard whispers... the Seers tried... it happens when two prism carriers lock their Solenscint."

"Lock?" Hoyt snaps.

I sit up again, pulse kicking.

Leon's gaze shifts between us. "Emotional resonance. High-intensity energy transfer. Water and…" He pauses. Too long. My heart thuds harder.

His eyes flick to Aaron. Hesitation.

"You'd have to be physically close," he goes on. "Very close." He clears his throat.

I shift, heat crawling up my neck.

Hoyt doesn't move.

"That doesn't make sense," Aaron says quickly. "They can't even touch."

Leon goes still.

My skin goes cold.

Behind me, Aaron's breath changes.

Leon's voice drops. "That's how the interlucence forms. It requires intent. Willingness. And… climax. Emotional, physical, magical… The stronger the surge, the deeper the bond." His gaze sharpens. "You would have known. Did you see them? The Solenscint speckles—bursting out, multiplying—when you were—"

The floor might as well split beneath me.

Hoyt says nothing. Just nods once.

Aaron stands. I feel his eyes burning into me.

Leon exhales. "Your prisms are locked. You can't undo it."

Hoyt's voice is low, bitter. "No. There's gotta be a way to stop these dreams!"

Leon meets his eyes. "There isn't."

Thirty-Two

I'm in the outdoor shower beside the shack. Wind bites my skin. The ocean crashes harder than usual—louder, closer, like it's angry. I promise myself I'll be quick. Just the important parts. Just enough to be clean.

But the second the soap drags across my skin, I feel it.

A hand. Warm. Firm. Pressing into my back.

Before I can scream, a second hand covers my mouth.

Panic spikes—until he turns me. And I see him.

Hoyt.

Naked. Soaked. Eyes wild.

His hand slides from my mouth to my throat. He doesn't squeeze—just enough pressure to remind me he could.

Then he kisses me—hard. Angry. Starving.

His right hand stays on my throat, keeping me suspended between terror and need. His left fist is in my hair and yanks, sharp enough to hurt, sharp enough to rip a gasp out of me.

He drags his mouth from mine, whispering against my lips, "You want forgiveness?"

"What?" I barely breathe.

"Get on your fucking knees."

I should fight him. I should walk away. But I don't. I sink to my knees.

The rest blurs.

Me gasping. Him relentless.

Rough isn't even the word—it's hunger with edges, and every second, I want more.

By the end I'm shaking. My name on his lips. His hand still tangled in my hair like he doesn't want to let go.

And for one dizzy second, I think it's real. But of course it isn't. Just another cruel dream.

When I open my eyes, the room is still. Pale moonlight cuts through the window silvering the floorboards. Everyone's asleep. My breathing is shallow, my skin damp with sweat. The dream clings to me—Hoyt's hands, his mouth, the way he made me beg.

Thank God this one was just mine. I can tell. The shared dreams hum with something otherworldly... This had no pull, no burn in my prism. *Just me. Old, horny me.*

Aaron snores from the couch, the sleeping pills I watched him take doing their work. Leon's quiet. And Hoyt—

I don't look. I can't.

I shift under the blankets, thighs sticky, panties soaked. The ache is still there.

I press my fingers to my lips like I can still taste him. My pulse won't settle.

Before I can think, my hand drifts lower. Half-dreaming. Half-remembering. A ritual I've lived on for months without him.

But this time it's different. Because he's here. Close enough that every shaky breath of mine might give me away.

The memory of his voice in the dream—rough, cold, *"get on your fucking knees"*—still echoes in my head as my fingers move slower. I bite my lip to stay quiet, half-lost in it, almost forgetting I'm not alone. But I'm so turned on that it takes nothing.

I'm right on the edge—heart pounding, hips shifting—when I hear him.

Not in my head.

Not in a dream.

His real voice, low and mocking in the dark:

"I guess Prince Charming isn't satisfying you..."

My whole body seizes.

He heard me?

I go still.

"Don't stop on my account," Hoyt murmurs, amused.

I want to disappear.

"I... wasn't..." The words trip out, broken.

"Sure you were." His voice is smug, like he's enjoying this. Like he's been awake long enough to listen.

"Go to sleep," I snap, whipping my back to him so fast I tangle in the blankets. Fabric scrapes my skin. Shame floods every inch of me.

Silence. For a moment I think—hope—it's over.

Then I hear him shift, moving closer.

"That was hot as hell."

My breath catches. I don't dare look. He's still in my head even when he's just inches behind me.

I feel the weight of his attention on the back of my neck like a touch.

"What?" I whisper, praying I misheard.

His tone drops darker, rougher. "If you were trying to get my attention... job well done."

Heat floods my face. "I wasn't trying to get your attention. When I am, trust me—you'll know."

Silence. Then a low, humorless laugh.

"Right... bullshit. You were moaning my name. Begging."

I squeeze my eyes shut, heart racing so hard I hear it. Aaron snores softly from the couch—steady, drugged. Thank God. Leon shifts once and settles. The night holds its breath with me.

There's the barest brush at my hip—fabric skimming fabric. I jolt. His finger has hooked the edge of my blanket.

"Don't," I breathe, warning that sounds too much like a plea.

He peels it down an inch—no more—but enough for the cold air to kiss the top of my thigh. He lets it fall back.

"Keep going," Hoyt says, low. "Might as well finish."

"I..." I fumble for words. Anything. But nothing makes sense when my whole body is already throbbing again.

He waits a beat, savoring it.

"Just tell me one thing." His voice is molten. "Was it my cock or his you were fantasizing about?"

My throat goes dry. I don't want to answer. But I need him to know. Need him to *believe* it.

"Yours," I whisper.

He leans closer. "Another lie?" he asks, voice sharpened to a knife.

"No, Hoyt." I turn to meet his eyes in the dark. "It was you."

A ragged exhale.

"Then by all means," he murmurs, "prove it."

I shake my head, pulse skittering wild. "I can't—"

He exhales harder this time, dragging a hand through his hair, fingers yanking at the strands like he needs the pain to anchor him. His chest rises and falls in rough bursts, like he's balancing on the cliff edge with me.

"Fuck, Iris."

"What?" My voice cracks on it.

His answer is raw, biting, desperate. "What's it gonna be? Do I walk out of here and jerk off alone, or do I stay—and make you watch me lose it over you?"

The words crawl under my skin, fire in my blood.

"You can't say things like that—" I hiss, glancing toward Aaron, toward Leon. "We're not alone."

His eyes pin mine, merciless. He doesn't even blink. "I don't give a fuck."

The silence stretches until it hurts.

"Go on. Keep touching yourself. Let's see who breaks first." He orders.

I blink. "What?"

"You heard me." His tone is a lash.

Heat crawls up my neck. Shame. Desire. Fury.

"That's what you want?" I scoff, but it comes out breathless. "A fucking contest?"

His mouth curves—something darker than a smile. His hand clenches the edge of my blanket, tugging once, hard enough to remind me he could strip it away at any second.

"No," he says. "I want proof."

"Proof of what?"

"That when you spread your legs in the dark, it's my cock you ache for. My mouth you want between your thighs. Show me I'm the one you want."

"Hoyt." My whisper breaks, already too soft.

For a second, I swear his glare cuts toward the couch where Aaron sleeps. The air sears my lungs. *Does Hoyt want him to hear this?*

His eyes snap back to mine, harder now. "Look at me."

I turn fully, locking on him in the dark. He shifts, his shoulders broad enough to block out the sliver of moonlight. His hand moves beneath the blanket—like he wants me to watch.

My whole body aches, a hollow hunger. I'd do anything to have his hands on me instead of my own.

"I told you," I whisper. "It's you I want."

His voice drops, a blade against my throat.

"Then prove it. Lick your fingers."

My breath catches. The command lodges in me, sharp.

"Do it," he says again, crueler now. "Don't look away. I want your eyes on mine when you come."

"I can't do this. Not here—"

"You already started. Don't you dare act innocent now. Tell me what you were thinking about."

"I... had a dream."

His eyes flick down my body, then back up. "Yeah?"

"Yes."

"About me?"

"Us," I whisper. "In the... outdoor shower."

"And?" His voice drops lower, dangerous. "What was I doing to you?"

My thighs squeeze together, instinctive, desperate. I look away, cheeks hot—

"Do not look away."

I jerk my eyes back and see his hand still moving beneath the blanket.

"You were fucking me," I whisper. My lips tremble. "Hard. Rough."

I brace for him to flinch. To falter.

He doesn't.

He blinks once. Then, steady: "Now, lick that middle finger. Show me."

My breath stutters. "You're out of your mind."

"Probably." His hand moves faster, sheets rustling with the rhythm. His eyes burn into me.

"And you fucking love it. Lick it."

The growl in his voice undoes me. Something in me snaps. If he wants a show, I'll give him a damn show.

I bring my fingers to my mouth. And I lick—letting my tongue circle, letting him see every motion.

His breath shatters, audible. He mutters a ragged curse. "Now touch yourself."

I do. My hand moves, slow and tentative, until I gasp. The pleasure hits fast and sharp, like it's been waiting all day.

His says with fury, "How wet are you?"

I can barely form the words. "So wet you could probably be inside me without burning."

He lets out a sound that's half a groan.

I turn my head toward him. "How hard are you?"

He shifts just enough for me to see the fire in his eyes.

"Hard enough to forget the rules," he snaps, like he's daring me to push him.

I bring another finger to my lips and smirk.

His eyes burn into me. "Hungry?"

"Starving," I breathe.

I move again, arching, my eyes fluttering closed—

"Eyes on me."

I force them open.

His gaze pins me.

Then the blanket moves.

At first, I think it's me, shifting. But no—his fist closes on the edge and he drags it down, sudden, ruthless. Cold air rushes over my thighs, my stomach, leaving me bare to the night.

I gasp, grabbing for the fabric, but he's already got it. His grip is iron.

"Hoyt," I whisper, panicked, desperate.

He doesn't stop. "I want to see you."

His eyes drop.

My skin prickles, every nerve alive under his stare.

The thin cotton of my panties is all that's left—damp, clinging, my hand still trapped between my thighs. I realize now that discarding my sweatpants hours ago in the heat of the night was a mistake

I'm so turned on that it terrifies me. The way he's speaking to me, looking at me—it's stronger than touch. Stronger than any dream.

I can't breathe. I can't stop.

"I'm close," I whisper, breath catching.

"Don't even think about it," he snarls. "Not until I say."

My body trembles. "Hoyt—"

"Another finger," he orders, low and vicious. "Now."

I let out a moan, louder than I meant to, biting down hard on my lip to keep from waking the others.

"Now," he growls. "Play with your ass. I want to see what it does to you."

My head jerks in a frantic no.

"You don't have to go further. Just trust me."

Something in me obeys before my mind can scream. My own fingers betray me.

I gasp, the shock electric, toes curling. A sound tears from my throat, raw, desperate.

"Feel good?" His eyes pin me, unblinking, merciless.

I nod, dizzy, undone. "I'm gonna—"

"Not yet." His voice slices through me, rough enough to wound.

"Hoyt—"

"Beg."

Humiliation scorches down my chest. "Please."

"Louder."

The word tastes like ash. But I'm too far gone. Shaking, I squeeze my eyes shut and whisper, "Please."

He leans in close, his breath shredded. "Now. Come for me."

The command detonates inside me.

It rips through me like a wave—violent, hot, unrelenting. My body shatters against it, every nerve burning. I lose myself in it, in him, in the way his gaze devours me whole.

But he doesn't let me collapse into silence.

"Keep going," he snarls.

"What—" I pant, trembling.

"I said keep going. Don't stop. Make it hurt."

My body jerks, sensitive to the point of pain. "I can't—"

"Yes, you can." He yanks his own blanket halfway down,

giving me the perfect view of his cock and his fist stroking hard, fast. My mouth goes dry.

"Look at me," he bites out. "Look at what you're doing to me."

I stare, helpless, drinking him in. The rise and fall of his chest, the flex of his arm, the tendons in his throat straining.

"Fuck," he groans, guttural. "You're gonna kill me."

The effort of holding it back claws through me. From the moment my fingers moved under the blanket I've been forcing my prism silent, strangling the shine in my chest so the others wouldn't see. Every gasp, every whisper, I kept it buried.

I can tell Hoyt's been doing the same. Both of us letting it slip on and off, fighting the glow every time it surged.

But I can't anymore.

The control shatters. My violet light bursts out in jagged pulses, staining my skin, flashing across the shack like a heartbeat too loud to hide.

And with it—he breaks.

His indigo glow detonates across the floorboards, bleeding into mine, the two colors tangling and writhing like they're alive.

We try to smother it, both of us, but it's useless.

Every time his fist jerks rougher, the light sears through. For a heartbeat it feels like the whole shack is alive with us—magic, sweat, hunger—all of it spilling into the air.

He strokes harder, faster, eyes locked to mine.

"Tell me again. Whose cock were you dreaming about?"

"Yours," I whisper, hoarse.

"Say it louder."

"Yours!"

A savage sound tears from his throat.

I freeze, transfixed. I should look away. I don't.

Every stroke is vicious, punishing. His knuckles shine with it. He tips his head back, jaw clenched, breath broken.

Then he comes—thick ropes spilling across his stomach, his

hand, the edge of the blanket. He grunts through it, a rough, strangled sound, like even release is war.

I can't move. I can't breathe. I simply watch him—every twitch, every shake, the way his muscles lock and tremble.

He slows, hand falling away. His chest heaves, damp hair plastered to his forehead. For a heartbeat, he looks wrecked.

His eyes cut to mine, dark and merciless.

"Too bad he slept through it," he mutters, voice hoarse, as he wipes his hand on the blanket draped across his hips.

He rises, slow and deliberate, dragging his own blanket with him. The fabric falls away from the floor where he'd been sprawled, twisted and damp, but he gathers it anyway, clenching it in his fist like he can erase what just happened by carrying it out the door.

For one wild second I think he'll look back. That he'll say something—anything—that proves this meant something.

He doesn't.

Hoyt yanks the shack door open, night air rushing in, then slams it shut behind him with a thud.

I'm left on the floor with nothing but my own blanket tangled around my legs, sweat cooling on my skin, heart still rioting in my chest.

A game. That's all this was to him.

THIRTY-THREE

"THE FARTHER BACKWARD YOU CAN LOOK, THE FARTHER FORWARD YOU ARE LIKELY TO SEE." – WINSTON CHURCHILL

Aaron and Leon leave early to pick up Mel. That means it's just Hoyt and me—alone. Left to practice, to pretend we're focused, to sit by the ocean and try not to feel anything.

We watch them drift away in the boat, Aaron surprisingly steady at the helm. Leon shouts something over the engine and waves. I wave back. Hoyt doesn't.

Then it's quiet again. Too quiet.

Last night presses at the edges of my mind. He hasn't said a word about it. Neither have I.

We're supposed to be keeping our lights off—controlling the magic. But all I can think about is the sound of his voice in the dark, the way his eyes pinned me while we both lost control.

I wrap my arms around my knees, try to sound normal. "At least you get to be by the ocean," I say, forcing a smile.

"Let's not... talk," he says, eyes fixed on the horizon. "We need to concentrate on the prism."

Right. The prism.

Another excuse not to speak to me. Another way to make last night disappear.

I shut up.

I turn toward the water, the way Leon taught us. Try to focus. To still myself. But when I manage to push Hoyt's voice away, all I see is James.

Leon said to treat each thought like a rock. Heavy. But throwable. I picture a black hole in the back of my mind, and one by one, I hurl the thoughts inside.

James. Gone.

Darion. Gone.

The boy. The maid. All of it—gone.

It takes more effort than I want to admit. The thoughts crawl back in like weeds, but I keep going. Again. Again. Like a game where killing memories is the only way to survive.

We keep at it for over an hour, so long my legs start to go numb.

Across from me, Hoyt is still. He makes it look easy, his crystal lying perfectly clear against his chest, the light off. I can barely keep mine down for longer than a minute.

And still, I can't stop watching him. The breadth of his shoulders, steady and unshakable. His hands loose on his knees, veins raised along his forearms. His mouth set in that stubborn line I've kissed in dreams and ached to bite in reality. A strand of hair slips across his forehead, damp with sea air, and my chest twists with the memory of us—together.

I shut my eyes before the wanting breaks me.

The rocks I keep trying to hurl into that black hole suddenly spill back out—faces, voices, screams. Marie's laugh. Tom's easy smile. Darion. Paris. Boston. My career. But mostly Hoyt. Always Hoyt. The weight of his eyes when they're on me—even when he pretends they're not.

My throat burns. My eyes sting. I dig my nails into my arms, willing myself to hold it back. To breathe. To not break.

But I do.

A sob claws out before I can stop it. Sharp, ugly, too loud in the quiet. I slap a hand over my mouth, shaking.

I can't sit here. Not across from him. Not under his eyes. Not when the weight of it all is caving me in.

Before he can notice, before he can say anything, I lurch to my feet and bolt. Sand shifts under me, clumsy and desperate, but I don't care. I need to get away.

I don't look back—until I feel it. Him watching me run, like he can see every piece of me.

By the time I reach the shack steps, I'm crying so hard I can barely see. I stumble inside, slam the door, and drop straight onto the springy couch.

I yank the blanket around me, clutching it tight like armor, but it doesn't hold anything back. Not the tears. Not the tremors.

I bury my face in the fabric, sobbing into the stale cotton. The sound is awful—too raw. I want to smother it, to swallow it, but it keeps tearing out of me.

All the dead people. All the secrets. My mother's voice. The necklace. The prisms. Hoyt. All of it floods me at once, it feels like drowning.

The door creaks.

I flinch, dragging the blanket tighter, trying to muffle my face. But it's too late. He's there.

Hoyt steps inside quietly, closing the door behind him. He doesn't say anything at first.

I wipe at my eyes uselessly, muttering, "I'm fine." My voice is shredded, a lie so thin it's pathetic.

"You're not fine."

The words are rough, but not cruel.

I shake my head, fresh tears spilling. "I can't keep doing this. Pretending. Surviving. Like any of this is normal."

His boots creak across the floorboards. He comes close, too close. He crouches beside the couch, reaching for the blanket. I try to hold it tighter, but his hand fists the fabric, knuckles white, and he rips it off me like he can't stand another inch of distance.

"Look at me," he snarls.

I do. God help me, I do. My vision swims, tears still running, but my chest still heaves at the sight of him this close.

A part of me wants to turn away, hide. I hate that he's seeing me like this.

For a second, I think he'll say something—comfort, denial, anything. Instead, he grabs the half-empty water bottle from the floor and twists it open. He holds it out like he's going to hand it to me. My lips part, ready to take it—

But then, in one sudden, reckless move, he tips it.

I gasp as the cold splash hits my chest, soaking straight through the blanket, dripping over my prism. He tilts it again, spilling the rest down his own front, his shirt darkening where the water trails.

Indigo and violet flare instantly—violent and unrestrained.

And a second later, his hand is in my hair, his mouth crashing onto mine.

It isn't gentle. It isn't careful. It's everything he's been swallowing, ripping out at once. I can sense our prisms thrumming against each other like they'll explode.

I clutch him back, half-terrified, half-drowning in him.

We break apart long enough for him to mutter against my mouth, raw and guttural:

"I'm not fine either."

Then his lips crush mine again.

I rip my mouth from his, breath ragged, his grip still tight in my hair.

"Stop—Hoyt, I don't want to hurt you."

He doesn't let go. The bottle is still in his hand; he tips what's left over us, water spilling across our chests, keeping the prisms alive, and drags me back to him like he can't stand the inch between us.

"I don't care," he rasps. "Fucking burn me. I'll wear your marks like hickeys. Go on—brand me."

My chest stutters. My body aches to believe him, but the terror claws louder. I push weakly at his shoulder. "No. I won't risk hurting you."

He grabs my wrist, yanks me closer. His eyes blaze.

"Don't you dare pull away from me again."

The words gut me. My throat closes, tears slipping free.

"I'm sorry, Hoyt," I choke out.

He steps back like I scorched him.

"We need to talk," I say, desperate now, hoping he'll hear me. "I never meant to—"

His eyes flash, sharp, furious. "To what? To fuck me up worse than I already was?"

"I—no—I never meant to hurt you, I was trying to..." The words crumble.

"What do you want, Iris?" His voice cuts, raw and unforgiving. "Do you even know?"

I wonder if he meant *who* instead of *what*.

"I want you," I whisper, broken. "I love you." My chest caves as the words leave me. "And I thought you felt the same for me."

He freezes. Silent.

"But from the way you've been acting..." I tremble slightly. "...I guess I was wrong."

Still nothing.

"Last night..." I force the words through my teeth. "I thought maybe you felt something. But you showed me—it was all just a game to you. A way to prove something to Aaron. To me. To— who the fuck even knows what?"

The silence after is unbearable. He doesn't move. Doesn't argue. Doesn't give me anything at all.

And that's what breaks me worst of all.

My breath shudders out, raw and shaky. "Say something," I whisper. It comes out more like a plea.

Nothing.

His jaw works once, twice, like he has the words but swallows them down. Our prisms dim slowly.

I wipe at my face, but the tears won't stop. "Fine," I rasp. "Then don't."

The door bursts open.

Laughter. Boots stomping on the wood. Leon's voice, too loud. Aaron's shape filling the doorway. Mel right behind them.

And there we are—Hoyt still too close, my blanket abandoned on the floor, the water bottle overturned, my face wet and swollen.

"You OK?" Aaron walks toward me, and I watch Hoyt step out without a word.

I swipe at my face with a smile that doesn't hold. "I'm fine."

It's Mel's face as she steps into the shack that saves us from the silence. She doesn't say anything right away. She stops in the doorway, scans the room, and exhales.

Leon's waiting with a sheepish smile.

"I know, I know," he says quickly, lifting both palms. "It's only for a little while longer."

Mel glances around—at the thin mattress, the blankets on the floor, the warped windowpanes, the table barely big enough for one person. She drops her bag with a thud and sits heavily on the edge of the cot.

"Leon, we're too old for this," she mutters, pressing her fingers into her temples.

"I think I made some progress today," I say, trying to cut the heaviness. He thinks I mean the prism. I just mean—finally—words were said.

"Good," Leon says, nodding like a teacher marking a box. "That's good. We'll push harder. Tonight we'll try bridging the prism. Hoyt already managed it."

I blink. "He has?"

"That's how I got him to come," Leon says simply, like it's no big deal. But it feels like one.

"Mel, walk outside with me?" Leon asks, already heading to the door. She gives him a long-suffering look, but follows.

Aaron paces by the window, phone pressed to his ear, voice

low. "I'll sign over the quarterlies to Clark. Tell him it's personal—no, don't elaborate. Just say I'll be back in a few weeks."

* * *

I must have fallen asleep somehow after saying I was going to shut my eyes for a minute or two. I wake up with the smell of garlic and seafood warming the small space.

I glance at Hoyt, sleeves rolled up, crouched by the battered log stove. Garlic skins curl off his knife, herbs scattered on the scarred table beside him. He doesn't look up. Doesn't say anything.

Aaron wanders shirtless through the room, glancing like he's begging for an audience. I notice. Everyone does. It's not even warm. And ever since he found out Hoyt and I can't touch, he struts like fate handed him a second chance. He makes sure Hoyt sees it too—brushing my hair back when it doesn't need it, steadying me by the waist when I walk past him, letting his hand linger too long when he hands me something. Small gestures. A quiet show of what he can do and Hoyt can't.

I should hate them both for turning me into a piece in their pissing contest. I should hate myself more for liking it. And still—I play.

I edge closer to the pot. "Can I help?"

Hoyt gestures to the bag beside him without looking. "Shrimp. Peel 'em."

"Got it."

We fall into a rhythm. Hoyt cooks, I peel. No words. Just the scrape of shells, the hiss of butter, the bubbling of water. His eyes stay on the pan. Mine keep trying not to drift to him.

It feels almost normal—almost safe—except my lips are still swollen from him, and my chest still raw from the fight we didn't finish. Every motion is a performance: peel, drop, stir, pretend. Like we're both staging a quiet lie no one else will notice.

Aaron settles into the far corner with Leon, asking sharp questions under the guise of conversation, as if he's determined to dig something loose.

By the time food's ready, everyone's inside again. Hoyt keeps his distance. Leon keeps the conversation moving. Aaron keeps pretending it's a hot summer day.

"You learned to cook?" Aaron asks with raised eyebrows, fork halfway to his mouth.

"It might be because I didn't have to make it myself," Mel adds, "but this might be the best pasta I've ever had. And we spent a year in Italy."

She shoots me a look, like she knows more than she's saying.

"Hoyt made it," I say softly. "I just peeled the shrimp."

Aaron chews a little slower after that.

"Thank you," Leon says, raising his cup.

Hoyt nods.

I start clearing the plates, gathering forks and stacking cups when Aaron crosses to the corner. He rummages through one of the boxes stacked there and comes back holding a small white one.

"I thought... well, since you probably spent your birthday alone..."

My hands freeze mid-motion.

"You got me a cake? My birthday was months ago, Aaron."

He shrugs, grin crooked. "Happy birthday. Sorry—I forgot candles."

The box opens to a simple chocolate cake, already sliced.

"That's..." My throat closes. Tears sting before I can stop them. "Thank you."

I hate that I'm this emotional. Hate that I'm also about to get my period. Hate that this moment, as sweet as it is, feels like it belongs to another life.

Aaron sets the box on the table, slides a piece onto a plate, and presses it into my hands like it's a gift.

"I hate that I failed you. I meant what I said all those years ago —I swore you'd never spend another birthday alone."

The words catch harder than I expect. I see him as clear as then: leaning against the lockers, finding me crumpled on the floor. It was the first year after my dad left. My grandparents were drowning in boxes, too busy with the chaos of moving to even remember my birthday. No cake. No calls. Just me, hollow and invisible. He crouched down, tipped my chin up, and swore—right there in the hallway—that I'd never spend another birthday alone.

I nod and take a bite. Too big. Chocolate smears at the corner of my mouth.

Before I can reach for a napkin, Aaron leans in. Close. His thumb brushes the smear away, slow, lingering a second too long. My chest stutters. Too close. Too familiar. His gaze drops to my lips.

The room blurs for a beat.

And then Hoyt's voice cuts through, sharp as a blade:

"You left her to spend her birthday alone?"

Aaron glances up, caught off guard. "What do you mean? She left."

"I thought you left together," Hoyt presses, gaze cutting between us.

"No," I say. "I was in Paris. Alone."

The table goes still.

"Until you met us," Leon says brightly, already digging into his slice.

I manage a smile. "I'm grateful. For all your help. Yours too, Mel."

"Repay us by learning this thing fast," she replies, sharp. "I'm not sure how long we can play house here."

Her words hang in the air like a dropped curtain.

And just like that, the room goes quiet again—each of us swallowed by our own thoughts, each of us pretending we're not terrified.

Thirty-Four

"Love is a fire. But whether it is going to warm your heart or burn down your house, you can never tell." – Joan Crawford

I'm in the outdoor shower behind the shack. It's nothing more than a rusted pipe stuck through a post with a valve on it. Hoyt propped up a couple of old planks when we first got here to give me some privacy, but they don't do much. The wind cuts right through the gaps.

The water comes out in a thin stream, icy cold, barely enough pressure to rinse the soap. My teeth chatter as I rush.

Then I hear it. A heavy thud. A scuffle. Raised voices.

I twist off the water and grab for the towel. When I step out, Aaron is on the ground with his hand to his face. Hoyt stands over him, chest heaving.

"Do not make me fucking regret saving your life," Hoyt growls.

"Hoyt! Stop!" I shout, panic rising as I clutch the towel around me.

He turns at the sound. And his eyes drop—once. The towel's slipped on one side.

His gaze freezes on the ink low on my hip. The fresh lines. The moth.

A moment. Barely a second.

But he just walks away without a word.

Aaron wipes blood from the corner of his mouth, pushing himself up slowly.

"What happened?" I ask.

"Nothing," he mutters, but his eyes give him away—flickering with something guilty before he looks down.

At the doorway, Hoyt's back goes rigid. He glances once over his shoulder, unreadable, and keeps walking.

A moment later, Mel steps into the frame, arms folded like she saw the whole thing.

"Boys will be boys," she says flatly. "Dry off, professor. It's time."

* * *

"This isn't complicated," Leon says, calm as ever, a small cup of seawater between his hands. "I'll travel to you—with water and flame. When my light appears, watch closely. You should see a silver thread. When you do, pull it. Gently."

The room goes quiet. Everyone waits. I try to keep my face neutral even though half of me is still convinced this is fantasy.

"That I've gotta see," Aaron mutters, leaning forward.

Leon lowers his hand into the cup, submerging the ring on his finger. Ripples spread and fade. For a few seconds—nothing.

Then it happens. A flicker.

The glow starts weak, like a coal catching fire. Slowly, a deep red light spreads out from his ring, steady and sure.

It looks nothing like mine or Hoyt's. My violet always sputters and pops, unreliable. Hoyt's indigo sparks like faulty wiring. But Leon's doesn't waver. It grows with purpose, like it knows exactly what it's doing.

I watch, transfixed, as he lifts his hand back out of the cup. Droplets stream down his wrist. The prism glows alive against his dark skin.

He brings it toward the candle on the table. The flame bends unnaturally, straining toward the light as though caught in its gravity.

Something in Leon's body changes. His chest rises with a sharp inhale—then stills. His shoulders slacken. His eyes roll back, white and empty.

He doesn't fall. He doesn't speak. He just... goes still.

And the light leaves him.

The red glow pulls free of the prism, rising into the air like it has weight. It hovers right above the cup.

My stomach drops. I've felt this before—done it myself—but never from the outside. Never watching someone else's light slip free.

Beside me, Aaron swears under his breath. He leans forward, wide-eyed, caught between terror and awe.

Hoyt doesn't move. Neither does Mel. They watch like it's old news.

"Pull the string," Hoyt says, voice low and certain.

I frown, not understanding—until I look closer at the glow. The red shimmers at the edges, like heat rising off pavement. And there it is.

A thread.

So fine it's nearly invisible, a strand of silver spider silk stretching from the center of the glow, pulsing faintly. I blink and almost lose it—but it's still there.

I reach out slowly, afraid even the air from my breath might snap it.

The thread doesn't stay still—it moves as I step closer. Like it wants to find me. It lifts, drifting with strange intent, curving toward my chest.

I don't even have to grab it. The thread stretches toward me on its own, drifting higher until it touches the violet prism hanging at my collarbone. The instant it makes contact, something snaps into place. The filament curls around my prism with delicate precision, binding itself there, and suddenly the red and violet are anchored —like they were always meant to be.

My prism reacts instantly. Violet bursts out of control, wild and erratic, answering my heartbeat—or my panic, or both. Sweat beads on my skin. My hands shake. I'm not doing anything. It's all happening on its own.

Then—without warning—every muscle seizes. Not with pain, but with connection. My chest locks tight. My mind empties. The world narrows to the silver thread, the red glow, the crackle of magic storming inside me.

I feel it before I understand it: a presence, sudden and warm, flickering inside my head.

I hear it but not through my ears. Clear as a whisper in a dream. *Can you hear me?*

My eyes snap to Leon. He's motionless, lips still, eyes half-closed, still rolled back. The voice didn't come from the room. It came from inside my head.

"Yes," I blurt, before it even occurs to me I could have tried to think it instead.

His voice hums again—pleased. *Good. That's all there is. We're connected now. You don't have to speak out loud—I'll hear you.*

You can hear... my thoughts? I try aiming the question directly at him, silently this time.

Sort of. Your mind's a mess, no offense. Too loud, too tangled. But if you focus—if you aim something at me—I'll hear it.

I blink, stunned. *This is impossible.*

Yes, he answers, and I swear I feel him smile. *Isn't it wonderful?*

I watch as the silver thread loosens its grip on my prism. It drifts back toward Leon, dissolving into the red glow still hovering around his ring. Suddenly—his eyes flutter open, and the light pulls inward, dimming until it's just a quiet pulse beneath the stone.

I stay frozen.

"That was…" My voice trails off. Words don't seem big enough.

Leon tilts his head, a knowing smile playing at his lips. "Magical?"

Aaron leans forward, eyes wide. "What the hell was that?"

"I…" I fumble. "I could hear Leon. And he could hear me. In my head."

Aaron stares like I've lost it. "What—like telepathy?"

"In a way," Leon says, blowing out the candle. "More like prism-to-prism resonance. But yes—the mind is involved."

He stands, claps his hands once. "Excellent. We're making progress."

Mel raises a brow. "Progress toward what, exactly?"

Leon looks at all of us. "Tomorrow's a big day. Get some rest."

"What's tomorrow?" I ask, wary.

His gaze sharpens. "Tomorrow we're moving to the haunted house."

Of course we are.

I could spend all day practicing magical rituals—but sleeping in a place where people were butchered? No.

"We can't," I say, watching the others already zipping bags and folding blankets. "This shack is fine."

They all stop to stare at me.

"We need space. Real beds. A bathroom," Leon says, like it's the most obvious thing in the world.

"We can't just break into that house. And it's probably as rotten as this place."

Leon shakes his head. "It's not in pristine condition, no. I looked it up. But the conservation group—the Shoals Marine Lab —they still maintain it as a historic structure. Only a few items are left inside, but honestly, anywhere will be better than here." He glances around the cramped shack, then at Mel. "I was willing to give this place a try when it was just us. But it's time to call it."

"I can't keep watching you sleep on the floor, Iris," Aaron says.

"She's stronger than you think," Hoyt puts in.

The compliment throws me off.

"I know she is," Aaron fires back. "But some of us actually want her comfortable."

"She deserves that," Leon agrees, clapping Aaron on the back. "Both ladies do."

"And some of us think women are strong, capable beings who can decide for themselves," I snap.

Mel exhales through her nose, arms crossed. "I don't care where we sleep. This place has mice in the rafters and rain in the sheets. The house might be haunted, but at least it's got doors that shut."

I roll my eyes. I don't care about a bed. I care about not lying awake with ghosts breathing down my neck. But it doesn't matter. I can already tell—I'm losing this one.

* * *

I wake to the sound of movement. Leon's crouched by his pack, folding blankets into neat stacks like we're leaving in an hour.

I slip outside for air—then freeze.

The boat is gone.

Panic scrapes through me. *Did Aaron leave? Fled, taking our only way off this rock?*

Before I can call out, Leon passes by with an armful of gear. "He's running an errand," he says, as if that explains everything, and disappears into the shack.

I'm still staring at the empty waterline when Hoyt appears, coming back from the outdoor shower. His hair drips down his neck, a towel thrown over one shoulder. His jeans hang low on his hips, like the waistband personally offended him.

Everyone's awake before me.

I tossed half the night, hoping for another shared dream. All I got were nightmares.

"Morning," I manage.

He nods, biting into a plum.

I can't help staring. The way he eats it—like it wronged him, like it owes him something—like I do.

Juice runs down his fingers. He lifts his hand to his mouth and licks it clean, slow, like he knows I'm watching.

It feels like a private show, though he never once looks at me.

I grip the edge of the windowsill, pulse kicking. *I need to get laid.*

He finishes the plum, tosses the pit into the dirt, and walks inside—like my entire nervous system didn't just short-circuit over a piece of fruit.

"You should both be training," Leon calls from the doorway, voice sharp enough to snap me back.

* * *

It's the simplest morning routine: wake up, skip caffeine, panic. By now, I've perfected it.

I walk down to the shoreline, deciding the effort of heating water for tea today isn't worth it.

Hoyt is already there, eyes closed. The man has been training nonstop. Staying up late, punishing himself like it's the only thing he has control over. I know the sound of his footsteps now, the weight of them pacing the old wood floors in the middle of the night. He's trying. Harder than anyone here.

I watch him from the side. He is getting better. We both are. But nowhere near the level of control Leon wants. Something tells me that's not a skill you master in days.

Leon appears a few minutes later, hands clasped behind his back. "Very well," he says. "Let's try something new."

Hoyt and I push up to stand.

Leon turns to him. "Come closer to Iris."

Hoyt moves, but only a step—keeping a safe two feet between us. The air tightens.

"Closer," Leon says.

We both draw in a breath.

Hoyt obeys—this time only inches away.

Close enough that I'm suddenly aware of every inch of space he *isn't* touching.

Our eyes meet. No words. Just tension. Just the weight of everything unspoken.

Leon's voice drops, "Now... let the prisms connect. Like you told me they've done before."

Hoyt steps in again, slightly. But it's enough.

With no effort at all, our prisms lurch toward each other—magnetized, bound by some command neither of us dares resist.

The lights spark to life between us. His indigo. My violet. Tangling. Twisting.

We barely need water today. The sea roars behind us, salt spray lashing our ankles, the tide angry and alive. Each wave slams into the rocks bigger than the last.

I try not to picture Aaron out there in a boat. Try not to imagine what those waves would do to something that small. Try not to—

"Stay like this," Leon says. "Don't move. Not until both of you can turn the lights off. You may come inside when you've achieved it."

He pauses, smirking. "I trust you don't need a chaperone."

It's just the two of us now.

We stand there—still. Awkward. Heat crackling between us, lights humming at our throats. Then Hoyt closes his eyes. A quiet dismissal. Clear.

I match him. Let my eyes fall shut too, pretending it doesn't sting.

The faster we figure this out, the faster we can—

The thought slips through me like the current. And then... an idea.

A wrong one. A reckless one.

What if I stopped trying to smother the light—and started feeding it?

I open my eyes.

I look at my prism, at the way it leans into his. Like it wants something. Like I want something.

Brighter, I think.

The light jumps.

My breath stutters.

Brighter, I demand, stronger this time.

It listens. Grows. Warms.

Brighter! I shout in my head—every nerve ending on fire now.

The violet erupts. A pulse so violent it bursts into white.

Hoyt's eyes snap open. He squints hard, shielding his face with one hand. "What are you doing?!" he shouts, blinking like he's staring into the sun.

"Sorry!" The word tumbles out, absurdly small against the blast I just caused. Instantly the light shrinks, like it only existed on adrenaline.

He lowers his hand, still blinking. "How did you... how did you do that?"

I gulp for air, my pulse racing. "I... yelled at it?"

His brow furrows. "Yelled. At it."

"Well, we've been trying to shut them off. I figured—maybe control isn't suppression. Maybe it's... permission."

He studies me for a long beat, something unreadable flickering in his eyes.

"You really do have a thing for breaking rules."

I can't stop the small smile tugging at my lips. At least he's talking to me.

"You try," I tell him.

"To yell at it?"

"In your head. See if it listens to you too."

Hoyt glances down at the indigo hovering near mine. His jaw ticks. He frowns, focuses.

His prism flares.

Not a flicker. Not a blink. A full surge.

So bright I have to throw up a hand, laughing through a squint.

Then it's gone. Snuffed like it was never there.

He exhales, almost amused. "Huh."

Something shifts in the way he's looking at my prism. Or maybe not the prism.

His gaze lingers—too low, too long. I glance down, suddenly hyper-aware of the thin tank top clinging to damp skin. I hadn't exactly planned on standing inches from him today.

If I had, I would've picked a bra that didn't scream unhinged academic on the run. Not that I have anything else left. I miss my clothes. My makeup. The version of me in the mirror who looked put together—who he fell for.

I haven't felt attractive in months. Not once since I left. Just bitten nails and shadows under my eyes. I shove my hands into my jeans pockets, like that'll hide me.

I clear my throat. "Excuse me."

His eyes drag up, slow, unapologetic. "What?"

I raise my brows. "Eyes. A little higher, please."

He smirks. "Right—because you don't want me to look?"

My stomach flips. "What?! Who said I do?"

He doesn't hesitate. "You've been throwing yourself at me since we met."

I blink. I blink again.

Did he really just—?

"What?" My voice cracks. My instincts scream to run, but I can't move.

"That's right." His tone drops—quieter, sharper. "I see it now, crystal clear." His gaze dips again, blatant. "The way you played your cards. I told you once—in the dream—you play this game well."

I open my mouth. Shut it. "I…"

"The gala," he cuts in, relentless. "God, I wish that night had come with a warning. Maybe it did—I just didn't listen. The late-night texts. The museum. You sought me out, Iris."

So much for the silent treatment.

"I didn't," I whisper. "It wasn't like that. I was looking for answers. About the prism."

His mouth twists. "You went all the way to Montana—while you were still engaged. Fuck. I should've known then—not to trust a… cheater."

His words hit harder than I expect. My throat tightens. I blink back tears—thank God for the ocean spray on my face. But what rises isn't shame. It's anger. My hand jerks up toward his cheek before I can stop it.

"Go ahead," he pushes, almost leaning in.

I drag it back down, every nerve on fire. He could've walked away if he wanted. But he didn't. Why didn't he?

"You… invited me," I bite out.

"You could've said no."

"Perhaps I should have," I snap.

He doesn't flinch. "Most definitely should have. But you weren't the first mistake I made. Won't be the last."

"You know what? Fuck you."

His mouth twists. "You have. And you're desperate for more— don't bother denying it." His eyes flick down again, bold, unapologetic. "But here's the thing."

He steps in closer, bending to my ear:

"As much as I enjoyed your tight pussy… liars aren't my type."

This time, I swear, he deserves it. My fist tightens, every inch of me ready to strike. But he's right about one thing—I can play this game. And I hate losing.

"You're right," I spit, "I am desperate. Desperate for that

cock." My eyes drop, lingering where I know it'll cut. "Desperate for you to stretch me again... for your tongue to swirl my clit like it's the best fucking drug you ever tasted."

His nostrils flare. Caught off guard.

"And you're also right—I lied." My voice rises, shaking with fury. "Why? Why the fuck did I lie, Hoyt? To save your fucking life. To protect your family. That's why."

I shove the words at him like blades. "I didn't have a choice—I had to leave. And I chose not to drag you with me. Do you get that? If Darion had known about your prism, it wouldn't just be death waiting for you. It would've been your whole life—gone. Hunted. On the run. Just like me. And not only you—Jo, everyone you love."

My throat burns. "So yeah, I lied. I broke it off. I let you believe I was still with Aaron, because it was the only way to keep you free. And I'd do it again. Over and over, even knowing what it did to me."

He just stares, silent, processing it.

I lean in, low and sharp. *My last card. My final move.*

"For someone who hates lies so much, you're damn good at it yourself. You can say I'm not your type—but we both know what happens in those dreams. So yes, I'm desperate. But you? You're pathetic."

I glance down.

"And from the looks of things, I might not be your type, but your cock disagrees. So tell me, Hoyt—why give me a fucking love sigil if you never meant anything by it?"

For a moment, the air between us is shattered. Stripped bare.

His chest rises sharply, breath stuttering, like I've ripped him open.

When he finally speaks, his voice is low, almost broken.

"I meant Mona. I meant what she symbolizes."

Silence cuts between us.

I laugh, bitter and raw. "Oh really? Bullshit. Who lets their supposedly soulmate walk away without a fight?" My voice cracks. "All I did was call to say goodbye. You didn't ask me to stay. You didn't come after me. You just... let me disappear. Went on with your life. Drinking in bars. With—" The memory chokes me. I cut myself off.

"I did come looking for you," he says, shifting his weight. "Akira told me you left. What the hell did you want me to do? You chose him."

"You should have tried." My voice breaks. "Tried harder. I was hurt. I was desperate."

He looks away.

"I..."

"You lied too," I say softly, like it's something I'm only just realizing. "Because Mona should have meant you'd do anything."

He exhales, slowly. "I let you go," he murmurs. "Because... some part of me thought you were better off. That maybe you could be happy in Boston—with your art, your future. With someone who could actually love you right. Touch you and take care of you the way you deserve."

His expression shifts—something soft, something undone flickers in his eyes.

But before either of us can say more, Leon's voice cuts through the wind. "Oh finally," he says, striding toward us with theatrical relief, scanning the waves. "I was starting to worry."

I follow his gaze—Aaron is back.

"By the way," Leon adds, pausing to glance between me and Hoyt. "Great job."

I blink. My eyes drop to our prisms. No glow. In the middle of that entire argument, we somehow managed to keep the lights off.

Leon claps his hands, delighted. "Now—go pack up."

Thirty-Five

"Monsters are real, and ghosts are real too. They live inside us, and sometimes, they win." – Stephen King

The house is colder than I expected. Not in temperature—though the drafts are sharp—but in memory. Wallpaper curls at the corners, dust clogs the grooves of the woodwork. A bed frame sits in the corner with no mattress, only the skeleton of iron springs. Back to the floor it is. At least this time I get four walls to myself. Or so they think that's what I wanted. Truth is, I'd give anything to go back to the shack—only to share the floor with Hoyt again. Turns out the pathetic one is me.

I'm rolling my blanket out when the floor creaks behind me. Aaron stands in the doorway, damp from the rain, holding something under his arm.

"Leon sent me out," he says, lifting the bundle a little. "He gave me a whole list—blankets, lantern oil, Mel's favorite biscuits... whatever he thought might keep her from bolting if this place feels too rough."

"I'm worried you're the one who's gonna bolt," I say.

He tries to smile, that crooked half-grin he always used when he was covering nerves. I used to tease him for it. Now it lands heavy, familiar in a way I wish it wasn't.

For a second I think I've hit too close. But he shakes his head.

"I won't. And—" he lifts the other bundle from under his arm, "I got you this."

He steps inside, sets the bundle at the head of the broken bed frame. A pillow. New. Still wrapped in plastic.

I glance up at him. "You didn't have to."

"Yeah, I did," he says quietly, like it's obvious. "You never sleep well without a soft one—the kind you can fold in half and hug. I remember."

The words knock something loose in me. He remembers. Of course he does. How many nights did we share the same bed? He'd always hand me the better pillow without asking. Little rituals I didn't realize I'd memorized until they were gone.

My hand brushes the plastic. "Thank you. Not just for this—for everything. For helping us. For helping me."

He shifts, rubs the back of his neck. Same nervous tic as always.

"I got your money—the transfer you made when I left." I tell him.

"I thought you might need it."

"I really appreciate it."

Then he exhales hard, sharp through his nose.

"Look, I know I don't belong here."

"Aaron—"

"I'm just the ex. The outsider. The fucking clown in this circus." He lets out a bitter laugh, shakes his head. "But if running errands, hauling the boat, training with him—if any of that gives you a chance? At surviving? At being happy?" His throat works. "Then I'll do it. Even if it kills me. Even if it means standing here, watching you look at him that way."

Something twists deep in my chest.

"I see it now... you never looked at me the same way."

I want to answer, but no words come.

He exhales, softer. "It's alright. But I still know you better than anyone."

"I'm sorry, Aaron. For everything," I manage, the words jagged.

He swallows. "I want to help, because what I've learned is… loving someone doesn't always mean you get the ending you want. Sometimes it means making sure they do."

I wasn't expecting that. Not from him. Not here.

"Aaron…"

He straightens, shoulders set like he's already shutting the door on what he just admitted. "Don't pity me, Iris. That's all I ask. I'm fine. And it shouldn't surprise you—I'd do anything for you. Always have." He forces a faint smile. "Now get some rest before the ghosts wake up."

He turns away and leaves.

I sink onto the bed frame, the springs groaning under me. I clutch the pillow to my chest. It feels softer than I deserve.

* * *

The pillow helps, but only a little. Sleep won't come.

I don't know if it's the storm or the possibility of ghosts—not that I believe in those things. I just don't want to find out the hard way. What I do know is that somehow, in a house with two of my exes, I'm sleeping alone. Someone should hand me a medal. Or a drink. Probably both.

The storm claws at the house like it wants in. Wind shrieks through the cracks. Windowpanes bow under the pressure. Floorboards creak like footsteps above me. Every time I close my eyes, I'm bracing for the glass to shatter.

We were lucky, if I had to say so myself, to move out of the shack when we did. By now it's probably being torn from the sand like paper.

Eventually, I give up. I wrap the blanket around my shoulders and slip into the hall.

The living room is already lit with a scatter of candles. Leon,

Mel, Hoyt, Aaron—they're all there. No one says it, but I can tell. They couldn't sleep either.

The house groans again, loud enough to make us all glance at the walls. The air smells of damp salt and mildew, old wood left too long against the sea. The fireplace dominates the far wall, wide and blackened with soot.

"What actually happened here?" Mel asks.

I sink down with them, clutching my new emotional support pillow.

"On a spring night in the 1800s, two sisters were murdered inside this house. Brutally. With an axe. Their older sister, Karen, escaped—barely. Some said she ran barefoot down the rocky shoreline, screaming for help. The man convicted was a fisherman, but even now, more than a century later, people argue whether he actually did it. The truth was swallowed by the tide, like everything else on this island. All that's left is this place."

I pause, feeling their eyes on me. "Not the kind of history I usually study. But it's history all the same."

Smuttynose is supposed to be peaceful now. People come out here to hike, birdwatch, take fog-drenched photos of seabird colonies. Sometimes the tours from the mainland bring curious wanderers. Other times, it's simply private boaters who want to act like they've touched a ghost.

Which means it's not impossible someone could stumble upon us—mid-training, mid-magic, mid-something we can't explain. I'm not even sure what we'd do. Scare them off? Lie? Keep them here? That last thought makes my stomach twist. I don't ask it out loud.

Leon clears his throat, breaking the silence. "If we're awake, we might as well be productive. Hoyt—bring the mirror closer."

I look at the mirror. It leans against the wall like it's always been there, framed in tarnished silver, the edges etched with sea creatures and vines. Still beautiful. I wonder where it used to hang —what wall it was meant for. Why this mirror, instead of the store-bought one we had before? Maybe because it's larger. Or maybe because Leon knows something he won't tell us.

I've learned to stop chasing every answer. There isn't enough time. And I'm starting to wonder if there ever will be.

Still, there's a strange comfort in it. Knowing there's a way out of this house—quick, if not complete.

I'm pulled from my thoughts when Leon cuts through: "I told you," he says, turning to Hoyt. "You can't come."

I catch the tail end of the conversation—enough to realize I'm the one going into the mirror with Leon this time. Hoyt clearly doesn't like being benched. But honestly? I'm relieved. I want out of this house. And more than that—I want answers. James was my student. If he's part of this... I need to know why.

We've all been begging Leon to use the mirror again. Starving for answers. But he keeps warning about pacing ourselves, muttering something about "overusing the Solenscint," like the prism has limits none of us understand. According to him, the light needs time to recover between crossings, the way lungs need air between breaths. "Push it too fast, and the Solenscint doesn't only weaken—it warps. Distorts the tether. Instead of finding who you're looking for, you risk ending up somewhere else. The eyes can't always bear the strain—things split, fold, blur. And once your breath falters in that place, it's too easy to lose the trail home."

The floor groans under my weight as I sit beside him.

"There's a problem," Mel says, stepping back into the room.

We all turn.

"The ice," she says. "It melted. And the cooler won't kick back on... too old, I guess."

"Shit," I mutter.

Leon doesn't answer right away, but his silence says everything. His eyes stay locked on the mirror—focused, calculating. Worried.

Mel crosses her arms, bracing. "No," she says before he can speak. "You're not doing it."

"We have to," Leon replies.

"We go with the flame then?" I ask, uneasy.

"We can wait another day," Mel snaps, her tone suddenly sharp —protective in a way that feels personal.

"We can't," Leon says calmly. "We've already been here for days, moving far too slowly. We've barely touched the basics. Every hour without answers increases the risk of being found. We don't know what happened to Darion. We don't know James's role in any of this. And we haven't even started…"

As if to prove his point, thunder cracks so close the floor trembles beneath us. The windows rattle. For a moment, no one breathes.

Leon doesn't flinch. "And at this rate, we may not have this place much longer either."

"I'll go." The words leave me before I can stop them.

All of them turn.

"I'll do it," I repeat, this time steadier. Harder. "Let me be the one to go find James."

Hoyt shakes his head instantly. "Absolutely not."

"It's too risky," Aaron says, already half-rising like he could block me. What the hell does he know about prisms?

"Iris," Mel says gently, but firmly, "you don't have to prove anything."

"I'm not trying to prove anything," I fire back. "I'm trying to move. We can't hide here forever. And none of you know James."

Leon studies me for a long beat. I can't read him yet, but I feel something shift in his expression. Quiet recognition.

"She can do it," Leon says finally. "In fact, she's the only one here who can."

"Leon—" Aaron starts, but Leon lifts a hand and cuts him off.

"She's already done it before," Leon says. "She found Hoyt. She survived Darion. And if there's anyone here who knows how James thinks, it's her."

Hoyt stands abruptly. At least he's done arguing out loud.

Supposedly, his prism doesn't work for this kind of travel. If that's true, lately though, I've started to question everything I thought I knew about him. Our last few encounters have... surprised me. Not always in good ways.

"I've done it plenty of times," I say.

Hoyt's eyes cut to me, sharp. And I realize what he's really wondering: how many times exactly have I spied on him.

Leon's shadow stretches behind him, long and alive, like it has a mind of its own. I'd almost forgotten he could do that. He's only let it loose a handful of times since we got here—enough to remind us it's real. Aaron nearly passed out the first time. Judging by the flicker in his expression now, he still hasn't adjusted.

"I thought that only worked if the person had a prism," Aaron says. He's been paying attention. That surprises me.

"It's different," Leon answers. "With two prism-bearers, the connection is natural. They're conduits—always sending and receiving unless you learn to block it. That's why they find each other so easily."

"Okay..." I say slowly.

"But to find someone without a prism..." Leon glances at the mirror. "That's harder. There's no signal coming back. You have to supply it. You can't reach for a stranger—you'll never find them. The prism only follows what's etched into you. The way they moved, the way they made you feel. Magic can't trace what you don't carry in your bones."

My stomach tightens. "And if I don't?"

"If we don't do it right," Leon says, calm but unblinking, "we can end up anywhere. Being seen by strangers in Times Square. Dropped in the middle of a desert. Underwater. We could get lost."

"Lost?" Hoyt asks.

"Or worse."

Hoyt's tone sharpens. "What's worse?"

Leon meets his gaze. "Trapped." Then he turns his eyes on me. "You've only done this to find Hoyt?"

"Yes. And..." I hesitate. "And the night with Darion, I also—"

"That time you found your own," Leon finishes for me, eyes sharp.

I nod.

He leans forward slightly. "Do you think you know James well enough?"

"I... think so."

Flashes of memory rise, unbidden—James in my classroom, always in the back row. Half-listening, half-staring like he already knew the ending. Leather jacket. Tattoos crawling up his arms, the rose inked on his right hand.

He had that sinister charm, the kind that unsettled me because I wanted to look longer than I should. A history nerd with an obsession for the dead, who read more than any other student I'd ever had. He once cornered me after class, asking about seventeenth-century ghost folklore. I'd been stupid enough to answer him for twenty minutes—not because he needed the information, but because he wanted to hear me talk.

And I remember his paper. The one I carried with me after Boston, pages folded and worn from being read too many times. He wrote about blood and sex like they were part of history, not separate from it. About rites that used the body as the altar. I told myself I was just passing the time, but every page pulled me back to him—to the way he'd once said in the library it was a shame people didn't read for *pleasure* anymore. The way he said my name, *Iris*, like he'd never once considered calling me professor.

Hoyt's watching me. I don't have to look to know it.

"I swear to you guys, he was just a student," I murmur. "I have no idea how he could be involved."

"We believe you," Aaron says, reaching for my hand.

I'm not sure which earns Hoyt's eye roll—the words or the touch.

"The book," Leon says. "The one you said he was writing. Think about it—his words. That will help."

I nod. I've read those pages a hundred times in the last few months. I could recite them now if someone asked.

"I only hope James actually wrote those pages himself," Leon mutters.

He studies me another long moment. "How about physically?"

"I remember," I say, maybe too fast. Tattoos, leather, eyes that never looked away.

Leon's expression sharpens. "Is there something particular about James that made you feel something? That's what you'll need to hold on to."

My stomach tightens but I nod. I think about the way his gaze locked on me during lecture. Like he wanted to see me flinch. I hadn't admitted it—not to anyone, not even myself—but James was trouble. He was bold, reckless, too sure of himself. And it wasn't just the tattoos or the leather jacket. It was the way he listened. Like every word out of my mouth was something he could use.

Across the room, Hoyt stands abruptly and grabs a bottle of water. I know him well enough to see it's not about thirst.

Leon claps once, softly. "Then we go."

"No," I say, rising with him. "I'll go."

He holds my gaze before nodding. "Right. Right. You go."

I close my eyes, trying to steady my breath. Trying to connect with my prism—whatever that means. Talking to it still seems ridiculous. But then, so does everything about our lives now.

I draw in a breath, slow and deliberate. They're all watching me. Waiting. Counting on me.

"And any tips to avoid getting trapped?"

Leon's gaze hardens. "You are in control there, Iris. You are the light, not the other way around."

My heart skips a beat, but I nod anyway.

THIRTY-SIX

I cling to James's words as I bring my prism closer to the flame. *If something in you stirs—low in your belly, sharp as hunger and fear—then you already know. You're already marked.*

The world convulses. Light folds, stretches, collapses—until there's nothing but white.

And then—black. Silence.

I drift there for a beat, unsure if I've gone too far, if I'll ever land again.

Then I'm here. Harvard. Of all places.

At least it's night—no students, no professors. Just the long hall stretching in front of me, lined with oil portraits and brass sconces that haven't changed in a century.

My prism's violet glow makes the hall look less like Harvard and more like some forbidden club after hours—the kind you should avoid, the kind where people drug you and punish you for misbehaving. But I'm sure this isn't a party. Whoever's here tonight won't welcome an uninvited guest.

The air presses heavy. I can't really smell in this form, but memory tricks me—wax, old polish, paper. I remember coffee stains on my sleeves from carrying essays through this hall. Flashes of a life that used to be mine.

I test the glow—*brighter*, I think, and to my shock the portraits flare, their painted eyes burning in sudden light. I freeze. *Did I actually... do that?*

Off, I order, sharp. Nothing. The glow clings stubbornly, humming around me like it doesn't understand. Panic needles my chest.

Dimmer, I try instead, hesitant. This time, the glow softens, pulling back until the hall is hushed in shadow again. My pulse steadies.

A flicker of satisfaction cuts through the unease. I've never controlled it before. At least I can manage this much. I hope it's enough to keep me hidden.

I pass polished cherrywood doors, gleaming like they've been waiting for someone important. Doors that practically sneer, *we only open for the chosen ones.* And back then, I loved feeling like I was one of them. Special. Now I see it for what it was—arrogance dressed as tradition.

Harvard was my second home. Here I was the professor, the nerd with too much coffee and too many books. Back then, I felt safe. Normal among people who loved the same things I did. Now all I feel is how far I've fallen from that life. And if the last few months have taught me anything, it's that tradition was meant to be broken.

I move forward, motion more memory than movement. Habit creeps in—even without a body, I almost pretend to skip the broken fourth step on the old stairwell, muscle memory echoing where no muscles exist.

That's when I hear them. They're too faint to make out, but close enough to follow.

I try to shrink myself, my glow dulling as I slide lower with the pull of the stairwell. *Off*, I command again—but the light only flickers, before dimming.

At the bottom, a door stands ajar. The old observatory. Supposed to be sealed for restoration. Tonight, it's wide open.

I slip through. And regret slams into me instantly. The room is too dark—any glow at all will betray me. Instinct drives me behind a tall stack of unused chairs, my pulse hammering like I still have veins.

I yell at my prism to turn off. I beg. Nothing.

Out of sheer frustration, I try reasoning with it—like it can even understand. *It's for your own good. You don't want to get trapped, do you?*

And just like that—like a candle blown—the violet snuffs itself out.

Relief rips through me like a breath I didn't know I was holding.

I shift forward, taking in the people and the room.

A massive tapestry looms behind the semicircle of hooded figures, the Radiant Eye blazing across its fabric—the same symbol I saw at Notre Dame. This is not a gathering of ordinary people— the Seers are here.

The silence holds until one steps forward, cradling a bowl of cracked glass.

When I glimpse what's inside, denial spikes first. No—it can't be.

But it is.

An eye. Human. Clouded and wet, staring blank at the ceiling.

The bowl is placed on a waiting pedestal. One by one, each figure slices their palm and lets a drop fall into it. Blood spatters the surface, streaking the iris until it looks like it's weeping red.

A chant rises. Not English. Not pure Latin either. Older. I catch fragments—*ignis, aqua, terra, aer.* Fire. Water. Earth. Air. Familiar roots twisted into something closer to Celtic rite than church Latin. Not worship. More like instructions.

A woman's voice cuts across the rhythm.

"Have you found her, Briar?"

And then—his reply.

"I found her family."

James.

"They're tied to my finger now," he continues, smug. "They'll lead me straight to her."

"She escaped once," a man snaps, irritation raw under the hood.

James scoffs. "Escaped because no one thought to mention her cousin was one of ours. That little omission wasn't an accident, was it?" His voice sharpens. "I know some of you are playing your own game. Maybe you'd like to see me fail."

The air thickens. A pause full of teeth.

A woman answers, cool and disdainful: "You lost her. Others had to pick up your slack. And now you claim control?"

His silence is taut. "I didn't lose her. She ran. But she's marked. That's permanent."

A chill rips through me. My prism light flickers—like it's flinching with me.

Are they—? They're talking about me.

Another Seer leans in, voice dripping doubt. "Confidence doesn't erase failure, Briar. Perhaps we should give her to someone else."

James laughs, but there's steel in it now. "Don't you dare. She's mine to take."

"Fail again," the reply comes, "and you know the punishment."

"I'm aware," James says. "And I'd remind you—I'm usually the one delivering it."

The silence that follows isn't agreement. It's wariness.

Finally, another woman smooths the edge.

"She didn't even know what she carried. If she had, she never would've stayed that long. How hard can she be to take?"

"She's stronger than she knows," says the silver-ringed woman. "Centuries of knowledge in her bones. The blood proves it."

"She's cracked now," James fires back, venom curling in his tone. "It's only a matter of time before she breaks entirely."

The group nods—but not with respect. With calculation. No one questions him further, but I see the balance shift. They don't trust him.

Another voice: "And the indigo?" The word drips like an insult.

"He's unstable," James says. "They're together." His tone sharpens, a challenge thrown at them. "And that's not all."

"What?"

"Comhghall is helping her."

The Seers murmur low. For a second, it almost feels like James has forced their doubt away from him and onto Leon instead.

They know.

They know everything.

A tremor ripples through me. For a second, my concentration falters.

The violet glow flares back to life—a small flicker, but enough. In that instant I know: I've given myself away.

Every hooded head lifts. Silence slams down, sharp and expectant. For one heartbeat, I hope—maybe they didn't see—

Snap.

Silver light detonates across the floor, racing toward me like a net. It slams shut before I can smother the glow, before I can even think.

I jolt back—too late. Something seals tight. Not air, not walls, but a surface that hums and holds, clear and solid, caging me in my own reflection.

My light bounces back at me, harsh and relentless, folding me inward.

No. No no no.

I push, claw, beg—but I don't have hands here. No body at all. Nothing but a light, sparking uselessly against the walls of the cage. Every flare drains me.

Cold seeps in, unnatural. My glow collapses tighter, like it's being wound up.

A cage.

The Seers don't flinch. Don't even whisper. One tilts their head, deliberate—as if they'd been waiting.

And then a voice slithers through the chamber.

"It appears... we have a visitor tonight."

My heart lurches in my ribs—at least, I think it does back home. Panic surges.

I beg the prism—plead with it. *Go back. Take me home.* I scream at it until thought splinters into static. But the trap holds, tightening the more I thrash.

Two figures step forward. Black-gloved hands clamp the edges of the invisible cube. I'm being carried with ritual patience.

They place me on the pedestal. The eye is gone.

I spin but it doesn't matter. The look in their eyes is clear.

I'm not going anywhere.

I try to pull my magic forward—reach through the light, let the prism burn—but it's too contained. Fear, so much fear. My light flares and fades, weaker every second.

And somewhere—back home—I know what this means. I'm bleeding. I'm not waking up. I'm not safe.

"Iris." My name rolls off his tongue.

He pushes his hood back. And yeah—it's him. Messy dark hair hanging in his eyes, jawline rough with stubble. Lean, all sharp angles and restless energy, like he hasn't slept in days and doesn't give a fuck if he ever does.

His smirk cuts sideways, that crooked mouth daring me. "Eavesdropping? Dangerous habit. You should know better by now."

His gaze drags over me and even without a body, somehow I still feel stripped bare.

"Looks like she's as dumb as the rest of that family," a woman sneers.

James doesn't even flinch. "Talia, Iris might be a lot of things, but dumb isn't one of them."

The woman—Talia—laughs, sharp and mean. "Then spill her now. End it before she gets clever."

"Shhh, Talia," another voice warns. "Don't rush. Remember the ritual. This is more than just stealing a prism."

"I want it, and I want it now," she snaps back.

"Quiet!" James's command cracks across the circle like a whip.

He circles the prism cage studying me like he's already chosen the method. Fast or slow. Painful or clean.

"Let's not forget our ways," he says. "Lira. Recite the vow."

And in that moment it's clear—James isn't their pawn.

The silver-ringed woman lifts her chin. "Seven call, seven will answer."

The circle echoes: "Seven call, seven will answer."

"The omen, we vow to see."

Echo: "The omen, we vow to see."

"Heart you must give. Heart's blood."

Their voices drop together, final, chilling: "Heart's blood."

"On your knees," James orders.

Hoods lower. The women sink before the men in eerie unison, their robes shifting enough to reveal glimpses of bare skin. Heads tilt back, throats bared. Each man presses a blood-slick hand to the crown of the one kneeling before him, sealing the vow in flesh and blood.

A low hum threads through the circle, not words but vibration.

The ritual shifts rawer, darker—before I can process what I'm seeing, James breaks away and comes closer.

"Meet me at your family's home," he murmurs, low enough that the others can't hear.

My light flickers, panicked.

"And Iris..." His head tilts, almost boyish, cruel in its ease. "Come alone. Unless you want anyone else to bleed for you."

The knife flashes. Quick. Practiced. He drags the blade across his palm without a flinch. Blood spills hot and dark, streaking the silver walls of my cage.

The cube hisses and smolders. Slowly, impossibly, the silver light begins to dissolve.

I can't scream, but inside I'm burning. The last thing I see before blackness swallows me is James—watching me fade with that same crooked smirk.

Thirty-Seven

"We are all broken. That's how the light gets in." – Ernest Hemingway

Everything feels heavy. My bones. My skin. My blood. Something is wrong. I try to lift my hand, twitch a finger—nothing moves.

Then—voices. Distant. Warped. Like I'm underwater.

"...she's back—she's trying to come back—" Leon?

Hands on me. Too warm. Pressing. Lifting. Shaking.

Stop.

I'm here. I'm here.

"She's not waking up," someone says. Panicked. Aaron. I'd know that edge in his voice anywhere.

I want to tell him it's okay. Just give me a second. Just—

"She's burning up," Mel says, clipped and low. "If we don't cool her, she'll seize."

A rush of movement. Water. Glass. The sharp twist of a towel being wrung out. Cold water on my neck. But it's not enough. None of it is.

The world tilts, shadows bending at the edges. James's smirk flickers there, wrong, out of place—quickly gone.

Another beat of quiet. Aaron's voice cuts in, soft and shaky.

"Hey. I don't know if you can hear me. But if you can... come back. Please, Iris. Please, open your eyes."

A chair scrapes. Footsteps. Someone walks away.

Then—Hoyt, from across the room. "If you touch her again, I swear to God, I'll kill you myself."

Aaron doesn't flinch. His hand is still there, pressing the cold cloth against my chest. Too close. Too high. Right over my breasts. Necessary—maybe. But I can't move. Can't push him away.

"Move your fucking hand," Hoyt snarls.

Aaron's voice cracks, unsteady but fierce.

"I'm helping her. What the hell are you doing?"

Cool cloth against my skin. I don't move. But inside, I scream.

Something else stirs—a dampness between my legs. Warm. Spreading. For a heartbeat I can't tell if it's blood or sweat. Shame burns hotter than the fever. I can't shift. Can't check. I just lie there, helpless.

"She needs a hospital," Aaron mutters. "She's going to die here."

"No," Leon replies. Calm. Cold. "She's still fighting. I can get her back."

The air trembles. A trick of the prism? For a second I see firelight flicker across stone walls, James leaning in, whispering: *Eavesdropping? Dangerous habit.*

I taste smoke. Sharp. Metallic.

"She's bleeding too much," Hoyt says suddenly. His voice closer, raw. "We should've taken her earlier—"

A pause. The kind of silence that hums with fear.

Footsteps. The scuff of a boot. Someone curses under their breath.

"She's on her period," Aaron says flatly. "I know she is."

Hoyt bristles. "How the hell would you—"

"She was eating Leon's chocolate stash," Aaron snaps. "She doesn't even like chocolate—she only eats it when she's on her period. I've seen her do it for years."

Another silence. This one heavier. Guilt-shaped.

Leon's voice cuts through, low. "She should have told me. I should have asked. I shouldn't have—"

"You shouldn't have let her go at all," Hoyt bites out.

"Enough," Mel interrupts, sharp. Then, softer, towards me: "I'll clean her up. Out. Now."

Fabric lifts.

I beg my body to wake up. Please. But I don't.

James's laugh ripples through the dark again, echoing where it shouldn't.

For a breath, there's only dark. Empty.

No more hands. No more towels.

Just air. And a heartbeat that isn't mine. Loud. Labored. Like someone's running out of time.

"Hurry," Aaron mutters. "She's getting paler—"

The scrape of glass. Water sloshes. A match.

"Careful," Mel warns. Her tone is calm but edged.

"I know what I'm doing," Leon snaps—sharper than usual, a crack in his calm.

Something tears through the air—red, blinding. My prism scorches against my chest like it's answering a call I can't hear.

I try reaching for the light—Leon's light.

Almost—

Gone.

"She won't take it," Leon breathes, strain in every word.

"Try again," Hoyt growls.

"She has to be awake for the thread to hold," Leon snaps, his calm fraying.

Something crashes—wood splintering. The sound rattles straight through me.

"Goddammit!" Hoyt's voice cracks, raw. "Don't you fucking say that. Don't you tell me there's nothing left to do. *Do something!*"

Silence. Thick. Unbearable.

His voice again—Hoyt, hoarse and ragged, closer than I expect.

"...What do I do?" he asks. "Just tell me what to do."

Leon exhales low. "The dreams," he says at last, as if testing the thought out loud.

Hoyt doesn't answer. But the silence speaks for him.

"Maybe you can reach her there," Leon goes on. "Find her in the dream. Pull her out."

Hoyt shakes his head, ragged. "They don't work like that. They just... happen. Half the time I don't even know it's a dream until I wake up."

"Then you'll have to know this time," Leon says, steady but sharp. "You need to try."

Hoyt's breath shudders. "I don't know how."

"Stop fighting it," Leon presses. "Don't summon. Don't force. Let it happen. Let her find you."

Hoyt lets out a strangled laugh. "How the fuck am I supposed to fall asleep like this?"

"Here," Aaron says quietly. A rattle of a bottle. The scrape of pills against plastic. "Take them."

Please, I think. Please let me back in.

"Just enough to sleep, Hoyt," Leon cautions. His voice is steel wrapped in calm. "You need to stay conscious enough to pull her through."

Someone touches my hair. Gently. Carefully. Like I'm breakable.

"I'm not going anywhere," Aaron whispers. "You hear me? I'm staying right here."

And I do hear him.

I hear all of them.

And I still can't move.

Thirty-Eight

Hoyt

I'm staring at the cards flipping. Red. Black. Red. Gold. The dealer's hand moves steadily. The air reeks of cigar smoke and expensive perfume. Somewhere behind me, whiskey sloshes in a glass I didn't order, and someone laughs too sharply.

Then I notice her hand. Not the way it moves. Not the way her fingers trail the edge of the velvet table. But the ring. The thin platinum band with its diamond like a weapon. I memorized it the first night I saw her. I searched for it, needing to know what line I was already crossing by just wanting her. And it wrecked me. Because that ring meant she was someone else's future. Someone else's choice. And I knew what that made me: a man with hands he shouldn't use and eyes that lingered too long. But still—I couldn't stop.

Music hums low from somewhere behind us. Sinatra. Slowed down. Warped. *Fly Me to the Moon,* maybe.

Her dress is deep black. Her lips—blood red.

She lifts the next card like she's handling something sacred. But it's not a playing card. It's a tarot card. *The Lovers.*

Not the soft Renaissance garden I expect. Two figures on

opposite sides of a burning tree, their hands reaching toward each other but never touching. She places it between us.

She looks at me and asks, "What are you betting?"

I glance down. My hand's already resting on a token I don't remember picking up.

"Everything," I say.

She arches a brow. "What if you lose?"

I lean in. Close enough to breathe her perfume—

"What if I win?"

Her smile isn't kind.

She lifts another card—*The Tower*. She presses it to her lips before laying it down like a verdict.

The table turns.

"What's taking you so long?" she says, like a spell.

I blink.

The cards scatter like ash. The table's gone.

And she's no longer sitting. She's standing barefoot in the middle of the ballroom. Her dress has changed—white, flowing, luminous.

In my hand—a glove. Black leather.

My prism hums on my chest. A pulse. A call.

I walk toward her slowly, like she might vanish if I move too fast.

"Dance with me," I say, holding out my gloved hand.

She takes my hand, and the ring is gone.

"What took you so long?" she asks.

The floor ripples beneath us.

The dream fractures—and reforms.

Suddenly we're barefoot in the sand. The sky glows a thick, honeyed orange, bleeding into a horizon too still to be real. The ocean swells behind us like it's listening—like it knows this moment matters. No wind. No birds. No distant voices. Just us, hand in hand, prisms glowing softly at our chests.

"What's taking you so long?" I ask her.

The words come before I can stop them. And somehow, I know—it's the phrase. The trigger. The one thing that makes me aware: *this is a dream.*

The world shifts again, seamless.

She's in a kitchen now—a little beach cottage. Placing a woven basket of fruit on the table like she does every morning in this place that doesn't exist. Bananas. Mangoes. Those little sugar-dusted plums she always pretends not to like but always finishes anyway.

She looks up at me with that half-smile. "Sorry! You know how they are—so curious about us. I had to answer a million questions again."

I just stand there, watching her. Trying to burn the image into memory. Her hair loose, her cheeks flushed with sun. I tried hating her. Tried cutting her out, forgetting her name, pretending I didn't know the exact pitch of her laugh when she's surprised.

Didn't work.

Loving her wasn't a choice. It was surrender.

"Come here. I miss you," I say, brushing a strand of hair from her face.

Her skin startles me. It's softer than I remember—warm from the sun, or perhaps from being too close to a version of her I never had. A dry version.

"I thought you were hungry," she teases, kissing me lightly.

"Starving," I murmur, sliding my hands up the smooth lines of her thighs and lifting her onto the countertop like I've done a hundred times in my head.

She kisses me back, and it's not teasing now. It's real. Like she misses me too. Like whatever tore us apart hasn't reached this corner of the dream yet.

"I think the water's warm today," she says, grazing my beard.

I glance over her shoulder, through the open patio doors. The ocean glitters beneath the syrupy sky, gentle waves lapping the white shore. The sun hangs high, casting golden light over everything. Too golden. Too perfect. Like it always does in the Bahamas —so flawless it almost looks fake. Well, I know it is.

My hands move on their own, as if they've waited too long to remember restraint. Her body arches into me, and the ache that builds in my chest is more than want. It's need. It's everything I couldn't say when she was gone.

"The water's always warm when you're in it," I whisper against her skin.

She smiles, fingers playing at the edge of my shirt. "Should we go?"

Before I can answer, she presses her hands to my chest—right over my prism—and pulls me closer by it, as if it's the only thing anchoring us. Her voice drops, barely audible.

"I'm sorry," she says.

I go still.

"For what?"

"For... leaving like that."

"Later," I say, kissing her collarbone. "I already waited too long."

I lift the edge of her summer dress and trail kisses up the inside of her thigh. She shivers, her hand tangling in my hair, holding me there.

"Hoyt?"

I look up. Her eyes are glassy.

"Don't," she says.

Something inside me breaks.

"Why not?"

"Because I want to feel it. Really feel it. When it happens in real life."

My hand stills. My breath stops.

"This is just a dream, isn't it?"

"I think so."

I rest my forehead against her stomach. "I thought I'd lost you."

"I'm still here."

I look up at her again, my eyes catching on the small inked shape on her hip—barely visible in the dream light. A moth. I kiss it slowly.

I breathe in, hard. "Promise me one thing."

"Anything."

"Wake up for me."

"What if I can't? What if this is all we ever get?"

Terror claws through me. But no—she's alive. I can feel it. I can drag her back. I have to.

"I can't stay," I whisper, even though every part of me wants to. "I have to go."

Her fingers clutch at me, desperate. "Stay... please. I don't want to lose you."

It rips me apart, but I force myself to rise, take her face in my hands. My voice breaks as I press my forehead to hers.

"Then wake up, Iris. Wake up and stop me."

THIRTY-NINE

"I won't stop until you wake up," Hoyt says.

It's not a dream anymore. His voice is in the room—close enough that I can feel the air move when he breathes. Real.

His hand finds my face and everything in me narrows to that touch. The heat spikes—raw, blistering. I smell flesh burning. Skin. Not mine. His.

"What the hell are you doing?" Leon snaps and I hear his cane scraping the floor.

"Hoyt—" Mel's voice, sharp, panicked.

There's a grunt. A scuffle. Someone tries to drag him back. Hoyt snarls through clenched teeth, half-feral. "I'm not letting her go!"

He's touching me. And I can tell, every second scorches him alive. His hand trembles. His breath stutters against my ear, half a growl, half a cry of pain.

"I need you," he rasps. The words are frayed, barely kept together.

The heat rolls off him, scorching, wrong. He's hurting himself. Hurting for me.

He doesn't stop. His hand presses harder, like he can force life back into me through pain.

"What are you doing?!" That's Aaron now, his voice cracking, horror pushing through every word. I hear him struggle closer, but Leon blocks him, barked orders sharp as steel.

No.

Hoyt is shaking. His breaths are jagged. I can almost hear his skin searing, the hiss of it, the way his body folds against the fire. Terror claws up my throat.

I slam my focus into the prism. I don't ask. I don't beg. I don't bargain. I command: *protect him.*

A jolt detonates through me. My chest locks. My fingers twitch. Something inside me cracks before igniting.

Violet bursts out of me, wild and erratic. For a heartbeat, it flares brighter than ever—and then, impossibly, it shifts. Deepens. Indigo. His color.

I don't need to open my eyes to see it. The world behind my lids is drenched in it, flooding my veins, painting the room in light so sharp I know it blinds them all.

Leon swears under his breath.

Mel whispers, "Don't let go."

Aaron's voice cracks: "What the fuck is happening?"

And then it rises over my skin. Cool. Clean. Like water wrapping me whole.

I know this feeling.

The veil.

Hoyt gasps, a sound I'll never forget—a sound of disbelief.

His burned hand is still on my face. He presses harder, desperate, like he doesn't trust what he's feeling.

A broken, half-sob laugh tears out of him. It doesn't sound like triumph—it sounds like something breaking. "No... no— come back."

Then both his hands find me, his grip hardens, frantic. He

touches me again—my throat, my shoulders, my chest—as if daring the fire to return.

But it doesn't.

Silence holds. For one impossible heartbeat, the whole room waits.

Something inside me bursts. My heart slams once, twice—

Air tears into my lungs. My throat rips open with a scream. My body convulses, every nerve dragged back to life.

And my eyes—open.

* * *

I see Mel, Leon, Aaron—hovering, pressing in—but not him. Not Hoyt.

Aaron crouches beside me, one hand hovering near my arm like he's afraid I'll break. "Water," he mutters, reaching for the glass. He tilts it toward me carefully, even though his own hands shake. "Slow. Small sips."

I obey. My throat burns, but the coolness anchors me. His eyes don't leave my face.

"You scared the shit out of me," Aaron says, voice cracking in a way that makes me ache.

I manage a whisper. "Hoyt. Is he... is he okay?"

No one answers. The silence is too long. Too pointed.

Leon leans forward, cane tapping once against the floor. His eyes pin me like a specimen. "What did you do?" The question cuts like a scalpel. "The prism—why did it change? What did you feel? Was it deliberate?"

"I—" My chest squeezes.

"Did you see anything? Hear anything?" His tone sharpens. "Iris. Tell me everything."

"I don't—"

"Leon," Mel says. Her hand lands firm on my shoulder, protective. "Enough. She just came back. She needs to heal, not be interrogated."

Leon bristles in frustration. "I need to understand. If we don't, we're blind."

"Not tonight," Mel says, sharper. A command, not a suggestion. "Not like this. She is not your experiment."

Aaron says gently, "You're okay now. That's what matters." His thumb brushes the rim of the glass before setting it aside. His focus never wavers from me. "Drink more if you can."

I nod, but I'm not okay. My body feels wrong, unstitched. Like I'm here and not here.

And Hoyt—

I push against the mattress, trying to sit. "I need to—"

Aaron's hand presses steady against my back. "You need rest," he says quickly.

"Rest. Everything can wait until morning," Mel echoes, softer but immovable.

But my pulse doesn't agree. Every beat is a question: *Where is he?*

* * *

It's been hours. They fed me. Forced more water down my throat. I lie under the thin blanket, pretending sleep. But my body thrums, restless.

They're wrong if they think I can just stay here and wait.

I sit up slowly, careful not to wake Aaron, who's keeping watch like a guard dog. My muscles ache—like I've been hit by a bus, even though I barely lifted a finger. The storm has moved farther out, but I can still hear the sea thrashing, restless as I am.

I don't know where Hoyt is, but I'm sure my prism does. *Take me to him,* I order.

The pull drags me outside. The wind cuts cold against my skin.

I follow the thread of light until I see it: a dim indigo shimmer, low to the ground.

He's sitting there, hunched forward on the wet grass, one arm clutched tight against his chest. His shoulders are rigid, his head bowed.

"Hi," I whisper.

He jerks upright, eyes flashing in the dark. "Are you okay?"

"Yes," I whisper back. "Thanks to you. Are you okay?"

The pause is enough to split me open. He lifts his palm. Even in the shadows I see it—raw, blistered, the cloth already stained through. His fingers tremble before he fists them to still the shaking.

"Hoyt." My throat closes. "God—you're burned. You need a doctor."

"Maybe."

"I'll go get Aaron. We can leave now—"

"No." The word cuts sharp. "Not tonight. I won't risk anyone in those waters because of me."

"You—" My voice shakes. "You saved me."

His jaw tightens. His eyes don't meet mine. "I didn't. Leon. Mel. Aaron. They pulled you back. I just—touched you. Burned myself. Watched."

"Don't say that. You did—"

His gaze snaps to mine, desperate, hollow. "Last year, in Alaska —you stepped out of the car for me. That was courage. That was something. This? This was nothing." His head shakes once. "I couldn't even hold on without breaking."

"Hoyt—"

"Don't worry about me. I'll be fine."

But I don't believe him. Not for a second.

The words clog in my throat. I want to stay, to tell him everything—how much I love him, how much I need him, how much it gutted me to walk away. But I don't. Because the truth is written all over him. He wants to be left alone.

So I turn. I force myself to walk away.

"Firecracker?"

I stop. He hasn't called me that since—since I left.

I look back.

"I like the tattoo," he says. His voice cracks on the edges, but he doesn't hide it.

I manage a small, shaking smile. "Me too."

FORTY

"I am not what happened to me, I am what
I choose to become." – Carl Jung

The town is quiet. Behind us, the island is already gone—
swallowed by dark water as if it was never there. The storm
has passed, but the weight of it hasn't.

I didn't sleep. Not really. After Hoyt sent me away with his
eyes, I paced the shack like a caged thing. Back and forth across the
warped floorboards until they creaked in protest. I kept waiting for
the door to open, for him to come inside, for someone to tell me
he'd let them bandage his hand properly. He never did.

When the sky finally bled pale, I woke everyone. I didn't care if
Leon groaned or if Aaron cursed—Hoyt was in too much pain,
and we weren't going to wait another hour. By the time the boat
shoved off, I was already rehearsing the arguments I'd use to make
sure the doctor saw him first.

As we walk into the inn, I can't help noticing how it looks too
quaint for what we've just crawled out of. We'd only driven a few
minutes from the marina in Hoyt's truck, but it might as well be a
different world than where we were.

I notice the faded flower wallpaper, the cracked brass bell at the
counter. The place is falling apart, but the beds are real. The power

works. And the bar stays open late. Hell—that's five stars in my world right now.

We don't even argue about it—one night here. Everyone needs it. Hoyt's hand needs tending. My body needs more than bandages. Mel looks like she hasn't slept in weeks. And even Leon, for all his gruff insistence on training, doesn't fight the idea of a bath, a hot meal, and a real roof over our heads.

At reception, Leon collects three keys—the only ones left. The innkeeper mutters about half the upstairs being shut down from a leaky roof. Leon grunts, takes the keys, and turns to us.

"Can you boys be men enough to share a room?" he asks dryly, handing one to Aaron and Hoyt.

Mel and Leon take another. That leaves me with the last key—alone.

The doctor arrives not long after, smelling faintly of tobacco. He tends Hoyt first, unwrapping the rough bandage with quiet efficiency. The skin underneath is raw, blistered, already peeling in places. Second-degree, maybe worse. It will scar, the doctor says, but he'll keep use of it. Hoyt doesn't flinch, but his shoulders go rigid. He doesn't speak, doesn't blink, just watches while the doctor works. When it's done, he takes the two small white pills pressed into his palm—swallows them dry—and pockets the rest of the bottle without a word.

Then it's my turn. The doctor checks me over, listens to Leon's clipped account of what happened. I nod through most of it, though the truth is harder to put into words than wounds are. He says rest, food, water. No strain. Simple instructions, as if any of this has been simple.

Leon presses me again for details about James—what I saw, what I heard. The same questions he's been circling since the fish shack, reshaped, sharpened, like perhaps this time I'll slip and reveal something new. I give him everything I can, the same answers as before, until Mel lays a hand on his arm and says firmly,

"Enough. She's told you all this already, over and over." For once, Leon actually lets it go.

We scatter for showers. For silence. For space.

By the time I come downstairs, everyone else is already waiting in the lobby.

"Leon and I will eat in the room," Mel says gently, slipping her hand into his. "We're tired. A movie sounds better."

Leon looks exhausted, but still sharp enough to snap: "No drinking. We train at sunrise. Keep your heads clear."

Aaron mutters, "We're adults."

Leon arches a brow. "Barely."

Mel only shakes her head and gives me a look that lands somewhere between warning and knowing. "Let them breathe," she tells Leon. Then, softer to me: "Keep it light, okay?"

I nod too quickly. "Of course."

The bar smells like wood varnish and fried things. It's small, dim, and tucked behind the inn's creaky dining room, but it's got charm. There's a jukebox in the corner, the kind that only plays songs older than the three of us, and mismatched tables scattered across a scuffed floor.

We claim one near the back, half-hidden behind a wilted fern.

The waitress shuffles over with a tired notepad. "Drinks?"

Aaron doesn't hesitate. "Whiskey sour. Make it a double."

She nods, scribbles, looks at me.

I glance at Hoyt. He shrugs, like *your call.*

"Sparkling water. With lemon," I say.

Hoyt adds, "Iced tea. Unsweet."

Aaron snorts. "You two kidding me?"

"We've got training," I remind him.

Aaron leans back, lips curling. "What's the fun in that?"

Hoyt doesn't even blink. "Staying alive."

Aaron ignores Leon's warning. "Suit yourselves." He leans back, stretching, his shirt pulling tight over his shoulders. "Then I'm drinking for all of us."

Dinner's decent—seafood pasta and garlic bread slick with too much butter. We pick at it while Aaron downs his whiskey like water, glass after glass. With each sip his voice grows louder, looser, words slurring.

Hoyt nurses his iced tea quietly.

When the plates are cleared, Aaron stands suddenly. His chair scrapes back too hard. "Be right back," he says, swaying on his feet, winking like a man trying too hard to prove he's fine.

He staggers toward the jukebox.

Hoyt leans in. "How many's that?"

"Three," I whisper.

"Four," he corrects, eyes flicking to the bar.

The jukebox screeches awake, the speakers coughing static before spilling Sinatra again. Always Sinatra. Something slow, crooning, too romantic for a room this small, too uncomfortable for what hangs between us.

Aaron turns back, eyes locking on me. His smile is lopsided, reckless. "Dance with me." He extends his hand like we're still at the Met and not stuck in a seaside tavern where the ceiling fans rattle overhead.

"Aaron..."

"Come on, Iris." He grins, charming. "It's just a dance."

"No." I keep my voice soft. "Not tonight."

The rejection slices clean through. I see it in his eyes—the way that one word fractures something inside him. The grin collapses. He nods once, slow. Drops his hand. "Right. Of course."

Aaron tips his glass at Hoyt. "Good job, cowboy. Something else you ruined for her."

Hoyt's eyes flick up, flat. "She said no because she wanted to."

Aaron leans back, sloppy grin curling mean. "No, she said no because of you. You're the reason she can't enjoy anything she loves —not the museums, not the dancing..." He swallows another mouthful, smirks around the rim. "Not even fucking."

The air sharpens. I want to step in, but Hoyt beats me to it—quiet. "Careful."

Aaron laughs, sharp and bitter. "What, cowboy? Gonna break my nose because I said what we're all thinking? Or because you're afraid she'll realize I'm right?"

Aaron pivots toward the bar, waving for another drink.

"Whatever loophole you two found... it'll never be enough. Do you even know how much she loves being woken up slow—half-asleep, begging when you push her panties to the side? You'll never fuck her in a soft bed the way she deserves. Not you. Not ever."

Hoyt goes still beside me. Too still. He doesn't say anything. He doesn't need to. His silence is louder than Aaron's stumble, louder than Sinatra's croon. Then—without a word—he pushes back from the table like he's about to leave.

Aaron goes back to the jukebox.

My pulse spikes. "Hoyt," I say quickly, "He's drunk. Don't go. Don't leave me alone with him like this."

For a second I think he won't listen. Then Hoyt exhales and sits back down. His chair creaks like it resents the weight of him.

The music keeps playing. The night stretches.

Almost an hour later, Hoyt and I are still there, watching Aaron circle the drain. His glass lifts slower now, his smile too wide, his words spilling faster, careless.

"Iris," he slurs, dragging out the vowels. "Did I ever tell you... about the invitations? About how many were already sent? The deposits I never got back? The goddamn band we picked?" His laugh breaks in the middle, jagged. "All for nothing. Just phone calls—everyone so sorry my fiancée cheated on me."

Hoyt doesn't move but watches every move. Arms crossed.

Aaron barks out a laugh. He slaps the bar. "One more!" he calls, voice too loud for the tiny room. The bartender hesitates, eyes flicking to me.

I shake my head. "That's enough," I tell her. She nods, relief in her face.

Aaron doesn't notice. "You remember this?" His hand sways like he's conducting an invisible orchestra. "She used to hum this song. You remember that, Iris? You used to dance barefoot on the kitchen tile—"

He laughs again, but it's broken. When he turns too quick, his knee clips the barstool and he almost goes down. He catches himself on the edge of the counter, glass sloshing. "God," he mutters, breathless. "I sound like a loser." His eyes blur past me.

The ache in my chest tightens.

"Alright, cowboy," I mutter to Hoyt, sliding off my stool. "Help me out here."

Hoyt doesn't argue but he sighs and pushes up from the bar.

We flank Aaron like handlers, one on each side. He protests, words tumbling out—"I'm fine. Just one more. I need... to talk to her..."—but his feet betray him, stumbling on the carpet. Hoyt steadies him with a firm hand on his shoulder.

"You heard her," Hoyt says flatly. "Time for bed, prince charming."

We haul him upstairs, down the narrow hall, into the room. He collapses backward onto the mattress like the strings have been cut out of him.

"Iris," he mumbles, eyes glassy. "You used to dance. You used to... love me."

Aaron tries to sit up and gives up halfway. "Don't..." His voice trails. His head lolls. Then he's out. Just like that.

We stand there in the room, door half-open.

I lean against the doorframe, one hand curled around the knob. Hoyt stands beside me, arms folded, watching.

"You can stay with me, if you prefer," I say.

He moves toward me and closes the door.

"He'll hate us in the morning," I whisper.

"Probably."

"We deserve it."

A pause.

"Maybe," Hoyt says at last. His voice is quieter now, rougher. "But I'm too tired to feel bad about it tonight."

I nod.

Neither of us say anything else.

Not yet.

Because the night's not over.

Not even close.

FORTY-ONE

Hoyt opens the door to the room next to Aaron's and holds it like it's nothing—like I'm not standing inches from him, still hearing Aaron's voice slurring my name.

He stops halfway into the room when he sees the bed. One. Small.

"I'll sleep on the floor," he says, stepping inside. His tone is flat. Controlled. Like always. But there's something underneath it tonight, something straining.

"No mountain of pillows?" I ask before I can stop myself, the memory slipping out.

His eyes flick to me. Brief. Sharp. Then he drops his gaze. "Too small."

I don't argue. I'm too tired. Too full of words I can't say. I move past him and sit on the edge of the bed, staring at the muted glow of the lamp bleeding across the wall. My mind is chaos—James, the dreams, the lies I haven't told, Hoyt's raw palm still vivid in my memory. Everything feels unsteady.

Behind me, I hear him moving—boots scuffing against wood, jacket rustling.

When I glance back, he's standing in the corner, holding something between his fingers.

"I... found this," he says.

A cigarette.

I blink. "Where?"

"Well..." he's looking anywhere but at me. "I asked for one. Bartender had a stash. You wanna share it?"

I take it. It's warm from his hand. I roll it between my fingers like it's something fragile. "I don't have a lighter."

"Shit," he mutters, already turning for the door. "I'll be right back—"

"Wait." The word slips out sharp. Too sharp. He stops.

I place the cigarette between my lips.

I look down. My hand drifts to my prism. It hums faintly under my touch, like it knows. Like it wants.

Hoyt watches me, unmoving.

I close my eyes.

Concentrate.

The room fades—the lamp glow, Hoyt's presence, even the sound of the water dripping from somewhere outside. All that's left is the hum of magic under my skin, coiling tighter the more I focus.

Two fingers press lightly to the crystal's smooth surface. My voice is only in my head now, low and sure.

Fire.

Heat blooms instantly. A thin thread of violet light sparks to life, dancing at the tip of the cigarette. It catches, crackles. Burns.

I inhale slowly. My eyes flutter open.

Hoyt's still watching. Frozen. His jaw tight.

"Holy shit," he says hoarsely.

I blow it out slowly, the smoke curling between us like a secret. "Didn't know it would work."

I hold it out to him.

He steps closer. His fingers almost brush mine as he takes it.

"How's your hand?" I ask softly.

My eyes drop to the bandage, barely visible in the muted glow. The fabric's stained a faint brown where the skin beneath is raw, angry.

"Fine," he says.

"Liar."

He huffs a laugh. It's rough. Uneven. Like it surprises him too. It's the first break in his armor I've seen since he came back into my life.

We pass the cigarette back and forth in silence.

Each time, his fingers almost touch mine. My chest tightens every time the filter touches his lips. I can see the faint imprint of mine there. He inhales, eyes never quite leaving me even as smoke unfurls between us.

It's maddening.

He doesn't look relaxed. He looks like a man holding a line that's fraying fast.

Finally, he breaks the silence.

"You're not drinking?"

I shake my head, eyes fixed on the ember glowing faintly between his fingers.

"You aren't either."

He looks down at the cigarette, then at me. "Trying to be responsible."

I huff a laugh that doesn't sound like me. "Since when?"

His lips twitch—not a smile, but close. He takes another drag, his throat working. When he hands it back this time, his holds on to it a beat longer. Just for a moment. But it's enough to make the cigarette tremble slightly in my hand.

I take another drag, watching the ember glow and die. "We used to be fun," I murmur.

He looks at me for a long, loaded moment. Then at the smoldering cigarette.

"I can do fun," he says.

But this time there's no humor in his voice.

Suddenly—he crushes the cigarette out in an empty coffee mug on the nightstand.

The sound makes me flinch.

"No!" I gasp. The word bursts out before I can stop it.

I'm on my feet before I realize what I'm doing. The cigarette is still smoldering in the makeshift ashtray when he looks up at me.

And then—he moves.

Like a predator who's been circling too long and finally decides to strike.

My legs falter as I take an instinctive step back—only to feel the wall at my spine. Solid.

"What are you doing?" I whisper.

Nowhere to go.

My heart slams so hard against my ribs I swear he can hear it.

He doesn't answer. Doesn't need to. His eyes are locked on mine, unreadable, but burning.

His boots stop inches from my bare toes.

"Don't move," he says.

Something in his voice—rough, edged with warning—roots me in place.

"Hoyt—"

"Don't. Fucking. Move."

It's not a threat. It's a plea wrapped in a command.

He lifts his one good hand—the other still bandaged, raw and useless—and without breaking eye contact, he leans in. Slow. Careful.

His mouth passes mine, almost brushing my neck, and goes straight to my prism. And then his teeth close around my violet light. Like he's testing its burn, daring it to scorch him. It doesn't.

I can't breathe.

He pulls back slightly, prism still between his teeth, the violet glow flaring in his mouth like it's alive.

Slowly, his good hand drops. Moves lower.

I don't realize what he's reaching for until his fingers curl around his own prism at his chest.

And before I can react, he presses it against my lips—hard enough that I can taste the cold, metallic edge.

I part my mouth slightly and he shoves it into my mouth.

Chains twist, but I don't dare move—not even when he leans in closer.

His bandaged hand comes up first, planting flat on the wall above my head. He's bracing himself—not for me, but against whatever this is threatening to do to both of us.

His fingers twitch slightly, like he's fighting something—himself, the curse, I don't know. He lets his palm hover near my throat. I can feel the heat of him before he even makes contact.

His thumb brushes under my chin—the faintest of a touch—and I flinch.

He presses a little firmer now, tipping my chin up, forcing my eyes to meet his. His gaze is a storm.

Slowly—agonizingly—he drags his hand down the line of my jaw, across the column of my throat, down to where my pulse is hammering wildly beneath my skin.

But instead of wrapping his fingers around it, he lets his hand drop.

And all the while—we're held together by magic, spit, and spite.

I can feel the prism between my teeth throbbing faintly, pulsing in time with my heartbeat. Or maybe his. I don't know where I end and he begins anymore. His breath is warm, his mouth so close I can taste it, even if he still hasn't kissed me.

Slowly, his good hand slides lower.

I stiffen as his fingers brush the waistband of my jeans. He pauses there, his thumb grazing the button—waiting, testing, like he's daring me to tell him no.

I don't. I can't.

His eyes never leave mine as he pops the button open with a soft click. The sound is obscene in the quiet room.

Then comes the slow rasp of a zipper sliding down. For once, my body's timing isn't a cosmic joke—my period ended last night. His face stays unreadable—except for the faint flare of his nostrils.

He pushes the denim down just enough—his knuckles ghosting over my hip bones. The fabric clings briefly before it surrenders, pooling low enough for him to slip his hand inside my panties.

His fingers brush my clit—light, testing—and I jolt. My violet light glows brighter between his teeth.

He doesn't pull back.

Instead, he drags his fingers over me again—slower this time. A single stroke that makes my knees threaten to give out. The calloused pads of his fingertips catch just enough to send another shockwave through me.

I choke on air. My hands slam flat on the wall behind me. I'm gripping it like it's the only thing keeping me upright. I'm unsure if I'm allowed to touch him back. Scared I'll hurt him. More scared he'll stop.

Hoyt's fingers press harder now, circling, stroking. Just enough to make my hips twitch before I can stop them. I don't mean to move, don't mean to tilt into his touch, but my body betrays me.

His eyes drop. He watches. Watches the way I grind helplessly against his hand. Watches the way the violet light flares brighter in his mouth every time my breath hitches.

And then—he fucking smiles.

It's a dangerous smile. Like he's been starving for this and now that he's tasted it, he's not sure he'll ever stop, or so I hope.

He gives me a wink right before he stops teasing.

His fingers slip lower. Slide inside.

I bite down on his prism, hard enough the edges dig into my tongue.

He thrusts deep—his good hand all he has, but it's enough. More than enough. His palm grinds over me with each pass.

I want to touch him. My hands ache to curl into his shirt, his hair, anything—but I don't. I can't. If I do, I'll ruin everything. I'll break whatever fragile magic is letting us have this.

So I stay plastered to the wall, shaking.

My hips move now of their own accord. Desperate, needy. His fingers curl inside me and I see stars. My vision goes white at the edges. My pulse crashes in my ears.

I break.

The orgasm rips through me—fast, brutal, all-consuming. My cry dies around the prism in my mouth. My entire body shakes as wave after wave wracks me, tearing me apart and stitching me back together all in the same breath.

And just when I think he might finally kiss me—when I feel his breath fan across my lips—he pulls back.

I'm still gasping for air. My thighs are shaking. My hands are still braced on the wall like I might fall without it.

Hoyt leans back.

His mouth parts, and my prism drops free, slick and glowing violet in the dim light. He catches it easily in his palm, his fingers curling around it like it's fragile. He holds out his hand—waiting.

Waiting for me to do the same.

My lips part. I let his prism slide from my mouth into his palm.

For a moment he simply stands there, staring down at the prisms lying in his hand—his and mine. The chains have gone slack between them.

He lets them go.

His index finger glistens in the low light.

And before I can even think, he drags it along his tongue. Luxuriously slow.

"You know what you taste like?"

I can't speak. I can barely breathe.

"Mine," he whispers.

FORTY-TWO

"LOVE IS AN IRRESISTIBLE DESIRE TO BE IRRESISTIBLY DESIRED." – ROBERT FROST

He turns away, leaving the room electric, every nerve in my body screaming, and none of this anywhere near enough.

He pauses in the doorway. Looks back once.

"Let me clean up the mess I made."

"What?"

"Get in the shower, Iris." His voice is hoarse and low. "You've kept me starving long enough."

The bathroom is already fogged with heat when I step inside. My pulse hammers as I take him in. He's standing at the counter, head bowed, his bandaged hand locked on the sink like he's holding himself back from tearing the place apart.

He doesn't move. He just stands there, steam wreathing his body, blurring the hard lines of muscle into something almost unreal. His eyes stay fixed on his reflection—like he's arguing with himself, debating if this is a mistake.

Slowly he looks up.

Our eyes meet in the mirror.

He watches me like a man on the edge of something he won't come back from.

"Take it off."

The words are quiet, measured—yet they land like an order.

I swallow hard. My fingers tremble as they find the hem of my shirt. The cotton clings damp from the steam.

His gaze follows every inch. Unblinking.

"Slower."

The word isn't a suggestion. It's a low growl, thick with need.

"I've waited too fucking long for this."

Heat sparks low in my stomach as I obey, peeling the fabric inch by agonizing inch. It drags over my flushed skin, snags faintly at the swell of my breasts. My nipples tighten under his stare.

When I toss it aside, he doesn't move.

His eyes roam.

"Fuck, Iris." His voice splinters. "Do you have any idea what you do to me?"

His gaze lingers—my breasts, my stomach. Then drops lower.

And lands on my hip. My tattoo.

"Like a moth..." he murmurs.

He steps back a fraction, but his hands go to his belt.

The soft clink of metal unfastening makes me want to beg. He undoes it with a patience somehow worse than urgency.

Then his shirt. He drags it off over his head, and I can't stop staring.

Every scar. Every cut of muscle. The way his chest rises and falls like each breath costs him.

His jeans drop next. The sound of denim sliding down his thighs is louder than it should be.

And then he's just there—massive, unashamed, his cock thick, veined, daring me to kneel, daring me to taste.

"Your turn," he says simply.

My fingers hook into the waistband of my panties. Slowly, I peel them down. When I step free, his tongue drags across his bottom lip.

Neither of us moves. My gaze slides to his hand.

"Your hand."

He glances down, then back at me, like he hadn't even thought about it. A sharp exhale. He grabs the plastic bag from the counter and ties the plastic off with his teeth.

"Better?" he asks.

I nod.

We just stand there—naked, breathing the same thick air, steam curling between us like it knows what's coming.

His eyes travel over me, unflinching. The weight of his stare presses against my skin, almost as tangible as a touch.

The silence stretches until it's unbearable.

Then he moves.

He brushes past me, straight into the shower.

I watch the water cascade over his shoulders, tracing every ridge of muscle. His hair slicks back. He leans against the far wall, one arm braced high on the tile, head tipped like he's perfectly at ease. Like he owns the space—like he owns me.

His eyes don't look away. "Get in."

I hesitate.

His mouth quirks—not a smile, more a warning. His finger curls once, slow and commanding.

"You're already soaked, Iris. Don't make me wait."

My feet move before my brain does. The steam swallows me whole as I cross the threshold.

His voice drops.

"Spread your legs."

"I—" The word breaks out of me, thin and useless.

His hand rises fast, firm but careful as it cups my jaw. He tilts my face up until I'm forced to meet his eyes.

His hand slides down, rough palm gripping my thighs. If I don't do it, he will.

I obey. My legs tremble as I shift, feet slipping on the wet porcelain. His gaze drops. He watches me open for him. Watches like he's memorizing every inch.

His calloused fingers skim down the inside of my thighs, slow and possessive. He grips just above my knees, thumbs pressing hard into tender skin as he pushes them wider.

"Perfect," he growls.

And then his mouth is on me.

The first stroke of his tongue is devastating. A single drag that makes my head slam back against the wall.

He doesn't rush. He circles lazily, tasting, teasing, every flick designed to unravel me.

"Hoyt—" My voice breaks on his name, more gasp than word.

He hums low in response, the vibration sending shockwaves through me.

His grip tightens on my thigh as his tongue drags harder, flat and unyielding over my clit.

The wall is cold at my back. Steam clings to my skin. I'm shaking so hard my palms slip against the slick tile as I brace myself. His mouth is merciless—flicking, circling, plunging—slow at first, then devastatingly fast, until I'm gasping, undone in his hold.

"Hoyt—" The name tears from me again, ragged.

He growls, the sound reverberating through my body.

"Say my name again," he commands, lips brushing me with every word.

"Hoyt."

"Louder."

"Hoyt!"

The name cracks like a whip in the steam-heavy air, raw and desperate. My legs tremble so violently I think I'll collapse. His tongue flicks, relentless, dragging me right to the edge—every muscle strung tight—

And then he pulls back.

Air rips out of me in a strangled cry, part protest, part plea.

"Don't—"

He rises slowly, water streaming down his chest. His eyes catch mine—green, unhinged.

"Turn around."

The words aren't a request.

I can't even think to move. His hand curls firm around my hip, guiding, forcing me to the wall. My palms press flat against the cool tile.

"Here's the thing, firecracker. You were always too wild for gentle hands."

His grip seizes my ass, hard enough to bruise. His palm drags up my side, over ribs slick with water, then back down again—kneading, claiming.

"This curse?" His voice drops into a growl. "It never stood a chance between us."

It's his time to talk because I can't even form words.

The blunt head of his cock nudges between my legs. I arch instinctively, a broken sound escaping my throat.

His hand slides up, fingers hooking the chain at my throat. He pulls it taut, the metal biting against my skin. With deliberate slowness, he drags the pendant down, twisting it until it lies flat against my spine instead of my chest. I feel him adjust it, angling it low, right where his own prism hangs.

The chains strain. The prisms align.

"Like a fucking leash," he murmurs.

The prisms connect. I gasp.

My thighs press together, desperate for friction.

He leans close, thick with hunger he can't cage anymore.

"You feel that? Your prism pulling toward mine? That's what you do to me, Iris. You've had me on a leash since the day we met."

His cock presses again—heavier this time, sliding just enough to make me whimper.

"Tell me you want it."

"I... I want it."

"Say it, Iris." His grip tightens at my hip.

"I want you to fuck me."

The head pushes harder now, parting me with excruciating slowness. My nails scrape uselessly at the wall.

"Please—" The word rips out of me.

"Shh." His hand clamps firmer on my hip.

He pushes deeper, inch by inch. The stretch burns, but it's the kind of burn I've been craving.

His voice is rough, strangled. "So fucking tight."

I gasp as he bottoms out, forehead pressed to the tile, legs trembling.

A moan rips from his chest, raw, as his hips press against my ass. He holds there, buried to the hilt; his whole body shakes like he's barely holding himself together.

"Hoyt—please."

"Please what?" His lips graze my ear.

"Move."

"Thought you'd never ask."

The first thrust is so slow. My mouth drops open, but no sound comes.

Then another—harder. His hips snap forward with a wet slap that echoes off the walls.

"Fuck, Iris," he groans.

His hand slides from my hip to my throat—not squeezing, just anchoring—as he drives into me again and again. The only rhythm is skin against skin, water pounding above us, my broken gasps between.

Each thrust tears a sound out of me. I can't stop.

"You're mine." His pace quickens, brutal now, his breath ragged against my ear. "Fucking mine."

"Yes—I'm yours—I'm—"

His hand drifts lower, his thumb brushing over the sensitive skin of my asshole—lazy, teasing circles that send a shock of heat straight through me.

"I'll claim every inch of you," he growls. "And I'm gonna make damn sure you never forget who you belong to."

The pressure grows firmer, more insistent, until he pushes just enough for me to gasp. Heat flares sharp and forbidden, my hips twitching helplessly back against him. He doesn't push further, just holds there, as though testing how much I'll take.

The shock passes through me, folding straight into the orgasm tearing me apart. I shatter around him. His arm locks tight around my waist, keeping me upright as he pounds deeper, his own control loosening.

But even through the haze of pleasure, panic cuts sharp. He's too close. I can feel it in the way his thrusts falter, in the guttural sound tearing from his chest.

"Wait."

The word rips from me, hoarse, desperate. He freezes instantly, every muscle straining.

Before he can ask, I twist, nearly slipping, and drop to my knees. Steam coils over my shoulders like smoke as I look up at him.

His eyes widen.

"I'm not on the pill," I whisper.

The faintest flicker of understanding—then hunger—flares in his gaze.

Before he can speak, my mouth is on him.

The taste of me lingers on his cock as I take him deep, lips sealing, tongue tracing every ridge. His hips stutter forward. A guttural sound bursts from him.

His good hand slams against the wall above me, his bandaged one curling useless at his side. "Fuck—"

I take him deeper, my tongue tracing every vein, working him until his control snaps.

He comes hot, hard. I swallow it all—every drop—because he's mine too. Because there's no part of him I don't want. And no part of me I don't want him to take.

For a moment, there's nothing but the sound of our breaths, tangled in the steamy air.

The water pounds down around us, but it can't drown out the sharp stutter of my chest.

My whole body shakes, overstimulated, still caught between the high of what just happened.

Tears spill hot before I even realize it. I jerk my face away, ashamed. But he sees.

He doesn't let go, but something in him falters. His hands hover now—still close, still trembling with restraint—but not possessive. Careful. Afraid.

"Did I hurt you?" His voice is raw, frayed at the edges.

The question undoes me. My dam breaks. Sobs tear out of me, shoulders heaving, palm pressed to my mouth.

"Fuck." He mutters it like a curse against himself. "I'm sorry..." The words are hoarse, like he's already twisting into apology.

"No." The word claws its way out of my throat. "You didn't hurt me. You have nothing to be sorry for."

His brows knit. He doesn't understand. Doesn't know where to put his hands.

"I'm the one who's sorry," I choke out between sobs. "For leaving. For lying."

His fingers barely graze mine—hesitant, like he doesn't know if he has the right to touch me anymore.

"Why did you leave, Iris?"

"I told you... I wanted to protect you. Darion found out about my prism. I thought if I disappeared, he wouldn't find yours. You have a life. A family. I couldn't let him take that away."

His thumb presses hard against my knuckles, not gentle. "So you just ran. Alone."

"Yeah." My voice fractures. "I thought it would keep everyone safe." The words feel hollow even as I say them. My throat tightens. "But I failed. He still got to Marie and Tom..."

His brows furrow, storm-dark. "Who the hell are Marie and Tom?"

"My neighbors. The only ones kind to me in Paris." My lip trembles. "And now they're dead because of me. I—"

"Stop." His voice rips sharp, but it's not at me—it's at the weight crushing me. Still, his eyes burn when they meet mine. "Tell me the truth. Did you leave me for him?"

The bottom drops out of my chest. "What?"

"Aaron," he spits, the name bitter on his tongue. "Were you with him? Did you end us because of him?"

The sob catches in my throat. "No! Hoyt—no."

The pain in his eyes guts me. For a second, I think he's going to press harder but in the next breath, he's dragging me into his chest, like he can smother every lie between us. His hand moves to my face.

And then—he kisses my eyelids. One. Then the other.

I sob harder against him. "I'm sorry—"

His mouth cuts me off.

He kisses me.

Not hard. Not rough. Soft—softer than I ever imagined. Like he's memorizing the shape of my lips, pouring months of anger, longing, and love into this single, devastating kiss.

And I kiss him back like I'll never get another chance.

I don't know how long the kisses last—minutes, hours, it all blurs—until I notice his hands. They're slick with soap, sliding gently over my skin.

He breaks away just far enough to breathe, his forehead pressed to mine. His voice is almost broken.

"God, Iris... I hate you for leaving me."

My breath catches. My hands grip his arms tight, terrified he'll let go.

"Do you know what that did to me?" His voice roughens, rising like he can't contain it. "I woke up every morning ready to hate you, and every night I still fucking wanted you. I tore myself apart trying to forget you." His jaw clenches, his breath hot against my cheek. "I hate you. But I hate myself more for letting you go."

His thumb brushes my cheek, soap and tears mixing under his touch. He swallows hard, like the words scrape his throat raw.

And then—like it guts him to admit it, he leans closer, whispering:

"I missed you. Too fucking much."

His hands move to my shoulders, kneading lightly as he spreads the suds there. I close my eyes, letting the warmth of the water and his touch sink deep.

"I missed you too," I whisper. Each stroke feels like he's etching himself back into me. "I was going crazy, actually."

Hoyt huffs a low laugh. "I doubt that."

I peek at him, a grin tugging despite the pain in my chest. "Why?"

"Because you're stronger than me." His hands drift down my arms, circling my wrists with his thumb. "I... I didn't handle it well, Iris."

My head tilts. "What do you mean?"

"It drove me mad. I even burned down my truck."

"What?" I blink, sure I misheard him.

"Yeah." His mouth hardens. "Didn't sell it. Didn't trade it in. I torched the whole fucking thing."

"Why?" My voice cracks on a laugh and a sob all at once.

"Because you picked the damn truck. You and your idea of cozy." His hands glide to my ribs, soap trailing slow, reverent circles. "Every time I got in, it smelled like your rosemary lip balm. Your hair tie on the gearshift. Your sweater in the backseat. It was you. Everywhere. And I—"

His fingers tighten on my hips.

"And?" I whisper.

"And if Johanna hadn't stopped me, I might've burned the whole fucking house too."

I laugh—a wet, shaky sound—as the water mingles with tears on my face.

"Hoyt... I never cheated on you."

He nods, thumb grazing the curve of my hipbone.

"Do you believe me?" I ask.

"I do. But I don't think I'm built to lose you twice."

His hands slide lower, cupping my thighs as he kneels, running the soap down the backs of my legs. His touch is firm, steady, but not sexual—like he's washing the months off me, every mile, every minute between us.

I stare down at him—this man on his knees, broad shoulders gleaming wet under the spray, his face caught somewhere between pain and devotion.

"I love you," My voice cracks.

He looks up through the steam.

I reach down, brushing the sharp edge of his jaw, tracing the stubble grown rough across his skin like it's the only thing keeping me steady.

He catches my hand, presses a kiss to my palm. Another at my wrist, lingering like he's trying to steady my pulse with his mouth.

"Good. Because I don't plan on letting you go again."

I smile through my tears, aching with too many emotions to name. "I want to know everything," I whisper.

He rises, towering again. Tilts his head. "What do you mean?"

"Everything that happened while I was gone. How's Mona? Jo? Broc?" My voice quickens, nervous, desperate to fill the air. "Can you believe Akira is there and—"

But he shuts me up with another kiss.

"Have I told you I missed you?" he murmurs against my lips.

And that's when I let go. Fully. Completely.

We fuck and kiss until I'm raw, until I can't tell where my body ends and his begins. The water runs cold long before we're done, but neither of us notices.

When we finally collapse into bed, it's quiet. Too quiet. The mountain of pillows is back between us—just like before.

We lie there, separated by inches and feathers, our breathing syncing in the dark. My chest aches with how much I want to reach for him.

"Do you think we'll dream tonight?" I whisper.

"I'm terrified this already is a dream."

Silence stretches, heavy.

"Want to know a secret?" He asks.

I roll closer, my pulse stuttering. "What?"

"I think I found my prism's gift."

I blink at him. Shock cuts through the haze. "What? What is it?"

He exhales, rough. "I'll show you tomorrow."

"Show me now."

"Not yet. I'm not ready. You're not ready."

I force a smile, but it doesn't reach my chest. Not with the weight pressing down there. Because I know what I'm about to do. And I need this—I need him to believe me, even when everything else will try to tear that belief apart.

"You believe me, right?" I ask him.

"About what?"

"That since the first gala, it's only ever been you in my head?"

A pause before, "Yeah. I believe you."

I swallow hard. "And even if sometimes I make you doubt that —I need you to know. You're the only one I ever wanted."

"I hear you..." His voice dips, grates. "But..."

"But what?"

"Maybe show me again tomorrow. In the shower?"

My heart breaks but I smile anyway. "You betcha."

"Firecracker?"

"Yeah?"

"I love you too."

The words split me wide open. My lips part like I might answer —but I don't.

Instead, I wait.

Wait for his eyes to close.

Wait for his breathing to even out.

Wait until his presence fades into the rhythm of the ocean outside.

And then I move.
Out of the bed.
Out of his grip.
Out of his life.
But this time, I know exactly what I'm doing.

Forty-Three

"Three may keep a secret, if two of them are dead." – Benjamin Franklin

The second the hallway door clicks shut behind me, I run. Not fast—just enough to keep from looking back. Enough to outrun thinking. I've done too much of that already.

I stop at Hoyt's truck, keys cold in my fist. No directions. Perhaps I should've stolen a phone along with the keys.

I could turn around. Slip back into the room and say I simply needed air. Pretend I didn't plan this. But I did. From the second I opened my eyes, I knew what I had to do.

I climb into the truck. My prism hums against my collarbone—a pulse that feels like yes. All I know is that Morgrave Hollow is located near the Permaquid Point in Bristol, Maine. But I don't need directions. Because my prism knows where to go. I don't know how I know this—I just do.

The pull isn't physical. It's turned inward, a tilt behind my ribs that points my thoughts instead of my feet. When I'm facing the right way, the prism warms. When I'm not, a faint wrongness creeps in, like standing at the edge of a drop.

The engine coughs to life. I grip the wheel. The prism answers with heat, gentle as approval.

Drive.

The tires crunch over the wet road. Headlights carve a tunnel through fog, the ocean breathing dark to my left, cliffs shouldering up on my right. The town disappears without a sound.

At the first turn, I don't guess. The prism tugs—left—and something inside me pulls tight, a line from my throat to the horizon.

I press harder on the gas.

Wind batters the truck, shoving at the frame, and I hunch forward, knuckles tight on the wheel. I'm shaking, but it isn't only fear. Not entirely. It's anticipation. Fury. A gnawing, electric ache that refuses to settle.

What does James want from me? What tie could he possibly have to my mother's family? Did he kill Darion?

The questions stack until I can't count them, but they don't matter. Not now. This isn't a choice—it's a summons. A challenge. A chance.

The road narrows, curling downhill. I ease off the gas, headlights splintering through trees that lean too close. My hands throb from clenching the wheel. My mind refuses to quiet. The prism hums steady, indifferent to my panic, its pull as certain as the tide.

My thoughts slip to Hoyt—inevitable as breathing. The way his voice cracked when he said he loved me. The weight of his hands, the heat of his body. Will he forgive me for leaving again? At least this time I left a note. *Don't come looking for me. Trust me, please. I know what I'm doing. I love you.*

But I can't stay there. I force myself to pivot, because James's game demands I be sharp, not lovesick. I rake through everything I know about him, about my uncle, about the last two years. About my bloodline.

Darion pretended ignorance—acted like he didn't know how to fuse a prism—but of course he did. My mother knew. He was too entangled in it all not to. So what could he possibly want from me? Why push for an answer he must have already had?

Who was the child Leon and Hoyt saw? What does my father

know? What did my mother confess to him? How did he find me on my birthday?

It's the not-knowing that drives me mad. Leon's lessons barely scratched the surface; I'm drowning in gaps. And James—James moves like a man who already knows the end of the story.

So why free me from the trap? The other Seers wanted me pinned. He cut me loose. Why?

I drive for hours without stopping. Every mile, every shadowed curve of road, I replay the moments, the clues. But it isn't answers pressing my foot to the gas. It's them. Hoyt. Aaron. Leon. Mel. Even Akira.

Aaron, when we were barely more than kids, rubbing slow circles on my back while I sobbed over everything I couldn't say aloud. And now, choosing to stay—choosing to help—even with me still holding him at arm's length.

Leon, dragging me out of Darion's grip, then coming here without hesitation, like my survival was reason enough.

Mel, setting food in front of me every time I forgot to eat, her quiet hands the only way she knew how to say: *you matter.*

Akira, pulling me all the way to Salem, her tears in that hospital room after Darion left me broken. She had carried more of my weight than I deserved.

Even Broc, patiently teaching me how to hold a brush, how to calm a horse, steady in ways I didn't know I craved.

And Hoyt. Hoyt, who burned himself to pull me back.

Every one of them stepped into the fire for me, shielded me, chose me when they didn't have to. Maybe I can't undo what's already been scorched. Maybe I can't fix it all. But I can try to end this. To stop the hunt. To make sure they get to go home—even if I don't.

I've already lost my job, my parents, my fiancé, my soulmate, my best friend, my home. Piece by piece, I've given it all away. But I still have one thing left to offer.

My prism.

* * *

The last time I stood at this house, I was running. I crept like a thief, stealing Aaron away. Not tonight. Tonight, I walk straight up the front steps like a guest.

For one suspended moment, I stop. The door looms in front of me, silent, waiting, like it might swing open on its own and devour me whole. *This is it.* No more hiding. No more being dragged. No more half-truths, broken rules, or running from a fate already knotted tight around my throat.

I lift my hand and hold it there. And though no one's watching, I do it anyway—I straighten my spine, tilt my chin, and breathe like it's the last inhale I'll ever take. Then I knock.

The sound detonates through the night, three hard strikes. Firm. Final.

For a second, nothing. Just the wind, just the dark, just me— standing like an offering. Because that's what I am. I don't know who will open the door—James, my uncle, a stranger, a ghost. But I know this: I am not afraid of being taken anymore. This time, I came willingly.

The door creaks open slower than I expect. And it's not James. It's a woman—older, hair pinned into a loose knot, flour dusting her sleeve like I've pulled her straight from a kitchen. She blinks, waiting.

"I'm Iris," I say, quick and steadily, though my insides riot.

Her eyes flinch at the name. She nods once, recognition sharp and pulls the door wide and steps aside.

I cross the threshold. The house smells of firewood and something faintly sweet, like orange peels left to boil too long. It isn't empty. It isn't abandoned.

She leads me into the same room where Darion's body once lay. Not much has changed besides the new rug.

"Just a moment, please," she murmurs, and slips away.

A black cat leaps down from the chair and follows the woman out. The sound startles me, and I jolt before forcing myself still.

I perch on the edge of the couch, its cushions sighing under my weight. My hands press to my knees. The prism pulses once beneath my shirt.

I feel him before I see him.

Footsteps. A presence pressing at the doorway like the house itself resists letting him through. He enters.

Tall, but not imposing. Thinner than I expected. Sharp-featured. Pale. He moves like someone re-stitched after being shattered, every step a wince he refuses to admit. But it isn't the limp that undoes me.

It's the eyes. Green. Her eyes.

"Hello, Iris," he says. His voice is almost gentle, almost pleased. "It's nice to finally meet you."

I don't answer. Not yet.

He lowers himself into the chair across from me, sitting like a man who's never had to ask permission. His gaze drags over me, soaking in every inch of my face, like I'm a puzzle piece he's waited decades to hold.

"You look just like your mother," he says softly, as if it costs him something. Perhaps it does. But not enough to stop him from saying it.

My blood spikes hot. How dare he—how dare he speak of her.

"We've been looking for you." His smile flickers, and for one fractured second, I swear he looks at me like I'm a ghost.

I don't flinch. I don't look away. When I finally speak, the words claw up from somewhere older than my bones. "Hello, Uncle."

His smile sharpens. Almost amused.

"So brave of you to come," he says. "Your mother would be proud."

Would she? *Would she?* Rage tears through me, bright and uncontainable. If he notices, he doesn't care.

He leans back, studying me like I'm a canvas he's only ever read about in letters. His eyes drink in everything—my breath, the twitch of my hands, the faint violet glow at my throat.

"You drove here?" he asks.

"I did."

"No one came with you?"

"No."

His head tilts, birdlike. "Good."

He settles back in his chair, considering me as though that answer decided something. "Well. We should make you more comfortable. There's tea. Or... something stronger, if you'd like."

"I'm not here to drink," I snap.

He chuckles, soft and knowing. "No. I suppose not."

His gaze lingers, slower this time, peeling me apart like pages of a book. Then—"You really don't know, do you?" he asks.

My pulse stutters. "Know what?"

He doesn't answer. He lets the silence stretch, a blade held at my throat. Finally: "James will be here soon."

I can't tell if it's a promise or a threat.

"Come," he says, rising with a stiff breath. "Let's get you to your room. You can rest until James arrives. Eat something."

I push to my feet. "What? No. I'm not here for a sleepover."

His smile crooks, amused—like this is exactly who he hoped I'd be. "You came for answers. You'll have them. But not all at once."

He gestures toward the hallway—the same one I crept through. Now I'm being ushered down it like a guest.

"This is your home too, Iris," he says. "You're welcome here."

The words slither over me, wrong. Too smooth. Too practiced. Like a line he's rehearsed for years, waiting for this moment.

"I don't want tea. Or a bed. I want to know what's going on. What James wants. Why he asked for me."

We stop at a closed door. My uncle turns, eyes soft—but not with kindness. Patience.

"James wants to tell you himself," he says.

I narrow my eyes. "So he's in charge now?"

Something flickers across his face—a faint smile that can't hide the anger beneath it. Or the resignation.

He swings the door open behind me. A bedroom waits.

"Please," he says quietly. "Rest while you can."

The click of the lock isn't loud, but it's unmistakable.

The room looks like a guest room. Fresh sheets. Heavy curtains. A vase with flowers already drooping. But it's sterile, staged. A set piece playing at welcome. No clothes in the closet. No shoes by the door. No sign anyone has ever stayed here longer than a night.

A knock. The door opens before I answer.

The maid slips in with a silver tray, sets it on the small table by the window, and does not look at me. "There's more if you want," she murmurs.

There is another click of the lock.

I test the handle—locked from the outside—but it doesn't spark panic. I know it's temporary. The door will open again— when he arrives.

I sit on the side of the bed. The food stays untouched. I don't eat. I don't move. What am I supposed to do? Wait? Run? Scream?

None of it comes.

Instead, exhaustion seeps in, heavy and relentless. First behind my eyes, then into my shoulders, settling in my chest like sandbags. I tell myself I'll lie back for a minute, just to rest my eyes.

FORTY-FOUR

"BEWARE; FOR I AM FEARLESS, AND THEREFORE POWERFUL." – MARY SHELLEY

A knock jolts me awake.

Morning. Bright. I sit up, throat sandpaper, limbs heavy. I actually slept? A whole night? Here, of all the goddamn places on Earth—this is where my body finally let go?

The door creaks open before I can answer. "Breakfast, miss," the maid says, too cheery for the weight crushing my chest. She sets a tray on the desk and leaves like this is normal. Like I'm not a prisoner with good pillows. The click of the lock is soft but final.

Beside the eggs and steaming coffee: clothes. A navy sweater. Jeans. My size. They knew I'd come. Not hoped. Not guessed. Knew.

I stare for a long time before I move. Then I eat. Then I change. Because when James walks in—when he finally faces me—I want to be ready.

But he doesn't come.

Not in the morning. Not by lunch. Not even after the second knock—sandwiches this time, a pot of tea already cooling.

I wait. And wait. Until the waiting frays me raw.

Three quick strides and I'm at the door. The handle won't turn. I yank, slam my shoulder into the wood. Nothing.

I back away, hands on hips, lungs shuddering against the static in my head. Pacing won't help. Screaming won't matter.

So I slide down the wall instead. Cold floor against my spine. *Be patient,* Leon would say. *Steady,* Mel would whisper.

I close my eyes. Find my breath. Feel the crystal at my throat— its weight, its warmth. *Control,* I whisper.

I don't reach for anything wild. Just a flicker. A shift. A tug at the current coiled inside me like some sleeping animal. It pulses. Listens.

And for a moment, it doesn't feel like a curse. It feels like mine.

So I talk to it.

When he comes. When they try to take you. Don't let them.

Don't hurt them. Unless you have to. But don't kill.

We need each other. I know you hear me.

It doesn't answer. Not exactly. But I don't need words. The prism and I—we're the same now.

So I talk to myself instead. *You can do this. You're ready.*

Time unravels. Minutes, hours—I can't tell.

Until the next knock.

I stand as the door opens. The maid slips in, but not with food. This time, it's a dress.

Deep green. Silken. Long. The kind of thing I used to wear to museum galas, to nights funded by other people's money, in the life I lived before blood and prisms and locked doors.

She lays it on the bed.

"Dinner will be served shortly," she says, not meeting my eyes. "Mr. Briar is here. He's requested your presence."

Requested. Like this is some Victorian courtship and I've been summoned for roast duck.

"About time," I mutter.

The maid doesn't answer. She simply slips out, lock clicking behind her again like a throat clearing.

I stare at the dress. No jewelry. No heels. I feel the soft weight of silk in my arms.

I hold it to the mirror. Of course it fits.

I change. Not out of fear. Not out of obedience.

I put on the dress because if there's one thing I've mastered, it's pretending.

* * *

The stairs creak beneath me as I descend, silk brushing against my bare legs, my feet whispering against the wood.

They're already at the table when I enter.

My uncle sits at the head, sharp in navy wool and silver cufflinks, posture carved from tradition. He looks like he belongs to the walls.

James is at the far end. No suit, no tie. Just a worn leather jacket slung across his chair, sleeves shoved to his elbows, black shirt clinging to muscle and intent. He looks like he rolled straight in from the street and couldn't bother to care. But I know better. His casual is as calculated as my uncle's polish. Different costumes for the same stage.

No sign of the boy. I scan once, twice. No footsteps, no laughter, not even the creak of another door. *Is he here?*

James looks up when he sees me. And smiles.

"Iris," he says, slow and heavy, savoring the name like it's wine. "You clean up dangerous."

My uncle shifts in his seat. "James."

James doesn't flinch. Doesn't correct him. Just smirks, tapping lazy fingers against the stem of his wine glass.

"Leave us," he says, eyes still on me.

The words hang, heavy. My uncle doesn't move right away. "That wasn't the agreement," he says, brows drawn.

James finally meets his gaze. "It wasn't a suggestion."

A pause before my uncle exhales through his nose, pushes back from the table, and stands. He straightens his jacket like it costs more than my freedom, then walks out. The door clicks behind him.

And just like that—

It's just me and James.

His eyes follow me as I approach the table, but I don't sit. I want to see what happens if I don't obey.

But James doesn't ask. He only smiles, like he's already won.

"Please," he says smoothly, gesturing to the chair across from him. "Sit. The wine—" he lifts his glass, inspects the dark crimson like it's holy—"they actually know what they're doing here."

I stand for one breath longer than necessary before I move. But I don't touch the wine.

"We both came a long way for this," I say. "Can we skip it?"

His brows twitch up. "Skip the fun?"

"Skip the charade. What do you want?"

"Take a seat, professor."

The word cuts. I want to tear it off his tongue. But I sit. Straight-backed. Spine like steel.

"You see..." James leans back. "This isn't simple. I could end your life with a flick of my fingers. But why waste you? That prism of yours..." His eyes drop to my throat like a lover's glance. "It's special. But it's only one."

Ice slides through my stomach.

"There are seven, as you know." His voice softens, almost reverent. "You think that one can shake the world? Imagine all of them—together."

"Nobody knows where they are," I snap.

He laughs. Low. Rich. Certain. Then leans forward. "Join me. Help me find the rest. We unlock power that makes gods jealous."

I don't flinch. But I want to.

"Join you?" I echo. "You mean the Seers?"

His smile falters slightly. "No. They're pawns."

"And if I refuse?"

James swirls his wine, calm as as if this is a minor inconvenience. "This was a courtesy. I don't actually need you."

I laugh, brittle and dry, pushing my chair back an inch. "You don't?"

His gaze locks with mine.

"So you know how to use it?" I ask, tapping the violet prism at my throat. "Lift and lower the Veil? Step through mirrors? Control dreams?"

Silence.

"Then go on," I lean forward, daring him. "Take it. End this."

My fingers close around the chain, my pulse a drum in my ears, but I won't let him hear.

"Because you know what?" My voice cracks like a whip. "I'm fucking tired of all of it."

I lean my elbows on the table, letting the prism catch the light between us.

"I never asked for this," I say evenly. "As you probably know."

He watches me. Silent. Waiting.

"But fate—" I flick my fingers through the air "—decided it was mine anyway. Bloodline, maybe. Genetics. Cursed inheritance."

Agonizingly slow, the smile slips from his face.

"But if you think you can find the others on your own—something men have chased for centuries and failed—then please." I shove my chest forward across the table, the prism swinging into the space between us.

"Take it."

Silence folds tight around us. His eyes drop. Not just at my breasts—but to the crystal.

"And when the voices start," I murmur softly, "when the world twists and nothing makes sense anymore..."

I sit back, smiling.

"Here's a tip."

My tone dips to a whisper.

"Laugh. Because by then, it's already too late."

That's when he smiles. Not like someone who's won—like someone who's been *waiting*.

"I knew you were worth it," he says.

And then he moves.

Before instinct even fires, he's on me—fast, brutal. His palm slams flat against my chest, right over the prism, pinning me back. His chair crashes behind him. My spine hits the wall.

My breath fractures. I don't think. I command. *Fire. Protect me.*

But nothing comes.

No glow. No hum. No resistance.

Silence.

I try again, louder this time, panic scraping my throat. *Light up. Burn him.*

Nothing. The prism lies dead against my skin, cold and uselessly. My stomach plummets.

James's mouth curves with amusement. Slowly, he sticks out his tongue—mocking, taunting—until I see it.

A glint. Not silver. Not gold. Black.

A prism. Cut like a diamond. Set into his tongue as a piercing.

My breath falters.

His hand shifts higher, thumb brushing my throat—just enough pressure to remind me it's there. Not strangling—worse: owning. Not my body; my power.

His voice curls. "That pretty little crystal of yours..."

He leans in close, breath hot against my cheek.

"It has no business around mine."

My pulse detonates. I whisper to the prism again anyway, desperate. *Come on. Do something. Anything.*

James presses the black diamond against his tongue. "The things I can do with this..." His voice drops, thick with threat. "... will have you screaming. Pain. Pleasure. Until you can't tell which is which."

I beg my prism. Scream inside myself. But it's gone. Absent.

James chuckles, eyes flashing. "Oh... Comhghall didn't tell you? This one's called a Silencer."

My chest caves.

A flicker. A ripple in the air.

So faint that anyone else would miss it. But I've learned to see shadows.

In the corner of my eye: slender. Still. Watching.

Leon.

He's here.

I don't look at him. I don't dare. I keep breathing, keep pretending I'm not about to break.

And then, steady as I can, I say the only words that will make James pause.

"I'll do it."

James stills. His grip on my throat loosens—just enough air, no more. He studies me like he's trying to decide whether I'm lying or if I've finally broken. His mouth twists into a slow, crooked grin.

"Didn't think you'd fold that easily," he says, smug.

"I'll join you," I repeat, careful now, my voice steady, my eyes fixed on his. "But only under one condition."

His brows lift, mocking. "Oh?"

"You leave them alone," I say. "My friends. My family. All of them. You don't touch them."

James tsks, shaking his head like I'm a child. "Ah, Iris. I'd love to humor you. But they're not just yours anymore. Some of them carry prisms too, which makes them mine."

Behind him, Leon's shadow shifts. Barely a ripple, but I catch it. I hold it, beg silently: *wait. Let me play this out.*

"I read your pages," I say.

That makes him pause. His hand slips from my throat, surprise flickering in his eyes. "You did?"

I ease one step closer to Leon's line of sight, lowering my voice so only someone listening closely will catch the edge in it. "You've got something rare," I say, eyes flicking briefly to James's mouth before sliding back. "Did you write it yourself? Or was the whole history-fanatic act another performance?"

James's gaze sharpens, hunger lighting behind his smile. "It was my research that led me to the Seers. That led me to this."

He tilts his head, tongue flicking out. The black prism glimmers, swallowing light.

"So the pages were yours," I murmur. "Impressive. I especially loved the part where you said history runs beneath the skin, like blood under flesh."

I let the words hang, my gaze sliding toward the shadow in the corner before drifting back.

"The ancients knew patience was part of the rite. Nothing worth power ever came quickly. They waited. Endured. And if your offer is real, than I must do the same. " I continue.

His grin spreads. "With you, me, and the Seers, it's simple. You draw them out, I track the histories, they do the hunting."

As he speaks, he circles me, slow and deliberate, then pulls me into him. His fingers dig into my arms just enough to make the point—control without a word.

"And when it comes to unlocking them..." His breath ghosts the side of my face. "...you already know the kind of rituals that require two bodies."

I smile. "How about this: we leave Hoyt's and Leon's prisms for last. Hunt the others first. Give me time to... forget." My gaze hardens. "See if I can stomach your world."

James narrows his eyes, weighing. "Now that, I might agree to. But if I find you playing both sides, Iris..." His voice drops, lethal. "Not only will I end their lives, right before I end yours—I'll make sure you watch what I do to them."

He leans in, the smile gone. "You might think you've finally met your match, but don't take this lightly. I'm always two steps ahead of you."

Something inside me shifts, clicks. The mask slides on. I move toward him—measured, deliberate—and lower myself into his lap. He doesn't stop me.

"You're right," I whisper. "I love them. But you know what they call me? A liar. A cheater."

James's smile curves. "And you begged. Didn't you?"

I drop my gaze, feeding him what he wants. "And they never forgave me."

He studies me, eyes sharp, searching for cracks. I look up again, meeting his gaze without flinching. The mask is solid now, sealed tight. "So you see... forgetting them benefits me too."

His grin widens, not with trust but with interest, as if he enjoys the performance. He knows I'm lying. I know he knows. The game is the point.

What he doesn't know is how far I'll go to win.

I lean closer, lips grazing his ear, my voice soft enough to sound like surrender, sharp enough to taste like a blade. "If we're doing this, we might as well enjoy it."

A Note From Blair

Dear Reader,
You finished *Crystal Iris II*. Which tells me one thing—you were
hooked.
If Iris and Hoyt are still lingering in your head, the best way you
can help me is with a quick review.
Thanks for being in this with me.

Come closer—
Instagram: @authorblairshadows |
TikTok: @blairshadowsauthor |
Newsletter: blairshadows.com

Until the next bad decision,
Blair

Acknowledgments

A huge thank you to everyone who told me
keep going—you'll never know
how much those words mattered.

WHAT TO EXPECT

Shared dreams. Dangerous mirrors.
Love that unravels. Secrets that consume.

Inside, you'll find:

Cult magic & creepy rituals
Family betrayals & locked doors
Murder, blood, and weapons
Drugs & alcohol
Child death (off-page)
Sex scenes that don't fade to black (rougher this time)

Read with care — or recklessness. Your call.

ABOUT THE AUTHOR

BLAIR M. SHADOWS writes mystical love stories packed with forbidden tension, devastating men, and heroines who don't beg —they bite. Crowned Queen of Mystical Romance (but she prefers Host of Bad Decisions), Blair is known for slow burns, sharp turns, and books that leave a mark.

Join the Shadows Society, where bad decisions are served on ice.
BlairShadows.com
INSTAGRAM: @authorblairshadows

* 9 7 9 8 9 9 9 1 8 0 0 4 6 4 *